Shadow World

Chris Impey

For Dinah

Published by Dark Skies Press, Tucson, Arizona
www.darkskiespress.com

This is a work of fiction. Names, characters, places, and incidents are
a product of the author's imagination or are used fictitiously. Any
resemblance to actual persons, events, or locales is coincidental.

Cover image "Wintery" designed and copyright © Kalle Törmä

ISBN 978-0-9898176-0-8 ebook
ISBN 978-0-9898176-1-5 paperback
1st edition 2013

Printed in the United States of America

CONTENTS

PREFACE

As Magritte might say: ceci n'est pas un livre. Like food and sex, fast writing offers at best rude pleasure. Books are to curl up with, pore over, and savor; writers should be similarly assiduous.

The boundary is a cruel enough box. Complete works of creation are not meant to fit into lunar cycles. But the pace was twenty five hundred words a day, eighty two thousand for the month. I started with four pages of hand-written notes. Suspecting formal constraints might spur invention, I added a few more. The work has twenty eight sections, written one per day, organized into seven chapters. The major and minor story arcs echo the motions of Sun and Moon. Each section is geographically specific, connected to and yet disconnected from the sections that precede and follow. Each chapter has a particular iconography: a celestial body, a substance, and an artifact.

It's unnerving to light the fuse and write, not have time to edit and know most of the words can and should be discarded. The flip side is a total freedom from hesitation and obfuscation. Some days, ideas were clamoring to get out; on others the track was laid down seconds ahead of the advancing train. These days, we multiplex and purity of purpose is hard to find outside a monastery. As hard as the writing was, I felt real sadness as the end approached.

If this is about anything, it's the boundary between creation and madness, art and science, the natural and the artifactual. Characters are fictional although some are inhabited by amalgamated aspects of real people. The science is factual but I insert plausible speculation in places. Conceived and executed in haste, it aged in a darkened drawer for six years. Then, with timidity and trepidation, I disinterred it to be massaged and edited over multiple iterations into this form. The first draft had enough holes to admit a howling wind. The final version has flaws and imperfections, but hopefully explores new terrain at the boundary between fiction, fantasy, and popular science writing.

1 THE DESERT SPEAKS

Big Gash

The donkey loses its footing and as I come to, my body swings lazily over the abyss. Stones clatter into space. I pitch forward and cling tightly to the donkey's neck, my legs grappling for purchase on its fat belly. Bristles poke my face. Shite.

Behind me, a low cackle. Night Owl. Bastard.

"What kind of beast did you get us?" I yell.

"He knows his business," says Night Owl. "He doesn't want to die any more than you. Scotchman needs to pay attention, needs to be in the real world."

The danger passes; the donkey resumes its slow and steady pace. I get comfortable with the lolling motion and gingerly sit up. Reaching forward, I grab the reins. The animal's back is a barrel covered by a blanket. Why hadn't I insisted on a saddle?

"Scotchman OK?"

"Like you care. If I'd paid you up front, you'd be happy to see me tit over arse off that cliff."

"A donkey is not a car," Night Owl's gaze is impassive. "He has his own mind. Not much, but he uses it if he can."

Now fully alert, I take in my surroundings. We're on a narrow rocky path etched into the side of a near-vertical cliff face. A pale Moon the color of egg yolk hangs over our heads to the left and we're in shadow cast by the rim of rock above. Down and to my right, only a foot away, is impenetrable blackness. Beyond that is an ethereal scene. Spires of slender rock. Endless cliff walls crumpled like curtains. And a huge rift bathed in jaundiced light. The Grand Canyon.

■

I work the leathery strap between my teeth. It tastes like sweat. We've stopped for a rest. I'm craving a Mars bar.

"You like the buffalo jerky? My uncle made it."

The old Navajo grins. I look at Night Owl carefully, this man I've trusted with my safety in a strange and inhospitable place. His face is smooth and unlined but seems ancient, like all the features have been worn away with time. In the moonlight his normally chocolate-colored skin is jet black. His long graying hair is tied tightly back. It's the eyes that unsettle me. Small and dark, they seem to admit no light.

"Where are you taking me, you old trickster?"

"Scotchman said he wants to learn the ways of the old world. I am taking you to places I take no other."

The ground is hard and unforgiving but Night Owl acts like he's in a comfy chair in front of the telly. He eats the jerky as if it were taffy. I've no idea how old he is.

"Aye. Like you said. But don't get it in your noggin to leave me to turn into jerky. My mates are waiting for me in Flagstaff." It's a lie. I'm alone. My friends and family are five thousand miles away. Nobody knows where I am.

"You are not trusting, Scotchman. That is a flaw." He grins and his teeth are small, nicotine-stained, and uneven, like cobbles; they lean against each other haphazardly. He has a lazy eye.

"I give it when it's due."

"You'll see. I'll earn a big tip!"

"Look how your eyes just got big, you bugger," I laugh. "When are we going to stop? I'm totally knackered."

"At the bottom. Then it will be too hot for your freckles."

■

An hour later the sky begins to pale, like a hidden giant is slowly lifting the lid on the world. The Sun is a swollen lozenge in the east, flinging shadows from every peninsula of the canyon. Its rays streak across the landscape with startling speed.

I stare, gobsmacked.

■

I'm McEvoy. Just that. McEvoy. Nobody calls me Ian but my

sis; even my mum calls me McEvoy. It fits. I can't remember how I got here, but that's nothing new, I've been dealing with it my whole life. This is a big trip for me. Stepping out for the first time. McEvoy takes on the world. Nineteen years on the planet. The lowland Scot leaves the mockers and the muckers behind.

■

"Time to go, Scotchman." Night Owl kicks the sole of my boot with his moccasin. "Let go your white flesh dream."

"OK. OK." I sit up. Under me is the fetid blanket I was riding on all day. It barely pads the rocky ground. I doubt I've slept more than an hour. The air is baked bone dry; it tastes acrid and smells bitter.

"Jesus. This place is brutal."

"You say so," Night Owl gives me an appraising look. "But you like milk and cars. We lived here for thousands of years."

"What the hell did you eat?"

"Maize. Squash. Meat of small animals. We lived like your kings."

"And drink?"

"There is water. If you know where to look. Top layers of canyon rock hold water like a sponge. We find seeps lower down, where the sponge rock meets hard rock. We plant even in dry years."

It's hard to swallow. The rocks grind down over time into red dust and the dust is everywhere—on my scalp, in the crevices of my body, and coating the inside of my mouth.

"God, I'm parched."

Night Owl pitches over the water bottle. "Easy, Scotchman. We have five hours before we get to the river." He regards me dolefully. "You are not made for this place."

He's right. I glance down at my arms and legs. They're pale and freckled and slathered with sunscreen. Using a canteen for a mirror, my face is pink daubed with white streaks, topped with a thick brush of short, ginger hair. I'm compact and well-built but I wouldn't last three days in the desert on my own. The only thing I have going for me is camouflage. I fit in well with the red rocks.

I fill my backpack and we're on our way. We've slept through the hottest part of the day but the air still makes my skin cringe and there are hours before the Sun quits. September in the Arizona desert and everything is harsh: bleached sky, angular rocks, and bristling cacti. I look for something soft, something forgiving, and find nothing.

Then, glancing up, I spot a solitary cumulus cloud in the expanse of sky, a modest statement of possibility and defiance.

■

"Why here?" I look quizzically at Night Owl. He smells like hair oil and saddle soap. "Sure enough, it's impressive. But this is a bloody hellhole. Even the lizards look pissed off."

Night Owl regards me and for the first time since I've met him his gaze softens.

"You are very young, Scotchman. What is a life? Is a life to be in a building, and move from one building to another? Is a life to bend the land to your will?

"That's civilization, man." I raise my voice. "It's why we're better than the beasts. We work our arses off to get loads of stuff and live better than the poor bastards who lived before us. That's progress. Don't you want to improve your life?"

Night Owl works a twig into the gap between his front teeth. "My life is no better and no worse than it needs to be."

"C'mon. Stop your havering, man. I saw your shack. Don't you want some bricks and a proper roof?" I'm exasperated. I think about the time I first met Night Owl and realize I can't remember the events leading up to it. They'll come back to me. It's like a painting where a few disconnected details are visible at first, and the rest slowly return to fill in the canvas.

"It makes no difference," he sweeps his hand expansively at the vista around us. "This is where we fit or don't fit. This is where we measure ourselves."

"Have it your way."

My shirt is soaked with sweat. I try not to paw at the heat rash on my thighs and neck. Something in the air is making my chest tight and my eyes itch. Right now all I want is to be back home in a noisy pub with my best mates, soaking up the beer with a haggis pie supper.

An hour later and we're on the canyon floor. The Colorado River snakes ahead of us, swollen and mud-brown with monsoon runoff. The cascading water emits a dull roar that echoes off the canyon walls. We walk downstream to a place where the low tiers of the canyon narrow like a throat. A rope bridge is strung high across the river, suspended by thick wire cables tethered in the rock walls above our heads. Many ropes are frayed and some are broken; it looks very dodgy. Night Owl steps forward.

"What about the donkeys." I gesture at the pot-bellied beasts that are chewing sage grass near the water's edge.

"They can find their way home." He flashes a crooked smile. "Now I'll teach you how to tread lightly, Scotchman."

He moves purposefully onto the rope bridge. I follow slowly, my body braced against the swaying under my feet. I look up and Night Owl is already far ahead. He isn't even touching the guide ropes on either side.

■

"Why are we eating this fancy crap?" I wrinkle my nose. "I was thinking you'd fix some rattlesnake stew like your ancestors used to make."

"This is best hiker food. You don't like the way I'm treating you?" Night Owl's voice lilts with mock concern. His good eye regards me while his bad eye drifts disconcertingly to stare at a point beside my head.

"You lifted this, you sly bastard."

It's true. We'd gone into a hiking supply store in Flagstaff to buy trail mix and as we hit the street I noticed Night Owl's bulging jacket pockets. He'd purloined a dozen sachets of gourmet, freeze-dried dinner. I'm chewing Beef Stroganoff. Night Owl's a petty thief and probably worse for all I know.

"I am just restoring nature's balance."

I arch my eyebrows. "I don't get you but I'm sure it's a crock."

Night Owl's face is as immobile as stone. He looks solemn. "To make food without water in a metal bag takes the work of many. We think it is simple but the land sighs and is poorer each time."

"Sure enough. I'll buy that. But what about the gloves?" Night Owl has also swiped a pair of fancy Goretex gloves.

"Also nature's balance. In my bones I feel a dry winter ahead for tips and extra income."

You thieving sod, I think. But I don't say it. I'm beginning to like Night Owl. I grin.

He grins back.

■

That night I follow Night Owl's admonition to drink plenty of water. After a few hours of tossing and turning on the corrugated ground my bladder tugs insistently on my sleeve. Our fire is down to a handful of dark red embers. Night Owl is lying straight on the ground, arms by his side, like a corpse prepared for burial. He's so immobile I bend over and listen. Nothing. No breath. No chest motion.

I'm about to shake his shoulder when his eyes flick open.

"Jesus H. Christ!"

"Night Owl is just resting. I am fully alert."

"I can see that now. You scared the shite out of me!"

"Scotchman needs his rest. Tomorrow he'll do some real walking."

"My poor bloody blisters."

"You'd rather stay in a motel? Watch TV?"

"No, no." The old Navajo is infuriating. "I'm here to learn."

"Good. Time to rest." His eyes flick shut again.

■

Corruscating light. So intense I keep my eyes shut tight. And pain. I hold my breath against its sharpness. Opening my eyes a crack, pure white seeps in. The pain is smooth and seamless and I can't tell if I'm being assailed by numbing cold or intense heat. I recall what a poet once said, about the world ending in either fire or ice. Is this how it ends for me? Bracing myself for what might be out there, I open my eyes. Darkness. Just a dream.

■

I stumble in the moonlight over uneven ground towards a beach at a bend in the river. My stream is gratefully accepted by the arid dirt. Then I notice something amazing. I'm casting two shadows. The first is in the opposite direction to the Moon. The second is much fainter and it takes longer to locate the source.

It's cast by the galaxy. I tilt my head back and look at the Milky Way—really look at it—for the first time in my life. It's crowded with stars, like bees hovering in an angry cloud. Arcing from horizon to horizon, the galaxy is a white lace strap holding the bowl of rock that both dwarfs and contains me. I imagine that a giant god might carry me away.

I imagine it's already happened.

Night Owl

Night Owl is sincere. Night Owl is treacherous. Night Owl does hard and honest work. Night Owl skates by, doing as little as possible. Night Owl's words fly straight and true. Night Owl is a compulsive liar. Night Owl is wise. Night Owl is shallow and craven.

After three days on the trail I have no idea who my companion is. My safe return depends on learning the answer soon. I met him in an IHOP in Gallup, New Mexico, a week ago. The International House of Pancakes: in the wee hours of the morning, a refuge for drifters and insomniacs. I was one of the sleepless souls.

He sat down in my booth as I nursed a cup of coffee and stared at the newsprint of a local paper without reading it. I thought he was a dosser so I fished for change in my pocket to get rid of him. He turned his head sideways in anger as I offered it across the table, showing me a proud and strong profile. I saw his high forehead, large triangular nose, fleshy lips, and smooth skin the color of milky coffee. His only adornment was a silver ring with a complex, braided pattern.

We did a little dance for the next hour. I was looking for a guide who could show me something special, something off the beaten track. He was looking for something from me but it didn't seem to be just the money. We shook on the deal and agreed to meet in Flagstaff several days later. I remember his hand was massive but light, the skin cool, smooth and firm like fine leather.

Then he got up abruptly and walked towards the back of the IHOP. Thinking he was going to the loo, I waited, but he never came back. A few minutes later, two Gallup police and a man in a blue uniform with ATF on the cap walked past the booth. I glanced up but didn't give it much thought.

■

Night Owl is the first friend I've had in the States, the first friend I've ever had from overseas. I'm a wee Scot, a lowlander, and this is my first trip anywhere. What's to say about me? What's worth saying about McEvoy?

I was born in Edinburgh. My mum Kirstie is a highlander and my dad John is a lowlander. I've a younger sister. When I was eight we moved to Galashiels, a small town in the Borders. Gala was total crap. School full of wankers. If you weren't into the gangs or thieving it was dead, sod all to do. My Dad buggered off so I lived with my Papa for a while. I left school at sixteen. Could do the work well enough, but was bored numb. I bummed around for a few years, working building sites and farms, odd jobs, just enough for a ciggie and a bevvy.

It's all in my wee book. That's what I call my journal. I started it when I was thirteen, summarizing anything epic I could recall. Now I add to it when I get a chance. With my cramped and spidery scrawl, the pages fill up slowly. The cover is frayed and taped over, and the pages are creased and stained with food and drink and God knows what else. My memory's iffy. The wee book tethers who I am.

When I turned eighteen I got the itch. Scotland was like a clammy jumper clinging to me. No air was getting in; I couldn't breathe. I met a merchant seaman in a pub down the Leith Walk. He said out West in the U.S. was the place to go. He put vivid pictures in my head: endless deserts, towering mountains, and magical light. He was totally pissed but he sold me. And here I am.

Those are the bare bones, but there's a fat, fleshy iceberg lurking below. Who is McEvoy?

Here's what the lads would say. McEvoy's a sport, a joker. He goes off sometimes but mostly he's steady. Got your back; good in a pinch. He's a mass of ginger hair and freckles. He's got a good face, an open face. And although the lads would roll their eyes before they'd say it, they might mention the eyes, the piercing green eyes.

The lasses? Not sure I'd want to hear it.

McEvoy is gentle. McEvoy is hard. McEvoy is loyal and true. McEvoy lies easily. McEvoy is fearless. McEvoy is afraid of himself. McEvoy can do anything. McEvoy is damaged beyond repair.

∎

The Sun is rising and my skin cringes. I've been lax and left a few patches uncovered. Those livid red scars throb and pulse each time I move. The desert as equal day and night approaches is as harsh to me as outer space. I slap on more sunscreen. Night Owl limits himself to a soft chuckle. My skin next to his is parchment next to mahogany.

"Scotchman, do your people live in caves?"

"Only in the winter. In the summer we come out to hunt Indians."

"You have much to learn about camouflage."

"And you wouldn't last half an hour in the New Town on a Saturday night."

"The Sun will forgive me but not you. We must go now."

"Tell you what," I say cheerfully. "You stop making me a cartoon of a Scotsman and I'll stop making you a dime store Indian."

Night Owl strides down the trail. He's inches shorter than me but covers the ground so efficiently I struggle to keep up. The broad river meanders to our left. After a mile, I spot a small aluminum shed, set back among the rocks at the foot of the cliff face. Sun-faded paint on the roof reads "Canyon Adventure Rafting." He walks over to it, picks up a fist-sized rock and pounds on the padlock securing the doors. I catch up with him as the padlock breaks and its pieces skitter across the ground.

"What are you doing?"

"The canyon ahead is too narrow."

"You're going to steal a boat?"

"Not steal, borrow."

"Someone might need it"

"They have others."

"Night Owl, this doesn't feel right."

"You like the alternative?"

He gestures downstream. The Big Gash is a tiered geological formation. At the level of the rim, seven thousand feet above sea level, the canyon is several miles wide. But here at the lowest level, the most recent erosion has carved a slender channel. The river is hemmed in by steep cliffs. Travel on foot looks impossible.

"OK. Let's go then."

Night Owl tilts his head. "You want to be captain or navigator?"

"Ha bloody ha."

.

We're unfolding the inflatable raft when I glance to the side where Night Owl has tossed his rucksack. I get a glimpse of dull metal.

"Fuck. Night Owl, is that a gun?"

He nudges the rucksack with his foot so I can no longer see inside. "Mind your business, Scotchman."

"For snakes?"

"You are safe with me."

"You're not exactly giving me the warm fuzzies." I wonder what else might be stashed in Night Owl's bag.

Luckily, the equipment is well-maintained. The motorized pump fires up and within ten minutes our gear is secured in the inflatable raft and we're drifting downriver.

.

"We're piddling, we're pathetic! Fucking insignificant!"

I'm lying on my back in the raft staring up at the sky. The edge of the canyon wall grazes the periphery of my vision. It seems impossible that time and nature could have sculpted something this vast. It's just as sensible to imagine that God or a race of aliens constructed it all for our benefit. I'm voting for the aliens. I crave a cold beer. Otherwise, everything's perfect.

"Not small. Not large." Night Owl says. He's not so much paddling as using the paddle to steer in the gentle current. He never expends more energy than needed. "Part of the chain of being."

"C'mon." I feel like testing him. "We're the top dogs. We can piss on anyone we want."

"You have the arrogance of youth, Scotchman. We cannot stand apart. Like us right now, part of a river flowing."

A single hawk wheels overhead, so high up it's just a dot on an eggshell blue canvas.

"And that hawk? Is he a part of me, of us, too? Seems like he's figuring if we're small enough to eat."

"The hawk too. All creatures are connected."

"Sounds like New Age crap. But, OK, I'll bite. If we're all one big machine with interconnected parts, how did we get here in the first place?"

Night Owl pauses, wondering if I'm taking the piss. He's not used to my sly humor yet.

"In my tradition, this is the fifth world."

"What happened to the first four?"

"The first world was filled with insects and insect-like people. It was so unpleasant the insects made themselves wings and they flew through a crack in the sky to the second world."

"OK, the second world."

"The second world was a blue world with birds who resented the insect people. So the insect people followed the voice of the wind to the third world."

"The third world?"

"The third world was yellow, with people and animals we would recognize. There were mountains at the four corners and the mountain people taught First Man and First Woman to plant corn. They also told the people not to bother the water monster."

I nod gamely. "Sure enough, the water monster."

"Coyote didn't heed the warnings. He kidnapped the children of the water monster. The ocean rose and began to flood. Everyone gathered on top of the tallest mountain. They planted a giant reed and climbed up it to the fourth world."

"Ah, right, the fourth world."

"The fourth world was beautiful, with races of people and different animals. First Man and the First Woman learned more about corn and about the difference between sexes…"

"…so they were diddling themselves in the first three worlds. That's too bad. And no telly to stay home and watch."

Night Owl ignores the crude jibe. "…Coyote still had the children of the water monster so the waters rose again. They planted a reed and climbed it but could not reach the dome or find a way through. The yellow hawk tried to scratch a hole in the dome but also failed and it was a locust that finally got through."

"One locust? Bit of a stretch, don't y'think?"

Night Owl stops storytelling and regards me balefully. "Scotchman comes from a wet country to the north. He is one of the mud people. Mud people do not understand metaphor."

Stung, I shut up. Night Owl continues in his sing-song cadence. "Spider spun a rope so that the people could climb up. The ants went first, carrying soil from the fourth world. The people followed, carrying seeds of corn and other treasures. And so they settled the New World, this world."

"And it's been hunky dory ever since?"

"Not quite. They had not been long there when the waters rose again. First Man and First Woman searched everywhere and rescued the children of the water monster from the Coyote. They kept them safe in a boat on the lake. Floods have never again destroyed man's world."

"The people in that story, they're your people?"

"Yes. The creators named us Lords of the Earth or the Holy Earth People. That got shortened to The People or Diné. We are Diné. The name Navajo came much later."

"C'mon man. You don't really believe that tall tale?"

"It is how I understand the world. The world makes perfect sense to me. It is people that make my heart sore."

•

The afternoon wears on. We drift lazily. Night Owl yawns. Four gold molars glint at the back of his mouth like sentinels in armor. He curls in the back of the raft and naps. The air shimmers. The sound of heat bugs wafts across the water. I steer for a while, then lie back and tilt my bush hat down over my face. I drift in and out of consciousness while locusts and giant spider webs play in my mind.

•

My reverie is broken when the raft suddenly lurches. I sit up. The river that's been glassy for so long is corrugated, with white water at the crests. The raft rocks slightly as it shimmies between the waves. Smooth rocks occasionally protrude from the water and we lurch when we hit one.

"Night Owl. What's up?"

He scans ahead. "We must leave the river. We walk from now on."

He hands me the other paddle, and points downstream toward the right bank, where there's an inlet and a sloping beach. "Paddle to that place."

We start paddling. Night Owl, who I've never seen break a sweat, is putting some effort into it, so I guess we've waited a little long to begin our maneuver.

Another rock looms on my side of the boat. I push against it with my paddle to fend us off. The paddle flexes and then snaps out of my hands and flies out of reach into the river.

"Shite!"

"Now it will be harder." Night Owl hasn't lost his cool but he ups his stroke rate. Despite his efforts our sideways progress is being eclipsed by our forward motion and the inlet slides beyond reach. Misjudgment and a mishap have cost us.

"Now what?" There's a metallic taste on the back of my tongue.

"Now we each trust our own god." He smiles blandly.

"For fuck's sake, man! What are we in for?"

"I don't know."

"You've never been down this river?"

"It's not advised."

"Then how the hell are we going to get through this?"

"By being calmer than you are now, Scotchman."

■

The raft bucks violently in white water. Soon it will be impossible to move around in the boat. Night Owl positions me in the front, with my feet wedged hard under the front pontoon and my hands gripping the side ropes. He gives me terse instructions on what to do if I get tossed off the raft. Then he sits in the back where he can use the remaining paddle to try and steer.

Maintaining my position and remembering his instructions keeps my mind occupied but I hear the dull roar of water up ahead and my stomach sinks. It's impenetrable, seamless white noise. It sounds like the end of the world.

"Now you get your adventure." His black eyes glisten.

The canyon walls converge and curve and we're pitched into the maelstrom. Drenched in water and buffeted from side to side by rocks, only the buoyancy of the raft gives me hope. I'm hanging on so tight I can't turn around. When I glance back Night Owl is gone. I'm doomed! But a moment later, I see him out of the corner of my eye, stabbing at the water with the oar and trying to keep us pointing straight.

Twice we tilt onto one edge and only keep the raft from capsizing by flinging our weight to the opposite side. Then it pivots onto its nose as a wave hits us from behind, and for one crazy moment I'm staring into white foam inches from my head while Night Owl and the bulk of the raft are poised above me.

My throat tightens and a wave of nausea floods over me. I conjure up the image of a water ride in North Berwick I used to go to with my mum, a tamer version of what I imagined they had in Disneyland. I pretend the river is just a ride and no harm can come to me because the builders have done their job well. With an act of will I keep panic at bay and reach a pale facsimile of Night Owl's stoic acceptance and fatalism. They'll make me an honorary Navajo yet.

Center of the World

"We're running short on supplies." I fish around in my backpack for some chocolate and find it's nearly gone. "We've just got shrimp pilaf from that fancy camper's food you filched."

"There's a trading outpost on the north rim."

"Can't do without sweets, Night Owl. I'll die."

"They have everything you need. You have money?"

The irascible Indian perks up whenever money is mentioned. I like him and he's just helped us escape the jaws of death but I've seen his light fingers at work.

"Just enough and no more, you sly bugger."

I've made sure he's never seen my cash; I saved for a year and I'm intending to travel the world. Even though it's uncomfortable, I sleep with my money belt strapped to the small of my back. I have an emergency hundred dollars folded up and inserted through a slit in the side of my boot.

We spend the day lounging by the river while our clothes dry out. I'm not sure how we got through the white water adventure. Night Owl's skill and strength helped though I'm sure it was mostly dumb luck. But having survived, hubris seeps back in. I'm pumped up and energized. McEvoy ascendant. McEvoy resplendent. Cock of the walk. King of the river.

Night Owl is feeling chipper too. He tells me some Navajo tales. And after we eat lunch he moves his hand across his face and tosses me something with one deft motion. My hand shoots out to catch it. I look down. It's a glass eye.

"Jesus! What do I want with this?"

"A souvenir. I have more."

"What happened?"

"A fight a long time ago. A lapse in judgment."

I look down at the small sphere with its dark brown iris, and then up at the Indian with his vacant socket.

"Night Owl, you're just a big softie. I'll treasure it."

■

The trail winds up high under the canyon wall. We get merciful shelter from the afternoon sun. The changing color of the rock is a constant delight. At noon, through a heat haze, it's dull brown. The afternoon wears on and tones of ochre and mustard emerge. But in the lengthening shadows, the colors vault through the rainbow from dull red to magenta and an improbable indigo when the last rays are extinguished by the Earth's inexorable motion.

As we ascend to the rim, the trail forks. The main route continues on and up while a branch heads back to the river. I'm about to follow Night Owl upward when I spot four figures in the distance down at the river's edge.

"Hang on, Night Owl. What are they doing?" I point.

"Maybe backpackers." He keeps walking.

"I don't think so." My eyes are excellent so I can make out a man in black trousers and a white shirt with long sleeves, and three women wearing plain frocks. It's strange attire for a hot day. They don't look like any tourists I've ever seen.

"Hold your horses, Night Owl."

"What is it?"

"I want to see what they're up to."

"If you must..." He trudges back to the fork in the trail, wearily, to make a point.

The setting sun casts the river into deep shadow. As we get closer, I see something unusual is going on. The man and two of the women are waist deep in water while the third woman waits on the river bank. I approach stealthily, motioning for Night Owl to stay put. He sits on a rock and seems happy to oblige. By walking quietly and keeping large boulders between me and the group of four, I get within earshot.

"...by revelation from the Righteous Lord, as anointed this day by his prophet."

Peering over a rock I see the man dip one of the women into the water. Some kind of baptism.

"Now you are a Child of Christ, guarded by angels."

The man is thin and tall, with a long face, sunken cheekbones, and a mane of black hair cantilevered up from his forehead and then swept back over his head. The women in the water are wearing old-fashioned petticoats and their dresses are folded neatly on the shore where an older woman waits. The woman he's just immersed stands calmly with water dripping from her hair.

"Sarah Winfrey Jessop, come forward."

The second woman in the water approaches him. She's must be a young teenager; she has a raw, strong-boned beauty. Her figure is full and her hair is so long it brushes the surface of the water.

"With this act, I wash away your sins with the blood of Jesus. Our Lord said he who believes and is baptized will be saved. In repentance and obedience..."

I listen quietly, a mere stone's throw away. When he's finished his incantation he lowers the second girl into the water. She rises up, her hair a glistening curtain, breasts and nipples sharply defined through the thin white cotton of the petticoat. Involuntarily, I catch my breath. Then I redden because at that moment she turns and seems to look directly at me.

．

Night Owl and I reach the trading post as it gets dark. I've been saving money by camping so figure we can afford a motel. There are only two to choose from in this small dusty town. We settle into the room and Night Owl spreads his blanket on the floor.

"You're not going to sleep in a real bed?" I ask.

"You are very trusting of the diseases of white people if you sleep there, Scotchman."

I stare at the bed nearest me and imagine all manner of invisible vermin. But I'm exhausted so I wash my face and fall asleep almost immediately.

There's not much to the trading post. As we walk around the next morning, apart from the motels, I count half a dozen general supply stores, several shops with Kachina knockoffs and bad Indian blankets, two diners, a rambling wooden barn selling horse supplies and fishing tackle, and a decrepit gas station. The only people out are a handful of tourists, some ranch hands and Indians who looked equally sun-baked and wizened, and a lot of people dressed like the four I've seen by the river.

"What gives? It looks like an undertaker's convention."

"They live apart, in a town north of here called Colorado City. The people here call them FLDS."

"FLDS?"

"I don't know what it stands for. They are Mormons. I don't keep track of the strange religions of white men."

I've a dim recollection of Mormonism as a misbegotten offshoot of Christianity that had taken root in the badlands of the American West. Joseph Smith. Tablets from God. A moronic angel.

"Why do they look so glum?"

"They are supposed to live a plain life. They spend a lot of time talking to their Creator."

I'm familiar enough with the extremities of religion back home to guess the answer to my next question.

"I don't suppose there's a place here to get a pint?"

Night Owl barks with laughter.

∎

We end up at one of the two diners where, sure enough, the strongest thing on the drinks menu is root beer. I order a BLT. Night Owl trumps that by ordering a double cheeseburger with bacon and mushrooms, a chocolate shake, and a side of onion rings. He's taking advantage of eating on my dime but I can't begrudge him. I've known hard times and you have to store fat to get through them.

"I thought you Indians were into nuts and twigs and berries."

"We have been corrupted by the diet of the white man." He sighs. "They might as well feed us heroin and cocaine."

"They'd do that sure enough if they thought it would keep you lot quiet." I gesture across the table. "Cadge an onion ring?"

The diner is noisy and full but as I chew I hear a dark, sonorous voice that's familiar. The tall man from the river is two booths away with his back to us. My chest tightens. The man shares his booth with the three women, and the younger girl is positioned so I can just see her past Night Owl's head.

"…the reservation doesn't have jobs for those who come out of treatment." Night Owl breaks off. "Scotchman is not listening. He has the attention span of a small child."

"Sorry, sorry." I redden. Then I redden more over the fact that I have reddened. My pale skin and sturdy capillaries telegraph every embarrassment. I hate it.

Night Owl looks back over his shoulder. "I see. You are held captive by your little warrior."

"I have to talk to them."

"Go." Night Owl waves his large hand dismissively while he chews on an onion ring.

My fists are clenched by my side as I approach. The body language is bad. The man talks in a low, angry voice and the women have their heads bowed. The young girl is hugging herself.

25

"Yes?" The man shoots me a hard look. His eyes narrow. "What do you want?"

It's now or never, I dredge up everything I'd ever heard from my mum, who is a lapsed Calvinist. OK, take a deep breath. Be calm and smile, I tell myself.

"Are you Latter Day Saints?"

"Why do you ask?" His voice is low and his eyes are hooded slits. His swept-back hair looks like a greasy helmet.

"I am a seeker. I have been on a path that is corrupt. I am looking for a new home."

"We are Apostolic United Brethren."

"Back home, I accused my church of corruption and was cast out. They have fallen so far from the Lord that I do not hear his word in their place of worship. They embrace paganism, and superstition, and finery for its own sake." I pause. Easy, McEvoy, easy. Don't slather it on too thick.

"Ah, the Great Apostasy." His face softens slightly.

"Did not Jesus say that many will fall away and they will betray one another and hate one another?"

"You speak a truth, stranger."

"I give myself over to you. I have heard you protect the Godhead." And God only knows where I pull that from, but it works. The tall man seems to make a decision. He stands and holds out a bony hand.

"I am Samuel Jessop, Prophet."

"Ian McEvoy, from Scotland."

"You may break bread with us tomorrow evening. If you work hard and submit to the Lord's will, there may be a place for you at our low table, but..." he hardens both his stare and his grip on my hand, "...if you're not who you say or what you seem, His vengeance will be swift and absolute."

On a napkin, he draws a crude map of how to get to his compound. I walk back to my booth slowly, stunned by my foolishness, wondering what the hell I've talked myself into.

Several hours later I'm tossing in the narrow, sagging motel bed. Night Owl is oblivious. For him, sleep is absolute and unequivocal. I've never seen him twitch a muscle while he's asleep. For a moment, I'm tempted to look in his rucksack, which lies next to him on the floor, never far from his sight.

The dusty streets of the trading post are deserted. The desert is radiating its store of heat and we're a mile high, so it's pleasantly cool and still. At the end of the main street, where it shades into the scrub, a small shadowy shape trots across the scene. A coyote? Shorn of my vice of drinking, I indulge my occasional other vice and light a cig.

■

"Ssss."

The noise is to my left, and down the street from the building I'm leaning against. A rattlesnake? Arizona wildlife makes me jumpy.

"Sssssss."

Slightly louder and more insistent. It's sibilant, halfway between a whistle and a whisper. Unlikely venomous. Probably human.

"Sssssssssssss."

I walk tentatively down the side street. It's pitch black. My muscles are taut and twitching. Suddenly a small hand reaches out, grabs my arm, and pulls me into the shadows.

It's her.

"You are…Sarah."

"Yes."

"You were at the river."

"Yes."

"Did you see me there?"

"Yes."

"I thought so." I pause. "Aren't you going to get in big trouble for being out here with me?"

"Yes." Her head sinks.

We're silent for several minutes. Then it tumbles out of her. The community she lives in, a breakaway fundamentalist Mormon sect with Samuel Jessop as the absolute leader. The harsh rules, rigid schooling, and absolute subjugation of women. Worst of all her fate to be the fifth wife of the Prophet now that she's been baptized. Jessop leads a group that practices plural marriage. Bigamy where I come from. It's illegal but I imagine people out here make up their own rules.

"How old are you?"

"Fourteen." She looks up at me. Her hair is pinned in a whorl. Her cheeks and lips are fleshy and perfectly formed. Her eyes are a deep brown, set slightly too far apart for her to be classically beautiful. She hasn't yet grown into her face. In fact, she's little more than a child. Sarah is wearing red lipstick and black eyeliner and I'm sure that's a major violation of the code of conduct of her clan. I'm conflicted; my juices and my protective instincts are equally aroused.

"You've got to get away!" I grab her hands. They're hot and very smooth. Her wrists are mottled with bruises. "He did this to you!"

She moves towards me and kisses me lightly on the cheek.

"You're sweet," she whispers.

Now she turns my hands over so the palms point upwards and says softly, "You're hurt too."

I pull away angrily and swing one hand hard against the clapboard wall behind me. My fist cracks one of the boards and the force drives splinters deep under my skin. I ignore the pain.

"Come with me. Leave this place."

Her face contorts into a mask of misery. "I can't. It's everything I know. It's my family, my people. This is my world."

"You can do better. Anything is better. Meet me at the top of the trailhead into the canyon tomorrow morning."

I plead with her for several minutes, to no avail. She says she has to go. Jessop will know she's away.

"You know where I'll be if you change your mind." I reach into my boot and give her my emergency cash. "If you need to you can get far away with this."

I'm taken aback when she rises onto her toes, reaches behind my neck, and pulls my mouth onto hers. It's a soft kiss, long and almost chaste, and I feel her hips and breasts gently grazing me. Her lips are liquid satin. She pulls away and melts into the shadows. I pull a white handkerchief from my pocket and press it firmly onto my cheek. It has a faint imprint of her lips from the first kiss. I fold it carefully and put it back in my pocket. I will go the ends of the Earth for a kiss this pure.

■

Turning the corner to go back to the motel, I pass a series of darkened shop fronts. Two men are walking towards me. One wears the dark blue uniform and cap with insignia I'd seen the week before in Gallup. The other has a square jaw and flattop haircut and wears a nondescript blazer and slacks.

ATF. I dimly recall the old American TV shows I've seen over the years. Alcohol, Tobacco, and Firearms. A quick mental checklist: I'm not carrying a bevvy, they're not going to hassle me over a few cigs, and I've never owned a gun. Then a wave of anxiety passes over me thinking of what's in Night Owl's bag. Should be OK. With what I hope is a casual nod I move to the side to walk past them.

AFT puts an arm out to block my path. "Late to be out."

Squarejaw stops walking and folds his arms. I look from one to the other. They're both a few inches taller than me and look strong and fit.

"Just catching some night air."

"Not from around here." AFT scrutinizes me.

"Aye, I'm visiting. From Scotland. Just up the road from England," I add helpfully.

"Let's see some ID." ATF's eyes haven't left my face.

I hesitate for a moment. They're not INS so they have no right to harass me, but the Feds are all in cahoots and I don't want to spend a night in a dingy, brightly lit room, so I reach behind my back for the money belt where I keep my passport.

With breathtaking speed, Squarejaw grabs my arm and spins me around and towards the brick wall to my side. I hit it with a sickening thud, sending a searing jolt of pain up my back. AFT slams a forearm into my chest and with his other hand he spears my neck between his thumb and forefinger until I'm gasping for air.

"Do it. Very. Slowly."

ATF releases his grip. Gagging and spluttering, I lean forward and rest my hands on my knees. Then, with exaggerated care, I reach for my money belt, unzip it, and extract my passport.

"Do you know a man called Winston Begay?" Squarejaw asks as he flicks the pages of my passport. ATF is still staring and his intensity is giving me the willies.

"No. Nobody by that name."

"What about Henry Chee?"

"Sorry."

"He has a lot of aliases. Navajo male, fifty five years old, long black hair streaked grey and tied back, prominent nose, and four gold back teeth."

"Nope. Not familiar with anyone like that."

"Someone matching your description was seen with him last week in Gallup, and then in Flagstaff four days ago." ATF drills me with laser beam eyes. "Not many people with your coloring come through here. Think harder."

"Umm." I gingerly finger my bruised trachea. "No. No bells ringing. Don't know the man. Very sorry."

ATF stabs his finger into my chest and leans in very close. His lips are drawn back into a sneer. He smells like cheap aftershave.

"Keep dangerous company and you'll get caught in the crossfire. Remember that."

With that, ATF and Squarejaw turn on their heels and leave, and I'm left on a dark and empty street nursing sore body parts.

I tell Night Owl a yarn to explain why we have to go back to the canyon trailhead early the next day. I say nothing about my run in with the Feds, but clearly he has a lot of explaining to do. I decide to bid my time. We arrive at the edge of the flat mesa a mile from the outpost, where trail descends into canyon. The appointed hour comes and goes and my heart sinks when Sarah doesn't show.

We're gathering our gear to leave when I see the dust cloud of a vehicle approaching. It swerves to a halt a hundred yards away where the road ends. I walk forward eagerly. But five dark-clad men emerge and run toward us, each carrying something I don't like the look of. Undertakers with guns.

I'm operating on pure adrenalin, and even though Night Owl has a slow pulse, he can get the lead out if the occasion calls for it. The trail zigzags gently down the hillside, but we're in a hurry so we scramble straight down the slope on heels and butts. I look back and see them brandishing their rifles. There's a loud crack and a cloud of dirt kicks up to my right. Fuck, not just brandishing. Perversely I think: where's the bloody ATF when you need them?

Night Owl yells across to me. "Scotchman should be careful of his smart mouth. By the end of this trip he may need somebody's god to protect him."

■

Back on the trail we fall into an easy rhythm. Lake Mead is fifty miles to the west; Flagstaff is seventy miles to the east. We haven't seen anyone all day. Trouble's far behind us. The majestic landscape infiltrates me completely and I feel that I belong here. We stop in the dappled shade of a mesquite tree and sip from our canteens. I never imagined I'd ever think water more precious than beer.

"I'm going up to that promontory to catch the view."

I've got bags of energy and I want to raise my pulse a bit. Night Owl nods and leans back under the mesquite with his rucksack for a pillow. I charge up the promontory and drink in the vista, then circle back up a gully to our rest spot. Night Owl is standing over my back pack, reading something.

"Bloody hell! What the fuck do you think you're doing?"

His hand drops to his side but he stands still.

"Godammit, that's personal!" My wee book's on the ground. I'm sure he's looked through it and now he's reading one of my mum's letters that were tucked inside.

I rush forward and grab the letter from his hand. My body is taut. My fists are clenched. We stand a few feet apart, motionless. It could all end here. As the silence stretches out his lazy eye stares at a point a few inches beside my head.

"You are lucky. I have no mother."

It's the first time I've heard him talk about his family. I'm still livid but I decide to back off.

"What d'ye mean? Is she dead?"

"She left me. I was five."

"Abandoned you?"

"She walked out. A family took me in. Then another. But they had nothing for me. I left when I could."

"What about your dad?"

He looks away with pursed lips and says nothing.

·

We settle into an uneasy peace. Finally, it's time to leave our rest spot. Night Owl heaves his rucksack onto his back. It's clearly heavy. I can't resist asking.

"You've been sticking your nose in my business, so what's in the rucksack, you old trickster?"

Night Owl looks at me evenly but says nothing. Heat bugs make a background din for our conversation.

"It's not like you change your clothes. And I'm lugging all the food and the cooking gear. It must be stuffed with something."

"A good guide must be well prepared."

"What a crock. Look, Henry or Winston or whatever your name is, you've pissed off the Feds in a big way. I'm not sure you're very good company anymore."

Night Owl's eyes narrow and I'm ready for him to get prickly but instead he smiles.

"You are a seeker, Scotchman. Nothing significant is ever gained without struggle. What kind of truth do you seek? Human truth is just a pale shadow. You want the truth that casts the shadow."

I look at Night Owl. He's a thief and probably a felon. I've no idea where he's taking me. A sensible lad would beat a hasty retreat. But I need to know who I am and I need to know what lies below the brittle surface of the construct of life I've encountered so far, and I sense he can help. So I gaze through the Navajo's skin and one good eye, past his stories and his artifice, to the place where his essence is inscribed. And I decide to continue.

■

Night Owl is becoming steadily more mysterious. Sometimes when we're resting by the trail or cooking over a small fire, I glance up and he's shifted position or moved yards away. These movements are so fluid and silent that I'm taken aback. Several times it seems as if the motion is instantaneous like he's vaporized and materialized in a new location. I have my lapses but this seems different. What power does this old Navajo possess? He's joked that he can freeze time in part of the world and then release it at will. Could it be true?

"You said you'd show me a special place, and tell me the secrets of the people who've lived here for a long time."

"Patience, Scotchman. We are getting closer."

"Who are they? Are they your people?"

"No. The people of this place are the Hopi. They called themselves the peaceful people, and they are farmers, but they have warred with my clan so I have no place for them in my heart."

I understand Night Owl is about to break a code that must bind all the native peoples to not divulge secret knowledge to white men. I'm uneasy; we're about to pass through a moral membrane.

"We are close to the village. I will find my last directions there."

I look around and see nothing. No buildings, no ruins.

"What village? There's bugger all here."

"Only mud people live near the river." A dig at me. "Look up."

I scan the canyon wall above. Amazingly, a settlement clings to an impossible rock face just under the canyon rim. It's constructed from perfectly camouflaged mud brick. Many of the buildings seem intact; some are even four or five stories high. It extends for a few hundred yards by following the sinuous curve of the canyon wall.

"Christ, Night Owl. Slow down a bit."

"You can rest when we get there. Plenty of shade."

He moves with grace and speed over the steep rubble and scree of the lower canyon. Then it's a hard slog up hundreds of feet of steeply sloping rock face to the settlement's edge. I struggle to keep up. It's embarrassing; I'm young and fit and he's more than twice my age.

I'm gasping. I rest for a minute. "This is brutal."

"Scotchman is soft. The women and children of this village climbed up and down several times a day, with heavy loads."

As Night Owl promised, it's cool in the village, which is set into an overhang of rock. The construction is vertiginous, with wooden ladders connecting adobe structures on half a dozen levels. There's nobody else here.

"When did people live here?"

"The villages were abandoned seven hundred years ago."

"Jings! Europeans were still living in crappy mud huts."

"When white men came, they had very little to teach us."

"Except about war."

"No," Night Owl smiles ruefully. "In that we are also expert."

"What are these holes?" Almost every major building had a sunken circular pit at its lowest level. "Fancy digs. Was that the Jacuzzi?"

"I will explain."

We clamber down into one of the nearby structures and sit on the perimeter of the lowest level, with our feet dangling into the pit.

"But first you must know how the Hopi viewed the world. The Hopi believed that the world existed there was nothing but empty, timeless, shapeless space. The creator used agents for his work. One was Spider Woman, who made people and the Earth itself. The first three worlds were destroyed by fire, ice, and water. This is the fourth world. It is being destroyed by drought and heat. There are three worlds in the future, so seven in all."

"That sounds pretty similar to your tribe's stories."

"Truth is the same in different voices, yes."

"You're not saying you believe it literally, that that's how the world was created?"

"Was Scotchman there?"

"No, but c'mon, Night Owl, these are just stories, myths."

"With humility, your grasp on knowledge might be more secure."

I flush. "OK, OK, go on. I'm listening."

"This is a kiva." He gestures around us at the circular room. "It's the ceremonial place where ancient wisdom is transmitted. The fire in the pit is the first world. The altar we're sitting on is the second world. The platform where the ladder rests is the third world. The ladder goes up through a hole in the ceiling to the fourth world, like birth when you leave darkness for light. Those small windows higher up align with the positions of the rising and setting Sun and Moon. See that hole?"

There's a small rectangular hole cut into the floor of the kiva.

"That is sipapuni, or navel. It links us by a cord to mother earth. A kiva holds the most important ceremonies and initiations. Only priests sit at the lower level. It is as close as we get to the underworld where all people emerged."

I absorb this information. There's something intangible here. The inhabitants embedded their cosmology and their cultural history into every house. They maintained a visceral connection to both sky and earth. We sit for a while, absorbing the stillness.

■

Night Owl has to explore seven or eight dwellings before he finds what he's looking for. In the kiva of an impressive four-story house at the center of the village there's an antechamber off to the side. I see something scraped into the top layer of mud, but when I try to follow him through the small entrance he holds his hand up.

"No. Only I can enter this place."

Reluctantly, I wait. Peering in I see that one wall is covered with glyphs and stick figures and pictograms of various sorts. Whatever he's trying to figure out, it takes him ages. I get bored so I explore some of the nearby houses.

"I have what I need. We can go."

"How far is it?" I'm completely in the dark about our destination. "Where are we headed?"

He ignores my second question. "It is two days from here. We will move quickly. Full moon is approaching. It is very bad to be at such a place when the moon is swollen."

■

He's not kidding. We keep up a blistering pace. Sometimes I'm so knackered I have to beg him for a rest. But as we ascend to the high plateau above the south canyon rim I get a new experience of the desert. The mighty Colorado has lots of water but the landscape is mostly bare rock with hardy grass and a few stunted mesquite trees. Up on the mesa there's little visible water but the flora and fauna are much richer. There are Douglas firs to make me homesick, Ponderosa and piñon pines, and mesquite and creosote everywhere. Best of all, there's shade and my blistering skin is getting a break.

In four days in the Grand Canyon I've seen little more than hawks, lizards, and a few ground squirrels. Up here are birds, rabbits, mice, and even deer—another reminder of home. After eight hours of hiking we make camp, eat some cold stew and trail mix, and I topple into a deep, dreamless sleep.

The next morning instead of an empty sky I wake to a canopy of trees. If the canyon is a place of light and shadows, this is a place of sounds and smells. My ears feast on birdsong and my nose feasts on the fragrance of pine, piñon, and mesquite. There's also a rank odor that Night Owl says is the scent trail of a javelina, a local wild boar.

A half a mile out from our camp Night Owl stops dead in the trail. He bends down and picks up a small object. He shakes his head.

"What is it?"

"A cone from a bristlecone pine."

"Is there a problem?"

"It should not be here. It grows hundreds of miles away."

"Perhaps a bird carried it. Or a traveler dropped it." But as I say this I know it's unlikely.

Night Owl furrows his brow. "No. This is not good."

He walks on. I can't imagine why he's making a fuss and being so superstitious, but the pine cone is beautiful and perfectly formed so I pick it up. I add it to the waterproof bag that holds Night Owl's glass eye and Sarah's kiss. My wee trove of treasure.

■

The two small figures move slowly across a forbidding landscape. Their motions barely register in the monumental scene. They move purposefully but they are insignificant and incidental. Everything is exactly as it should be.

■

Around noon we take a side path and descend into a red rock canyon, a miniature version of the Big Gash. There's no river on the floor of this canyon but there are tortured volcanic formations and remains of ancient lava flows. For the first time since I've met him Night Owl is distracted and unsure of himself.

"Are we lost?"

"No." He looks around like he's in an unfamiliar place. "But we are very close to the underworld. The energy unsettles me."

I try to feel what he's feeling but can't. No doubt my finer senses are dulled by lifelong ingestion of sugar and fried food. We wander in and out of side cuts in the canyon until we stumble on a large, ruined building. None of its walls are more than waist high.

"Here, Scotchman."

I go to where Night Owl is standing, in the middle of the ruin. A gust of air whips my bush hat high into the air.

"What the hell was that?"

"Come closer. Look."

I see a small hole in the smooth rock, two inches across. As I lean over it a jet of fast-moving cold air makes me flinch. Reaching down, I try to cover the hole with my hand but the air flow is too strong.

"That's brilliant!" I realize why there was once a building here. "Air conditioning."

"Yes, an underground cavern. At night cool air falls in. During the day it is forced out."

"Very nifty, Night Owl. Is that why you brought me here?"

"No. Follow me."

We walk another half mile. Night Owl has his bearings now so he doesn't waver. But I sense his trepidation. He stops near the canyon wall at a place that looks no different from dozens of others in this trackless wilderness.

"There." He points to the ground fifty yards ahead.

I walk in that direction but Night Owl doesn't join me. He slumps to the ground, like a marionette with its strings cut.

"Oh my God."

There's a large hole on the canyon floor, four feet wide. I can see a few feet in, but beyond that is total darkness. No air rushes out of this hole. What does emerge is amazing and much more difficult to accept. Sound. Not the low thrum of air moving in a large cavity or the whine of small protrusions of rock vibrating like reeds. This is a rich web of sound that evokes voices and music and souls in torment.

Logic, McEvoy. Logic says that you're imagining, projecting. Logic says it's an underground cave, a natural geological formation that can generate complex sound. Logic provides many reasons why the Hopi might have chosen such a place to spin their tales of emergence from the underworld.

But the cool cucumbers who invented logic aren't with me in this primal landscape. They can't hear with my ears the voices of those who must stay behind to pay for the sins of those who were able to bring the world into being.

Snakebit

"Shite!"

They're buzzing about my head in a lazy cloud, moving just slowly enough to see their long stingers, trailing like the landing hooks of fighters approaching an aircraft carrier. Wasps. God, I hate wasps.

"Fuck!"

While trying to get away from the wasps, I flail my arms and swing my hand into a barrel cactus. Dozens of evil barbed hooks sink deep into my flesh. One goes so far through my index finger that it pokes out the other side.

Night Owl!" I yell plaintively.

He ambles over and holds my hand firmly with one hand while he tries to extricate spines with the other. I wriggle like a child.

"Desert wildlife minds its own business. If the Scotchman is calm, the cactus will not bother you."

"Jesus H. Christ, Night Owl, will you can the lecture? I'm a shish-kebab here!"

"Then be still. Each one that breaks will send a piece into you on a long and unpleasant journey."

That settles me. I take several deep breaths and watch as Night Owl expertly removes the needle-sharp spines. His large fingers are able to get purchase even when only a stub shows above the skin.

"Cacti! Just don't get me started. These barrel bastards are cruel enough. Then there's the kind I backed into yesterday…"

"Prickly pear. Good jam."

"You people are loony tunes if you eat them. All I know is that the fine needles stuck into me like fur. I was itching and rubbing at them half the night. Then there's the one that jumps up and attacks you."

"The cholla."

"Whatever. The bastards have it in for me."

I ease off on my rant and try to calm down. I have a cumulative sense of dislocation from being in the desert. It's utterly alien from the drab houses and tidy suburban predictability of the town where I grew up. It fits Night Owl like a glove, but I'm an interloper operating past my date stamp. Never mind; we've started the long trek out. Feeling better, I take the three-inch long spine that skewered my finger and store it with my treasure trove. Trophy of war.

■

I'm lost in the rhythm of my breathing and footfall when a sound penetrates my cocoon. A low hum at the edge of the audible range. Night Owl has already heard it and has picked up his pace. He lopes along the trail in long, effortless strides.

The throbbing hum rises to a dull roar and four helicopters sweep over us, barely a hundred feet off the ground. I glance at the closest and see a U.S. Government seal on its belly. FBI. Holy fuck. Big bad trouble, McEvoy.

"This way! Move quickly."

Night Owl has left the trail and he's heading down a gully, running in a low crouch. We're in a badlands of red and brown rock with few trees and almost no cover. Tortured volcanic formations undulate in every direction, with cuttings and gullies where erosion has etched a lower level. I see no reason to run and no way to escape.

"Night Owl. Stop! Give it up, man. Whatever you've done, it can't be that bad."

He's fifty feet ahead. He stops and turns to face me. I think of him as an older man, but his body is taut and leonine.

"You must choose."

It shouldn't be a close call. I've done nothing wrong. They'll give me a hard time and let me go. But here in the badlands, bad things can happen, with no witnesses. Loyalty tilts my hand.

"Wait up, you old bugger. You've got me huffing."

"Follow me! Move quickly."

■

Just before I follow Night Owl into the gully, I see them, maybe half a mile away. A dozen federal agents have fanned out and are bearing down on us.

"It's hopeless. They'll take us down like skittles."

The fractured terrain has seams and crevasses and crumpled piles of ancient lava, but there's nowhere to hide.

"This way." Night Owl beckons urgently.

He's on the gully floor near a dark opening a yard wide. He climbs in. With trepidation, I follow. I scramble down a scree slope in total darkness, scraping my head and shins on the rocks several times. At the bottom, I pause. My heart is pounding.

"Wait until you can see." Night Owl is barely discernable.

"Oh shite." I hear the faint but unmistakable sound of voices.

"Go that way." Night Owl points in the gloom. "Do not follow me."

Then he's gone. Tentatively I step into the cool darkness with my hands groping in front of me. Enough light leaks in from the entrance to see an undulating tunnel ahead. It's a lava tube. Brilliant!

Progress is slow. I keep my arms out and above me to protect my head. Some parts are large enough that I can slowly walk, other times I crouch, and in a few places I crawl on hands and knees. Slivers of light enter from above. Unintelligible sounds from a bullhorn and a scrabbling in the distance tell me I must keep going.

I enter a part that's totally dark and I'm forced onto my belly. It gets so tight I have to pull with my hands and push with my toes, a fish swimming in rock. Then I'm stuck fast. Nausea and panic flood me like a rip tide. Gripped by the anus of hell, Tartarus waits on the other side with endless torments.

Be calm, McEvoy, or be asphyxiated in this rocky tomb. I slowly release my breath and wriggle as I imagine a snake might. Inexorably I inch through the constriction and emerge into a spacious part of the tunnel.

"Agent Sperling? Are you there? Don't follow me in. I'm stuck."

The voice is faint, some thirty yards behind me.

"Agent Jackman? Frank? I need some help!"

I want to push on but the urgency in the voice makes me

hesitate. Cautiously, I retrace my steps. I think I recognize the voice and now, in the feeble light from an overhead crack, I see a familiar face. ATF. His arms are pinned to his sides and he's stuck fast. His head pokes through the hole like meat from a sausage roll. Well, how the tables have turned.

"We're going to catch you and put you away for a long time." He's glaring at me but his face is softened by fear.

"No. You're not catching anyone for a wee while. Not done up that way, like a pig in a truss."

"We have this entire area surrounded." Given his predicament, the bluster is quite amusing.

"I'll tell you what," I say, reaching past his startled and indignant face into his inside jacket pocket. "I'm just going to borrow your ID."

"Goddamn you! Put that back!"

I fish his ID out of the small wallet. Special Agent Henry Firestone. Hmm, he probably goes by Hank.

"If you want to do some good in the world," I roll the "r" for extra Scottish effect, "there are some lassies you can help out. They're being beaten by a religious nut job called Jessop. He should be taken down. Here's where they are." I slip the map that the Prophet drew for me on a napkin into the agent's pocket.

ATF is speechless.

"And I'll be writing a letter to your field officer to make sure you did your duty, Hank. So please don't be derelict."

∎

Night Owl is waiting as I exit the lava tube. He knows this entire labyrinth and has taken his own route to evade our pursuers. We have a tense few additional hours walking through the late afternoon and twilight, but we don't see the helicopters again and Night Owl's keen working eye doesn't spot anybody who might trouble us.

We're scouting a place to spend the night in semi-darkness when we hear a high-pitched whine. I hope it's not human; I've had quite enough excitement for one day. Between two mesquite bushes I spy a bobcat caught in a trap. The poor creature is in agony; the clamp has completely sheared off one of its front feet. Night Owl sets down his rucksack, pulls out the gun, and calmly kills it with a single shot to the head. It's the right thing to do but I'm taken aback by the clinical way he dispatches the animal. I'm not sure why, but I locate the severed paw, wrap it in a Kleenex and add it to my treasure trove. We make our camp.

"To the fourth world!" I take a swig from the hip flask and pass it to my traveling companion. We've just feasted on the final sachet of freeze-dried food, a lip-smacking chicken Florentine.

"I do not drink."

"Shame. You're missing a killer bevvy. Laphroaig. Laid down the same year I came out the spout. My special travel treat."

"It dulls your brightness, Scotchman."

"Why Night Owl, coming from you, that's almost affection."

His face flickers in the campfire light, but reveals nothing. I take another sip from the flask.

"Sure enough, you've shown me some grand things. But I cannae make head nor tail out of some of them."

He tilts his head. "You think too hard, Scotchman."

"What d'ye mean?"

"The answers to your questions are in your little book."

I sigh. It suits the old Navajo to talk in riddles sometimes. The fire also sighs as it settles. The embers give off a dull red-orange glow and there's a chill in the air.

"C'mon Night Owl, what's in the rucksack?"

He chews his food but is silent.

"It can't be drugs or guns. You wouldn't have the bloody cavalry after you for that. It must be something much bigger."

He keeps chewing. His eyes, good and bad, give away nothing.

"And what did you take from the kiva, the one you wouldn't let me go in? Oh Night Owl, you are a Man of Mystery."

∎

I wake up and lie still while I get used to the pale early light. We are on an upper tier of the wedding cake of mesas, half a day's hike from the south rim and Grand Canyon National Park, where we came in. We're in the shelter of a scooped-out indentation in a rock wall. Night Owl is fixing a lace on his moccasin.

I blink. He's gone.

I must have fallen asleep, but it doesn't seem like it. I glance at the shadows on the rock. They haven't moved. No time has passed.

I look back. A coyote is standing where Night Owl was a moment before. The Trickster.

Uneasy now, I raise myself onto my elbows. The coyote turns and pads away making almost no sound. I crawl on all fours over to a flat rock and reach behind it for my pile of clothes. Two things happen in the same instant: I hear a loud, bone-chilling rattle and I feel a sharp stab in my hand.

My yell echoes off the rock walls. The rattlesnake keeps an eye on me as it warily slithers away. I want to say, it's OK, I didn't mean to bother you. But I can't breathe because a seamless wall is pressing down on me.

The pain is stunning. I push it back just enough to clear a small oasis of thought. Stay calm. Night Owl will be back soon. But then: what if he takes too long? Go and get help. But then: if you move, you'll work the poison through your system. Stay. Yes, gather your strength for a while, let the pain subside, and then go and get help. But the pain doesn't diminish. It sharpens and crashes over me like waves pounding a beach until I enter a delirium.

■

In the nightmare, my world is upside down. Sky is below me and rocks lurch up and down over my head. I'm doubled up in agony. My snake-bit hand is swinging high in the air. It's black; gangrene has started to set in.

Then a realization: McEvoy is upside down. I'm draped over the shoulders of someone carrying me at a slow, steady pace up the trail. My limbs loll like those of a rag doll. I consider resisting but it seems like too much effort so I fall back into my nightmare.

■

"You're a lucky so-and-so, sure enough."

I'm on a small cot in a semi-darkened room. Through a window there are groups of people milling around in what looks like a lobby with exhibits. It must be the tourist center for the National Park.

"The ambulance will be here in a jiffy. Fix you right up."

The woman speaking is standing over me. She wears the green uniform of a park ranger. She has curly brown hair and a wiry build and looks to be in her mid-forties.

"How did I get out of the canyon?"

"That would be me." She says this matter-of-factly.

"Excuse me?"

"I carried you out. Well, most of the way. They met me with a stretcher at the trailhead."

I look at this slender woman, who's probably four inches shorter and thirty pounds lighter than me. It's hard to believe.

"Nora Walcott. Park Ranger. Thirty years service."

"McEvoy. Ian McEvoy. I...I don't know how to thank you."

"You owe your friend a debt too. He must have been the one that left the message about you, but nobody saw him before he left. He saved your life most likely."

"What do you mean?"

"Sucked the venom out. By the spacing of the punctures, that was a big fella. Western diamondback, the most venomous in the country. You're not showing much hemotoxic reaction so your buddy must have done a thorough job."

I don't want to look, but I raise my hand. As in the nightmare, it's discolored and black.

"Am I going to lose it?" I ask tremulously.

"Heck no. He did you a good turn there. He rubbed medicine of some kind into the wound. It's hardly swollen at all. You'll probably be out of hospital tomorrow."

It's a lot to take in. The park ranger leaves me for a while and I look through my stuff. Sure enough, my money belt is empty. I know

I've seen the last of Night Owl.

I'm aware of an unusual sensation on the hand the snake didn't bite. It's caused by a ring on my fourth finger. Night Owl must have put it there before he left: it's the silver braided design I noticed on him the first time we met. I take the ring off. It neatly unhinges into five pieces like a Chinese puzzle. I rustle in my backpack for the bag with my treasure trove and place six objects on the bed.

■

A bloody cat's paw
A glass eye
A pine cone
A cactus needle
A braided silver ring
A kiss on a handkerchief

■

I search for meaning in this selection of artifacts. Are these clues or omens? They are telling me something about my journey, not just through the desert, but my bigger journey. It's hard to concentrate; there's still toxin in my system. So I gather them and put them in the plastic bag on my bedside table. I lie back and close my eyes. After a while, Nora the Ranger comes back with a glass of water and we chat while I wait for the ambulance. I get a new take on the Grand Canyon.

"Do you lead tours down there?"

"Sure." Nora leans in conspiratorially. "But I have to tow the party line, tell people what they want to hear."

"What d'ye mean?"

"I tell 'em it's millions of years old. Heck, this is a good job. I'll tell them turkey buzzards can do math to keep this job."

"I don't get it. What do you really think?"

"It's six thousand years old." She says this brightly. "Like the good book says. The Lord probably carved it in a few hours."

I groan inwardly. I'm weary of all religions and their need to jockey for the right story. While people squabble over myths Nature just goes about its business. Nature just is.

The Greyhound station in Flagstaff. My ticket says San Diego but I don't know where I'm headed after that. We're sacks of water; one of my fantastically distant ancestors crawled onto land and after a week in the desert I feel far from my roots. I crave the ocean.

I take a seat and do an inventory of the contents of my backpack before putting it in the overhead rack. My clothes are rank and they've taken a beating in the past few weeks. I pull out my wee book and the letters from my mum are tucked inside. Good. I reach deeper and feel nothing. My treasure trove is gone! With dismay I realize I must have left it on my bedside table back at the ranger station. I'm disconsolate at the loss of these objects; to me they had totemic power. Memories of my time in the desert are already getting fuzzy and dreamlike. I try to focus on them but as I do they shape-shift and morph.

It's like those sand paintings Night Owl once told me about, where the story is erased as soon as it's been told. If I had to tell the story of the last month right now I'm not sure how it would come out. Luckily I have my wee book as a testament. Without it I'd worry about my grip on reality, which sometimes slips through my fingers like grains of sand. I can handle my memory lapses but I'm much more unsettled when I sense that I'm a character in someone else's play.

■

I turn my attention to an irritating sensation in one boot that I've noticed ever since I left the hospital. Maybe a pebble or small stick. I struggle to remove the boot with my good hand. Shaking it, nothing falls out. There's something in the lining which once held my secret stash, the money I gave Sarah. Among other indignities, I'm broke. The hospital staff passed a hat around to get me enough money for my bus fare.

Finally I snag three objects with my fingertips. They're small flat stones, perfectly circular and cool to the touch. Night Owl must have put them there—the bastard even knew about my stash. The Navajo took hundreds of dollars and left me with his eye, his ring, and three stones. Now all I have is the stones. I'm Jack of beanstalk fame.

But as I turn them over in my hand I see they're unusual. One side is plain grey. On the other side there are alternating rings of pale and dark shades of grey and brown in concentric circles. The edge and the center are connected by jagged brown lines, like lightning bolts.

I peer at one closely and it's perfect. It doesn't seem to be painted. If this is inlay it's the most masterful job I've ever seen. I take out my pocket knife and try to score the surface, but it resists the blade. They have the heft and texture of stone but aren't made of any material I'm familiar with. Did they come from the secret kiva? Are they natural or artifacts? Did they reach me from one of the five worlds of creation or a different world? Night Owl leaves me with these and other questions as the bus travels through the high mesa towards the sea.

What was it that Night Owl said? You want the truth that casts the shadow. I feel that I've been chasing shadows and am no closer to the truth than when I began my journey.

2 CANYONS OF STEEL

Golem

"Can I help you to a seat? Except I think you're supposed to ask me that."

I'm flat on my back on a carpet staring up at ornate ceiling molding high above my head. An old man peers over me. He's plainly dressed, wearing black from head to toe.

"I don't know what…I was just…" It's taking me time to recover my bearings.

"You passed out. Toppled over, like a tree felled with a single blow. Someone's gone to get you water."

My head throbs. Feeling for any damage I notice white gloves on my hands. It starts coming back. This is Avery Fisher Concert Hall. I'm an usher. I work here.

One of my co-workers arrives with a glass of water. I scramble to my feet, embarrassed. The concert-goers give me a wide berth, acting like nothing has happened, not wanting my episode to intrude on their evening. New Yorkers.

"Can I help you to your seat?"

"Good recovery, young man. Certainly."

We walk to near the front on a side aisle. The old man's a season ticket holder, a regular. I've seen him before. He has a compact and craggy face composed of haphazard, intersecting planes. Hair dyed jet black and eyebrows so bushy the top of his eyes are in shadow. He's old and perfectly erect, but he walks with a limp and carries himself stiffly, as if his body harbors ancient injuries.

"Ari Zeeman." He shakes my hand. I feel dry and papery skin.

"McEvoy."

"That's it? Just McEvoy?"

"Yes. Nothing more."

"Well, McEvoy. You look well-built but maybe you're not

eating. I'm sure they don't pay you much. Please let me buy you a sandwich after the show. Hal's Deli, round the corner."

I thank him and take my seat up with the gods, where I listen to all the concerts.

■

"I have seen the worst that man can do to man. But every morning I wake up optimistic about the world."

Ari Zeeman cradles a cup of coffee. I'm plowing through a platter piled high with blintzes. I can't take my eyes off his hands.

"What's your story, young man?"

"Nothing much to tell." I say, my mouth still half full.

"I suspect that's not true. There is life in you. And pain. Let me guess. It's a skill I've developed over the years. May I?"

"Be my guest." But I wish he'd just drink his coffee and keep the conversation light.

"You have the color, complexion and speech patterns of a Celt. That's obvious. Some time in the Navy? Twenty four years old?"

"Twenty five. Merchant marines. You saw my tats."

"True. That was also easy."

I listen and try to keep an even keel.

"You are smart but untutored. A traveler. Many trades."

"Fair enough."

"Now, going deeper. The pain I see doesn't emerge from you. It comes from somewhere nearby. Your family. You have lost a close relative. Maybe other tragedies."

I chew very slowly.

"That episode in the lobby. It has happened to you before, perhaps many times. It colors your life."

I try to bore holes in him with my eyes so he'll stop.

"And some things dwell in a man and shape how he moves through the world. You may not have had a drink for weeks or months, but you are an alcoholic."

■

I avoid Zeeman for weeks after that. I'm busy, working odd jobs in the Daily Post newsroom, then traipsing uptown to my evening job at Avery Fisher. I spend as little time as possible in my tiny apartment in Bed Sty, with its faded paint and linoleum bearing the imprint of sad lives. Each weekend, I devour all the city has to offer: museums and galleries, free concerts, vistas of Central Park, soulful street food. And everywhere I go there are endless people, a maw of humanity.

But Zeeman is lodged somewhere inside me and I can't shake him loose. He's managed something that I've been trying to do most of my life. I'm no stranger to hubris but I have a lot to learn.

"Mr. Zeeman." I approach him in the lobby at the intermission of an all-Mozart concert.

"Mr. McEvoy. Are you enjoying the lightness of the master? Those who make it seem effortless also make us forget it's anything but."

"I like it fine, but he's not one of my favorites."

"Yes. More moody, melancholic. Mahler? Sibelius?"

"Brahms. Debussy."

"Ah, a closet romantic, with your tattoos and red brawn."

"Mr. Zeeman?"

"You've been avoiding me. My directness scares you."

"Yes."

"Now maybe we can really talk. Get past the formalities."

"I'd like that."

"Splendid."

"Mr. Zeeman?" I hesitate. "What happened to your hands?" The first time we met in the deli I'd noticed his pale and gnarled hands. Now, looking closer, his fingers are all skewed and his knuckles are bulbous and swollen. His hands are like ghostly banyan trees.

"Severe arthritis, I'm afraid." A tight-lipped smile.

"Wow. I'm sorry."

I'm thinking that I don't buy his explanation when a strange scene plays out at the periphery of my vision. A young girl and her mother are heading back into the concert hall on the other side of the lobby. The mother is well-dressed and the girl is young, maybe ten or eleven. The girl looks in Zeeman's direction and waves tentatively. He shrugs and raises his eyebrows. A query. The mother shoots him a withering glance and pulls her daughter sharply into the auditorium.

■

We take a cab to Central Park later that evening. Zeeman has difficulty walking very far but in every other respect he's as strong as anyone I've ever met. It's early winter and we're bundled against the chill wind. We find a bench near the band shell. Looking skyward, a handful of stars twinkle and struggle to be seen against the city glow. One light doesn't waver: Jupiter. I smile to myself—the god of cosmic justice watches over us.

"I survived the gulag because I couldn't embrace death. Death seemed such an easy retreat. There were people there who needed me, people who had lost hope. I had enough to go around. It's such a simple gift."

"Why were you there?"

"A Jew, of course. A writer. Active in my town, patron of the arts. Stalin didn't actually want to destroy people, though he killed many. He wanted to destroy the glue, that connective tissue that separates us from simpler animals. When that glue is gone, we become those simple animals. It was a cunning strategy. Quite brilliant."

I look at his face in profile as he speaks. In the jaundiced light of the street lamps his hooded eyes are looming and intense. I sense he can tap a line into any broken part of his body and be transported four thousand miles away and half a century back in time.

"We were such a mixed bag. Artists and musicians thrown in with murderers and vagabonds. For a while, the calloused laborer had an advantage over the soft-handed banker. But once the flesh and finery had been rendered, when we had all been reduced to our fundamental chemical form, we were all the same thing. We were all mud."

"Was there ever any pleasure?"

"Yes! There was profound pleasure, made more exquisite by its evanescence. A starry night bright enough to read by. The music of a violin made from scraps of wood peeled from the barracks. The joke told and retold and always funny, like gum that never loses its flavor. Perhaps a single orange, passed around segment by segment like a gift from God. People who spurned these pleasures or couldn't grasp them always died. They always died."

We watch the sky in silence. A jogger passes by, then an inline skater being pulled by a dog. I sigh.

"You find it hard to talk about yourself, McEvoy. Why is that?"

"Because it doesn't matter!" I say fiercely. "Whatever I do—good, bad or ugly—it's insignificant. It doesn't fucking matter."

"But it does matter to you," Zeeman's voice is low, soothing. "And I would hazard a guess it matters a lot to those you love."

The quiet stretches out like a slender thread between us. Zeeman is patient. He waits.

I take a deep breath. "My dad was a bastard."

"Explain."

"He was a jobber. Always moving on, always getting fired, always uprooting us. We moved all over Scotland while I was a kid."

"But that's not all."

"No. He was mean. He was a prick."

"Go on."

"That's enough. He didn't cherish my mum. He never had a kind word for my sister. He only cared about going down the club, playing darts, ogling tarts, getting pissed. He was a piece of shite."

I fold my arms to signal the end of this line of questioning.

"You use the past tense. Is he dead?"

"No. His black heart beats on."

"Here you are, thousands of miles away, living your own life, and he still has a hold on you. Why?"

"I haven't a fucking clue."

"Your sister, you mother. What do they do?"

"My mum lives with her sister. My sister? She struggles."

"And you, McEvoy. Is this what you want?" He sweeps his arm past the Manhattan skyline.

"What's not to like. The Big Apple. Fancy cars. Fine art. Important people. Canyons of steel and glass. It's the financial epicenter of the world." Inwardly, I wince. The cheap sarcasm is unbecoming.

Zeeman tents his fingers to form a pale, bony labyrinth. "I teach the violin. I also teach evening classes at Columbia. Russian History. European Politics. You could run circles around most of my students. You are passionate and you are very sharp."

"My schooling wasn't exactly a roaring success."

He surprises me by reaching out and gripping my hand so hard it hurts. His eyes blaze in their sockets like coals.

"You must never give up on learning, Mr. McEvoy. Never!"

I pry my hand from his.

"I appreciate your interest, Mr. Zeeman, I really do. But I'm not looking to make any major changes right now."

He breaks into a smile. "To an optimist like me, that's virtually a signed contract." Then he winks. "My lawyers will be in touch with your lawyers, as they say."

■

The notes soar up to meet me like balloons released in the park, each one a splash of vibrant color. I'm folded into the crawl space at the crown of the concert hall, looking over the heads of the crowd to the two men and two women in their cocoon of concentration on the stage. Bartok's third string quartet. The pinnacle of dissonance. I've long ago given up trying to parse music or discern the intention of the composer, or even ape the popular expectation of what their intention should be. Rather, I absorb the music through my skin. Based on the reaction of my body, I say "This is total shite" or "I don't give a toss" or "This is brilliant."

I seat people at the last intermission and clamber back up to my perch where I can look straight across at the art deco chandeliers. I settle on pillows I've purloined from the fancy box seats. When the first notes hit me, I freeze. It's Shubert. Death and the Maiden. I'm not superstitious but I shiver like someone is walking over my grave. My throat tightens and a wave of nausea crashes over me. I scramble down the stairs and rush from the concert hall into the cold night air.

■

There's a game I play when I'm on the job. I scan the crowd from above and look for someone who piques my interest. It might be the way they're dressed or a gesture or the glimpse of a distinctive face. Then I tell myself a story about who they are, what they do, and what kind of drama might go on in their life. At intermission I mingle in the lobby and seek them out. But I'm not so brazen as to talk to them. I linger nearby and eavesdrop on the conversation and hope that clues emerge.

Usually they do. And quite often I'm right. Much more often than if I had just guessed.

I don't know how it works and I don't want to. Thinking too hard or playing Sherlock Holmes by analyzing visual clues leads to failure. It's much more effective when I have a light touch and use averted vision. It's a brilliant feeling when I cipher someone who was no more than a distant figure in a crowd.

■

"You're looking natty, Mr. Zeeman."

"I am, McEvoy, I am. Normally I care so much about the internal that I neglect the external, but a well-meaning friend has arranged a date for me, and I must do my best."

"A date!" I laugh. "Sorry, I didn't mean…I just thought…"

"…that an eighty year man wouldn't be interested in such things. I've been a widower for twenty years but I'm not quite dead yet. And the camps didn't destroy my libido or my equipment."

I blush and cast my eyes downward.

"Quite right. You should hang your head. When my generation is ready to hand over the planet to you, we'll let you know. I'll be mud soon enough."

"I suppose we're all mud monsters." I'm thinking of something that a crazy Indian called Night Owl said to me years ago.

"The Golem!" Zeeman squeezes my arm hard.

"What's that?"

"An unshaped form. In the Talmud, Adam is created as a golem when his dust is kneaded into a shapeless hunk. Originally, golems could only be created by someone very holy or very close to God. But every golem is a shadow of the being that could be created by God."

"Then why make them?"

"They've had their uses. In the 16th century, the Emperor of the Czech nation issued an edict to eject all the Jews from Prague, or kill them. The Rabbi fashioned a golem from the mud of the Vltava River. The golem came to life after the Rabbi chanted special incantations in Hebrew. But the golem grew and used its power to kill innocents. The Emperor promised to stop persecuting the Jews but begged the Rabbi to destroy the golem. To destroy the golem, the Rabbi rubbed out the first letter of the word "emet" or God's truth from the golem's head to make the Hebrew word "met" or death."

"That's a helluva story."

"Story? The golem is still stored in the attic of the New Synagogue in Prague. I tried to see it once but they wouldn't let me in."

"I suppose scientists still do try and make life from mud."

"There is hubris in creating life to do your bidding. Another Rabbi created a golem that grew so big that he was unable to kill it without trickery, whereupon it fell on its creator and killed him."

"Like Frankenstein and his monster."

"The end of the story is not yet written. Do all that you can in life before you turn to dust, as one day you must."

Zeeman turns somber and directs his riveting gaze towards me. I'm like a butterfly pinned to green baize.

"Near the perimeter of the camp they piled the dead in shallow graves. They decomposed quickly in the short Siberian summer. In winter that area was mud; nobody wanted to go there and have it clinging to their boots. But in summer the top layer turned to dust. One rare hot day I remember basking in the Sun watching the dust whipped up by a breeze and carried over the fence. To freedom."

White Heat

I try to hold the basis for Nietzsche's withering critique of Kant in my head but the professor's words slip away.

"…we recognize in his work the philosophy of the hammer…"

My attention is trapped like a bug in amber by a girl sitting near the front of the classroom. She's tall and slender with jet black hair cascading down her back. Her skin has a Mediterranean hue of pale olive, and she has fine cheekbones and a perfectly straight nose. The package is made complete by black tortoiseshell glasses rimmed with rhinestones.

"…an aphoristic work, jumping from one assertion to another…"

I try to conceal my attention by looking ahead while staring at her obliquely across the room. She's like a taut bow—bristling with energy. She fidgets and twirls her pen, her foot jiggles incessantly, and every few minutes she swivels her head and arches her neck. The long arc of skin from her chin to her collarbone is making me weak.

"…resorting to ad hominem attacks and emotional appeals…"

She asks pointed questions several times in that first class and I find her impatience and directness thrilling. Other times she looks exasperated or disgusted, but never bored or disengaged. She has cat-like grace and a sinewy elegance. I'm smitten.

"…his claim that language should be the army of metaphors."

When class gets out I head downtown and walk the Park as I do whenever I'm gloomy or obsessed with an idea or image that I can't shake. Central Park isn't completely safe at night but I avoid gang areas and can take care of myself if trouble comes calling.

Zeeman has persuaded me to take some night classes and start exploring options for a degree. First there was the small matter of getting a GED, since I'd never finished high school in Scotland. That was months of torment with textbooks and workbooks that appeared to be written by cranky pedants for small children. I sneaked through that and now I'm at Columbia, taking one of the few classes that fit my Avery Hall schedule. The campus intimidates me. Its monumental architecture and well-shod students proclaim loudly that I'm an interloper, a pretender.

■

"I should have two holes in the side of my head."

"Excuse me?"

"You might try and be a little less obvious. I feel like your personal aquarium."

I wince and the mercury in my thermometer rises. I feel my pallid skin redden like litmus paper.

"But someone who's so transparent in their discomfort can't be all bad. Men are obtuse; sometimes the direct approach does work. I'm Rebecca. Rebecca Meunier."

"McEvoy." She's intercepted me at the end of class the next time it meets. "I'm sorry I was staring. I forgot myself."

"That's charming too, in its way. You're not some obsessive stalker are you?" She's tall, eye to eye with me. Her voice and face are stern, betraying none of the irony in her voice.

"Not sure I'd admit it if I was. Then you wouldn't come and get a coffee with me."

"True. Was that an invitation?"

Can the diffident approach, McEvoy. That's pure insecurity.

"Yes. Please have a coffee with me. I'd like to talk."

"Well, I suppose after an hour of listening to words about words, we might as well make some of our own."

■

The coffee shop isn't ideal for an intimate chat. It's jammed with students, a jazz trio plays in the corner, and sound careens off the metal surfaces, keeping the volume just short of a din. After fifteen minutes of yelling fruitlessly at each other we give up and spill back onto the street.

"This might work." I point a few doors down.

It's a Korean supermarket with a deli in the corner and several tables and chairs set out, almost as an afterthought. The lighting is garish and the ambience nonexistent, but at least it's quiet.

"What leads you to the Great Philosophers?" she asks.

"It's as good a place to start as any. I've been looking for a new direction."

"What was the old direction and what was wrong with it?"

"Too many different jobs. Too much traveling. Some time at sea. But I was at sea metaphorically as well. I've been blundering around and I've stumbled into some truth, but not as much as I hoped for. I need to take a direct approach."

"A seeker. Mmm. That's attractive." She smiles. It barely dilutes her intensity.

"What about you?"

"I'm doing a Ph.D. in astrophysics here at Columbia. We've lots of courses to take, but it's a monotonous diet. So I take the occasional evening course: art history, ecology, philosophy."

"Do you have a boyfriend?"

She raises her eyebrows. "So you do know how to be direct. I'm probably too busy to have a serious boyfriend. To be honest, most men my age can't handle the seriousness of my subject and my commitment to it. Boys do come calling, but very few men."

"Tell me what you study."

"I'm working on the cosmology and the early universe…"

As she talks, I lock in on her eyes; they dance and sparkle behind the tortoiseshell glasses. Rhinestones seem to be a theme; apart from the glasses, they feature in her jewelry and also on her belt buckle and shoes. She's wearing black pants and a black turtleneck sweater, with a high collar that makes me yearn to see her neck again.

"…ripples in the radiation left over from the big bang…"

Her face treads the delicate line between beauty and severity.

Her nose is strong and straight, the planes of her cheeks are smooth and classical, and her eyes are the color of burnt umber. I hear hints of a French accent in her voice, like molasses with a hint of gravel.

"…and have you been listening to me at all!"

"Sure. You're testing the big bang by looking at the microwaves left over from the early hot phase of the expansion." I grin. "OK, you did lose me a bit after that."

"And I can tell it's not because you couldn't keep up. You seem distracted." Her face softens. Her eyes are now large, the dark brown irises flecked with green.

"True. Maybe we can go somewhere else?"

She gestures at the sacks of rice and jars of kimchi. "This isn't intimate enough for you?"

■

We find a row of small galleries open late, one of those unlikely clusters of culture amid commerce scattered all over the city. I play the fool, riffing on the sculptures and paintings with a mixture of mock erudition and bawdiness that she seems to find amusing. We spill onto the street and as we're walking down the street I brush lightly against her arm.

That's all it takes. Like drunken sailors we stagger into a doorway pawing at each other. I find her mouth. She pulls me hard into her so that my hipbones meet hers. I wrap her hair around my hand and pull her head back to better taste the skin of her neck. My other hand has reached under her sweater to cradle her breast. She grabs me around the waist and squeezes me tightly. Our tongues meet and dance. She exhales with a sound that's halfway between a sigh and a moan, then pushes me away.

"Where do you live?" Her breathing is fast and shallow.

"Bed Sty. Half an hour on the E train."

"Too far. My place." She takes my hand and pulls me forward.

A brisk walk in the chill autumn air just manages to keep the lid on. But as the door closes behind us, we fall into each other again. I peel her sweater off and fling it to the side while she scrambles at my belt. She unbuttons my shirt and I reach around and cipher the brail of her bra clasp. Then we take that surreal and momentary time out from the flood of passion to remove our shoes and socks and ask each other about birth control.

Clutch reengaged, we're back in gear. I delay as long as I can the delicious moment of penetration. It's all happening too fast; I might never see her again. We both ease back, savoring the moment. Blood courses. Her nipples are like tiny unopened flower buds, standing out from the perfect meringues of her breasts. She hooks her legs on my shoulders and we end the shuddering ride in a tight embrace.

Never bolt your food, my mum used to say. So I savor the second course. She chews her lower lip in concentration and I'm wearing only a sloppy grin as she straddles me and plants her hands on my chest. The sinews stand out slightly on the inside of her thighs. I watch her rise and fall, eyes half closed. Looking up, I cede her the keys to my castle and its estates.

In the grey early light, I spoon Rebecca and bury my face in her tangled hair. We juxtapose well. My body is thick and muscled while hers is long and willowy. My head is massive and topped by a flaming crown of curly hair while hers is elongated and graced with a river of flowing black tresses. My skin next to hers is like strawberry mousse mingling with iced coffee.

I gather my scattered clothes and reluctantly dress. Rebecca keeps grad student hours. She can sleep until noon but I've got to be at the news desk by eight o'clock or I'll be fired. She stirs and stretches like a cat as I pad to the door. She looks at me with heavy-lidded eyes. Her voice is slurred by sleep.

"We're lovers, McEvoy. Now do I get to know your first name?"

■

We meet the next day for an Italian meal on the upper West Side, before she has to head off to work on her research project and I have to go to the concert hall. She starts with a reality check.

"I don't normally behave that way."

"Is sex an aberration for you?"

"Don't be annoying."

"So wanton sex with a near stranger is an aberration?"

"It takes me a while to trust someone. I'm a little embarrassed. I don't know what came over me."

"Aye, the coming was more than a wee bit of fun."

"Don't be crass."

"I'm sorry. Rebecca, you can't live by equations alone. I may be laddish at times, but I'm liberated enough to know that women get horny too."

"I just feel we got into this so quickly."

"Fair enough. You dial back your sexual magnetism and I'll dial back mine."

"McEvoy, be serious!" She purses her lips. "I don't know much about you."

"Are you saying you don't want me to come over after work?"

She reaches across the table and pinches my arm, hard.

·

That's how it goes. Intense physicality set against a backdrop of intellectual yearning. I'm no fool. I know from day one that the pure metal of her intelligence may grow weary of my unrefined ore. A time may come when she wakes up and decides she's been slumming. But hubris and lust keep those thoughts at bay.

I toy with pumping myself up, telling her grandiose stories of my past that she can neither confirm nor deny. Elevating up my status at the Daily Post to a copy editor or better. But I've never been one for Walter Mitty fantasies. If she wants me she'll have to get used to the tatty paint and chipped varnish. There's no bright, shiny McEvoy.

·

"You're so smug, you can barely contain yourself." Zeeman looks at me suspiciously over the rim of his coffee cup. "I know you don't have the wherewithal to come up with a cure for cancer so it must be a woman."

I smile.

"Your IQ has lowered 20 points. It must be a smart woman."

I beam.

"She's not only stealing your soul, she's stealing your mind."

I grin like a damn fool.

"McEvoy. I don't keep your company because of your effervescent wit or your deep knowledge of world culture. I like you because you're young and hungry and full of infinite promise. If you disappoint me, I'll look elsewhere to live vicariously."

"Oh, lighten up, Zeeman. You're brilliant but sometimes you're just a crabby old man."

"Such ingratitude."

"Listen to us; we're like an old married couple." A light goes on. "Why Zeeman, you're jealous!"

His mouth purses like he's just sucked a lemon. But I want the two most important people I know in New York to meet, so I fix a meeting at Rockefeller Center the following weekend on what turns out to be a bright, chill morning.

∎

It doesn't go as planned. I imagine it will all be about me—them comparing notes on why McEvoy is a great guy. But Rebecca wants to go skating on the outdoor rink and I don't know how so Zeeman steps gallantly forward. They twirl elegantly over the ice for an hour while I nurse a glass of flat, overpriced beer.

"That was delightful, Ms. Meunier."

"I enjoyed it too. I haven't skated for years."

"You grace the ice like a swan."

"Oh knock it off, Zeeman." I'm a real sourpuss.

"McEvoy's not himself. But I don't know who else he could be, and I doubt anyone else would have him." Zeeman is unusually jovial. He's enjoying himself far too much.

As Rebecca sits down she reaches across and touches my arm. It works; my hackles settle.

"Mr. Zeeman, what do you do?" I've not told Rebecca because I actually know very little.

"I've had many jobs. Teaching the violin pays some bills, but not enough to live in this great city. My pension was cancelled by a stroke of the pen of one of Stalin's minor functionaries. Now I live off blood money."

I regard Zeeman with new interest. "What d'ye mean?"

"When I was a teenager my family abandoned everything and fled to Riga. Latvia had been in and out of the hands of the Nazis and the Soviets, and at the time it was struggling for independence. We were harbored by a family of sympathetic Jews in the basement of their big house. For months, we lived secretive lives, only coming out at night for an occasional walk or to see a movie."

"What happened?" Rebecca pivots to face him and leans forward on her elbows.

"The father of the host family must have had a better offer. One day the Soviet soldiers came and shipped my parents and my seven siblings off to the camps. I escaped because I'd been sent to buy milk minutes before."

"Where's your family now?" Rebecca is transfixed.

Zeeman is matter-of-fact, as if he's talking about people he barely knows. "One sister did survive but she died ten years ago."

Nobody speaks. The sound of children's laughter and the scrape of skates are very distant.

"What does that have to do with your retirement?" I ask.

"It's most strange. About thirty years ago I received an unmarked envelope and a key, with directions to a safety deposit box on Canal Street. Every year, in January, ten gold Krugerrands are waiting for me. I cash them in and it's quite sufficient to live on."

I whistle softly. "Someone in their family tracked you down."

"The sins of the father." Zeeman is preternaturally calm. "I bear the family no ill will. I accept the gesture with grace."

Who is this fierce yet tender old man? He put me on the defensive when he asked about my family, but my gut tells me there's more to Zeeman than the stories he's told so far.

■

"Welcome to my world."

The ceiling is so low that neither of us can stand up but Rebecca is impressed. We're in the elevated crawl space under the rococo ceiling of Avery Fisher Hall.

"As long as you don't mind sharing it with the pigeons, and rats with no fear of heights."

"It's wild! I love it."

"It's my home from home. I'd love to live here, but I'm near six feet so it would turn me into Quasimodo."

"Are you sure nobody comes up here?"

"Never. The janitor's afraid. Something about operatic ghosts."

"McEvoy, you're full of surprises."

"Mmm, try me."

Rebecca crawls further inside. The opening is three feet high and ten feet wide and opens onto the upper reaches of the hall. It's an eighty foot drop straight onto the mostly balding or wigged heads of the concert-goers below.

"The acoustics are brilliant."

"I can't wait."

From our eyrie we hear the buzz of the audience subside. There's some rustling and a few scattered coughs, then restrained applause as the performers walk out. A voice radiates outward and upward, a pure and sultry mezzo-soprano. Mahler's Liede von der Erde.

"Oh, how beautiful."

"The best seats in the house, because music has wings."

At intermission we have a picnic, huddled in a crawl space grander than any attic. We're open to the world, yet completely private. I slice apples and brie for Rebecca, and pass grapes from my mouth to hers. We sip champagne that I lifted from the bar downstairs during a shift change. Instead of crystal we have Dixie cups.

In the second half of the concert, Mozart's Jupiter Symphony wafts like balm up to the ceiling. It's very close to perfection, written at the peak of his powers, less than two years before he died. Zeeman told me he never saw it performed.

Rebecca is still on her hands and knees, projecting slightly over the abyss. I'm on my back letting the sound wash over me. I roll over and crawl toward her, then turn onto my back again and wriggle between her legs until I'm staring under her silk shirt onto her navel and she's straddling me. I slowly undo the buttons of her jeans and work them down over her hips. I feel between her legs. The dominant tone rises under the fundamental tone.

"Oh. Oh, no." But she doesn't move.

I ease her panties down over the curve of her ass. Her skin is cool to the touch. Her leg muscles quiver. Patiently, I remove her jeans and panties leg by leg and inch by inch.

"No. Mmm. No."

After a lyrical response to the fundamental tone, the aria insertion theme is repeated and extensively developed. Her breathing is shallow and irregular. My tongue flickers in a series of fanfares. I pull on her haunches and her breathing rises in rapid arpeggios. I gently press my finger on her perineum, skin as sensitive and pink and wrinkled as that of a new-born baby. The floodgates open.

In the cavernous space beyond our heads, the five-voice fugue of Mozart's stunning finale unfolds. Notes rise and expand like perfectly-formed, miniature worlds. Each note is a bubble that, no matter how beautiful, can't last forever.

War of the Worlds

"Your stuff is in a box. I've already assigned your desk to someone else. Go get your last check, hand in your keys, and be out of here by noon."

The city editor of the Daily Post spins on his heel and walks away briskly. A busy man. No doubt he has lots to do and many people to fire before lunch.

I've no one to blame but myself. There've been a few too many mornings sleeping in with Rebecca to keep a job that's built around deadlines and the presses running on time. It wasn't glamorous work, but I had enjoyed the hurly burly of the news room. Wearily, I pound the pavement, and by lunchtime I snag a job bussing tables at a busy bistro nearby. It's tiring and the tips are shite, but it will pay some of the bills.

Just not enough. New York is insanely expensive and I need two jobs just to keep my head above water. With a classy girlfriend my spending has ratcheted even higher. Cheer up McEvoy, at least you get to experience amazing sex and music almost every day.

■

"McEvoy, where were you?"

"Sorry?"

"You just went away. You weren't asleep; your eyes were open. But you checked out for a minute."

"Just daydreaming."

"No, it was stranger than that. I called your name and waved my hand in front of your eyes and you didn't react."

"I'm an all or nothing guy, Rebecca. When I daydream I take no prisoners."

"Well, I suppose…"

She isn't convinced, but I distract her by running my tongue along the inside of her long, elegant leg. From her toe with the silver ring to her upper thigh is a journey of a thousand miles. Her bed is too narrow for lollygagging so we're lying on a duvet with lots of pillows tossed on the floor.

"Cherie, tell me about your family."

After a bivouac on her navel, my tongue continues its long and arduous journey. It runs through the fine down on her stomach then does the modest ascent of the escarpment of her rib cage. The gentle mound of her breast lies just ahead, a hillock on the horizon. It's soft and pliant to the touch. I circumnavigate her large and dark aureole, which are the color of burnt umber. My tongue teases her nipple and registers a slight metallic taste, alien yet pleasing. I take the nipple into my mouth and it puffs up proudly.

"Stop!" She pulls my head up and holds it in her hands, inches from her face. "Really. I want to know about you. I can't completely trust you when you're such a cipher."

I sigh. Rebecca's a keeper. Time to come clean.

"I like to think I take after my mum, Kirstie. She's a highlander, from Nethy Bridge. That's where I get my tendency for a good tan. She's a freckly redhead with a big heart and the saddest and most beautiful eyes you'll ever see. But she made some poor choices. One was my dad."

"Where is she now?"

"She lives with my aunt in Aberdour on the south coast of Fife. All her adventures are behind her now. It's a very quiet life."

"And your Dad?"

"I've no idea where he is and I don't care. We left him when I was eight and went to live in Gala, outside Edinburgh. He was a mean wee man."

"He can't be all bad. Didn't you get anything from him?"

"My sweet tooth and the gratitude of dentists everywhere I live." I think for a minute. "And my love of travel. He's a wanderer."

"What about your sister?"

"Annie's seven years younger than me. She lives in Edinburgh."

"She must be just about to leave school. What does she want to do with her life?"

"Rebecca, my sister's a heroin addict. She's in a shelter. She has no life. Before I left home she went on a binge and sold all my stuff. That helped me to travel light."

Rebecca squeezes my hand. "I'm so sorry."

"It is what it is. I don't look back. I don't feel false sentiment about my family." Bluster and bull shit, McEvoy.

Her voice rises. "It's not just sentiment to care about people, even if they're flawed."

"Annie and I are solid. We can't be torn asunder."

She pulls my head toward her again. "Those eyes! Those

fabulous green eyes. They're your magnet and your shield. What do you really care about, McEvoy? Who do you love?"

■

Two days later, it's Rebecca's turn to be caught off-balance. We're in a used bookstore near Columbia University when a young man and woman walk up to us. I peg them right away for students, most likely grads in Rebecca's department. They sport the standard issue winter uniform for students in the city: jeans, dark sweater, wool coat, and thick scarf. The look is generic but the quality is good, Abercrombie and Fitch rather than Old Navy.

"Hey, Becca."

"Hi, Frank, Jenny."

"You missed the department meet and greet, and also SciFi movie night. Lawrence made great eats." This from the man.

"Yes, I was busy both times."

"Shapiro is asking after you," he continues. "He's got a simulation project he says is perfect for your skill set. Cold dark matter. Better talk to him or he'll steer it to someone else."

"I will. Thanks for the tip."

The conversation continues, with me part of the circle but feeling increasingly like a fifth wheel. I cough.

"Sorry," Rebecca reddens. "I'd like you to meet McEvoy. He works at Avery Fisher."

"Pleased to meet you." I shake their hands.

"What instrument do you play? Or do you work in the front office?" This from the girl.

"More of a floater. I help people to their seats."

There's an elongated pause, and after a few pleasantries they take their leave.

"Are you embarrassed to be with me, Rebecca?"

Normally so direct, this time she says nothing and avoids my gaze. I have my answer.

"I enjoy the romps, but I don't want to be your dirty secret. Maybe when GED meets PhD it's a mismatch."

She reaches out and touches my arm. "No, no. You're very smart, that's one of the reasons I was attracted to you."

"Aye, well, my intellect's rough-hewn, more native art than what you'd see hanging in the Met. But we never go out with people in your department and I've never met your family. I think my crust hangs too low for you, Rebecca."

She looks miserable and I leave her on the hook for a while.

■

Zeeman nurses a coffee while I try to get my jaw around a corned beef sandwich of monstrous girth. We're in Hal's Deli and I'm telling him about my awkward conversation with Rebecca the day before.

"I'm in deep. She's all I could ever want."

"She has the power to hurt you." As always, Zeeman's analysis is crisp and accurate.

"If all I am is her walk on the wild side, we're doomed."

"So dramatic, young man." He cackles with amusement. "Perhaps you should be yourself and not worry about perceived obstacles."

"I feel like I need to raise my game."

"Then do so."

"The first thing I need is a job with a future. Clearing tables and shepherding arses onto seats is getting me nowhere. I'm still skint. When I get to night class I can barely keep my eyes open."

Zeeman leans forward conspiratorially. "I have an idea."

"I'm all ears."

"The public school system in the city is in disarray. Contract talks have just failed and many teachers will lose their benefits. They're all fleeing for the suburbs. I've heard they're turning substitutes into head teachers."

"What's that got to do with me?"

"McEvoy, sometimes you're very obtuse. You'd make an excellent teacher. You are broad, well read, and you have passion for learning."

"Thanks for that. But there's the small matter of an undergraduate degree, a Masters, and a teaching credential."

"The middle school near me is desperate. I know the principal. He would probably—how shall I say—make an exception and turn a blind eye to the lack of letters after your name."

"Zeeman, you're a hero!"

"You are a project, McEvoy. Clay that I would like to help mold. My own golem."

■

Something else is preying on my mind but I don't mention it to Zeeman. He knows I share his gift of discerning truths about people I don't know or have barely met. I've told him that it sometimes works from a distance and he got excited when I recounted my experiments at Avery Fisher. But I've had moments in my flat or Rebecca's where I'm relaxed in a chair and I think I can see the interiors of neighboring flats. They're mere flashes, but very vivid, with the heft of reality. As tight as I am with Zeeman, I don't want to tell him I can see through things and into people. Since I'm not a superhero from a Marvel comic I may be delusional.

■

Rebecca surprises me with an invitation to her mum's apartment for dinner. We've been luxuriating in a cocoon of lust, but after three months I've finally advanced from secret sex toy to boyfriend. I'm not sure we'll survive the transition but I'm game to give it a go.

"Ah, the mystery man. You've been keeping Rebecca in a ferment. Bienvenue."

"Sorry to be so tardy. The E train decided to sulk in a tunnel."

"Pas de problem!" She holds out a slender hand. "Je suis Chantal Meunier."

"Grand to meet you, Mrs. Meunier."

"Not Madame Meunier. Chantal. Je t'en pris."

"OK. Chantal it is."

Rebecca's mum is striking and has French style in spades. Simple but elegant emerald green dress, the auburn hair piled high, teardrop earrings, and just enough makeup to draw out and enhance her lips and cheekbones. Her features are softer than Rebecca's but the fire behind the green eyes is very familiar. The entire effect is debonair, vulnerable, and coquettish.

"Cher amis, voici l'homme énigmatique. Ian McEvoy."

There's an awkward moment as I enter the dining room and nine pairs of appraising eyes swivel in my direction.

She purses her lips. "I'm sorry; in my family we slip easily in and out of French. We'll try and behave."

Everyone's already seated. I've momentarily punctured the bubble of wine and conversation. Rebecca beams at me and pats the empty chair next to her. But first, Chantal goes around the table. Rebecca's two older sisters and their husbands. Her aunt and uncle. A neighbor couple. And a woman Chantal introduces as her dearest friend.

"Do we call you Ian? Rebecca says she calls you by your surname." Chantal looks at me skeptically. "Un peu étrange."

"Ian's fine. McEvoy's better. I'm not bothered." I smile equably.

"And what is it that do you do, Ian?" Rebecca's sister Hélène asks. She's dressed primly in dark blue skirt and white blouse; her tidy face is framed by a bob haircut. She and her husband are lawyers.

"I'm taking night classes. And working to pay the bills."

"Mmm. And what is your career path."

"Up for grabs," I say, finessing the fact that I only just passed my high school equivalency. "Maybe history or philosophy."

"Très bon." Chantal gives me an earnest look. "It's good to study while you explore options."

"Becca finds the real world too dull. Ennuyeux, n'est pas?" This is Louise, the oldest sister. She's immaculate in a fawn pants suit. I've already forgotten what she does; something with financial derivatives. "We're still waiting for her to come down to Earth."

I glance at Rebecca. She looks calm but the muscles under her jaw have tightened.

"Och, I don't know, but a Ph.D. in astrophysics is fairly

impressive where I come from."

"Bien sur." A bright smile from Chantal. "She always did take the path less travelled."

∎

And so it goes. Cultured and articulate, the well-shod rels diss us singly and sometimes lance us both with the same bon mot. I figure my meager accomplishments are fair game, but it gets my goat that they discount Rebecca's intellect and ambition. Ah well, at least the plonk's first rate.

"…the Fauré was well done, but I do prefer Berlioz…"

I blink.

"…Pierre and I first met at the Cloisters…"

And chew my filet en croute.

"…outrageous what they charge for parking…"

I blink again.

"…was trying to steal our clients, imagine…"

Then glance at Rebecca.

"…a Seychelles, mais l'hôtel c'etait décevant…"

She's gone.

"…d'accord, c'est l'enfant chéri de tous les politiciens…"

I reach for my wine.

"…Charles Edward Stuart, isn't that right, Ian?"

I concentrate.

"…so of course we'd love to know your opinion."

Chantal's face comes into focus.

"Ian, are you alright?"

The chatter and clatter subside. All eyes turn to me. My sense of time has fragmented into disconnected shards. Marooned on a small temporal island, I struggle to get my bearings. It would be easier to accept if I was drunk, but sadly, I'm not. Parts of my existence have simply been elided.

"The Young Pretender, aye, he's OK if you like your heroes tragic and inept." When in doubt, be confident. "We both had our chance to save England from the English and we blew it."

Later, in the kitchen, a strange evening gets stranger. Rebecca and I help her mother fix coffee. French press, naturellement. They thrust and parry and I keep body parts out of the way.

Chantal is arranging bone china cups in saucers. "Darling, Henri and I don't talk much, but we worry about you."

"Maman, you don't get it. I'm doing what I love. It's not a phase. It's not a dalliance."

"Of course, mon ange. But what will it lead to? Shouldn't you have something to fall back on?"

"Maman, I love you, but you're infuriating! I've no desire for the kind of affluent, predictable life that Louise and Hélène have."

"I just want you to have the best future possible. And make the best possible match."

Almost instantly, my cheeks are burning. Realizing her faux pas, Chantal covers her mouth with her hand. She busies herself pouring the coffee.

"Darling, please take these out. And put liqueur glasses and the liqueurs on the table."

Rebecca gives her mother a scornful look and leaves the kitchen. Chantal shrugs and sighs heavily. I'm filling the kitchen sink to soak the pots and pans. It's silent except for the sound of the tap and the sloshing water. She turns towards me and reaches across me for a sugar bowl on a shelf above the sink. I'm enveloped by a cloud of perfume. Her body brushes mine. I feel her thigh and breast through the satin of her dress. She leans toward me and tilts her shoulders inward, increasing the roundness of her breasts and the darkness of the hollow between them. A languorous glance and she pulls away.

∎

The air in my apartment is stale and smells faintly of fish. There's one window and it looks out on the rusted fire escape of the building across the alley. To create an illusion of space I've removed almost all furniture. Looking down, I see my slippered feet. Under them, a faded Mexican rug and a parquet floor. And under that, laid out in the literal perspective of foreshortened vision, eight stories of anonymous lives. I see them all as if there were captured on multiply exposed film: a man in a white t-shirt playing with a short-haired terrier, a family sitting motionless in front of a flickering TV, a teen lying on his back reading a comic, a dark and empty room, a woman with eczema trying not to scratch it, a bald man eating spaghetti with a spoon, a couple pacing at a pause in an argument, a teenage girl staring at the wall in quiet desperation. And above them all, McEvoy, a ghost in the machine.

■

The air crackles with electricity. After my silly bouts of jealousy I thoroughly enjoy the times when Rebecca, Zeeman and I get together. The old Russian Jew and the patrician New Yorker of French extraction get on famously and sometimes the sparks fly.

"Where is God in your story? Tell me." Zeeman leans forward in his seat in the coffee shop. Anticipating argument, his body quivers like a tuning fork.

"There's no God in my story. There's no need." Rebecca is serene and in full control.

"What is the narrative then? What makes it a story?"

"It's beautiful in its way. Everything we see around us, all the other planets and stars in the Milky Way and in all the other galaxies formed from vast clouds of gas and dust billions of years ago in the expanding universe."

Zeeman nods. "From dust and vapor, everything is possible. Yes, I do like that."

"Before that, long ago, the universe was featureless particle soup. Everything emerged in the big bang: infinitely hot, infinitely dense, a singularity."

"A singularity! Pure sophistry. Scientists fit angels on the head of a pin and dress it as logic."

A flash of annoyance flashes over Rebecca's face. I'm enjoying this. They're on opposite sides of the booth, face to face, titans of thought engaged in battle, while I slouch in the corner licking the sugar off a jelly donut.

"Ari, we have plenty of evidence for the big bang." Her voice is soothing, almost a singsong. She knows it raises his hackles to be talked to like a child by a beautiful woman. I gaze at her admiringly. She's wickedly playful.

"There are the microwaves from the early hot phase, the remnant radiation that surrounds us," she continues. "There's no other way to explain that. There's the helium fused in the first few minutes, more than could ever have been made by stars. And there's the expansion that Hubble discovered, all galaxies are moving away from each other, pointing to a time in the past when everything was denser and hotter. It all makes sense."

"Sense? Sense? No, it's a bloodless story told by people who have computers where their sinews should be." I wince. Zeeman has gone over the top but he doesn't know the amplitude of Rebecca's temper. "Who was there to witness this extravagance?"

"The universe doesn't need witnesses. It leaves us with evidence. At least for those with eyes to see. Do you doubt your birth because your eyes were too new and gummed shut to see it for yourself?"

Ari cackles loudly. "McEvoy, take care of her. She's a gem. Keep her hidden so no one steals her."

This is for Rebecca's benefit. Zeeman knows she hates being talked about as if she isn't there. But Rebecca keeps her cool.

"It's the joy of science, Ari. I can sit here and be bounded by the Earth and my limited lifespan, yet know that universe is much, much larger and much, much older than I am, and know that the origin was 13 billion years ago in an iota of space and time that held you and me both, Ari, and everything there is."

"And the iota. What came before the iota?"

"We don't exactly know."

"And the expansion of the iota. What caused that?"

"There are ideas, but the theory doesn't fully explain it."

"Ha! There's your God. Just as his Son could multiply fishes and loaves, so the Holy Father could take an iota of space and multiply it into myriad stars and galaxies."

Rebecca smooths the tablecloth. Her slender fingers sweep crumbs to either side. They're galaxies and we're in a bubble universe of our own construction within the bustle of the coffee shop.

"That's totally ad hoc," she says. "It's quite plausible the universe emerged due to quantum processes."

"I like my explanation better. God set everything in motion and scattered galaxies like seeds to the wind. Then he made it interesting enough that the creatures he created would have a challenge for their big brains."

"Your explanation has the charm of a bedtime story, Ari. Maybe you'd still like to think that Jupiter is a capricious Roman god, who moves among the stars by whim. But I'd rather follow Galileo and think of Jupiter as one world among many. If you want to know how nature really works, turn to science."

■

The next round breaks out with no warning on the Staten Island ferry. It's a blustery day with flat grey scudding clouds that promise rain. We eat hot, salty pretzels in Battery Park and walk the financial district. Then we lean against the railing and enjoy a view of canyons of glass and steel. Looking toward New Jersey, Ellis Island and the Statue of Liberty are visible across water studded with white caps.

"It wasn't an accident to suggest this," says Zeeman. "Fifty years ago today I came to this country, and got my first taste of possibility in the shabby halls of that building." He points a misshapen finger at Ellis Island.

"That's bloody brilliant. Many happy returns, you old bugger. How did you con them into letting you in?"

"I had nothing. No passport, no identity card. Just a few scraps of family correspondence, enough to prove my name and age."

"It's no problem," I say. "America is the perfect place to reinvent yourself." Rebecca flashes me a strange look.

"I remember the smell of grease and disinfectant. I remember the brusqueness of the official who gave me my papers. I wanted him to take his time, to make a ceremony—this was my future! I remember the line took five hours, my penalty for having a name at the end of the alphabet." Zeeman falls silent.

"You've been through a lot, old man."

"No matter where I was," Zeeman says, his voice far away, "I've always been in His hands."

"Do you mean you've not been in control of your life?" Rebecca, the arch-rationalist, senses a debate.

"In a sense, no. The mud that I am is sculpted and animated by the Creator anew every day."

"Where is free will in this?"

"It's not a useful concept."

"Ari, surely you aren't giving up your birthright as a human being, to make decisions moment by moment, with full responsibility?"

"That's not precisely how it feels, young lady."

"I don't want to denigrate your worldview," she says, and I know she's going to do exactly that, "but these are just traps of the mind, tricks of psychology."

"Explain."

"Suppose you're in a cell in a prison, thrown in there for life and forgotten. One night a sympathetic guard slips the bolt of your cell, without you knowing. You wake up in the middle of the night, and for a moment sink into the deepest despair at your plight. At that instant you think you're not free, and yet you are."

"Intriguing…"

"Or say you're sleeping in the familiarity of your own room. In the middle of the night, quietly, so you can't hear it, some nasty person bricks up the door and window so you are sealed inside. You wake up in the middle of the night and think of what you'll do the next day. At that moment you think you're free, yet you're not."

"Provocative…" Zeeman winks at me, "It must be interesting to be with someone who loves philosophy so much."

"My point is," Rebecca continues, "religion paints itself as the way to live a better life, but we all know how much death and destruction has been wrought by people following their Gods. I think too often it's an excuse to give up autonomy, to cede control of your life."

"A person without faith, like you, will have difficulty accepting and understanding this. Let me explain. My god is not a conventional god."

"I thought you were a practicing Jew."

"That's how I was raised, but I actually follow the Gnostic faith, a precursor and inspiration for all the Abrahamic religions: Christianity, Judaism, and Islam."

"How does it work?"

"Gnosticism accepts the world as flawed and filled with suffering. But unlike those conventional religious traditions, it does not blame this on Man and his failings, but on the imperfection of the Creator."

"Isn't that blasphemous?" Rebecca is taken aback.

"Perhaps. Gnostics also take the view that scripture is myth, but not in the sense that you might mean by myth: stories that are not true. In the sense that the truths embodied in these myths are more profound and on a different order than the dogmas of theology or the statements of philosophy."

"How can you say that? A story is a story however you choose to interpret it. Why should the Gnostic interpretation have any special validity?"

"It springs from our view of deity. Gnostics believe in an ultimate and transcendent God, who is beyond all created universes including your big bang. He, or It, emanated the substance of all worlds, visible and invisible. But this divine essence has been corrupted over time and distance. To worship the cosmos, as you do, or nature, as many others do, is tantamount to worshipping the taint of corruption."

"I don't worship the cosmos. I know it exists and I can explain it, and your supernatural entity isn't needed to do that."

"Hence the human flaw. We each contain a fragment of the divine essence, but we also have a perishable component that is flawed by secondary creation. Earthbound and materialistic beings like you are not ready for Gnosis and liberation."

"The dualism's a clever twist, I'll give you that, but it still smacks of the same "Just So Story" to defer the responsibility we each bear onto a metaphysical construct."

"What say you, McEvoy?" Zeeman gives me a baleful stare.

"An honorable draw. Can we go get a snack?"

■

"What's the book by Hegel about consciousness?"

"Phenomenology of Spirit."

Rebecca looks over her glasses at me from where she sits cross-legged on the floor. "I don't get it. I never see you reading. You never crack a book. Yet you do just as well as me on the tests. This is hard stuff. How do you do it?"

"I'm abundantly and effortlessly talented." I toss my head back and preen my hair.

"I'm serious!"

"I know, and you really should lighten up."

A pillow flies through the air and glances off my head. "McEvoy, you can be a pig."

"But I know where to find those truffles."

She yells in exasperation and returns to her reading. Rebecca is smart and competitive. Our philosophy class doesn't count toward her degree but she won't settle for less than an A. It bothers her when I handle the work so easily. I let her off the hook.

"I've an unfair advantage."

She looks up quizzically.

"I've read all these books before."

"The way you describe the schools in Scotland I'm amazed you're even literate. When did you do all this reading?"

"The merchant marine."

"Ah, yet another hidden compartment of the Chinese box called

McEvoy."

"Not hidden, exactly. Not much to tell."

"Tell anyway." She smiles mischievously. "I'm sure all these secret places are laid bare in your journal. What do you call it?"

"My wee book." I smile wanly.

"Yes. You've mentioned it, but I've never even had a glimpse of it. Where do you keep it? I'm sure it's fascinating reading."

Each time this happens, and my interior spaces are opened to the light or fresh air, a small tide of panic rises in me. I'm afraid that the spaces aren't filled with my life. I'm afraid that the spaces are hollow. Rebecca is hard to deflect. That's the trouble with dating a scientist; they're interminably curious.

"Four years, lots of time on my hands. Those books about the sea, they're always painting it as infinitely varied, as having a personality with many hues. That's bollocks. The sea is fucking boring. On a trip lasting sixty days, it'll look exactly the same for fifty five of them."

"So reading was your recreation."

"Aye. At each port the lads would go off for a bevvy and some slap and tickle, while I'd roam around the town with my backpack of books and swap them at used book stores."

She arches an eyebrow. "So you were a choirboy? You never joined "the lads"?"

"Och, never say never. But not very often."

"They must have made fun of you."

"Aye, but as quirks go, it wasn't interesting to them. Some would even come sheepishly to me for a loaner. By the end of my tour, my little cabin was cheek by jowl with books."

She laughs. "The best library on the high seas."

"Probably. I found that I was swapping out most of the novels but hanging onto the philosophy and science. That's why I know my Hegel from a hole in the ground."

"It sounds almost idyllic: curled up with a good book and a shot of brandy, with the rhythm of the sea to lull you to sleep."

"Parts of the life were hard. The loneliness."

She purses her lips. "But you got used to it and probably learned to like it. That's why you escape into your head so often."

"Aye, but it's no teddy bear's picnic in there, I can tell you."

"And all those tattoos?"

"They're not that bad, like a swarm of mosquitoes biting. No, I meant the carousing and partying, the wear and tear on the body."

"I don't understand."

"Rebecca, it's why I can't drink."

Inside the Machine

The teaching gig barely lasts a month. I'm thrown in the deep end teaching world history to an 8th grade class at P.S. 121 down in the meatpacking district. Mostly hardscrabble kids, a combustible mix of poor white and black, with some Koreans and Puerto Ricans tossed in. I know the subject well enough; all the skill comes from motivating them and maintaining control. Just as the bike stops wobbling and I have a lick of speed the principal pulls the plug. He apologizes and tells me I have talent and potential, but his head would be on the block if the shirts ever find out a neophyte's in the classroom.

Zeeman is philosophical and says he'll look into programs to pay my way to get trained and certified as a teacher though he thinks the fact that I'm an alien might be a problem.

Meanwhile, waiting tables at the bistro isn't paying near enough. The tips are lousy and I can only do the lunch shift, unless I give up my usher job. So I start working as a bicycle courier, ferrying time-critical packages all around Midtown between law offices, businesses, and ad agencies. It pays better and I get the occasional fat tip plus I can stay in shape. But dodging the traffic is hellish.

I'm ill at ease. The seams between my world and Rebecca's are starting to show. Her life seems effortless. She's smart and works very hard, but her parents pay for her cozy Westside apartment and money is as abstract to her as the big bang is to me. Each of my decisions is weighed against the brutal calculus of living in the most expensive city on Earth. Columbia classes cost money and mean two nights a week I can't work. It's touch-and-go to make rent every month and I'm weary of living in a wee hovel.

∎

"I remember when I was in third grade, our teacher said a penny thrown off here would make a dent in the cement."

We're bundled up against the cold on the observation deck of the Empire State building. All summer the lines to get in are four or five hours long but in the winter New Yorkers get to play tourist.

"So what did you do?" I've already guessed the answer.

She laughs. "Well, it seemed ludicrous to me, so I persuaded two of my friends to come with me after school to do the experiment."

"What about innocent bystanders?"

"We had that covered. One of my friends stayed on the street with a walkie-talkie to tell us when the coast was clear."

I laugh at the naïve precision of the idea.

"Yes, it was foolish. And I did have a pang of anxiety when I tossed the coin over the railing."

I look somber. "So that was your first murder…"

"Probably not. Years later, when I was studying physics, I worked out that the terminal velocity of a penny in air is 65 mph. It wouldn't hurt any more than if someone threw it at you hard. And of course the wind would've blown it way off course or onto one of the ledges so it's unlikely it ever reached the ground."

We take in the city, its majestic grid laid out below us, yellow taxis like corpuscles moving along linear arteries, a low din of activity rising up to meet us. Just before we turn to go, I have a strange sensation. Looking uptown, I see streets and cars that are hidden from view by intervening buildings. I've had a similar experience inside, but never outside and on this scale. I muse on the power of imagination.

We head uptown to the Guggenheim and then into the park for an ice cream. Rebecca opts for a coffee instead and watches me shiver with amusement.

"Why do you eat ice cream when you're already cold, McEvoy?"

"Hard to explain. It's an ancestral thing. As a kid, having an ice cream meant you were having out a good time. So you always did it. Didn't matter if it was sleeting or blowing a gale."

"I thought you were hardy."

"Hardly. I was miserable in the cold and the damp. My mum used to take us to North Berwick and we'd go in the sea in most seasons. It took ages of her rubbing Annie and me hard with a towel to get rid of our goose bumps and blue lips. Making myself cold still reminds me of a good time."

"You're a strange man."

"Aye, it's been said of me."

The ancient elevator takes ages to come. We've bags of groceries to make dinner in her apartment but the pot is already simmering. As the door slides shut we paw and claw at each other. We're wearing far too many clothes.

Rebecca moves her lips over my shoulders and chest, lingering at the large freckles. Compared to my splattered canvas, her body is a seamless expanse of soft pale brownness. She takes me in her mouth and I ascend a slow arpeggio of the scale of pleasure, keeping me at the subtonic just short of resolution. Then she eases me into her and leans backward and forward. Her hair drapes like a black curtain on my neck and face. I feel her tremors, like waves on a far shore.

We no longer talk when we have sex. There's still hunger but no dinnertime conversation. This time we're both quiet afterwards too. We lie next to each other in separate worlds.

■

I give up evening classes to take a third job, placing orders and restocking shelves of a Korean supermarket near my apartment. It's yet another small wedge between Rebecca and me, losing the activity that had brought us together. I read the entries in my wee book that trace our few months together. It's like a chronicle of chemistry: fast combustion followed by the slow separation of immiscible fluids.

Zeeman misses a concert so I have my eye out for him at the next one, an all-Beethoven evening.

"Mr. Zeeman, can I help you to your seat?"

He smiles and clasps my elbow tightly. Is it my imagination or are his lips thinner and his fingers bonier than usual?

"I missed you, old man. You OK?"

He waves his hand dismissively. "I am like an ox."

"Let's leave your personal hygiene out of this. Maybe the coffee shop after?"

"Certainly. Will the young lady join us." His eyes shine.

"Don't think so. Something going on in her department."

"I see." He purses his lips. "I hope you're giving her your very best effort, young McEvoy."

"I'm not sure my best will be good enough."

I have a feeling of a disconnect approaching and the void that lies beyond. It's disconcertingly familiar.

∎

Zeeman misses two concerts in a row. It's unlike him; I'm worried. I ask one of the sales clerks to look up his address in the season ticket subscriber list. It's a no-no, but I cajole him until he relents. Soon I'm standing in the lobby of an upper West Side brownstone. The area has seen better days and is in transition; on the sidewalks I see a mixture of long-time patricians, Koreans, Cubans, and a few gang-bangers. His name is there on a tarnished brass plate, but the button is missing and the door is wedged open. The stairwell smells of urine poorly masked with disinfectant. I start climbing.

"…treat him this way. He's a good boy. He wants to learn but you ask too much."

A woman's agitated voice. I pause below the top landing and peer through the bannisters so I can observe the scene.

"…in tears after he's had his lesson. You came highly recommended but Zach is miserable. We're not coming back!"

Zeeman's response is inaudible.

"That's completely unreasonable! You shouldn't be working with young people, Mr. Zeeman. You're harsh. Zach's scared of you."

More words I can't make out.

Her voice is a crescendo. "Enough. Enough! Just keep the money for the last lesson. I'm amazed you have any students left!"

I move to the side. She brushes past with her head down. Zeeman stands motionless in the open doorway.

"What was all that about?"

He doesn't answer but turns and walks inside. I follow and close the door behind me. The apartment is one room with a tiny kitchen and a bathroom off it and a bed along one wall. There's a music stand with a naked light bulb above it, a few boxes in the corner, nothing on the walls, and no other furniture.

"Moving out? Just moved in?"

He shakes his head. "I've been here for fifteen years."

Now it's my turn to shake my head. "Christ, Zeeman. This is sad. The phrase get a life comes to mind. Who was that woman? She was pretty pissed at you."

"Another parent who is failing to give their child a love of learning. The children are very raw. I can shape the clay. But the passion has to come from them…"

His voice trails off. He sounds defeated.

"How many students do you have?"

He waves his arm vaguely. "Three? Four? Once, I had many. My best students played Avery Fisher and Carnegie Hall."

I sigh. "You owe me a story." I sit cross-legged on the bare floor. "C'mon old man, I'm not going anywhere. Let's hear it."

■

"I had been in the camp for a year. Two long winters stitched together by a pitifully short summer. People died and new prisoners arrived to take their place. We depended on each other, but it was dangerous to make friends. That created an opening for cruelty and betrayal. I kept to myself. I endured."

"To keep going we accepted the grim rhythm of life. The guards were cruel but disengaged. Their life wasn't much easier than ours. They died from dysentery and typhoid as we did. Then a new camp commander arrived."

Zeeman paused. He stood in the middle of the room. Light from the bare bulb made him look wan and cast deep shadows from his brow onto the planes of his face.

"Viktor Grogin. A pedestrian name for someone of such refined evil. The posting was a punishment to him. He didn't sit back and wait out his term. He changed the rules and invented arbitrary punishment. He picked favorites and bore grudges. It became an extra task for us to avoid his displeasure."

"Grogin liked music. He had appreciation but no understanding. He played the violin serviceably but with no sensitivity. In St. Petersburg he had gone to concerts regularly so our camp was cultural purgatory. When he found out I played the violin I was a marked man. At first he made me play for him. I did my best but the violin he had sent in from a town a few hours away was cheap and tuneless. One day he took it from me and smashed it on the floor then struck me in the face with his gun for good measure. Then we had no music for a while."

"Sometimes silence is golden."

"In this case, yes. I faded back into the woodwork. But one day crates arrived from Moscow. Grogin was visibly excited. We saw the guards unload violins, violas, cellos, and basses. Enough for a string orchestra. Even at a distance I could see the instruments were very high quality. We found out later they belonged to an elite chamber orchestra dating back to Peter the Great. The regime considered the players to be intellectually suspect. So Stalin had them liquidated. Literally, I believe."

I whistle softly.

"I played for Grogin, but he got bored with the solo work of Bach, Scarlatti, Paganini. He made me teach him instead. He was a mediocre student, stubborn and surly. He set himself the goal of playing a short piece by Tchaikovsky, written for piano and transposed to the violin. I despaired that he would ever master it, but after a few months he set the date, and one sharp winter morning he assembled the entire camp in the exercise yard. I remember that the Sun was pale and low on the horizon, like an egg yolk. It was bitterly cold. We prisoners shivered in our rags; the guards stamped their feet like horses."

"Grogin played. It was not good and not bad. But it didn't match the sounds he had in his head. He was humiliated. And of course his humiliation was my humiliation. I was brought to him. Two guards held my arms and two held my hands. I tried to concentrate on the clouds of breath rising from each person and disappearing into the blue sky. Joint by joint, finger by finger, bone by bone, the guards broke my hands."

The pit of my stomach tightens. I want to get up and grab onto Zeeman and hold him. He stands as rigid as a board. I wait.

"I cannot play and he cannot play but Grogin must be entertained. He declares that each week there will be a performance. That I must select the music and train the players. That music is all that separates us from beasts. We had use of the extraordinary instruments from the chamber orchestra. One of the violins was a 1732 Guarneri. I cradled it in my hands and was heartbroken that I could not play it."

"My life became about one thing. That helped me forget my hunger and other ailments. I picked short but elegant pieces that were not too difficult to play. I favored ensemble pieces where the shortcomings of a single player would not be too obvious. I scoured the camp to find anyone with a musical background. With some success; my first group had talent and after practicing for five or six hours a day the first short concert was a success. Grogin arranged for the lead violist to be sent back to Moscow and released."

"The mood in the camp was electric. I was inundated with people who wanted to train with me and play their way to freedom.

But I was very selective. With good reason, as it turned out. The second concert also went smoothly and the cellist got his release papers the next day. But Grogin sat stone-faced through the third concert, even though the music was quite well-played. The next day the violinist who had been weakest player did not appear for grog and bread. Yet no car came to transport him from the camp."

"He wasn't good enough, so the bastard offed him?" My voice is loud and raw. "That's fucking diabolical!"

"It was a world apart, with its own rules and logic. We have done this for millennia. In a place they had just conquered, Roman soldiers killed every tenth villager to instill order and obedience. Grogin would not allow anyone to perform twice. Every week I had to prepare a new set of recruits, to mold them from clay. The talent pool was shallow so I trained my recruits for twelve hours a day or more, until their fingers cramped and bled and they fell asleep while practicing. They had to learn, but I had to teach them well. I had to teach them well."

Again Zeeman stops. His eyes are blazing and his misshapen hands slowly clench and unclench at his sides.

"Prisoners avoided me. I was a pariah. But hope is a sturdy weed, hard to destroy. If they were lucky they would play their part and be unnoticed and return to more familiar daily hardships. A few did shine and were released. It's the others I can't forget. Their reward for the gift of music was a bullet and a shallow grave."

■

In my dwarf-high eyrie I lie on my stomach on cushions and edge forward until my chin rests on the lip of the vast chandeliered concert space. I never totally relax when I'm up here because I have to be in place to usher during the intermission and escort people out of the building at the end of the concert. I'm expert at racing downstairs a dozen bars before the end of a piece.

But as the first notes of Beethoven's "Great Fugue" reach me I know I'll be immobilized until the final chord has evaporated into an imperceptible shimmer. The jagged, leaping dissonance reaches right into my gut. When the music finally releases me I'm exhausted, like when Rebecca and I have a wee tumble.

■

I get up to leave and look out over the heads of the crowd filing demurely up the aisles. Something extraordinary happens. I can see through the seats, stanchions and barriers. The walls are transparent; I see staff in their offices and walking down corridors in other parts of the concert hall. I see through the walls of the building to cars on the street beyond. Groups are talking on the sidewalk and I can see their expressions and almost read their lips. In earlier moments similar to this I was able to forget what I saw. I could tuck it away or treat it as a momentary hallucination. But this vision is precise, richly detailed, and implacably real. It can't be denied. Just as suddenly, the window on this hidden world shuts tight.

■

"No donut for McEvoy?" Zeeman raises one eyebrow.

"Some new health kick. Rebecca's convincing me of the importance of cruciferous vegetables. But I'm a Scot. Haute cuisine is a deep-fried Mars bar. She's swimming against a brutal current."

The coffee shop buzzes with conversation and laughter. Zeeman is opposite me in the booth. We're both still blissed out on the music. He reaches into the pocket of his great coat and hands me a folded piece of paper. The edges are yellow and it's brittle with age.

"You're too old to pass me secret notes. If you love me, just come out and say it, you old bugger."

But Zeeman isn't in the mood for levity. I open it carefully. It's a crudely stamped picture of a pile of shell casings on a backdrop of a red star with Russian script above and below. It looks like the label from an old case of Red Army munitions.

"The other side."

I turn it over. Musical notation in a cramped, spidery hand fills the reverse side, running up to each edge of the paper. I look up.

"It's for you. A sonata. It was my attempt to show that the quaver is more powerful than the bullet."

I stare at the tidy notes, written it a world run amok. The color is not black or blue; it's more like rust.

"Zeeman, is this written how I think it was?"

"Blood. For music, worth every last drop."

The clatter of the coffee shops sounds like it's far in the distance.

"What is it, Zeeman?"

He's immobile and silent.

"What?"

He stares at a point beside my head.

"What!"

"They tell me I have pancreatic cancer. Stage four. I have a few months to live."

■

"Ari, your god has a lot to answer for, however well you protect him by declaring his remoteness from the worlds' imperfection."

"Creation is an act of love. Can you not accept love?"

"It tastes too often like a poison pill. Maybe we'd do better if we stopped waiting for salvation, accepted our responsibilities, and set about fixing things."

Rebecca and Zeeman are in fine form. It's Washington Square in December, and the oak and beech trees lifting their shivering arms in a plea to the leaden sky. We sit on the cold hard ground and chew deli sandwiches. Pleasure mingles with sadness—Zeeman is one of the few reasons Rebecca and I are still together. I feel like we're entering our coda, the last, brief phase of a sonata. If life mirrors art, this cadence will achieve complete harmonic and melodic closure.

"Ari, believers like you still don't have a good answer to Epicurus, who asked these questions two thousand years ago."

Rebecca's on a roll. It's thrilling to listen to. I still love her fire and steel. She barrels on.

"Is God willing to prevent evil but unable? Then he's impotent. Is he able but not willing? Then he's malevolent. And if he is both able and willing, why evil?"

"Yes, theodicy. The problem of evil." Zeeman nods earnestly. "But your complaint is based on a misunderstanding the nature of creation and action in the Gnostic cosmos."

"You can't have it both ways, Ari. Is God angry at us because we are sinful? Is he making us suffer to test our faith? If he tortures and maims and murders people to see how they'll react this doesn't seem to be a God worthy of worship."

"The target of your frustration is the demiurge, the creator entity of the universe, known to my people as Yahweh. It's a category error to confuse the demiurge with the Monad, the absolute essence, the spiritual source of everything."

"You say I sweep all my uncertainty under the rug of the big bang. Well you sweep all the perfidy of the world under the rug of your faith. What's redemptive about Ethiopian babies dying of malnutrition?"

The debate continues for an hour. The sandwiches are untouched on the grass. I have a sloppy smile on my face for much of the time. I'm in a state close to bliss.

■

The next evening, I feel much heavier as I closed the accordion gate on the elevator in Rebecca's building. At her floor I step out and am stopped in my tracks as a vision crackles into view. I can see not just through the walls of her building, and the next building, and the next, but through street after street. Like an X-ray through a canyon of glass and steel, the skeleton of the city is laid out before me, etched in flickering rectilinear light, a grid converging to a vanishing point in the distance. Is that why I'm here, why I exist at all: to see the hidden pattern of the world?

The vision is sharp and overwhelming. I stagger back against the elevator door and catch my breath. It's not at all dreamlike, but what accompanies it is even more striking. Like a radio dial locking onto a signal I tune into a cacophony of sound, a babble of conversation and argument, the din of thousands and thousands of people in the vast metropolis. That's followed by a wave of inner thoughts and emotions but as it rises I panic. With an act of will I shut it out and the vision vanishes like a TV image collapsing to a dot.

■

"I hoped you'd come to the Beethoven."

"We had a visitor in the department. He's in my field; I had to join the group for dinner." Her arms are wrapped tightly around her torso. Her brow is furrowed. "We've had less chance to hang out since you stopped coming to class."

I'm exasperated. "You know I have to work. I don't have the luxury of parents who can pay for my apartment. It's all just come so easily for you, Rebecca."

I say this but know it's not true. Rebecca has obstacles of her own. My words are hurting her and pushing her away.

"All you try is easy. You never stretch yourself; you've always been afraid to find out what you could do. For all your bravado and bluster, you're scared, McEvoy."

Wilful misunderstanding on both sides. We stare at each other.

A long pause. I speak first. "Is this how it ends?"

She tilts her head until her chin rests on her chest and I can't see her eyes. Her voice is almost inaudible. "Yes."

■

I think: this is where I came in. A city filled with arcs of happiness and pain. Something about Nietzsche and eternal return. He asks us to imagine life that doesn't end with our death, but repeats over and over for eternity, each moment recurring exactly the same way. If we loved and valued life suitably, we'd be happy at the prospect.

I cradle her face with my hand. With my finger I wipe a tear from the corner of her eye and touch it to my tongue, tasting her one last time. For a moment I fool myself by imagining we'll meet again far in the future or even stay friends, but in my heart I know I'll never see her again.

3 MIDDLE KINGDOM

Shifting Sands

The first thing I notice is the taste of grit. Not coarse sand but fine particles ingratiated into every part of my mouth, covering my teeth and coating my tongue. I'm incredibly thirsty.

Then I notice the pain. Pulsing pain in my forehead. Reaching up, there's a lump and a crude gash over my right eye, caked over with dried blood. Shifting onto my elbows I wince again. My ribs are very sore and one arm is scored and blood-streaked. Looking down, I see every part of my body coated in dust. My clothes and my skin are a uniform shade of dull brown. I feel it on my scalp as well.

I peer beyond the physical pain to my surroundings. I'm lying on packed dirt, under a tree that looks like a mulberry. It's a wasteland of scrub and stunted trees. There are a few scattered houses but they're very primitive, more like huts or mud shacks.

McEvoy, what happened and where the hell are you?

▪

Waking up in a strange place and being disoriented isn't new to me, but my setting this time is totally unfamiliar. I can't think of any chain of events that could have brought me here, wherever here is. Another unwelcome discovery: my pockets are empty and I've no ID or money. I don't have my journal either and I'm more bothered to be missing my "wee book" than I am to be missing my passport. Only my inimitable sense of being McEvoy keeps me from panicking.

I pick myself up, discovering several more bruises and abrasions along the way, and walk to the nearest group of huts. I'm barefoot and wearing baggy drawstring pants and a tee shirt, both originally white but both now filthy.

"Do you speak English?" A blank look.

"Excuse me, do you speak English?" Another shaken head.

"Sorry, hello, can you help me?" Each request is met by an averted glance or a shaken head. Some people veer away from me. I'm like a leper.

At least I can guess where I am. Everyone I see has the black hair, fallow complexion, and short stature of an Asiatic race. The hegemony of the Han. I'm in China. The Middle Kingdom.

Finally, one small boy doesn't scatter like a skittle as I approach.

"English?" I ask. He smiles brightly but says nothing.

"No. I suppose not. Take me to your family?"

A fragment of meaning gets through because he grabs my index finger and leads me through the village to a dingy hut that's just like all the others. An old man sits on an upturned pail carving a piece of wood.

"Ah, the patriarch. Fine sir, do you speak the Queen's English?" I query, fairly confident that he does not.

He smiles broadly, revealing a handful of nicotine-stained teeth surrounded by large tracts of pink gum.

"Regrettably, my otherwise excellent education omitted instruction in the noble Mandarin language."

He continues smiling. The boy, now standing beside him, beams. I'm still utterly lost but we're getting along famously.

And so I do a little pantomime. Pointing to my sad face, looking around quizzically, using the universal hands-upturned query, then pulling out my pockets to show how empty they are. Almost as an afterthought I add the tongue-out, I'd-love-a-drink gesture.

The boy brings me a tin ladle of water and I gulp it greedily. Soon he's pulling me through the village again by my forefinger to a dusty square. Men in drab pajamas and sandals sit idly or talk in groups. I see no women. The boy crouches on his haunches. I assume a similar position—when in Rome, squat like a Roman.

We wait amiably for what seems like half an hour when an ancient bus lurches into the square trailing a billowing cloud of dust. The boy talks to the driver for a minute and I'm let on, even though I've no money. The destination on the front of the bus is cryptic but

I figure we're bound to go through a bigger place eventually.

Sitting in the cramped seat I realize how beat up I am. I feel like total shite. Every bump in the road—and there are many—makes an echo of pain reverberate in some part of my body.

The countryside is almost featureless farmland broken up by the occasional huddle of huts. There are few trees. It's unremittingly flat. The clear sky is stained smoggy brown, shading without demarcation into the horizon and the boundary with the land.

■

I've no master plan. One step at a time. That'll do fine, McEvoy. I'm here for a reason and now I have to figure out what it is. Several hours later we enter an urban area, more town than city, with legions of bicycles and few cars. There are no tall buildings but many small boxlike dwellings and offices. When it looks like we're approaching a commercial center, I get off.

I head for the nearest bank. I need money and surely in a bank someone can speak English. No such luck. But a teller takes pity on me and leaves his cubicle to escort me to a different and larger bank. Goggle-eyed stares in the street; I look like a mess. The first teller I approach shakes his head but then he disappears and returns with another man who also wears the Chinese banker's apparent uniform of an over-sized grey jacket and plain blue trousers.

"Hello. You must be the guy who speaks English." I say hopefully.

"Little bit. English not good. Schools here bad."

"Never mind. I'm bloody glad to meet you. Name's McEvoy."

"I am Yang. Yang Xue."

We shake hands. "So what do I call you?"

"Yang is my family name," he says. "Call me Xue."

Xue is about a foot shorter than me, with a small nose, flat face, and high forehead that conveys openness and intelligence. His short black hair is so dense it looks like fur. His teeth are dazzlingly white.

"Xue, here's the problem. I've suffered a mishap and been left with nothing: no money, no passport, no ID, no clothes, no shoes. Is there any way I can make a phone call to the UK? I could get some money and get back on my feet."

He frowns. "This is bad." He glances toward an office in the back. "Only one phone in bank can call overseas but…"

"…it's in there and you're not allowed to use it." I guess.

"Yes." He frowns again. But then he appears to make a weighty decision. "My boss not here right now. Come."

He stops to talk to another teller, presumably asking him to act as a lookout. Xue shifts his weight from one foot to the other.

"I appreciate this. I really do."

"Come. Quick."

Xue talks to the operator to get an international line and I give him my best friend Robbie's number. It's probably late in the evening back in Edinburgh and Robbie might be out but he's my best bet to get this sorted. The phone rings for a long time.

"Hullo."

"Robbie, you beautiful bastard! It's McEvoy. I'm in a huge fucking jam, too long and gory to get into, but I need your help, pal."

"No problem. Name it."

"Right. I need cash, a few hundred quid. Let's say three. That's it, then I'll get this mess sorted out bit by bit."

"Where are you? Sounds like Timbuktu."

"Might as well be. China."

"Aye, I heard you'd been on a wander. You dropped off the map. So where do I wire the cash?"

I ask Xue for the information.

"It's a town called Lintong, near Xi'an, in Shaanxi province. Get it to the People's Agrarian Bank."

"Sounds obscure, but will do."

"Robbie, you're a fucking hero. Thanks a ton."

"Sure enough."

"I've lost everything, Robbie, so I'm starting from scratch. It'll take a wee while to pay you back."

"Nae bother. I'm flush right now and I know you're good for

it."

■

Getting the money takes two days. Reconstructing my life will take a lot longer. Xue lends me flip flops and a shirt and pair of pants. The local shops are dire; their clothes won't fit a burly Scotsman. I have to get pants that float above my shoes and shirts with sleeves that ride up my arms. It's either that or a Mao jacket and a coolie hat. I need a new passport and that means a trip to Xi'an, the regional capital. They say it will take a week. I fill in the forms, pay the fee, and head back to Lintong to chill.

Xue is my tour guide, not that there's much to see. Just a dusty archeological museum with pottery shards and relics from a nearby Neolithic village, a puppet factory, and a children's water park that's short on water.

"Xue, what about the night life?"

He giggles. Which I notice is a disarming habit of the Chinese.

"What, no exotic dancers? No burlesque theater?"

"We have go clubs."

"Clubs with go-go dancers? Sure, that'll do just fine."

"No, go clubs. Clubs with go."

"Aye, clubs with oomph, pizzazz, I'm with you."

Exasperation breaks through his tranquil demeanor. "No, no. Go is game. Big game in China. In go club you play go."

The next few evenings we head for Go Clubs where Xue is known as a player. With no pubs, it's either that or stay in my room knitting. I've got no clue about the game so I sit on the sidelines and learn by watching. The board's got 19 squares on a side. The pieces are flat stones, white and black. The goal is to create contiguous patterns, surround your opponent, and control territory.

"I get it," I say after watching him for a while. "Sort of a battle game. Looks pretty simple."

He frowns. "Not simple. Mr. McEvoy has much to learn."

We're in a sprawling lounge with a half dozen go tables on one side. Xue is playing a very old man whose fingers are so warped by arthritis I'm amazed he can handle the small game pieces. I have a sudden recollection of an old man I once knew with such gnarled fingers but the image disappears before I can lock into it. On the far side of the lounge there's a bar and a black and white TV showing a cheesy travelogue set somewhere in China. At least I can get a drink.

"Let me have a go at go. I'm a dab hand at chess."

Xue smiles patiently. "Not simple," he repeats.

He's dead right. I sit across from the old man; we clear the board and begin to play. With amazing and humiliating speed all my black stones are outflanked, outmaneuvered, and then usurped by his white stones. The game barely lasts ten minutes. Next time I lose even more quickly. A third loss leaves me bewildered and frustrated.

"Chinese players very good. We get practice."

"How much."

"Go four thousand years old. Emperor Yao had a son who liked to be naughty, get in trouble. He had his teacher invent game to teach him discipline, how to think hard."

"Bloody hell. Why didn't someone show me this ten years ago?"

"Big board makes many possibilities. Stones together are safe, can avoid capture. Stones apart gain territory, but are weak. Good player must do both."

"Yes, I see it now." I watch Xue play a new opponent, and I gain vision of the game slowly. The board churns with possibilities. Go is simpler than chess in its rules and pieces but the situations are far more complex. Go is to chess as chess is to checkers.

"Not like chess." As if he's reading my mind.

"You got me there, Xue. It's a wicked game."

"Chess is like combat, rows of soldiers. Chinese people say: man against man. Go has handicap system, many layers of strategy. We say: man against self."

Later in the evening the bar's lively and then grows rowdy. Men in plain worker's uniforms are drinking, laughing, and arguing. The racket doesn't seem to put a dent in the go players' concentration.

With time to kill I come to the club during the day while Xue is at the bank. It's better than hanging out in my Spartan hotel room. The players are either old men or young boys. No matter—I get my butt kicked every time by everyone. The week wears on. I improve. And just occasionally, I eke out wins against boys so little their feet don't touch the ground.

■

We're at the club every evening. It's a pleasant diversion, though sometimes the rowdies at the bar set my nerves on edge. I focus on the go and my new pal Xue to dodge the unpalatable fact that I woke up penniless on the far side of the world with no shred of memory of how I got here.

I ask Xue for scratch paper and a pen to continue my journal. I've no idea if my wee book is in Scotland or if it was stolen in the incident that left me banged up and bleeding, but I feel the urge to document my life. As always, I make succinct notes on important incidents and omit idle blather. It's therapeutic but it's also a backstop—I'm worried I might suffer an episode that wipes the slate clean. Then I watch Xue playing a wizened man with a Fu Manchu mustache. I'm getting bored; it's time to get myself home.

"Xue, do you have a girlfriend?"

He covers his mouth with his hand and giggles. "No girlfriend."

"What else do you like to do?"

He's solemn. "I have bank. I have go. That is enough."

"No family?"

"Parents dead. Two brothers live far away."

"How old are you?"

"Thirty years old."

"Not much older than me. I'm twenty seven. But don't you want to get out there, see the world?"

"No. My own country is big enough."

Not everyone has wanderlust. And compared to the rural peasants in the place where I first found myself, Xue lives a life of luxury.

The day my passport arrives at the consulate in Xi'an I have a day to kill so I go to see the famous terracotta army. Under a canopy the size of several football stadiums, eight thousand clay soldiers stand in rows in dug-out trenches. Each one is life-sized, distinct, and unique. It's a staggering act of hubris, taking half a million people forty years, all to help their leader rule another empire in the afterlife. How badly we want to believe.

I tell Xue I'll head out the next morning, by train to Shanghai and then a plane home. I take him out for a fancy meal to thank him for all his help. A Chinese feast is an endless cavalcade of dishes: dumplings of many varieties, various mixtures of meat and vegetables, and then the weird stuff: whole fish staring up balefully through syrupy sauce, unidentified internal animal organs, greenish duck eggs served after being interred underground for several months, and the feet, probably of the very same ducks, cut off at the ankles, cooked, and arrayed on the plate like a miniature marching army. I imagine them garnished with tiny terracotta booties.

·

Then, as usual, on to the club. I get a couple of wins in before the serious players arrive. Then I prefer to watch Xue. I've learned enough to recognize that he's a master tactician. Many of his moves surprise me because I can't recognize the potential opportunity or hazard they allude to.

The bar area is raucous. Xue says today is payday, so the laborers are drinking the first day or so of their wages.

"When you get home? What then?"

Xue knows my checkered work history. I've still not told him that I have no idea why I was here or how I got here.

"This and that. I might teach."

A couple of voices rise above the rest, loud and argumentative. I glance over toward the bar and see a table of men and—surprisingly—a woman. Even more unexpected, it's a white woman. We're the only non-Chinese in the place.

"I'll be back in a minute."

I slip away from Xue's game and walk through the back of the building to the outside urinal. On my way past, I glance at the noisy group and take in the scene. The woman is thin and has a thatch of sandy hair. She's wearing a khaki shirt and pants and looks to be in her mid-thirties, with the bronzed and weathered skin of an outdoors person. The accent is American. The Chinese man next to her is more well-dressed than the rest and he seems to be a colleague or a friend. The other six men around the table are laborers and all are in various states of inebriation.

Coming back from the urinal I size up the situation again. It has moved beyond discussion; two laborers are standing and shouting. The woman projects a sense of control but her eyes betray that she's nervous. A fist thumps on the table. I make a snap decision.

"How are we doing here?" My best megawatt smile.

"We're fine," says the woman. "Thanks for your concern."

"It sounded a wee bit heated. I thought I'd check."

"Like I said, everything's under control." A tight-lipped smile.

Riding over the top of our conversation, the woman's friend and one of the workers are arguing. Their staccato words sound like an exchange of machine gun fire. I don't understand the meaning but I recognize the tone and the implications. He turns to her.

"They're insulted. They say the wages are adequate but the other terms are punitive."

"They can take it or leave it." She talks in a low voice. For a small woman, probably five feet five and 120 pounds, she radiates a lot of authority. "We can find porters and diggers anywhere."

"They think you don't trust them."

"We've got a lot of valuable equipment."

"They think you're a looter."

"I don't expect them to understand my line of work."

With that she stands up, declaring the negotiation over. Around the table the laborers all rise, but it's not to bid her and her friend a fond adieu. Bodies are tensed. The air is thick. The situation is poised on a knife-edge.

I step forward with a wide, reassuring smile. My fists are

clenched and I keep Phobos and Deimos poised for a second so they'll know the spirits of fear and terror are ready for a rumble. Then I open my hand and pick up an empty shot glass from the table.

"Drinks all 'round, eh lads?"

I turn to the woman's Chinese friend. "Translate this for me, will you?"

Then I turn to the workers, who are still standing. "Here's to China, emperor among nations."

They look surly, but sit down and drain their glasses. I order a bottle of the local fire water and refill the glasses. Menace leaches from the air. I see Xue out of the corner of my eye, looking anxious, but I wave him off and hope he'll go home. A corner has been turned but I still have to follow through.

"Here's to the Chinese worker. Noble and industrious."

"You don't have to do this, you know." She looks annoyed.

"Trust me, lady, I do." I meet her eyes. "And if this is how you treat the locals, your minder's going to have his hands full."

The evening wears on. A second bottle, and a third. Endless toasts and dull-eyed smiles. And I slip into the warm embrace of a friend I know too well.

On the Edge

I lie with my eyes closed tasting grit in my mouth. The same grit coats my skin and scalp. I'm sure I was once in a hot place with dust like this. I haven't bathed in over a week and haven't left the room in almost as long. I don't give a fuck.

Loess. It's fine windblown silt. The word's German but it should be Chinese because there's more loess in China than tea. Lintong is on the edge of a vast plateau covered in loess. It's an almost featureless terrain spanning hundreds of thousands of square miles, big enough for bonnie Scotland to fit into ten times over.

Some days I go out, find a dingy bar, and drink. Other days I stay in and curl on my cot. I drink swiftly and efficiently. Food is irrelevant. Oblivion's my lover and my only friend. I welcome her with open arms. I've shifted hotels so Xue can't see me in this state.

∎

Dimly, in the distance, knocking.

Louder, now, and closer.

It's my door. I lie still, but the knocking doesn't stop. Slowly and gingerly, I go to the door. The American from the bar.

"God, look at you."

"Thankfully I don't have to."

"Can I come in?"

"I wasn't expecting company." I wave my hand at the squalor behind me. "Otherwise I'd have put the doilies out."

I sink back onto the cot. There's no other place to sit so she just stands. She's wearing a safari suit that's functional rather than stylish. She's slim and pretty in a boyish way. Her fair brown hair is thick and cut short. She radiates calm confidence.

"You were hard to find."

I don't reply. Just having a conversation is a huge effort. She is dressed simply and wears no earrings or makeup. There's just one flourish: in a silver setting on a silver chain, an animal eye, its black pupil within a gorgeous iris of flecked gold.

"Look. I wanted to thank you for what you did. It doesn't happen often but I lost control of the situation. You got me out of a jam."

"Aye, whatever. All in a night's work."

"Now I feel terrible. You're a mess."

"Don't beat yourself up. This is an old demon, not your doing."

"But it happened because of me."

My skin is crawling. "Look, I don't mean to be rude, but I've got to lie down. I helped you out; you thanked me. We're square."

"OK. But here's my card. My hotel number's written on the back."

I peer at the card and the print slowly swims into view. Dr. Helen Matson. Professor of Anthropology and Archaeology. The University of Wyoming.

"Why are you giving me this? I don't need any bones digging up."

"I'm going on a new expedition. We're heading into the field in a couple of days."

"OK. So?"

"I'm inviting you along."

"Sorry, but I'm in no shape for tourism."

"Think about it. There's no better place to dry out than the driest place in China."

■

Three days later I'm speeding across the loess plateau north of Lintong in the second vehicle of a convoy of five Range Rovers. We're literally eating the dust of the lead car. I have a familiar, grainy taste coating the inside of my mouth. It's slightly acidic, mostly metallic, and entirely unpleasant.

The bloke to my right is a sullen local, who looks like he doesn't speak English and wouldn't if he could. The bloke to my left seems to be southern European.

"I guess the view's always the same if you're not the lead dog."

"You get used to it." He shrugs.

"The name's McEvoy." I offer my hand.

He shakes it. "Giovanni Brusa. From Bolgona. Just call me Gio."

"Grand to meet you, Gio. What's your role in this little circus?"

"I am a climatologist, with a government research institute."

"Do you know where we're headed?"

"A distant part of the plateau. It's perfect for taking samples and looking at the history of the climate."

"Aye, but the scenery's a bit dull. Wake me up when it gets more interesting, or when lunch is served. Whichever comes first."

We stop for gas in an anonymous, sepia-toned village, just like all others we've driven through. Everyone gets out to stretch their legs or buy soda and I take a closer look at the expedition personnel. Gio is so tall he has to unfold himself from the back of the Range Rover. He has oily and chaotic black hair, an equine nose, dark five o'clock shadow, and a lugubrious air.

The lead car holds Helen Matson, her Chinese fixer, and five other Americans. Gio and I are sharing our car with three other European scientists plus one from South America and one from China. The third and fourth cars are stuffed with local laborers, including the six I saw at the altercation in the bar. Two dozen of us in all. Bringing up the rear is the car holding the gear—suitcases, food and water supplies, and the valuable scientific instruments. I'm the nimble traveler in the group, with a small backpack holding the ill-fitting Chinese clothes I had to buy.

At the rest stop Matson moves easily among the groups, directing and organizing. She projects a crisp air of authority. She is collegial yet slightly bossy with the scientists. However, it's finely judged and their personalities seem to prefer having someone in charge. With the locals she lowers her voice and it acquires a slight edge. Although her words are going through a translator she's establishing her dominance with every utterance. I'm impressed but then I remember the situation she let unfold back in Lintong.

"Gio, what's the story with the boss lady?"

"Helen Matson? She's a bit crazy. Fuori di testa." He taps his head.

"I mean her work, her reputation."

"She's at the top of her field. In fact, she's at the top of two fields. She's a big name. Il formaggio grande."

"But nobody likes her much."

Gio shrugs. "Research isn't a popularity contest. She publishes a lot. She gets the big grants. When you want to do field work in tough parts of the world, she's the best ticket."

"What do you mean?"

He smiles. "In Africa, in Asia, and in Central and South

America, it takes a long time to get permission for field work. She makes wheels turn faster."

"Gotcha. Bribes. Backhanders. Maybe the odd forged document?"

"I tried to get a permit to come here more than three years ago. My government supported me; I had all the right letters and forms. But if I hadn't bought into this team, merda, I'd still be waiting."

It's not the genteel academic world I imagined. Matson has a few researchers from her own university with her, but all the researchers from elsewhere have paid to be here. The Chinese scientists, including the sour man to my right, are mostly window dressing to appease the government. I've no doubt she'll get full measure from the local labor in the trailing car.

■

We pull off the road again just as the Sun slides below the rugged horizon, like a blood orange slipping into a rumpled brown pocket. The locals set to work pitching a camp and cooking our evening meal on a portable propane stove. The landscape stretches off into the distance, unbroken by any human habitation. As the light fades I'm surprised to see a sprinkling of lights on either side of the road.

"You probably thought it was empty, a literal desert." Matson is standing next to me, looking into the gloom.

"What's out there?"

"Not what, who."

She reaches down and puts some of the soil on her fingertips, then illuminates it a flashlight.

"Loess is made of rock ground up by glaciers, but it's not just dust and dirt. Look."

I peer closely. The tiny grains are angular; they sparkle and glint in the beam of light.

"Loess is quartz, feldspar, mica and other minerals," she continues. "It's porous, with lots of air space. When it's deposited in layers and dries out it's quite rigid and strong."

"So those lights are people?"

"Thousands of people. They dig their homes into the hillside. Some are little more than caves. Others have many rooms and several levels and channels carved into them to carry smoke outside. They're called yaodongs."

"I didn't realize how poor they were here."

"It's economical. A yaodong stays warm in the winter and cool in the summer. Mao lived in one for thirteen years before he started the Revolution."

"Nature's perfect building material."

"Almost. Back in 1556, an earthquake in this province made the yaodongs collapse for hundreds of miles. It was the world's deadliest, killing almost a million people."

■

After another day and a half of driving we're truly in a wilderness. Apart from the odd low mountain range, the flatness is unremitting. Suddenly, and without warning, the lead car pulls off the road and heads at an angle across a lunar landscape. A few miles further and the convoy stops. Most people pile out but I'm strung out and feeling like shite so I stay put. I hear a heated debate. Then Matson's voice rises above the rest and we resume the journey.

"What was all the commotion?"

"The GPS is giving us bad readings," Gio says. "Tanto peggio. Then everyone disagrees over the best direction to go. It is—how you say in English—a cluster fuck."

"Don't tell me. Matson rode roughshod over all you nancy boys and got her way."

He shrugs.

"Is she always right?"

"Often enough that nobody challenges her."

"That must be nice."

When the convoy finally stops and we start unpacking it doesn't look different from any other place we've been in the last few hours. The scientists move into high gear. Aluminum boxes are unloaded and delicate equipment is assembled. The Chinese workers pitch tents and set up a camp. I've got a brutal headache, like someone's working on my skull with pliers, so I stay out of the way until the blinder wears off. Being on the wagon is spoiling my natural bonhomie.

Over the next few days I get to know the other scientists better. It's a very interdisciplinary team. In addition to anthropologists and archaeologists, there are geologists, climatologists, archeologists, and even an epidemiologist. These smart researchers know their stuff and some have healthy egos, but they all accept Matson as their leader and also defer to her in more subtle ways. In this crew, there's only one alpha dog.

"Do you want to see why we come here? Che brutto."

It's Gio. He hands me what looks like a test tube with the closed end cut off and sharpened. It's a small transparent cylinder.

"Go ahead. Push it into the ground."

"Where?"

"Anywhere. It's all the same. Tutti uguali."

I press the tube into the ground. It meets some initial resistance, then moves easily, like a knife through cake. I pull it out. There are alternating bands of orange and paler material, each an inch thick.

"Look closely," he advises.

I put my eye near the glass and see delicate horizontal striations. The layers are incredibly thin, barely discernible. Each of the broad bands is made of hundreds of the razor-thin layers.

"This is the climate history of the planet. In a dry year, the only material deposited is from wind off the desert. The layer of loess is only one hundredth of a millimeter. But in a wet year, with normal monsoon, the material is soil and the layer is a bit thicker."

"What do the colors mean?"

"Loess is pale and mostly crystals. The soil is darker and has more organic material and fine particles."

I do the math in my head. "So this is forty thousand years worth?"

"Yes. Most of human history is in your hand."

I whistle softly. "How far down can you go?"

"There's 22 million years of undisturbed loess under our feet. With our equipment we can measure changes of salinity and the flipping of the Earth's magnetic field. We can see the ice ages come and go and look for small variations in the Earth's orbit or the Sun's energy. Che formidabile, eh?"

"Fuck, that's amazing." It's hard to believe you can learn so much from a pile of dirt.

"Look near the top." Gio is animated, so rhapsodic he might have been talking about a lover. "See the dark layer?"

A fraction of an inch from the top one slice is almost black.

"That's China when she emerged as a civilization. Fuliggine. Soot. We can always see the mark of pre-industrial humans because they burn wood and charcoal."

■

The field work continues for a week. We've come this far to reach a place where the loess is undisturbed, where the local topography and wind patterns are stable enough to ensure the strata contain a reliable record of climate.

Some days my desire for a drink is overwhelming. I want to weep or crawl into a loess cave and be put out of my abject misery by an earthquake. Other days it's merely chronic, like a toothache. Luckily, Matson runs a dry operation so there's little temptation except for the fire water I know the locals have hidden away in their own camp. I'm proud of myself for not joining them and getting shit-faced. I like to think Xue would be proud of me too and I feel a pang of guilt for not telling him what happened and why I was leaving.

Anti-camaraderie is infectious. The Chinese workers do their work sullenly and grudgingly; their resentment is like a smothering layer of loess. I also sense a schism among the scientists, but not one based on nationality. Some people seem to be more in the know than others. One the second day out two of the Americans and a South American get into a shouting match.

"What is it?" Gio is walking away from the scene in disgust.

"Guai. Troubles." His vowels elongate and flatten due to his strong accent and he waves his arms expressively.

"Serious?"

"Bambini viziati. Spoiled children. You might say it's like bald men fighting over a comb."

"But something big's happening, right? I can feel it."

"Yes. Matson's deciding who will go with her on the next stage of the expedition. Nobody knows exactly what it's about. She really likes to keep people guessing."

"Are you going?"

"Non lo so. But I'm going to make my case this evening at dinner. In boca al lupo."

"What does that mean?"

"In the mouth of the wolf. Wish me luck, McEvoy."

I'm weary of the tension, so after dinner I walk across the plateau until the camp is a small huddle of shadows and lights in the distance. The loess crunches underfoot. I tilt my head upward and am stunned by the enormity of the sky. The stars are ablaze. Mars, the blood-red warrior, is hanging low in the southwestern sky. That's in the direction we're headed, so I hope it's not some kind of omen. I imagine that my distant ancestors stood here thousands of years ago and saw the same magnificent view.

On my way back to camp I pass our vehicles and the piles of boxes containing testing equipment. Between two of the Range Rovers there is movement. I'm dark adapted and close enough to make out details. It's Matson, or at least I think so, and Gio, there's no mistaking his lanky silhouette. They're locked in a steamy embrace. Alpha dog and the Italian. I never saw that coming.

Relics

I cling grimly to the arms of my seat. At one particularly violent lurch I hear a collective groan from behind. We're flying on a small plane, an ancient over-wing turboprop, from the far western city of Urumqi to the oasis town of Kashgar. Clear air turbulence kicked in where warm air over the Taklamakan Desert met cold air flowing off the Tibetan Plateau. I try not to think about the age and condition of the plane or the prodigious power of moving parcels of air. I try not to think of anything at all.

With four of us on sitting on each side and one pilot up front, the plane feels like a toy being tossed around by a malevolent god. Maybe he thinks we need reassurance, because the Chinese pilot looks over his shoulder once to give us a wan smile. Well, he's Chinese, so he's probably always wan. It's not much comfort to watch him wrestle with the steering column. Several people are throwing up. I'm spared that indignity—my stomach is empty because I have a hangover. I fell off the wagon our last night in Urumqi.

The only person who seems unperturbed is Helen Matson, who sits across the aisle from me with her head tilted back and her eyes closed and her face serene.

"This doesn't bother you, does it?"

"Not really. It'll be over in a while and when we get off the plane we'll quickly forget it happened." Her eyes are still closed.

"Aye, and now I can cross Disneyland off my list."

As suddenly as it started, the turbulence ceases and the plane fills with conversation and nervous, relieved laughter.

I'm feeling mischievous. "So, you and Gio?"

She looks at me calmly with unblinking, brown eyes. "You seem surprised."

"I thought you were gay."

She laughs. "It's none of your business. But who said I wasn't."

Now it's my turn to laugh.

"I like strength and I like confidence. In men and women." She looks reflective. "Even I get lonely sometimes."

She reads my mind.

"Don't worry McEvoy, you're not my type. You're strong and you're interesting, but you're damaged."

And with that she closes her eyes. End of conversation.

•

Alpha and Gio get a car and supplies while the rest of us cool our heels in the hotel in Kashgar. I amuse myself at the ping pong table. By dinner they still aren't back so we check out the buffet. The food is dreary and institutional, heavy on tough, highly spiced meats and piles of overcooked, indeterminate vegetables.

"Who here knows where we're headed?" I ask cheerfully, thinking I'll get to know my traveling companions better.

"It's a new site that Helen's found. Her email was cryptic. That's all I know." It's Royce Ostriker, a Princeton anthropologist who specializes in early Asian civilizations. He's ruddy-faced, jowly, and overweight. Although we're only a mile high, his breathing is labored.

"I don't know much either. But I was asked to bring my portable carbon dating machine." This is Alex Farnsworth, a geologist from Colorado. He explains that he's developed the only radioactive age measurement technique that can be applied in the field.

We all turn to our last companion, a woman who I've not heard a peep from all week. She's so quiet she's invisible. As she is now. She slowly chews her vegetables. All I know is the name: Sonja Escobar. She's a Peruvian epidemiologist. There are no serious communicable diseases here, as far as I know. So why the hell are we dragging an epidemiologist around with us?

•

The journey from Kashgar further west takes us onto the Tibetan Plateau. Most of the terrain is high tundra and mountain ranges of shattered rock. We pass salt lakes and catch a glimpse of K2 in the distance toward the south, its profile a perfect triangle of snow and ice. Alpha drives our Toyota Land Cruiser. I'm sitting up front and the others are sleeping or dozing in the back.

"Don't we need we need local help?" I ask.

"We'll recruit them closer to the site. I want people with detailed knowledge."

"If you need any help with diplomacy, just holler." I mutter this mostly to myself. I never thought I'd hear myself say that.

"McEvoy, you don't know me, so stop judging me. I get the job done. When I negotiate, everybody gets something they want. If you don't like how I work, you're welcome to get out and walk." Then she softens the message with a prim smile.

"No problem. I'm having a grand time."

"You don't like me, do you?"

"You're not really a people person," I say carefully. "On the other hand, you persuaded these high-powered academics to come halfway round the world pretty much on spec. That's impressive."

We drive for a while in silence. There are scattered yerts on the tundra and I see occasional camels and yaks in fields ringed by stone walls. The people are dark and Asiatic. It doesn't feel like China any more.

"What's your story, Helen Matson?"

She smiles briefly before she answers. "It's funny how I dislike talking about myself. I'm a doer, McEvoy. I've been doing since I was five. I'm from Ohio—the heartland, with God-fearing people. I grew up on a farm. My dad dropped dead behind the thresher when I was little, and my brother had emphysema, so it was up to me and my mother. We did our best, but it wore her out. She died when I was sixteen."

"But why did you pick this?"

"I was always handy. I could fix things. I liked science. The plough sometimes turned up bones and pot shards and I wondered what their story was."

"So their story is your story."

"In a way, yes. Research is easy for me. You home in on the most important idea and pursue it. Most people don't know what they want, so they get out of your way."

"I've noticed."

"It's how the world works, McEvoy. Nobody remembers who

came in second."

Another long silence, broken only by the arpeggio snoring of the Princetonian in the back seat. I look at Alpha's profile as she drives. Her face and body are perfectly arranged for action. She's right—power is attractive.

"McEvoy, are you staring at my chest?"

"No. But I am staring, at the necklace."

She fingers the glassy eye. "I got it in Kamchatka."

"That's Russia. Siberia." I'm shocked. "Is that…"

"Yes, it's a tiger. But don't worry, I didn't kill it. I was at a dig out in the tundra. I happened to find the place where the son of the elder of the village had been killed in an accident. I brought him his son's bones. He gave me this, his most prized possession."

■

We roll into Tashkurgan after eleven hours on the road. Our digs are clean but primitive. The next morning I get up early and explore the town. It's a small trading post with a long history as a stop on the Silk Route. A stone fortress on the edge of town has a commanding view of the flanking mountain ranges.

Walking back into town I pass a large Chinese garrison. I see several phalanxes of soldiers jogging on the streets, all chanting in rhythm. This is the visible, muscular projection of Chinese military strength. Tashkurgan is in what the Chinese euphemistically call an autonomous province. The Han race is a tiny minority; most people here are Tajiks, plus small pockets of Uzbeks, Uyghurs, and Tibetans. There's no missing the tight grip the Chinese keep on all local culture and customs. Theirs is an army of occupation.

"Coffee, please." I point to the small copper pots simmering on a bed of charcoal. I'm wandering the downtown market as people are starting their day.

The stall-keeper gives me a toothless grin and pours viscous liquid into a tiny cup. It eases down my throat like coal tar. I try striking up a conversation with the Tajiks nearby, who have been staring at me suspiciously.

"Here's to yaks!" I presume that they're abundant mainstays of the local economy. Sort of like a sheep to a Scot. No response. They might not speak any English.

"Here's to yerts!" That doesn't work either. Stupid man McEvoy, nobody toasts their house.

Then I realize my kinship to these people. I'm from a tiny nation five million strong sitting on the rump of a country ten times larger. They're the marginalized inhabitants of a country of a billion ethnic strangers. I'm actually quite fond of the English but there's a principle at stake.

"Fuck the English!"

One tentative voice replies, "Fuk angrish?"

"Fuck the English!"

More join in. "Fukri glish."

"Not quite right, lads. Fuck the English!"

A ragged chorus now. "Fuk Ri Lish."

"Close enough. Let it ring out. Give it your all. Fuck the English!"

"Fuk Ri Lish!"

"Fuk Ri Lish!"

■

We set up camp fifty miles down the valley, within an hour of the Pakistan border. Two Chinese military jeeps join our convoy. Alpha says they're old models sitting idle in the garrison outside town. She has bribed the town mayor handsomely, who in turn has bribed the military commander to let her borrow them for a couple of weeks. I'm impressed by her brass.

I'm less impressed by her choice of a crew. She seems to have picked strong-looking locals pretty much randomly from the open air pool halls and coffee houses. The dozen men gathered at the edge of camp included six Chinese, four Tajiks, and two Uyghurs. One of the Tajiks, a man called Farzam, has just enough English to serve as a translator. They eye each other uneasily. I have a bad feeling about assembling potentially immiscible fluids.

Suddenly, my unease sharpens to a point and the hair stands up on the back of my neck. Call it second sight, call it intuition, but I'm able to see the twelve hired hands clearly, although they're strangers separated from me by a gulf of language and culture. One of the Tajiks and one of the Chinese are pilferers and are not to be trusted. Another Chinese man, who has a pinched face and fidgety hands, is capable of extreme violence.

Alpha takes Farzam aside and talks to him for a while. Then she surprises me by going back to the crew and talking to each man, with Farzam interpreting. I expect it to be perfunctory, the general giving a nod to the foot soldiers, but it's more than that. She seems genuinely interested. The men are very hesitant but several show her pictures, presumably of family members. The three I pegged as problems hang back and don't respond to her overtures. I assume this is just Alpha's clever way of getting local knowledge to help the expedition.

On her way back to the main tent, she pauses in front of me.

"Want to earn your keep, McEvoy?"

"Well, I'd more hoped to be Stanley to your Livingstone."

"Aloof and keeping a journal? No, I want you to get your hands dirty. I think you can help with the dig."

"What's the pay?"

"A lot better than the locals are getting."

I think for minute, but I do need the dosh to pay back Robbie for getting me out of my jam.

"Alright. I'm game."

"Good." Her gaze is direct. "Stay sober and follow my rules."

I can't resist getting in the last word. "Aye, and I'll try not to unionize your labor force."

∎

Later, I lie awake for a long time in my tent, listening to muffled conversations outside. On this high plateau the temperature drops sharply after dark and I've borrowed a sweater from Gio to stay warm in my thin sleeping bag. This expedition is making me uncomfortable in many ways. I concentrate on my breathing.

Darkness. Bright metal. A twisted body. Loud noise and large rocks tumbling. Stench. One eye staring. Something sharp moving quickly. Wetness. Two eyes closed. Sleep finally comes.

■

Each day we split into the three groups and fan out to places on the edge of the valley floor. The instructions are to look for signs of ancient human habitation. Alpha doles out the information sparingly, so we know little else. She hands out detailed maps with destinations and each group has four locals along to carry equipment and act as diggers. Ostriker, the corpulent Ivy Leaguer, is nailed by the altitude, which is over 11,000 feet, so he stays at base camp to analyze data and keep the logs. That leaves Gio, the geologist Farnsworth, and the silent Peruvian chick to lead the three groups. Alpha's a floater, joining a different group each day, which I recognize as a clever way to keep her finger on the pulse of the work.

And McEvoy? Part of me wants to hike into the high country and avoid all human company. I've a splitting headache before lunch each day and it's a coin toss whether it's caused by altitude or detox. Part of me wants to find oblivion with the liquid opium I know I can find in the seamy bars and smoke shops. On the other hand, I've had no ruptures of memory and time since the disaster that landed me in China, so I'm grateful for that. And Alpha's paying me, so I grab a shovel and join a different group each day.

On my first day, to my surprise, I find the work comes naturally. Digging for small items that look little different from the surrounding dirt is easy. It's like I've peeled through layers of history before but I have no recollection of it.

■

I take a break and sit on a flat rock watching the rest of the crew work. After the sensory flashes I had last night, and the déjà vu of a moment ago, I have an even more disconcerting feeling. Perhaps we will make discoveries and find amazing artifacts. But what if it's all a shadow play? Why am I here, near the edge of the roof of the world? Waking up dusty and bleeding in a small village I could have just gone home. Why did I intervene in Matson's dispute and why did I tag along with her team? If these were choices why does it feel like everything is pre-ordained and inevitable? Solipsism is a small step from insanity so I try to banish these thoughts.

∎

"What do you mean old? Help me out here." I've no reference for what we're looking for. It's dinner time and we're gathered around a fire. The flames cast dancing shadows back into the night.

"You know the Silk Route? It passes through here." Ostriker eyes me distastefully, as he would an lowlife student whose parents have scammed him into the Ivy League.

"I know about the game where you can't be last to jump out of the pool. Marco Polo."

"That's the 13th Century. Marco Polo was one of the first Europeans to travel the Silk Route and then write about it. However it had already been a prosperous trade route for centuries. It was a vital artery for the Roman Empire and for Alexander the Great before that."

As Ostriker speaks and his plummy diction pours all over me like syrup, the magisterial strains of Masterpiece Theater's theme music reverberate in my head.

"Before that, the evidence is fragmentary," Ostriker continues, and we might have been in a cozy seminar room in Princeton rather than in one of the most wild and remote places on Earth. "Jade and lapis lazuli were traded from the Middle East to China in the 2nd millennium B.C. But as we reach back to pre-dynastic Egypt, I reach the limits of my expertise, so I defer to Professor Matson."

Alpha takes over with my lesson. "The earliest artifact pointing to trade is charcoal from the tomb of the Egyptian king Nekhen, around 4000 B.C., that's identified with cedar from Lebanon. The route was likely used for trade as soon as the donkey was domesticated, about 5000 B.C. Beasts of burden are critical. The Asian steppes are covered with grassland and water, so donkeys can graze and prehistoric people could carry a lot of goods and cover a very large range."

"Bloody hell. D'you mean people have been tramping up and down this road for 7000 years?"

"Maybe even longer."

"But what's the origin of trade itself?"

"You're asking about the civilizations that could gather and store merchandise. They started with what's called the Neolithic Revolution, the development of agriculture in the Fertile Crescent in the Middle East. There's evidence of a granary in Jordan in 9500 B.C. Humans made the gradual transition from hunting and gathering to living in large fixed settlements ten to twelve thousand years ago."

"But who's to say that they…"

We're interrupted by shouts from the worker's camp fifty yards away. Alpha and I walk quickly that way. As we approach I see two of the men shoving each other while two others yell nearby. There's a flash of metal.

On pure instinct, I break into a run. Covering the ground quickly I launch myself into the air. I hit the man with the knife from his side as his arm is poised high. I'm much heavier than he is so we fly through the air and crash to the stony ground with a thud. The knife clatters into the darkness.

■

The next morning we get visitors. We've barely finished breakfast when two jeeps bounce along the dirt road toward us. The occupants are all Han Chinese. Two men get out of the lead jeep and approach. They're dressed in ill-fitting suits. The four men in the second jeep are wearing khaki and all but the driver have automatic rifles on their laps. Alpha and her Chinese fixer stride out to meet them. I strain to hear the conversation.

"You are Matson?"

"Yes. Is there a problem?"

"This valley is under contract to the Qinghai Mining Company and your operations violate our exclusive rights here."

Matson plants her hands on her hips. "No. We have papers

signed by the Minister of Culture. This project is official and approved."

"That is not my concern. We have approval from the Ministry of Industry for testing and exploration."

"Maybe we can come to some arrangement." Matson changes tack. "I've not seen any sign of your operation. We'll only be here for a few weeks."

"That's not possible. Mining rights take precedence. You and your team will have to leave."

Matson speaks through clenched teeth. "We'll see about that. My team has a right to do their work."

The suits ignore her. They turn and leave. Matson is furious and stalks off fuming. Gio walks up to me.

"What's going on, McEvoy?"

"A pissing contest with a mining company. Alpha's good but she may be out of her league."

"Cosa vuoi dire? What do you mean?"

"The Ministry of Industry trumps the Ministry of Culture. She paid off the mayor but the mining company is regional. We have old army jeeps but they have goons with guns. Game, set, and match."

"I just came here for research. Sono solo uno scienzato. But it's such a labyrinth." He shakes his head.

"Or a Chinese puzzle."

■

The dig settles into a routine. Alpha sets up a relentless pace that keeps everyone fully engaged. The groups set out after a breakfast of rice cakes and coffee and return at dusk, dirty and exhausted. We're at the edge of a river valley two miles wide so the river's too far away to be useful. Every three days we go into Tashkurgan for supplies and to use the feeble cold showers in the municipal building. Alpha peels off and does her own thing on these trips; nobody knows where she goes. Not a word is said about the visit from Qinghai Mining.

The flare-up in the worker's camp is over but not forgotten. The man I nailed has four broken ribs and a broken wrist. I got off lightly with a chipped tooth and some bruising. Alpha consults with Farzam and replaces the four men who were in the heat of the argument, but ethnic tensions are simmering and I don't see an improvement in the demeanor of our local crew. I envy Alpha's supreme confidence, and the way this small woman effortlessly organizes groups of men. She tries and connect with them individually. But the currents of conflict arising from culture and history among them are very strong. It all may all end in tears.

I talk to Farzam, and our facilitator and translator tells me the group contains kin of the man with the knife, so we have a festering problem. Alpha is paying Farzam more than the rest, enough to keep him on the job for now, but he's unhappy. In the field, everyone is occupied by the hard physical labor but there's palpable and surly resentment each time scientists come into contact with workers. I'm never able to let my guard down.

"So, Gio, are we famous yet?"

In the rotation, I've joined Gio's group to help out. The thin Italian is friendly and approachable, so the atmosphere is fairly calm.

"Peccato, no. Out here we've found some pottery and jewelry, but it's all from the classic period. Meglio di nulla. Better than nothing but not what we came for."

"Just what did we come for?"

He strokes his stubbly chin; Gio shaves morning and evening and still looks like someone has taken charcoal to his chin. "Helen thinks there might be a precursor culture here. She scouted out the location in several trips she made solo in the past few years."

"How's it going with her? Does she ever let you be on top?"

He wags his finger at me. "You're a bad, bad man, McEvoy."

The afternoon wears on. I dig for a while then sit against a rock and daydream. Cued by the Sun's rays grazing corrugated mountains on the far side of the valley, the team is packing up the equipment to leave when Gio bursts on the scene, gesticulating. His excitement scrambles his English.

"To come with! McEvoy, you must. Che appassionante!"

I scramble over the scree to a flat area behind a spur of rock. It doesn't look different from any other area we've been assailing with shovels and pickaxes.

"Guarda. Look. Look!" He waves his arms wildly.

At first I see nothing. Then I notice the ground is traced with a subtle, irregular grid. It's a just hint of a pattern, but unmistakable. With my eyes now tuned I see it extends for a hundred yards until it hits the rocky slope that leads to the river valley floor. I'm looking at the shadow of an ancient town.

"Is this what I think it is?"

"Yes. Che bella! It's a settlement, very extensive. But that's not what makes me excited. Come. Come!"

He gallops across the flat area to where it meets the rising slope where the mountains began. Suddenly, he disappears.

"Gio? Gio!"

"Here." A head pokes out of the ground. He's in a cleft in the rocks that seem to lead deeper underground.

When I reach him he opens his huge hand. In it are several glass beads, ceramic disks with some kind of writing on them, and a couple of fragments of gold jewelry.

"There is so much here, it's spectacular. Stupendo!"

"Can I come in?"

"Sure, sure. But step carefully."

The cramped area is a natural underground cave, with a floor five or six feet below the ground level outside. Small artifacts, none bigger than my thumb, are scattered all around. As well as the glass beads and ceramic fragments, there are pottery shards and wisps of what seem to be woven fabric.

"McEvoy, look here." Gio points to and picks up a small chunk of dull metal. It's unremarkable. I shrug.

"Bronze. They were working metal, making alloys."

"Gio, we'd better get back. It's almost dark. This will all be here in the morning."

■

The mood at dinner is electric. Alpha rarely shows emotion, but I can sense the coiled energy of her anticipation. All the others are as animated as Gio. Even the taciturn Peruvian is smiling and adding to the conversation. This is what happens when scientists open presents on the biggest Christmas of their lives.

The entire team heads back to Gio's site as soon as the Sun rises the next morning. We spend a long, exhausting, but exhilarating day gathering, mapping, and conducting exploratory digs. By day's end the enormity of the finding is confirmed. This large settlement dates to the dawn of civilization. The artifacts aren't of any recorded style. We're unraveling history that's not in any history book.

Just before we leave, Alpha surveys the scene from the top of a hillock. She's master of her domain, legs apart and arms akimbo.

I walk over to her. "This must be pretty special."

She's exultant. "I know how Schliemann must have felt when he found his golden hoard. The Troy of the Iliad is real!"

"I wish you experts would give me some background," I say over dinner around the fire. "I feel like everyone's getting stuck in at the orgy and I'm the wallflower on the side with my clothes on."

"What do you want to know?" asks Alpha.

"I need some benchmarks. I slept through history at school. It was so badly taught it made me want to push pencils into my eyes. I need to know enough to know what I should be surprised by."

"We found glass. Similar glass beads date back to 3500 B.C. in Egypt and Mesopotamia. Actual glass containers weren't made until 1500 B.C.; they're found in tombs of the Pharaohs."

"What about pottery?"

"It probably developed in both the Middle and the Far East around 8000 to 7000 B.C. By 5000 B.C., it had reached a level of high craft in China and Japan. Tradition puts the origin of all important transitions—first agriculture, first pottery, first ceramics—in the biblical area of the Mediterranean. But now it's clear that similar advances in the Far East may have been contemporaneous or even earlier."

"And metal?"

"That's complicated. Pure metals like gold and copper are found throughout the Egyptian period, but the way different cultures used metals varies. Conventional wisdom talks about three ages of early human technology. For a million or more years, the only tools were made of stone. After several thousand years of primitive agriculture, the first use of bronze is recorded around 3500 B.C. in Anatolia in Turkey. Writing starts around then too. The last transition is to the Iron Age, around 1200 B.C."

"But I can tell you don't like the conventional wisdom."

"It was always too tidy," she says. "And it was based only on what happened in Europe and the Middle East. Some cultures skipped steps or didn't follow the transitions. Some Amazon tribes are still Neolithic, using stone tools, while south of the Sahara there was no Bronze Age; they went straight from stone to iron."

A memory fragment intrudes on my train of thought. I've loved a woman who loves bronze, a woman who is a mistress of metal.

I summarize. "So basically, we're scrabbling around eating grubs and berries until ten thousand years ago. Then, in order, we master clay, glass, and metal. Viagra and sex videos come later."

"You're crude as always, McEvoy." She gives me a grudging smile. "But accurate, and I suppose crudeness is part of your charm."

"But where does what we found yesterday fit in?"

"That's the big question." She looks around the group to make sure the import of her words sink in. "This has been a human thoroughfare for seven thousand years, yet there's no record of major habitation on this site."

"So the things we've found must have come earlier, which upsets the whole apple cart."

"Exactly."

It's quiet except for the crackling of the fire. Everyone watches the flickering flames and retreats into their own thoughts.

The next weeks are a blur of activity. Long tiring days bleed into each other. Alpha has selected well; the science team is efficient and organized. We're working flat out, so it's a relief when she declares a day off. Most of the team is happy to kick around the camp and read or catch up on their correspondence. I tear paper out of a lab book to catch up on my journal, having mislaid my wee book, then catch Alpha in time to go into Tashkurgan with her.

"Walk around the bazaar for a while, McEvoy. I have business to attend to. I'll be back in an hour."

A single Western woman is an oddity in this provincial ethnic town and many eyes follow her as she walks past the stalls of bright fabric and cheap brassware. She seems oblivious to the wake she's creating. Curious, I follow her at a distance. She ducks under the blanket that acts as the doorway to a small shack and emerges ten minutes later. The pattern is repeated. Each time she enters a small, anonymous dwelling and stays only a few minutes. I wonder how she knows her way around; she's only been to Tashkurgan a few times that I know of. Worried that she'll notice me, I move off in a different direction to sample the multi-sensory pleasures of the bazaar.

We make two stops on the way back. One is to buy plastic bags, plastic containers and boxes. The second is at a dusty building with a sign identifying it as a regional office of the Qinghai Mining Company. I get out of the jeep but she sharply indicates for me to stay put. When she comes out her face is a mask of fury.

"Still a stand-off?"

"Worse." She slams the jeep into gear. "They want us out today."

"But I thought you had permission, from near the top."

A grim smile. "Yes and no. I found a ministry official who was willing to sponsor our visas and get our equipment in. But he used channels that were unofficial."

"There's no mining going on anywhere in the valley."

"Doesn't matter. We've seen enough while digging to guess the value of the land to a mining company. Rare earths alone are worth billions. We know too much and us being there is inconvenient."

"So what are we going to do?"

"Our work." Another tight-lipped smile.

"This is all messed up."

"Agreed. It's how China works, McEvoy. The local government is very corrupt."

I point to the bags and boxes in the back seat. "Should I bother asking if you have an export permit?"

"Here, an arrangement works better than a permit."

We drive in silence for a while. The upper reaches of the valley are lush farmland with a short growing season. The dirt paths are dotted with people carrying wood or hay or water on their heads.

"What were you doing while I was in the bazaar?"

She looks at me sharply. "Did you follow me?"

"Not exactly. Well, OK, yes. Do you know people here?"

"McEvoy, it's none of your goddamn business." She gives me stony silence then her face softens. "You've probably noticed that the ethnic minorities here aren't doing too well."

"Yes. Our first trip into Tashkurgan, I went to the Cultural Heritage Museum. I thought I'd learn something but it was a whitewash built by the government. Faded photos of women in fancy dress and shots of the locals thanking smiling soldiers. I gagged."

She nodded. "They're well and truly screwed. I've nothing against the Han but the government is engaged in ethnic cleansing. With the recent replacements, our crew is more mixed than ever. It includes Tajiks, Uzbeks, Uygurs, and a Kirgiz. Farzam has been translating for me. They've got some serious health problems at home."

"So you were visiting their families?"

"Twenty dollars goes a long way out here. It's more than they'll see when Qinghai Mining takes their land."

∎

Back at the dig, I keep my finger on the pulse of our workers by talking to Farzam, and the feedback is sobering. Pre-existing tensions in the group are simmering just short of a boil. Nobody can get away from anyone else. The stress level is exacerbated by the intensity of the work. The scientists are all in their element, turbo-charged with excitement, but also oblivious to anything going on in the very real world just outside their heads.

"Che ti prende? What's the matter with you?" Gio asks me. We're bagging items from a recently excavated room and mark each bag with a grid coordinate within the site.

"I've got a bad feeling, Gio."

"Yes." He looks somber, his long face elongated in seriousness. "She's driving too hard, no?"

"It's frustrating. She's not the cold bitch I thought she was a few weeks ago, but she's relentless and it means she misses parts of the picture."

Gio purses his lips. "She's not that easy as an inamorata, I can tell you. But I can't resist her. Come una falena alla fiamma. Like the moth to the flame." He smiles sheepishly.

"You all don't see it. We're on the edge. The knife fight wasn't an isolated incident."

"I understand." Then he shrugs. "But what can we do?"

"Keep our eyes and ears open. If it gets dodgy, I may need help."

"Garantito."

■

Traces of a bustling community are everywhere under our feet. We'll have to be selective. Like pretty shells on a beach, there are so many items to choose from that we can't bag them all. I get a better sense of the site from Farnsworth, the geologist.

"Why are we only finding tiny bits?" As an amateur, this is my main disappointment. "Why not whole pots and full skeletons?"

"A river flowed through here. There was runoff from the mountains behind, and erosion. Large objects are never intact in so much running silt and sediment."

"How big is this site?"

"We don't know. You have to use your imagination."

"OK, but how?"

"The wide ledge we're standing on was the level of the river valley thousands of years ago. The level is now a hundred feet lower."

He sweeps his hand across the vista of the valley dotted with yerts and yaks. "Most of the evidence has been swept away. We have to find what we can at this level, at the edge of the erosion."

That evening, Alpha hatches a bold new plan. Tomorrow the three groups are to leave the site that's been so fruitful and fan out across the valley. She tells one to go a mile further down the valley to the south, where it seems there are similar flat outcroppings. The other two are to go to separate locations on the opposite side of the valley, two miles away. Not everyone signs on with this plan.

"Matson, our visas will expire in a month." The outsized Ostriker speaks first. "I think it's more sensible to be thorough in documenting the site we've already found."

"I have to agree with him." Now Farnsworth chimes in. "The formations on the far side are not nearly as promising for preserving the strata. I think the same layers we're studying here will be eroded over there."

Gio is quiet. His loyalties are divided.

"This is not a debate." Matson sets her jaw and her voice acquires a slight edge. I can tell she's going with her gut. She's feeling a sense of urgency and I know why. "Plus, there's the matter of carbon."

"What does that mean?" I whisper to Gio.

"It means that we've been unlucky in one way. In all the artifacts we've found so far, there's no wood or charcoal."

A little light bulb goes on. "Ah, so we've no easy way to measure the age of all this."

"Correct."

Alpha rises, signaling the end of the discussion. "Everyone get some sleep. Tomorrow's a big day. Good night."

■

I stay put and have an easy day for a change. I help Ostriker for a while then walk across the valley to the river. The clear water burbles through dense tufted grass and reeds. I lay back and the stress seeps out of my body. I let the sound lull me to sleep.

Escobar is the first to return. She's gone a mile further down the valley along the same rocky slope we're camped near. Success. She says it's not as extensive as the original site, but she's seen traces of similar dwellings and found beads and pottery that match.

Alpha is next back, in the group with Farnsworth that struck out directly across the valley. Their faces tell the story. Nothing.

The wait for Gio's team seems interminable. We eat and nobody can muster more than idle conversation. It's dark when we see his headlight's wavering approach as the jeep bumps over the dirt road. Walking to the fire with shoulders slumped, he's clearly exhausted.

"Well?" Alpha stands like a coiled spring.

"The first place, there was no outcropping at the right level." Gio's face is weary, he seems defeated. "We went a mile further down and had trouble with the car. That took a few hours to fix. There was an easier approach another few miles down so we went there, and…"

Everyone's staring at him but his face offers no hope.

"…we found it. Everything! Just the same as this side." His face splits into a grin.

The group erupts into a cheer. Alpha rushes over and hugs him, then remembers herself and disengages.

"Mio dio, that's not all. Look!"

He opens his clenched hand. It's hard to see in the flickering fire light so we move in closer. Five, small, misshapen dark objects are lying on his palm. They don't glitter, but I know at once they're far more valuable than gold nuggets. Charcoal!

■

The next day Alpha, Gio, and Ostriker lead groups back across the valley. Gio will return to his find while the other two will explore areas at the edge of the flood plain, where the cliffs rise up. We've already got a triangle of data telling us of an ancient settlement that extends for several miles in both directions, but what's the full extent? Alpha hopes we'll find new small caves with trophies that can be retrieved without back-breaking labor.

I intend to bum around camp again, but Alpha sends me off with Ostriker. The rotund Princetonian isn't much good for physical labor, so really I'm there with two of the local helpers to dig and lug samples. Ostriker is fastidious and methodical in preparing his materials, so I have some time before we leave. Farnsworth is assembling his solar-powered gizmo for measuring ages. I try not to interrupt him but I'm curious.

"How does your contraption work? Has it got you a date yet?"

He ignores my wee dig. "Carbon has a radioactive cousin with two extra neutrons in its nucleus. Radioactive carbon is very rare: about one atom for every trillion normal carbon atoms."

"You can measure that?" I'm impressed.

"Actually it's trivial." He nods in satisfaction—geologists aren't just cowboys with rock hammers. "Every living thing, every plant, every animal, takes in radioactive carbon along with normal carbon while it's alive, but when it dies the radioactive atoms start to decay."

"How does that let you measure the age?"

"Radioactive decay is a random process, but for large numbers of atoms the behavior is very well-defined. After 5600 years, half of the radioactive atoms will have decayed. After another 5600 years, half of those remaining will have decayed, leaving a quarter of the original number, and so on."

"I think get it. If the dead thing has half the number of radioactive carbon atoms as the living thing, it died 5600 years ago."

"More or less, and it works for organic material that was once alive. Like cotton or paper or wood…"

"…or flesh!"

"Indeed. Egyptian mummies have their ages measured this way."

"What's so special about your gizmo, Farnsworth?"

"Until a few years ago, machines to measure the concentration of radioactive atoms filled a large room. I developed the first portable device." He puffs up with pride.

"How reliable is it?"

A cloud passes over his face. "Well, it's only been tested a couple of times in the field. It's reliable up to ages of 50,000 years, at which point there's so little radioactive carbon left that it's hard to measure. Now, if you'll excuse me, I need to concentrate."

■

I drive the jeep with Ostriker in the passenger seat and two Tajiks in the back. We bounce across the wide of the valley to a place where the river level was thousands of years ago. Now it's a rocky area under steep cliffs. It's the second day this site has been examined. There's a perimeter staked out with wire and with string crisscrossing it to mark out squares roughly ten meters on a side.

It's backbreaking and slightly dull work. We find some beads and shards but no jewelry and no charcoal. I'm aching as we sit on some flat rocks to eat cold canned stew. The Tajiks are a few yards away, gnawing on yak jerky. The light is fading; we'll head back soon.

Suddenly we're jolted by an explosion above and behind us. We all freeze. Then there's a low rumble, growing in intensity.

"Get up! Run!"

I grab Ostriker's arm and haul him to his feet. Looking over my shoulder, the rock face is in motion. Huge boulders are careening downwards towards us. The Tajiks start moving away from the cliff. I'm pulling Ostriker forward.

"Move! Faster!"

Then everything's a blur of dust and flying rock. Something slams into my shoulder. Ostriker is wrenched from my grip. The searing pain is only broken when consciousness seeps away.

I come to. Not much time has passed because it's still light. I hear moaning. Trying to sit up, I gasp. My collarbone is probably broken. I lie still until my shallow breathing becomes more regular. Then I get up slowly. One of the Tajiks is nursing a gash in his leg.

Otherwise, he's unhurt. The second is under a pile of rock. I burrow in, moving rocks with one hand, until I find an arm. No pulse. Ostriker lies face down ten yards away. His head is a bloody pulp.

As I grimly drive back to camp, each bump in the road sending searing pain through my upper body, I fixate on the fact that mining companies have lots of dynamite.

■

The rest of the team is waiting for us as we pull up.

"What happened?" Alpha barks. "We heard the explosion."

"We were right under the rock fall. We had no time to get away. Ostriker's dead. One of the Tajiks is dead. I'm pretty fucked up."

There are gasps. Gio helps me out of the jeep and she and Alpha clean my wound and strap my shoulder as well as they can.

"We leave at first light. Pack everything up. And Farnsworth," she fixes him with her intense gaze, "Keep doing your work."

He's too stunned to argue with her so he heads back into his tent. The bulk of the camp is broken down and packed up in near silence. Farnsworth works on the samples in his tent, using the only powerful light we have, powered off one of the car batteries. Alpha paces the camp like a caged tiger. We're relieved when she says she's going to walk along the river path by moonlight and will be back in a while.

Time drags. Gio and I play a few games of chess on the pocket board he has with him, but we can't concentrate. Farnsworth finally emerges.

He speaks crisply and carefully. "I ran the calibrations three times, and checked each against a control sample I brought. The machine is working perfectly. Each of five samples gives the same answer."

We stare at him, waiting.

"The site is 35,000 years old."

■

Incredible. But the moment of triumph is muted by tragedy. We're all still absorbing the events of the evening. Then Gio says,

"Where's Helen? She should be back by now."

He and I head down the path at a brisk clip. We can see clearly by the moonlight. We nearly reach the road when I stop.

"Gio, look at this."

At right angles from the path, there are parallel grooves in the gravel, heading towards some large boulders.

We break into a run. I round the corner of a large boulder and stopped in my tracks, my heart pounding.

She's on the ground, motionless. Her legs sprawl and one arm is trapped behind her back. She's like a rag doll someone has discarded. Her neck is wrapped with a leather cord and her head is bent at an awkward angle. The eyes stare out at the night.

Blackout

Gio and I look at each other leadenly. Like robots, we follow the ritual of Chinese drinking, with all its gladiatorial elements. Show the label of the bottle, that you do not dishonor your companion with an inferior brand. Fill the glass. Lift the glass. Toast your companion and pay him more honor than you would yourself. Drink as one. Then tilt the glass toward your companion, to show that you do not insult him by leaving a drop.

Reload. Repeat.

Reload. Repeat.

I see Gio's tearstained cheeks and feel nothing. My neck is in a brace after breaking my collarbone and I haven't taken pain meds but the alcohol is doing its job. I'm numb. This is good. This is why I drink. It makes perfect sense.

"Buona notte al secchio."

"English, Gio."

"Good night to the bucket. It means we're screwed. Screwed."

"Aye, you've hit that one on the noggin."

"Come la mettiamo?"

"English, Gio."

"What are we going to do?"

"Too hard. Ask me another one."

We stare across the crude wood table and take petty comfort in each other's helplessness and misery.

The next day is no different. And the day after. I dimly remember the events that follow the deaths of Ostriker and the Tajik and Helen Matson's murder. Stunned silence as we absorb the losses. Fear tilting into despair as the implications for the expedition and our discovery sink in. Knowing that we're very much on our own. Discovering that the workers have scattered to the winds—and the likelihood that one of them has killed her. Was he paid off by the mining company? We have more questions than answers and too much to assimilate.

∎

We're back in Kashgar, the bustling oasis. It's a better and more anonymous place in which to lick our wounds. The local police come the next morning. They take away the bodies. We've no illusions that they'll bother to investigate. They cart off the boxes of artifacts. They confiscate our equipment. I imagine a local official of the Communist Party scratching his head as he ponders what to do with a portable carbon isotope mass spectrometer.

Farnsworth takes the easy route: the first flight home. No doubt he's secreted some glass beads or a bone fragment into his luggage, but who could he tell and who'll believe his story? Without publishing all the evidence the discovery will sink like a stone and the academic waters will smooth over without a ripple. Escobar is still here, staying at our hotel. She's one cold fish. We see her occasionally at the buffet and she barely makes eye contact.

∎

Time is splintering again. I'm crouching behind the door, on my tiptoes, so I don't make a sound. She's against the wall with wide eyes. She's against the wall because his hand holds her there, holds her neck. You stupid bitch he says. You stupid fucking bitch. He lets go. She drops like a marionette with the strings cut. You fucking cow. I'm still behind the door. But I must move. He can't see me. He can't ever see me again.

■

Gio and I are locked in an unhealthy embrace. I can handle this life. I've done it before and no doubt I'll do it again. But it may ruin the Italian. Farnsworth knows Gio's reputation and he's told me how brilliant he is. After two postdocs, Gio was offered a professorship in Pisa. In Italy, universities are seized up like a rich man's bowels; jobs are hard to get and most young researchers just give up and leave the game. Gio got offered a plum job and he turned it down. He didn't like how it would make him conform and prune back his wildest ideas. He didn't want to fit the expectations of the Academy.

Sonja Escobar stands at our table. I almost forgot she's still at the hotel. Her voice sounds strange; I've hardly ever heard her speak.

"There's something you should see."

Gio looks at her dully. "Lasciami stare. Leave me alone."

"What is it?" I ask.

"I can't explain."

She stands, and I realize she won't go away until we go with her. Wearily, I get to my feet and drag Gio to his. In her room we sit on the bed. She takes a cardboard box from her suitcase and opens it. Then she puts four pale brown objects on the blanket between us. They're like curved fragments of pottery.

"Skull casings. From two different locations on our dig. One is a child, the other three are young adults."

We look at her, bewildered.

"Look more closely at the inside. What do you see?"

Gio just holds his head in his hands, but I pick up a fragment and stare at it. The outside is smooth like an eggshell but the inside has a faint undulating pattern imprinted on it, like the interlocking pieces of a curvy jigsaw. It's a clue, part of the biggest puzzle of all. I know I'll see this again so I pay close attention.

"Look at the others."

I do. They're all the same. They all have the pattern. I recall the time with Gio when I saw the faint outlines of the settlement on the ground. This is important too.

"What is it?"

She exhales slowly. "What does kuru mean to you?"

A blank. "Nothing."

"It's a disease first noticed in the Fore people on New Guinea a century ago, where it was spread by cannibalism. It's caused by a prion, which is a tiny folded protein, smaller than a virus. The prion eats the brain, leaving it like a sponge. The imprint of the ravaged brain looks exactly like the patterns you see here."

"What happens to people with kuru?"

"It's a progressive neurological disease. There is memory loss, personality change, and hallucinations. Then comes impairment of speech, jerky movements and seizures. Death follows within weeks. The disease is always fatal."

I struggle to understand. "Do you mean these people ate each other?"

"No. There was no sign of cannibalism at any of the sites. This disease spread either by contact or in the air. It was a contagion."

∎

I'm safe but not for long. She's above me, cooing softly. He comes in, smelling rank. He leans over the crib. What do you want? What the fucking Christ do you want? He's looking down at her. I imagine he can see past her, through her, and see me. He slaps her. It sounds like a fish hitting the kitchen counter. She cries out. Another slap. Much harder. Another. I can't help her. I'm safe but not for long.

∎

We've chosen the rowdiest bar in Kashgar. I'm with my drinking buddy Gio. I'm trying to cheer him up. But his face is so long it looks like someone turned the heat up in Madame Tussauds.

"She knew." I lean across the table and whisper. "She knew. She brought an epidemiologist along for the ride."

"It makes no difference."

"Waddya mean?"

"We have no evidence; we can't tell anyone. Non vale un cazzo. It's not worth shit."

"True." The glaze of alcohol is fading. My neck and shoulder are throbbing. I wax philosophical.

"We've turned the world upside down, Gio, but who really cares? We found a culture eons ahead of their time. If they'd persisted, who knows where we'd be now? But little weevils got into their brains and no doubt we'll have our own little weevils soon enough."

"Va bene." He says. "Every civilization gets a day in the Sun."

"It's all too neat. Evidence of a previous culture. Laid out for us to find and piece together. Like someone salted the mine. What if it's all a clever ploy by someone or something smarter than us?"

He stares blankly at me. "McEvoy, you are truly crazy."

We drink in silence.

"To Mars," I toast. "To owning a sword and a good kit of armor. Life's one fucking battle after another."

He raises his glass. "To prions."

"Aye, the meek shall inherit the Earth."

He looks across the room. "Gatta ci cova."

"What?"

"I smell a rat."

I follow his gaze and see tables of men drinking hard, all the multi-ethnic hues of the Xinjiang Uyghur Autonomous Region. But on the far wall, one group catches my attention as it has Gio's. Two of them are men from our work crew. My fog lifts quickly. I rise.

Gio clutches my arm. "What are you going to do?"

"Nothing, my friend." I remove his hand. "I'm just going to see if these folk know something."

I've seen one of the two head outside to the urinal so I follow him. There's no plan. I'm thinking exactly one moment ahead. He finishes and turns from the stinking trough of piss and cigarette butts. I grab him by the throat. My hand fits neatly around his neck.

"What happened to the woman?"

His eyes bug out and then narrow to slits.

"What happened to the woman?"

It's no use, a waste of time. I'm walking away when I hear motion on the tile floor. I turn.

First I see the knife. A second later, I see the tiger's eye pinned to his belt. I lunge. My first blow spins him to the side, sending the knife flying from his hand. Then it's in my hand. I clasp him behind the neck in a half-embrace while the other hand presses the knife into his gut. I twist and feel warm, pulsing wetness. He's mouthing words, but none come. I rip the tiger's eye from his belt. One of us shudders. All color leaches from the world and the light ebbs. The iris shrinks to black.

4 THE PAMPAS

True Blood

He stands on the platform of the station at Ushuaia in Patagonia, with unkempt ginger hair, wearing tartan trousers and Doc Martens, as if it was the most natural thing in the world.

"McEvoy, you beautiful bastard." I say.

"Dr. Livingstone, I presume." He replies.

He's filled out. McEvoy's always been partial to pie and a Mars bar. But the smirk and the broad, swaggering stance masked by a wee bit of earnestness are the same as ever.

"Did you really come to see me?" He asks.

"McEvoy, I'd follow you to the butt-hole ends of the Earth."

"Such a smoothie." He looks thoughtful. "But how d'ye know I'd be here?"

"Silly bugger," I say. "You wrote me three weeks ago, don't you remember?"

He furrows his brow and looks lost. "Robbie, there's so much I don't remember I can't begin to describe it."

∎

We stand on the platform and catch up for a while. It's natural talking to Robbie, as natural as slipping on an old glove, even though I've not seen him for five years, since I was at sea. We fall into the old speech patterns. I have a sharp memory of the anticipation of a rowdy night out, or an afternoon spent soaking up the feeble winter sun at a football match. Robbie's tall and skinny, with a mop of shaggy black hair restrained by a red bandana.

"Breakfast, eh?"

"Sure," he says. "I'm famished."

We hoist our backpacks and hit an easy stride. The town is a mile away, down a slight hill, and we can see the broad curve of the bay. Ushuaia is the capital of Terra Del Fuego and the southernmost town on Earth. The houses are plain, with sloping roofs of corrugated metal. A dozen piers project into the blue-gray waters, all hosting clusters of fishing boats and freighters bristling with cranes. The sky's slate grey and spitting rain. A raw wind howls in from the sea. This must pass for summer at the foot of the planet.

"What d'ye fancy?" We're looking at menus in the first small café we spot.

"Dunno, the meat looks good."

"Aye, but check out over here. Meat."

"Mmmm. I'm feeling a bit meatish."

"It could be the meat, then."

"Unless we go the other way."

"With meat?"

"Aye."

Argentina is a country of colonic heroes. Every day, forty million people chew the charred flesh of animals and sent it through turbo-charged stomachs to cast-iron bowels that discharge their duty with brio and panache.

Our plates arrive piled high with brown mounds. Two eggs are on the side as a garnish or afterthought. Like jaundiced eyes they watch us tuck in.

I'm earnestly solicitous. "How's your meat."

"Mmm, rather meaty. Yours?"

"Ditto. Do you know what any of this is?" I ask.

"Not really." Robbie pokes at the meat with his fork. "There's steak and sausage, of course. Pork cutlets. I see tripe and blood pudding. Then it gets a bit blurry."

"Tasty, though."

"Aye."

"Trust the meat?"

"Absolutely. Words to live by."

We draw the line at the beverage that's part of the folk culture of southern Chile and Argentina: ñicha. It's a mixture of cow's milk and lamb's blood. Beloved of the Scythians and Alexander the Great, as I recall. Robbie seems partial to the idea and is smacking his lips. But I demur—the blood is warm and it's supposed to be fresh, but how can we be sure? I thumb Egon Ronay but he's no bloody help at all.

Ushuaia is the meeting place but it has little allure so we head back to the station. The town feels leaden and sullen. Not surprising, as it was built in the early 20th century by the convicts of a notorious high security prison modeled on Devil's Island. The station master regards us suspiciously through the iron grille.

"What do you think, Robbie? North?"

"Aye. It's a possibility."

"You seem torn. Perhaps we should head north instead?"

"That would be fine too."

"Shall we toss a coin?"

"I don't have a coin."

"It's decided then."

■

The train leans left and right as it navigates the sinuous contours of the river valley. Hundred-foot high spruce and Douglas fir flick by the windows. Each time we cross the river the trestles groan and the cataract rages below. Snow-covered mountains loom over the valley, which is unscarred by roads and nearly untouched by people. This is nature untrammeled.

Patagonia looks like the Scotland of my imagination. But all the piss and vinegar was knocked out of my homeland a long time ago. There are few primal forests left and most of the wild animals have been eradicated or marginalized. Now it's little more than a large holding pen for sheep. The Scots.

Robbie is staring out of the window, absolutely engrossed. I've always envied his ability to shut out distractions and lose himself in simple pleasures. My monkey brain doesn't have an off switch. It's endlessly peppering me with questions or carrying on a commentary. McEvoy, what's the point? That was a stupid thing to say. You're not going to get laid, you know. Why did he say that? They don't respect you. Why am I in this godforsaken job? McEvoy, wake up!

"How are you earning a crust these days?" Robbie asks.

"Teaching. I'm a sub."

"Teaching what?"

"History. Geography. Whatever they need. Whatever I can fake."

"Is it good?"

"Good enough. I like kids. Especially at the age before they realize what their parents have done to the world and just how fucked up it is. They ask questions. They wriggle in their seats. Their faces are open books. They have hope, Robbie."

"I see it's not contagious."

"Oh, I still have moments when I think I can change the world. But they're thinning out."

"Then you move on?"

"Can't abide attachment. Must be a Buddhist thing."

"The Phantom McEvoy. You never leave much of a footprint."

I want us to get on back the light stuff. I want to shoot the breeze, riff on the quirks of our mates, and act snidely superior. I want us to find a football and indulge our jock fantasies. I want to regress. But I need an update from the home front first.

"How is she?"

"Your mum is…doing OK." Robbie isn't good at weighing words.

"Does she go out much?"

"Hardly ever. That's what your aunt said."

"How does she look?"

"Much the same." He's very uncomfortable. "No, that's not true. She's declining, McEvoy. Skin's sallow. Hair's coming out in clumps. It's not good."

"How long?" My voice is weak, hammered flat.

"God man, I don't know. You can pick up a phone! Your arm's not broken." His voice falls. "Sorry. That's partly why I'm here."

"And…"

"You don't want to know."

"Tell me anyway."

"Annie's a user and abuser. McEvoy, I know your sis has had some rough luck, but she's burned her bridges with me and everyone else I know. She looks like shite. If she wasn't so well pickled, I think she'd check out before your mum." Pause. Grim smile. "Sorry again."

"You shouldn't be. They're my sodding family. I'm the one that's got them on my plate."

That's self-righteous crap. I've seen to it that I'm either on a boat in the middle of an ocean or five thousand miles away ever since I left home. Abandonment may be too strong a word but willful neglect hits it on the head.

Robbie guesses my thoughts. Sometimes it's like he's in my head with me. "You deserve your own life, pal. Christ, if I had your smarts I'd have buggered off years ago."

■

"What about the FB?"

"Don't ask about the FB."

"Tell me about the FB, Robbie."

"Don't ask me about the FB, McEvoy."

The FB. John McEvoy. My dear dad. The Fucking Bastard. When John was your friend, you were cock of the walk. When he said he'd got your back, bullets would bounce off you. His talent was to create then squander trust and goodwill. His real marks were in the world of business. He just used his family for target practice.

I remember him spending all afternoon one Saturday playing with me on the living room rug. I must've been four or five. We did building blocks and Lego and Meccano and the trains, exhausted them all, and he had infinite patience and all the time in the world. But next day, as we walked the footpath of the Lothian canal on a blustery winter's day, he whisked me into his arms but then he held me over the near-frozen surface of the water and said, "You love your Dad, don't you, wee boy, you love your Dad? You really do, don't you? Don't be afraid, why are you afraid? Tell me how much you love me, tell me. Tell me."

"The FB."

"You're like a dog with a fucking bone, McEvoy, I swear you are."

"The FB."

"OK, OK, you win." Robbie takes a deep breath. "He's got a shop on the Easter Road. I drove by it a few times. Home improvement. Attic and loft conversions. Subdividing houses into flats. Does pretty well. I've seen him in a red Mini Cooper. T reg."

"Girlfriend?"

"Aye. She's a slag, though. Not a patch on your mum."

"Do you believe in justice, Robbie?"

"Not really. Haven't seen much evidence of it."

"That's two of us. What about a moral underpinning?"

"Come again?"

"Right and wrong. The sense that someone's guiding the ship, that the world knows its tit from its arse."

"No way. Lunatics are running the asylum. Shite happens. You just duck, take cover, and get by as well as you can."

■

We sleep in our seats on the train that night and wake up cricked and tweaked. Outside, the forest thins out and shrubs and tall grass take over. We're approaching the boundary between Patagonia and the Pampas. The rolling prairie disappears into morning mist suffused by ochre sunlight. I see my first gaucho, cantering alongside the train for a few hundred yards. His seat is so good he doesn't bother to hold the reins.

Robbie's still dozing so I pull out my wee book and make some notes. The Chronicle of McEvoy is the size of a paperback, two inches thick, bulging with inserted pages and covered with fraying duct tape. It's almost half full of my spidery scrawl. I hope that doesn't mean I'm half done with adventuring because I'm barely 28 and feel like I have another wee book or two in me.

"Am I in your wee book?" Robbie's eyes are still half-shut.

"It's riddled with you," I reply artfully.

Late that evening we roll into a coastal town called Bahia Blanca. Not wanting to face another night on the train, we pile off. We're the only people on the platform.

Big mistake.

The town's shut up tight. We walk down the dead streets feeling like ghosts. Nobody's out and even the canonical stray dogs seem to have something better to do. The few hotels we pass are boarded up or closed for the winter season.

"This is dire." Robbie's dragging.

"Aye, nobody wants our money and our scintillating company."

"We're going to have to doss, you know that?"

I sigh. "I can handle it. I'm asleep on my feet already."

We're near the city center. It's as deserted as if a plague had hit. I spot an ornate Spanish colonial building with a courtyard. The wrought iron gate is closed but we climb it easily. In the dark we can make out the outline of an elegant formal garden. Aisles of grass pass between neatly trimmed hedges, flowers and fruit trees. A full moon casts the picture in cool yellow light.

"Will a thousand star hotel do you, McEvoy?"

"Only if there's a mint on my pillow."

"Do you think they have room for a couple of lunatics?"

"Of course. Madness occupies no space."

Having no sleeping bags, we pile on every layer of clothing we've got and try to find comfortable positions on the cold, hard turf. I toss and turn for ages and in my exhaustion I'm just beginning to drift off when a light goes on and an upper bay window is flung open. We see the silhouette of a massive man clad entirely in black. By bearing and demeanor he can only be a priest. When he speaks it's with a heavily inflected Spanish accent.

"I assume you're strangers and speak English. You can be woken by the sprinklers at 5am, or you can come in for a warm bed, and be woken with a sweet roll and coffee for Matins at eight."

Maybe there is a God.

Marking Time

The Mission of San Ignatius is better than any B&B. The beds are comfy, there's hot water in every room, and they serve huge portions of vegetables to stop your innards from seizing up from the meat that accompanies them.

There's just the small matter of services. In return for room and board we have certain duties. I teach English at the mission school and once they find out Robbie is a wizard who can fix anything he becomes the indispensable handyman. But we're also expected to partake in the spiritual life of the Jesuit community.

We learn about this in our first conversation with Father Carlos, the man who flung open his windows and invited us inside. We do our best to conceal the fact that we're wastrels and heathens.

"Life here is simple and hard, but rich with inner reward. We rarely have visitors, let alone emissaries from the far north. Welcome."

"Thanks, Father." I speak for us both. "You've got great digs here. We might just settle in for a bit. We were headed for Buenos Aires and then home, but we have no great plans."

"In light of your duties, I will reduce the requirement of the Liturgy of the Hours. Since you start work at dawn, you can forgo Matins. The main sustenance for the soul will come at Terce, None, and Vespers. You may also join me for Compline at midnight in the Lady of Santos chapel."

"Ah, excuse me, Father." Robbie's shifting nervously from foot to foot. "Are you saying we have to go to Church four times a day?"

"Yes," he says simply.

"That's a bit steep, isn't it?"

"The Psalms tell us: seven times a day I will praise you. They say: Evening, morning, and at noon I will cry and lament."

"You see, Father, my friend Robbie, his dad was a Presbyterian but not a very serious one, and Robbie's pretty much agnostic," I try not to ramble but the priest's placid demeanor is unnerving me. "While I," And here I pull out my trump card, "grew up in a Wee Free house."

"I see."

I hope that means we'll be free and clear. To a Catholic, Calvin had slightly smaller horns than Luther himself and Wee Frees are the most virulently anti-Catholic sect among Protestants.

"No sin is too large to forgive. He welcomes all back to the flock."

I size up the priest. Bulk is a part of his intimidating authority. He wears an unadorned black cassock with white collar and he fills it like a mountain. With his sloping shoulders, massive shaved head and lack of discernable neck, he looks like he could have built the mission with his bare hands, effortlessly hoisting the huge stone blocks.

He's implacable, so I cave in. "Right then, I guess we'll see you at Ponce, or Tone, or Vespa, or whatever the next one is."

He inclines his head slightly and gives me an economical smile to acknowledge both the crude attempt at mockery and its utter failure. I'm outmaneuvered. The features of his face crowd towards the center of its great expanse. There's keen intelligence there, and an iron will.

Father Carlos is a twin. How do I know this?

■

"With one balletic move, he leaves the defender flat-footed."
I nutmeg Robbie and dance around his outstretched leg.
"The thuggish full back is left to eat his dust."
Robbie gets up ponderously and chases me, huffing.
"His ball control is so good it's like he has Velcro on his boot."
Darting left and right, I close in on the goal.
"Avoiding the crude tackle, he unleashes a lethal volley."
I catch the ball flush on the laces, while Robbie catches air.
"His rocket finds the top corner. The crowd roars. Gooaaal!"
This is where script and reality separate. I get under the shot and the ball sails over the hedge and shatters a window of the Our Lady

of Guadalupe Chapel. There'll be hell to pay. Or if I'm lucky, merely limbo or purgatory.

■

Robbie's in a sulk.

"What's up, Robert the Bruce?"

"You can be a right bastard, McEvoy. Why d'ye have to humiliate me when we play footie?"

"Sorry. Really, I am. I've no idea why you put up with me."

He's mollified and gives me a knowing smirk. It's our lunch break and having worked up a sweat, we tuck into meat pies in the shade of the courtyard.

"D'ye think he's trying to convert us?" Robbie sounds worried.

"Of course he is. Like some pretty women with gays. They've got something great the guy should want so they have to try and flip him. I would too if I were in his shoes."

"Maybe we should leave."

"Robbie Robertson." I give him my most disparaging look. "Is this the man of the scam, the lad who couldn't be had? I do believe you're scared, a timorous beastie!"

"That man can't intimidate me." He blusters unconvincingly.

"Could it be, sweet pea, that you not only have a soul but think it might up for grabs?"

"Lay off, McEvoy."

"Well, do what you want, but I'm more than willing to chew the wafer with the fat man if it'll get me a soft pillow and meat pies."

■

We eat quietly for a while, enjoying shadowed coolness and the aroma of birch and lavender. We're far enough north that the air has lost its sharp edge. It's quiet except for a wavering hum of bees.

"Hello," I nudge Robbie. "Spring has sprung. Time for the badger to come out of his winter hidey-hole."

He follows my gaze. A young woman is picking flowers across the courtyard. She has a full, pretty face and wavy auburn hair cascading onto her shoulders. She wears a simple flowered dress that she fills nicely. Robbie and I slip into a state of heightened anticipation. Our breathing is regular and synchronized, all previous conversations are forgotten. Men are such simple creatures.

"Stroll." I nudge Robbie again. "Time for a stroll."

"Absolutely. Got to get the kinks out."

We walk sedately across the courtyard. For the immediate purpose, we engross ourselves in a dissection of the relative merits of McEwans Eighty Shillings and India Pale Ale.

"Hello!" I say brightly. "You've got a beautiful basket."

Robbie elbows me hard in the ribs.

She turns and shines a smile at me. Full lips. Small, well-formed teeth. A pert nose. "For the sacristy."

"I am McEvoy, and this is my best pal Robbie."

"I am Letitia Mantovani."

"We're guests of the mission and visitors to your fine country."

"From where you come? I hear the accent but don't know."

"The frozen north. Scotland. Land of kilts and haggis."

She smiles to herself. "Excuse my English. Not very good."

"Better than our Spanish, fair maiden." Ease up, McEvoy, you're slathering it on with a fat knife.

"Well, I have to go. Please excuse me." She turns and glides from the garden, leaving us grasping at straws: the receding rustle of her dress and the sway of her hips.

"Oh God." Robbie is rooted.

"And you were just about to sign on. Shame about the vows."

■

The small town of Bahia Blanca is not much livelier on an average weeknight than it was when we arrived on a Sunday evening. There are many joints serving asado, the barbequed meat that seems to be essential to the Argentinean constitution. There's one Italian and one Chinese restaurant, and that's the full gamut of the world cuisine. As elsewhere in South America, families and couples like to promenade on the central boulevard. It runs the length of the town and is lined with large clay pots containing spring flowers and a tented canopy of cypress trees.

We gorge on grilled, braided intestines and leave the barbeque joint with bellies stretched and aching. Our own intestines will have some work to do, which is poetic justice.

"Best walk this off a bit, eh?"

"Aye. Reckon we can find a pint?"

"Easier out here than back there." I laugh. "Trust us to choose the only monks who don't make booze in their spare time."

Bahia Blanca is laid out on a grid so is easy to navigate. We head away from the central square toward the port. It's spookily quiet and everyone seems to be tucked in with a cup of Bovril by 8m. But as we hit the waterfront there are signs of life. We walk into brightly lit bar wedged between two warehouses.

Robbie turns to me. "OK, d'ye reckon?"

"Aye, we'll have our drinks, mind our own business, and be as quiet as mice."

"Fair enough. What about Elvis over there?" He jerks his thumb towards a group at a large table in the corner. Their apparent leader sports a slicked-back rockabilly hairstyle. Very retro.

I shrug. "I've no beef with him, as long as he doesn't gob on my blue suede shoes."

We sup a couple of pints and take in the scene. It's working class and rough, but the buzz is fairly friendly. So far—the night is young. After watching them out of the corner of my eye, it's clear the corner hosts local thugs and fences. Several shoe boxes on their table seem to hold nipped car stereos. Elvis is unduly full of himself for a small time, small town thief.

I tilt my head. "OK?"

Always good to stay ahead of the game. Robbie and I drain the remains of our pints and head for the door. But they intercept us a block away as we're turning the corner to head back into town.

"Donde vas, maricon?" It's Elvis, with curled lip. His confederates are arrayed beside and behind him.

I size up the situation. We can handle ourselves, but the

numbers are against us. Speed and surprise are essential. I relax and smile as if I had all the time in the world.

"Just taking some ocean air."

Then my boot rises swiftly into Elvis' groin and he gasps with pain and crumples to the ground. By the time his gang has reacted we're fifty yards away and running hard.

■

Disaster averted, we reach the central square, winded. Just then the town clock chimes.

"Shite. I said I'd help the Incredible Hulk at Nones. I'd better go; he'll break me like a twig if I'm late." I look at Robbie suspiciously. "How did you get out of that one?"

"I said I was fixing the heating in the chapel." He's unconscionably smug. Then his eyes widen like a wee boy's at Christmas.

A block away, Letitia is strolling with a woman we guess to be her mother. They're arm in arm. Even at this distance, the roll of her waist makes me feel like the drunken sailor I once was.

"So sorry you have bugger off, old chum." Robbie apes a hangdog look for my benefit.

"If you get off with her, I'm leaving you out of my massive will."

"So suspicious. McEvoy, you're such a lowlander. I'll merely offer my rippling physique to protect two vulnerable women walking alone."

Muttering under my breath, I hot-foot it back to the mission. I've already discovered Father Carlos doesn't appreciate it when I sneak in the back in the middle of a service. But to my surprise, services are very calming. Since I don't understand a word of the Latin, it acts like a mantra, and the sonorous chant from the choir of seminary students is a balm rubbed deep into my body. McEvoy leaves chapel in as close as he ever comes to an exalted state.

Walking to my room I see a monk and a young woman talking at the corner of the courtyard. It's her! She's not only given Robbie the slip but has had time to stop off at home and change her outfit. She's wearing a dark blue velvet shift that's stylish and simple but manages to leave little about her fulsome figure to the imagination. I bide my time until she's free then make like a cruise missile.

"I'm really pleased to see you." I say, with the earnestness knob cranked up to eleven. "Frankly, I was concerned for your safely. My friend did a tour in the Amazon before joining me, and he has some sores that have the doctors scratching their heads."

"Friend? I am confused. I have never seen you with a friend."

"OK, OK. He's got you wrapped up. I'm man enough to accept it."

"I don't understand. You are upsetting me. I have to go."

"Wait." Now I'm confused. "You do know who I am, don't you?"

"Yes, Señor McEvoy. Padre Carlos said you were staying here to do penance for your many sins."

Many sins? I make a mental note to give Hulk a piece of my mind, but even as I register the thought I know I'll chicken out.

"I'm sorry. Look, Letitia, I just want to see you again."

She erupts into peals of laughter from a joke I'm not privy to.

"You're talking about Letitia. I am Patricia. Somos gemelas."

"Come again?"

"We're twins, Señor McEvoy."

More peals of laughter, and this time I join in. Not one, but two beauties of her caliber! I'm gobsmacked of course, but not so much that I forget to ask her to go for a walk. As we stroll down a quiet street near the mission through puddles of lamplight, I breathe in her delicate scent and become intoxicated. Her ravishing hair, her supple lips, her bosom lifted up as an offering to the angels: all these are so familiar. Am I disloyal to double purpose my lust? Is this a vicarious form of infidelity?

Later that night, Robbie and I share a hip flask of cheap whiskey. The male force has fissured; we must repair the damage. Robbie and I have come to blows several times in the past over a woman and we've smoothed it out each time. The lunatic, the lover, and the madman are of imagination all compact.

"What if it's a crock?" Robbie looks thoughtful.

"What d'ye mean?"

"Neither of us has seen them together," he says. "So how do we know they're actually two people?"

"Good point." I muse. "In that case she's grabbing the attention of two so she must be a larger than life woman."

"Or, they really are twins."

"If they're devout we're fucked." I say sadly.

"But if they're not devout we're really fucked." He gives me a sly look and we laugh.

■

"Your thirst for knowledge, Mr. McEvoy, it gives me hope for you. There's a collection you might be interested in"

Father Carlos stands in the doorway of the classroom as I gather books and papers I have to grade. His massive frame fills the opening and admits little light. His physical presence always unnerves me; it's so uncompromising and absolute.

I follow him up a spiral stone staircase to a part of the mission that I know exists but have never visited. Passing through a massive oak door we enter his personal apartment. His bedroom door is open. It's Spartan inside. Plain white walls hold a single cross and the cot barely seems wide enough for his girth. Then we enter his private study and my jaw drops.

"Holy crap!" I redden. "Oh, sorry Father. I've never seen anything like this."

The room is lined with bookshelves but there are no books. Every shelf and every surface is covered with fossils. There are skulls no bigger than an egg and ammonites the size of a car wheel. The coffee table is supported by four sauropod leg bones the size of tree trunks and the hat stand is made of six mastodon tusks bound together and facing outward. With pride of place over the tall arched window is a triceratops head frill.

"It's brilliant, Father." I walk around the room touching piece after piece like a giddy child. I look at him quizzically.

"Does the Bishop know I indulge in this hobby? Yes, he does. The Society of Jesus has always valued knowledge. We've been suspect in some eyes within the Church because of this. But science is a worthy companion on the path of humility and service. It teaches us that we can't know everything and it reveals our small part in God's plan."

"So you don't think He knocked all this up in six days?"

He rearranges his face in a temporary smile. "It's a challenge, I agree. No, we accept that the wonders of nature dwarf our meager existence. Pierre Teilhard de Chardin, a member of the Society, was involved in the discovery of Java man. George Lemaître, who rose to the rank of Abbé, predicted that the universe began in an enormous explosion called the big bang billions of years ago."

"Did you find all these?"

"No, I merely dabble. My brother is a paleontologist in Mendoza. Most of these are from his expeditions."

"You chose very different paths."

"Perhaps. But I live his life as he lives mine. I to the world am like a drop of water that in the ocean seeks another drop."

"I don't understand."

"He is my twin."

■

Robbie's cough has a jagged edge to it.

"That sounds dire; you'd better have them see to it."

"Och, I'm fine, nothing a little meat won't fix."

"Ah, the meat cure. Doctor's orders?"

"Even the side orders are meaty."

"That'll see you right."

We banter, but it's forced. Robbie's sliding into illness and lethargy and I'm getting itchy feet after three weeks in Bahia Blanca.

"Maybe they'll serenade us tonight from the courtyard."

I put on a falsetto. "Dromio, Dromio, wherefore art thou. Deny thy father and refuse thy name."

"Sure enough, the Hulk would kill us if we sullied the twins."

"Why can't we get a double date?"

"Lettie says they have to trade off evenings with her sick mum. But she promises we will next week."

I'm dubious. "I dunno, Robbie, something's not right here."

■

The next evening it's Patty's turn to come up to the mission and I have her to myself. Robbie's laid low, in his bed. Something nasty has taken up residence in his lungs; he's sallow and drawn. The Hulk got a doctor to come but all he did was stand over Robbie's bed and mouth platitudes. I'm diminished when my alter ego is so compromised.

In the absence of the balm of hot romance, I practice my Spanish in the mission library with Patty. Or is it Lettie? Wrapping my tongue around the strange words is hard enough, but the meaning of the passages I'm reading from Don Quixote entirely escapes me.

"...Si de la amistad y amor que Dios manda que se tenga de al enemigo, entraros luego al punto por la Escritura Divina..."

I'm on the edge of a dream state, hypnotized by the cadence of my own voice speaking a foreign tongue, and by a hint of her vapor.

The door opens and Father Carlos approaches. His eyes weigh the scene carefully for impropriety and, sensing none, the granite face softens to mere sandstone.

"An opportunity has come up for you."

"Yes?"

"My brother is going to the pampas on an expedition. I told him of your untutored but enthusiastic interest in science and he says he can use you. You will have to decide quickly. The next overnight train for Mendoza leaves at nine tomorrow morning."

"I'd like to, but..."

"It's good to be loyal. The doctor visited me again today. Robbie has had pleurisy and now he has contracted pneumonia."

The color drains from my face.

"Don't be alarmed. He's out of danger. But he needs three to four weeks of bed rest. It will be a while before either of you…" He gave me the look that bypassed with skin and flesh and penetrated right to the darker pockets of my heart. "…can indulge in any activities that might jeopardize your immortal souls."

•

I'm gathering my belongings for the trip to Mendoza when I get word that the Hulk wants to see me urgently. When I enter his office I know it's bad. He's sitting rigidly at his desk with his fingers tented in the form of a miniature chapel. His face is stern and implacable.

"We had a theft last night."

"Sorry to hear that. What was lifted?"

"Silver from the sacristy. I don't care about the value of the metal. But these pieces are relics, some hundreds of years old."

"Hold on." My voice rises. "And you think I…think we…"

"I don't know. But nothing was broken. Apparently the thief or the thieves had a key."

"Father Carlos, I suppose I can't blame you for being suspicious. But there's no way Robbie and I would ever betray your trust."

His gaze is unwavering. There's a long pause. Faint birdsong spills in through an open window. He makes a decision.

"Yes. I think my initial judgment was correct." A thin-lipped smile. "Enjoy your trip."

Birth Order

The train ride to Mendoza is long and uneventful. For hour after hour the undifferentiated, rolling grassland slides by the window. The pampas. I miss Robbie and conduct both parts of the dialog we might have had in my head. I share my small compartment with a taciturn businessman with a pinched face who is in no mood for conversation. As night falls we pull the seats out to make rudimentary beds that span the full width of the compartment. I sleep fitfully. Each time the rhythmic clacking starts to send me off, the train groans or lurches sideways. It's a long night.

Mendoza is a bustling city one million strong, Argentina's fourth largest. It has a European flavor with tree-lined streets linking squares and piazzas. The Andes loom in the distance. I don't have any time for sightseeing so I grab a cafecito at the station and follow the directions Father Carlos sketched on a piece of paper.

Turning the corner of a quiet residential neighborhood, I see the University of Mendoza. I get lost several times trying to navigate the labyrinthine campus but eventually find a building where two people are piling boxes onto two minivans at a loading bay. I see one man's massive form, looking like the Hulk stripped of his cassock, and know I'm in the right place.

"Professor Gutierrez? McEvoy. I think you were expecting me."

He turns. The resemblance to Father Carlos is uncanny but it stops with physical appearance. He smothers me with a bear hug, breaks into a wide grin, and pumps my hand energetically.

"Yes! The Scotsman who loves fossils. Carlito told me. Welcome!"

"You're sure it's no bother, me coming on this trip with you?"

"Absolutely not! We'll put you to work. You'll learn a lot. It will be excellent for everyone."

He has sonorous, deep, slightly gravelly voice. His ebullience is invigorating but disconcerting; I'm accustomed to the stern and dour ways of his brother. Perhaps the Hulk better fits my secret Calvinist tendencies.

"You're thinking I am so different from my brother, yet we have the same DNA. How can it be? We're products of our environment too. If you take two shoots from the same plant and put one in the pampas and the other in the mountains above Mendoza, they grow differently. Carlito grew up with the cold stone and spiritual rigor of the seminary and the Jesuit Theological College. I preferred an academic field where nobody knows the answers and I like the wind and rain in my face too much to be stuck inside."

He looks thoughtful for a moment.

"The rest is birth order. We are the last two boys in family of six. In my country, in my social class, one boy is given to the Church. It was either me or Carlito. Luckily, it fit him like a glove. A big glove!" He bellows with laughter at his own joke.

"You look the same, but as people you seem quite different. Are you sure about the DNA?"

Another gust of laughter. "Yes, we have the same genotype, our genetic instructions are identical. But then we chose to follow those instructions in quite different ways. That's known as the phenotype. Differentiation starts at conception, not birth. Mama said that when she was pregnant one of us moved very little while the other twisted and turned like a gymnast. That was me! I fought to get out first; I couldn't wait. But Carlito had to be coaxed by the Doctor and then pulled with tongs. He liked the dark and quiet place. Birth Order!"

He unleashes another gale of laughter, belly quivering under a faded denim shirt. A member of the group talks softly in his ear.

"They tell me we have to get on the road. The site's a little tricky; we need to get there by tomorrow evening, before sunset."

"Thanks again for having me along, Professor Gutierrez."

"No ceremony here. You left that behind at the mission. I'm Pablo. Pablito. Call me that!"

■

Having traveled all the way from the southern tip of Argentina to Bahia Blanca on the coast, then inland to Mendoza, I have a sense of the vast expanse of the country. Now our small convoy heads south, back across the pampas to the northern edge of Patagonia. The snow-covered cordillera looms on our right. Pablo points out Aconcagua, the highest mountain outside Asia at just under 23,000 feet. All day long we follow the spine of the Andes. Stratocumulus billows high over the cordillera.

We pile out to eat a simple dinner and stay in a Spartan barracks-style lodge after twelve tiring hours driving. Pablo and a colleague, a geochemist called Esteban, are the only faculty on the trip. The other six people are graduate students in his department. Their rapid-fire

Spanish is intimidating but they enjoy practicing their English so I'm included in their conversations and get lots of chance to practice my rudimentary Spanish. Most of them are living out their childhood dreams to be fossil hounds.

The next day is another long drive and late in the afternoon we turn east away from the mountains. Esteban drives the lead van and by dusk he's anxiously looking for a dirt road that will take us to the first site. The last hour is an undulating ride across low hills and dry stream beds. We pitch our tents under the canopy of stars and a full Moon bright enough to read by. My tent mate is a grad student called Miguel with bad breath who snores loudly. I'm so road-weary I don't give a toss and sleep without trouble.

•

"Pablo, how do you know where to look?"

We're on a rough trail through scrub forest. The vegetation looks parched but the ground is damp—this is the monsoon season when rains lash in from the Andes and flash floods are a danger. Pablo's in the lead and he keeps up a surprisingly swift pace, given his girth. I can't bring myself to use the diminutive form Pablito with someone who weighs two hundred and fifty pounds.

"We find the places where bones are preserved in sediment. In the Mesozoic this entire area was under a shallow sea. We're heading for the place that was near the water's edge back then."

"Is Argentina good for what you do?"

"Ha! Good? It is the best!"

I expect some automatic chauvinism and resist a comment about kicking their butts in the Falklands.

"OK, I'll bite. Why is it the best?"

"The shallow sea and swamps that covered the country plus our huge area means every period in the fossil record is found here. Do you like dinosaurs?

"Is the Pope Catholic?"

"Fifteen percent of all dinosaur species were found here first. We have the largest carnivore, the largest herbivore, the largest bird, the largest mammal…"

"I get the picture. Is that what we're after? Dinosaurs?"

"Not just a dinosaur. Something special. A dinosaur that rewrites the story of life!"

We continue the conversation at a rest stop. Pablo lights up. His combination of weight and smoking doesn't auger well for longevity but his lust for life is infectious.

"When we first met, you said you went into paleontology because so little was known. Surely we know lots. Museums are stuffed with fossils; why your brother must have hundreds! When they drilled all the geological eras into my thick skull at school they all had animals attached. So we must know when tiny creepy crawlies tuned into big bad dinosaurs."

"Young McEvoy, you have much to learn, but you've come to the right place. Fossilization is rare! Only one in a hundred creatures that die gets entombed in the right way to turn bone into stone. The rest are ground to dust by erosion and geological forces and scattered to the four winds. We are reading a book where almost all of the pages are missing."

"Now you make it sound totally impossible. I don't see how you can know anything at all."

"It's a wonderful puzzle, a detective story with just enough clues. The fossil record spans the last five hundred million years. We see a progression from the first small amphibians that came ashore 400 million years ago through reptiles and insects 300 million years ago and then giant dinosaurs 150 million years ago. Alongside dinosaurs there were mammals and birds. This is the early tree of life. We're a recent twig after half a billion years of animal evolution."

It's a new way to revel in my ignominy. I'm familiar with thinking of myself as a pathetically small sack of atoms in a universe stuffed with a vast number of atoms. Now I'm an inconsequential twig on the enormous tree of life. It's enough to make a sensitive Scots soul seek out the sonic solace of a Bach partita or a John Coltrane solo, or the gustatory consolation of a chocolate bar.

The team finds their previous excavation and begins work quickly and efficiently. Graduate students are paired up; Pablo and Esteban move among them to make sure work goes smoothly. Watching, I'm certain I've done this or something like it before and it ended badly. But scouring my brain for memories I come up empty.

I watch. Then I offer to get stuck in with a hammer but it's clear that an amateur could do a lot of damage out of ignorance. Early on the first day in the field one of the grads discovers a skull in what had once been a salt marsh. She painstakingly chips and chisels the pale brown rock and a smooth curved surface steadily appears, identical in color and texture to the surrounding rock. To my untutored eye, she's a sculptor creating the skull rather than unearthing it.

By the fourth day I realize that genuine Eureka moments are rare in paleontology. It's mostly tedious. A few scattered bones have been found, but all from well-known species and well-understood sections of the geological record. Attention increasingly focuses on the skull that's being worked free of the rock that grips it. I marvel at the patience of the students as they dislodge the fossil flake by flake. If I had a mallet it would be a different story.

I also experience a wave of emotion partway between wistfulness and regret. The graduate students are my age or slightly younger but they've already spent eight or more years in studying in a university and are now becoming highly trained professionals in an exciting field. By contrast, I've bounced around the world and never quite settled on anything. I have some disconnected pieces of a big, brassy life under my belt but I'm not sure what they add up to.

"Excellente, Sofia!" Pablo is standing behind her like a one-man cheering section. "It's a spectacular find. This is not just your thesis; it's the beginning of a beautiful career."

The Sun is setting. Everyone gathers to watch. Nobody offers to help. It's clearly important that Sofia finish the excavation herself like a deep-sea fisherman must land the huge marlin no matter how tired they are.

Several hours later it's dark and chilly. Nobody's eaten and three other grads hold flashlights to illuminate the scene. At last the skull breaks free and Sofia holds it aloft like a triumphal gladiator.

"Bravo!"

"Olé! Olé!"

As everyone devours empanadas at our camp near the minivans, Pablo carefully measures the skull with calipers and writes numbers in a notebook. It's about the size of a rugby ball.

"Fully grown," Pablo is triumphant. "An adult. The largest we have found yet!"

I'm feeling left out of the party. "What is it?"

"It's a new species of flying dinosaur. We found the first specimen near here three years ago. Very exciting!"

"Aye, I believe you, but why?"

"First, it's a true dinosaur. Previously known flying lizards like the Pteranodon and the Pterodactyl were in a class called pterosaurs."

"I don't get the distinction."

"Pterosaurs were vertebrates whose wings were formed from a membrane of skin, muscle and other tissue. They had small legs to perch on and they hunted by scooping fish or amphibians from near the surface of the water."

"What's a dinosaur then?" I'm amazed at my own ignorance.

"A dinosaur is an erect or semi-erect reptile, so they have both arms and legs."

"You're saying this creature had arms and legs and wings?"

"Yes! This was a great advantage because it could hunt both on land and sea and it had an extra pair of limbs for manipulation."

"Just how big was this beastie?"

"We didn't know until tonight because we'd only found nestlings. My quick calculation says larger than Quetzalcoatlus, the previous record-holder. So a weight of two hundred kilos and a wingspan of fifteen meters."

"Jesus H. Christ!" I'm flabbergasted. "That's the size of a small Cesna. It could've carried away tasty small children, if there'd been any to carry away."

"Yes. It's remarkable. We tried to publish a finding based on the first skeleton. But the reviewer insisted we'd confused remains from multiple species. Now we have more evidence—there's no doubt."

"What are you going to call it?"

Pablo pauses, then lowers his voice for dramatic effect. "For the extra pair of arms and the ability to hunt on land and sea, just one name fits: the destroyer. Shivasaurus."

∎

The prize finding is wrapped carefully in muslin bandages and then packed in foam padding in an aluminum crate. A few smaller items are numbered and labeled and we begin the slow overland journey to the next site. I note the find in my wee book and—influenced by Pablo's enthusiasm—I'm unstinting in my use of exclamation marks!

Miguel snores louder than usual the next night. I know I've been set up when I mention his snoring to a couple of other students and they snicker. I try to shut out the sound with an act of willpower, by summoning up a vision of Letitia's face. I lock in to her large brown eyes and creamy cheeks and the slight dimple in her chin. She tilts her head forward and a lock of her raven hair falls forward in an inverted question mark. The image melts away. In frustration I put on a jacket and crawl out of the tent.

The moon bathes our camp and the surrounding grassland in an ethereal light. Bats gyrate overhead. I wander towards a nearby dry river bed and see an unmistakable human form lying face down just off the path. Pablo! A seizure? Heart attack? The poor bastard. I rush over and fall onto my hands and knees beside him to check for breath. But he turns his head sideways and in his normal husky voice says:

"This is quite special, young McEvoy. Look closely."

An exposed shale surface lies just below his head, on the sloping bank of the dry river bed. He points to a spot inches from his nose.

"There! See?"

I put my face as close to the rock as his. In the dim moonlight I see tiny paw prints. I wonder how on Earth he's been able to notice them in the dark while walking. The familiar claw pattern and spacing suggest one thing.

"A mouse?"

"Almost! But a mouse is a recent creature. Meet one of your most distant ancestors. This is a species from the taxon Euheria. I believe it is an example of Eomaia. It walked across here when the surface was mud and left its mark. Then the mud was buried and transformed by heat and pressure into stone. Recently it was revealed by erosion. It's so beautiful it makes my heart ache."

"When did it leave these tracks?"

"Approximately 100 million years ago."

"You're bloody joking!"

"Paleontology is no laughing matter," He laughs from deep in his belly until he's shaking on the ground. "We came here because the exposed layers all date from 100 to 110 million years ago."

"What do you mean, ancestor? I'm OK with descent from an ape, but not a mouse. A wee cowering, timorous beastie. With apologies to my pal Robert Burns, no fucking way. Pardon the expletive."

But it's liberating to know that I don't have to rein in my potty mouth with Pablo; his brother would have me scrubbing the chapel steps with a toothbrush for such a transgression.

"About 300 million years ago, a time we call the Carboniferous, vertebrates split into two lines: the sauropsids, from which lizards, snakes, dinosaurs and birds are descended, and the synapsids, with mammal-like properties. The large lizards, especially the dinosaurs, did very well—it's called the Triassic Takeover—but synapsids stayed small and also did well and by 100 million years ago we see the first signs of true mammals."

"Sorry, Pablo, I am one so I suppose I should know, but what's a mammal again?"

"Mammals are warm-blooded. They have hair, sweat glands, and milk glands, and they give birth using a placenta."

"Some days I do feel a wee bit mousy."

"We parted company with Eomaia about 70 million years ago. It's plenty of time to evolve and develop our own ape-like features."

"It doesn't look like we were very bossy back then."

"Lizards ruled the world for 150 million years."

I stare at the tiny shadowy markings in the shale and wonder at the chain of inference that stems from such meager evidence.

"Right, Pablo. I'm going to get some shuteye." I get up and look down at him. I think he might actually be crazier than I am. "Did you come out here for a reason?"

"I make some of my best finds under a full moon."

"Fossil-hunting by moonlight does sound like lunacy."

"That's where the term comes from. Before gas or electric lights, people could only venture out at night by moonlight, so trouble and interesting things have always happened under a full moon." Then he looks completely serious although his eyes are twinkling. "But I don't think I'm crazy."

"What about sleep?" I ask.

He gives me a puzzled look.

■

For another week the work's uneventful. The monsoon is fitful but several days bring drenching storms in the late afternoon. I'm just an amateur and fossil-hunting loses its charm when the ground is muddy and you're cold and soaked. Several times we have to remove socks and shoes to ford rivers swollen by monsoon runoff. One afternoon, at a third location in the seemingly endless pampas where an escarpment rises up vertically, excitement builds again. One of the grads has found another rich set of fossil deposits in a stretch of brown rock.

"Lagerstätten!" Pablo bellows, as if he's just won the lottery.

"What's that?"

"It means resting place in German. These are very special places. Animals near the water's edge are buried in a sudden landslide or rock fall. The mud has so little oxygen that even soft parts are preserved. And many animals feed near water so lagerstätten are miniature zoos from the prehistoric Earth."

The entire team descends on this stretch of mud turned to stone and starts chipping and chiseling blocks and then using sharp blades to gently pry open the thin layers. Some rock sandwiches are empty and others hold the delicate imprints of leafs and fins and legs and claws. It's like photography; a positive impression is adjacent to a negative impression.

The work is excruciatingly slow. I watch one student spend three hours liberating a single sauropod thigh bone. Dozens of species from the Cretaceous are represented, but a few days later at dinner, newly discovered Shivasuarus is still hogging the limelight.

"Tell us what you found, Roberto." Pablo gently nudges the shyest member of the student group into being more assertive. "And please speak English so our visitor can understand."

"It's a large group, almost certainly."

"How many, and how do you know?"

"Six or seven. I found four distinct skulls and the fragments of five breastbones."

"What does this mean? Anyone."

Miguel, my noisy nocturnal companion, pipes up. "They weren't solitary and they weren't mating pairs. They were carnivores and they probably hunted in packs."

"Yes!" Pablo gives Miguel a playful punch in the arm that makes him wince. "Shivasuarus was a social, flying carnivore with a big brain. Interesting, caballeros…"

The following day it gets even more interesting. Pablo and Esteban ask me to join them in hiking to a new area, while the grads continue harvesting the lagerstätten for more gems. I'm itching to revisit the topic Pablo raised yesterday evening.

"When you say Shivasuarus had a big brain, you mean it's smart. But how smart?"

"I would love to know. Herbivores like the stegosaurus had

brains the size of a walnut. In fact, some of the larger sauropods didn't have brains large enough to control their limbs; their nervous systems had distributed control centers to do the job. However, smaller theropods like the veloceraptor had a brain casing the size of ours. Shivasaurus seems to be similar."

"But brain size doesn't mean you're a smarty pants, right?"

"It might, but behavior is a better guide."

We reach a place that Esteban wants to explore in more detail. There's a rock wall where the face has been cleaved by uplift and the strata are neatly exposed. He begins to investigate. I follow Pablo, wondering where his remarkable nose for rock is taking us.

"Here!" He stops dead in his tracks.

"What? I don't see anything special." I never see anything other than rocks and dirt and more rocks and more dirt.

"Look under your feet. What do you see?"

"It just looks like smooth hard rock and dirt. For some reason the plants don't like growing here."

"Look closer. What does it remind you of?"

"Well. It's grey and slightly rough but generally smooth." I say the first thing that comes into my head. "It looks like a road surface."

"Exactly!" He claps me on the back with his bear paw. Ouch.

"So some ancient tribe built a road to nowhere?"

"Almost. Long ago there was a seam here that leaked thick tarry deposits onto the surface. It turned over time into asphalt."

"I get it. Like the La Brea Tar Pits. Animals might have got stuck and died in the tar."

"Yes, yes."

And with that he ignores me for six hours and enters the tunnel of his work. A hundred yards away Esteban neatly extracts a sample of layers from the nearby rock face. He says I have to visualize quite a different terrain a hundred million years ago, when the asphalt pools lay at the bottom of a narrow cutting that had since been worn down by erosion.

Whatever Pablo has found he's so preoccupied he doesn't talk all the way back to camp.

■

The next day we split up to explore the site more efficiently. I'm paired with my tent-mate Miguel. A shallow river runs swiftly through the middle of the tar bed. It's silty brown and flecked with white caps. The escarpment is ten yards away and Miguel goes there to look for a promising place among the jumble of rocks at its base.

He's off in his own world so I clamber up a gully to the top of the escarpment and find a shady spot to sit and catch up on my Borges. I'm startled by a sharp crack of thunder. Blow, winds, and crack your cheeks. Miguel and I scan the sky; its dark and foreboding but only spitting occasional drops of rain, so he keeps working. Then the rain stops, though I can still hear thunder in the distance. I lay the book down and close my eyes.

■

Brown rocks and a river valley. A foreign language. Patiently digging. Unearthing the past. Rewriting history. An unexpected pine cone. I struggle to make sense of these fragments. Are they from a dream, my imagination, or memory? When I can't connect them to any experience, the images melt away. On their heels come stronger images, and colors so vivid and real they create a sharp taste in my mouth. Green. Soft, lush, moist fields of green. White. A seamless expanse of pristine, bright ice. Then black. The void.

■

When I open my eyes I'm shocked to see the river has swollen to twice its previous width. It's moving swiftly and its surface roils with waves a foot high.

"Miguel." I yell. "Time to clear out, pal."

He looks up. "Claro, claro."

I see the water level rising moment by moment.

"Miguel! Pronto, the rocks can wait."

"Momentito."

He starts to gather his tools and samples but he's dawdling so I head over to help him. I hear muffled shouts from people upstream.

"Holy crap! Miguel!"

A three foot wall of water appears in the distance, moving rapidly towards us. Miguel wastes vital seconds trying to stuff samples into his backpack. By the time he looks up it's too late. He's swept away. My reflexes take over. I dash over to the churning water and dive in.

For a few seconds I turn somersaults and swallow water and think I'm going to die. Then I emerge spluttering on the surface and start swimming with the current. Miguel bobs like a cork ten yards ahead. We're lucky there are no rocks but the water is moving insanely fast. Steadily, I close the gap between us. I grab him by the collar and pull hard toward the slower water. Moments later we tumble on the shore, muddy, battered, bedraggled, and exhausted.

■

It's the last evening before we load up the minivans and head back to Mendoza. I can't imagine how the vehicles will handle such a rough road once they're loaded with thousands of pounds of rock. Melancholy pervades the group. Part of it's a reaction to the narrow escape Miguel and I had. But it's also sadness for leaving the immediacy of the field. I get it: field work is where you truly live; at the Uni you're tapping on a keyboard or pushing paper.

Pablo cheers us up. He tells rapid-fire stories in Spanish that have the students in stitches. He plays cheesy Argentinean lounge music on a boom box and gets us all dancing the tango. The sight of him with hands clasped and cheek to cheek with a student half his weight raises extra mirth. He's a natural showman and he has one final, large trick up his sleeve.

"What do we know about Shivasaurus?"

People call out the basics. Warm-blooded. Carnivore. Six limbs. Flight. Large brain.

"What about food sources?"

Again, the students reel off the Latin names of species that have been found associated with Shivasaurus as prey.

"You've named all the major Cretaceous taxa. Shivasuarus had no natural enemies. She was top of the food chain."

He lets the thought sink in.

"Now. Three more pieces of the jigsaw puzzle. Sofia?"

The girl who found the first intact skull of the trip speaks next. She's clearly a budding superstar.

"Here is a Shivasuarus skull fragment from the lagerstätten."

She passes around a piece the size of a slightly cupped hand.

"What do you see?" Pablo asks the group, eyes sparkling.

"Not much," Someone says. "Wait, there are markings inside, very light. I can't tell…"

"Let me!" Another student has the fragment. "There are definitely curving marks on the inside face."

"Anyone?" Pablo asks. Nothing, so he continues. "You're looking at folds in the cerebral cortex. Only a lagerstätten can preserve delicate features like this. Elephants have brains four times the weight of ours, but they aren't four times smarter. What counts is the total area of the cortex and the degree of folding."

You can hear a pin drop. He has everyone's full attention.

"Now, let me tell you about my day. I found a nice collection of remains in a tar bed about a mile from here. Maybe a dozen species, usually complete or nearly complete skeletons. I also found parts of Shivasaurus, but only teeth and a few broken claws. What does that suggest to you?"

A student volunteers. "Shivasuarus was feeding on animals that were trapped in the tar?"

"We can't be sure but it's a good guess. However, the geography of this location 100 million years ago is also relevant. The tar ponds were in a narrow cutting between two cliff faces. That means that…"

I blurt out. "…Shivasuarus chased or herded them to their deaths. It was a hunting strategy!"

■

The atmosphere is turbo-charged. It's left for me, the outsider, to say what everyone else is thinking.

"This beast was smart, social, adaptable, and had no rival. It was like us just before we developed technology. So what stopped it?"

It's as if Pablo has somehow conspired with me to orchestrate the final revelation. He turns to his colleague. "Esteban?"

"I took a clean core that runs from 130 to 80 million years ago. We've only got a handful of specimens but the youngest Shivasaurus dates to about 95 million years. The portable mass spectrometer saw most of the usual isotopes, but one unusual one: Iron-60."

Everyone looks at him blankly. They're paleontologists and he's talking geochemistry. Such is the specialization of science.

"Iron-60 decays in a million years or so and it's rare in the Solar System. But it's a standard product in a supernova when a massive star dies. I found a spike in the concentration of Iron-60 at a layer corresponding to 92 million years ago."

We try to absorb this information. I feel Iron-60 pounding its way into my unfossilized skull.

"Let me get this straight," I venture. "You're saying Shivasuarus was killed by a dying star 92 million years ago?"

"Yes. We know the K-T mass extinction 65 million years ago was caused by a meteor or comet, and others like the Permian extinction 250 million years ago were probably caused by widespread volcanism. But there's also good evidence for a mini-extinction two million years ago that synchs up with a dying star in the Scorpius-Centaurus star cluster. And there are other extinctions that might have been caused by a nearby dying star. The problem is that the star leaves behind a neutron star or a black hole and the residual gas dissipates so millions of years later there's little evidence of the event."

"A nearby supernova oxidizes the ozone layer." Pablo chimes in, or rather, booms in. "That lets in UV and cosmic rays, causing mutation and cellular damage. Flying creatures are the most vulnerable."

■

At this point, silence falls. Each person tries to understand what the discovery means. Even the irrepressible Pablo retreats into his head. For me, the primacy and inevitability of humans and eternal progress are thrown into question. Octopuses and orcas are pretty brainy but we're the lords of the planet. Was it just a roll of the dice that snuffed out Shivasuarus and stopped their descendants from sitting where we sit now? What if a different species, not yet found in the fossil record, surpassed our brains but did so without developing technology? Or maybe they did invent technology and we just haven't found or recognized the artifacts. Like a Bard long before me I thank the lucky star that let us be the paragon of animals, the quintessence of dust.

Skin Deep

Equinox.

Today is the cusp of equal day and equal night. Back home right now I'd be heading into the long gloom of winter, but here on the far side of the world winter's grip is relenting. Crocuses and daffodils are starting to bloom in the mission gardens and I need one less blanket at night. I sit on the courtyard grass under a large oak tree and the sound of the monks chanting Vespers flows over me like a balm.

I pride myself on living in the moment, on taking it one step at a time. Ah, McEvoy, the existential anti-hero. But the equinox gives me pause. Is my journey a full circle or will I always be a wanderer? Am I heading into darkness or into light? I've seen out in the pampas with Pablo how the "book of life" has veered in expected directions. What happens in the second half of my wee book?

I will keep traveling. I will shape young minds. I will learn things that I never could have imagined. Three women will be important to me. One will break my heart, one I will leave, and one will tilt me into a crisis that reduces me to my essence. What began with fire will end with ice. How do I know this?

∎

"S'good to be back."

"S'good to have you back."

"Knees worn out yet?"

"Aye, it's brutal. The Hulk won't let up."

"He just cares about your soul."

A petulant look. "It's mine to squander if I want."

I slip back into the routine at the mission with ease. The kids have missed me and I've missed them. Their good manners and their prim uniforms are reassurance that there's order in the world, although it's hard to imagine how much trouble you could stir up under the watchful eyes of so many Jesuit priests and Benedictine nuns. They're nothing like the rude and thieving rabble I went to school with. I regale them with tales of ancient monsters and cataclysm from the sky.

The Hulk tells me the local police came by to investigate the stolen silver. But with no clues and no suspects they displayed little interest in the case. He thinks the relics are gone forever.

■

"Hail Mary, full of grapes."

"Give us this day, our jelly bread."

"And lead a snot into temptation."

"OK, that was good for a warm up."

"Full anagram version?"

"Aye, you're on."

"Help Rosy Retard."

"The Lord's Prayer."

"Warfare haunt thine Hoover."

"Our Father who art in Heaven."

"By the lewd, mean halo."

"Hallowed be thy name."

"Bed the lily now."

"Speaking of bedding the lily…"

"Don't start…"

"Time to meet the meat."

"Behave yourself…"

"The meat we like to greet and eat."

"Stop it. You're incorrigible."

"Have you seen herselves since you got back?"

"No, but the mere thought's giving me a wee stiffie."

I enjoy the repartee but he seems barely there, a shadow of the person I left only three weeks ago. Sad.

■

One afternoon I'm leaving the refectory when I see her near the gate at the corner of the courtyard. She's talking to someone and the conversation is heated. I reposition myself to see better. Elvis! Lettie and the town spiv; I'm gobsmacked. Why is she slumming with that buffoon? I'm almost sure it's Letitia. I've not seen much of a physical difference but Lettie favors flowery dresses that reveal a bit of leg and cleavage while Patty wears plainer, simpler clothes.

She turn on her heel and walks quickly across the courtyard, head down, clearly upset. She enters a large wooden door. On impulse I run across the courtyard and follow her. I ascend a spiral stone staircase, treading quietly and keeping my distance. She continues to the top, a place I've never visited. Seen from the ground the top floor has small gable windows cut into the sloping lead roof. When the mission was first built these would have been the servant's quarters. She enters a room and closes the door. I test it and it's not locked so I push it open a crack.

She's sitting on the floor, sharing sweets with two small children and talking to them in a pleasant lilting voice. She shifts position and I can see them more clearly. Twins! Looking carefully, these boys seem to resemble her.

Letitia has a secret.

That's why she's at the mission so often—not the wayward charms of a roguish Scotsmen. A scenario takes shape in my head. There was a youthful indiscretion with Elvis. I can't bring myself to think he was ever her boyfriend, but he's well-dressed, good looking, and a player. She was headstrong and resisted the idea of adoption, so there was a compromise involving the assistance and complicity of

Father Carlos. Patty visits less often but the twins clearly get attention from their auntie too. Maybe my arithmetic is faulty, but Lettie has a key to the sacristy, so I put two and two together and draw another conclusion about Elvis the greaseball.

．

That evening I help out at Vespers, grade some homework, and don my warmest, darkest clothes. I look for Robbie but he's been no bloody use lately—never around when I need him. I go solo.

There's an alley across the street from the pub where we had our run-in with Elvis and his rabble. I stand in the deep shadows where I can't be seen. The cold night air seeps into my bones. I've a meat pie to tide me over but it's miserable waiting. People come and go.

Finally, not long after the town clock chimes eleven he leaves and walks down the waterfront road. I follow at a discrete distance. After ten minutes walking through a run-down neighborhood, he ducks into the front gate of a small semi-detached house. A minute later, a light goes on upstairs. I climb up a low brick wall and hoist myself onto the garage roof. Moving quietly and slowly I ease along the wall until I can peer into his bedroom window through a small gap in the curtains. I'm feeling very exposed but there's no turning back now.

I see electronics and car stereos on the floor and piled on a table. Elvis has been a very busy young man. Then he turns on a television and slumps into a chair with a beer. I consider my options.

I can play the hero: knock on his door, overpower him, and search his place. But the fight could turn out badly. Even if I won, recovering the silver might point the finger at me. Worse, the police might close ranks to protect a local. Or I can follow him around and when he next goes to the bar, come back here and break in to check out his room. But if I get busted they'll lock me up and throw away the key. While I'm pondering I get lucky. He walks over to his closet to put away his jacket and on a high shelf I see something.

Jackpot. The unmistakable glint of silver.

I still have work to do. If I rat Elvis out it may backfire if he argues the silver was planted. The next morning I sneak into the Hulk's office while he's in mid-mass. All I take is a sheet of paper with the mission letterhead but I'm sweating buckets afterwards, as if I'd committed a mortal sin. In town, I find a woman in a travel agency who has decent English. On the pretense of chatting her up and maybe booking a trip, I carry on a conversation that gives me all the fragments of Spanish I need to write a terse note pointing the police to Elvis' address and his bedroom closet. At the bottom I add a florid, hopefully indecipherable, signature. Then I drop it in the police station mailbox while the office is closed for the early afternoon siesta. Hopefully, Elvis's next hit will be jailhouse rock.

■

"Mmmm, Letitia."

"Mmmm, Patricia."

"Letitia. Lettie. Let."

"Patricia. Patty. Pat."

"Will you let Lettie?"

"Only if I can pat Pattie."

This reverie is broken by the looming presence of the Hulk. He addresses me sternly.

"Father Scalfini is visiting the Prelate in Buenos Aires for a week. I need you to fill in for him at Matins."

I groan silently. Four services daily is stiff penance for an agnostic. I've memorized all the mumbo jumbo but my heart's not in it. Still, it's not worth resisting his implacable will.

"Sure, Father." I wait a beat. "So you'll be round with a sweet roll and coffee at six?"

He smiles blandly. "No. But I do have something to give you."

I follow him to the study of his private apartment.

"I have a feeling this time is coming to an end," he says. "Pablo was pleased to have you on his team. He says you have an eye for rocks and he says that of very few." He sweeps his arm around the fossil emporium. "You may take any item."

"You're yanking my chain. Really?"

"Absolutely. Any one."

"Wow. That's incredible. But aren't they special to you?"

"Their stories are fascinating, but Pablo can get me more. I took a vow of poverty. This will be a gift from the Church."

I roam around the room excitedly, wishing I knew more about the stories behind the rocks.

"What's this?"

"The cochlea or inner ear of a whale, ten million years old."

"It's brilliant. And this?"

"Part of the bony frill of a Stegosaurus."

"Is this what I think it is?" I picked up a small item that looked like petrified, soft serve, chocolate ice cream turned to rock.

"A coprolite. Fossilized feces from a small mammal, probably about four million years old."

I grin beatifically. "And not a hint of a pong."

I'm drawn to the teeth and the claws and the small tusks. Then I notice a small fossil that's like half a ping pong ball with the flat face polished. The outer surface has the exact texture of a pine cone."

"This." I'm sure.

"You have excellent taste. This specimen is from Cerro Cuadrado in Patagonia. There was a pine forest there in the late Triassic, about 230 million years ago."

"It's stunning. And it hasn't changed!"

"God's creation is timeless. And even though the restless hand of evolution constantly changes life, some species are perfectly adapted. With all our failings, I doubt humans will endure another million years let alone prosper for a quarter of a billion."

■

Lettie's avoiding me so I intercept her one evening as she leaves from a visit to the secret nursery.

"Lettie, we haven't read together for ages. I miss it. I miss you. Is anything wrong?"

"I cannot." She looks uncomfortable. "You're a very kind man, and a funny man, but..."

"I know about your twins."

She glowers at me and I think she's going to walk away. But she stands with her arms tightly folded.

"It's OK. Really, it's OK."

"No, nothing is OK. You don't understand." A tear rolls down the side of her nose. "You can't understand! You are a man. You move here. You go away. You travel. You make jokes and do what you like. It's all easy for you. My life is horrible. If it wasn't for Padre Carlos…I don't know what I would do."

"What about their dad? Is it the guy I saw at the gate a few days ago just before you went to see the twins?"

"So you spy on me?" She's angry and hugs herself even tighter. "I'm sorry I ever talked to you."

"I apologize, Lettie. I was curious."

"Ricardo is not the problem." But she looks miserable and it's clear he's a big problem.

"Your sister helps."

"My sister! Yes, she helps. But she's the good one. She's not cast out. She doesn't have to deal with the stares and the not belonging. I have no future. I hate this place. I hate it!"

I want to tell her that the world beyond Bahia Blanca is bigger and better. That it would be hard to get by but she could find people who are open and accepting. That she's young and pretty and smart and brimming with promise. Instead the words come out different.

"I'd stay here with you, Lettie. I could help you with the twins. No commitment; you don't have to be my boyfriend. We'd just see what happens." I surprise myself. I really mean it.

Her eyebrows rise, then her face softens and her shoulders slump. Tears are coming in a steady stream. She meets my eyes.

"You are a good man, but no. It's my life. It's not your life."

She wipes away the tears and gradually composes herself.

■

"Come."

She beckons me to follow. She goes to the corner of the

courtyard and climbs the stone stairs. At the top she pushes the door open a crack. Her boys have abandoned their beds and they're playing with building blocks on the floor. Their voices are low but eager; they're breaking the rules and want to get away with it as long as possible.

"Come."

She pulls me across the corridor and into another room. It's a garret used for storage. Boxes are piled against the walls and there are a few pieces of furniture covered with drop cloths. The full moon casts a pale slab of slab of light across the room. I realize it's exactly one month since I joined Pablo's dig and two months since my first night in the courtyard of the mission.

We stand in the middle of the room, face to face, for a long time. The moonlight illuminates our profiles and casts them on the far wall. She stands perfectly still. Then she leans forward and tilts up onto her toes and kisses me very softly. Only our lips touch.

An insistent voice rises up in me. It's driven by raw desire and her musky scent. I want to unleash the beast and devour her voluptuous body and penetrate her until we're one thing. A second voice rises up, equally loud and insistent. It tells me to treasure this woman.

"You don't have a sister, do you?"

She looks down, more in sadness than shame. "No."

I return the gentle kiss. Then my lips move over her face, hovering above the surface of the skin, brushing against her hair and eyelashes. Her eyes are open wide and their hue darkens to burnt umber.

She slowly unbuttons my shirt and pushes it over my shoulders. I let it slip to the floor. She traces her finger over my chest and follows the outline of my tattoos. Like a child with a picture book she traces the tiger on one bicep, and the anaconda on the other, and the Celtic knot below my clavicle. I think of the delicacy of her touch compared with the needle that put them there. She leans forward and breathes me in. She kisses my arms, my chin, and then the tip of my nose. Her breath is hot and damp.

I reach behind her and unzip her dress. I slip it off her shoulders and it falls to her waist, where it stays, held up by its belt. I ease my fingers under the thin straps of her slip and pull them outwards and over soft skin of her shoulders. The slip falls to her waist with a slight, silky sound. Her breasts are swollen and heavy, the veins just visible under translucent skin. I trace their curve with a finger. I move closer and trace my tongue lightly over her shoulders and neck and I slowly paint every inch of her face with my lips. I gently cup her breasts and meet her mouth.

Then I step back, sated and delirious.

I reach down and touch a vertical scar that traverses for six inches under the swell of her belly. It's a C-section, the ugly and livid mark of small town doctoring.

"They hurt you." I say.

She pulls my arms out, turns my palms up, and runs her fingers over the network of scars inside my forearms.

"Someone hurt you too." Her voice is a breathy whisper.

Beyond this room, there's silence. The low chatter has stopped, her boys are asleep. I pull her towards me until her soft flesh presses into me and we're in a tight embrace. The setting moon edges our shadows up the wall almost imperceptibly.

■

He stands on the platform of the station at Bahia Blanca, with his unkempt black hair, wearing tartan trousers and Doc Martens, as if it was the most natural thing in the world.

"Robbie, you beautiful bastard." I'm smiling but I'm sad. "I thought I knew you."

We're saying our farewells.

"Aye, fair enough. I could say the same." He replies.

"You've changed. You don't connect with people any more."

"I've a lot on my plate." He looks somber.

"You were important to me. We shared everything."

"Don't get soppy on me now."

A sudden thought. "Can I have your bandana?"

"Sure." He peels it off and tosses it to me. "Wear it in good health."

He smirks. "Ah well, I'll always remember the meat."

That's more like the old Robbie, I think.

But Robbie has already gone.

■

The station master hands me a letter that's been waiting for me at the little post office in the station. The postmark reads Edinburgh. The sender is Robbie Robertson. I open it and read the short note in his cramped hand: "McEvoy, you know I'd like another adventure with you. But I'm in the middle of starting my wee business and I'm totally skint. Next time, alright? Your pal, Robbie."

5 EMERALD ISLE

Green

"Pull over! Pull over!" She's screaming in my ear. "For fuck's sake, you're going to kill us!"

My hands are on the steering wheel of a small car which is heading downhill fast, right into the path an oncoming tractor. The hedgerows are flicking past on either side. There's little room to pull over and no time to stop.

Still yelling at me she wrenches the wheel to the side. With that and a violent move sideways by the startled driver of the tractor we pass each other in a blur with nothing worse than the sickening sound of metal scraping on metal.

The wheel is turned to the left so we shudder along the steep embankment that rises up from the edge of the road. We come to a stop near the bottom of the hill with dirt and stones and vegetation flying up around us. For a moment, everything's still. Then all hell breaks loose again. She unleashes a torrent of curses. I see in the rearview mirror that the tractor driver has clambered out and he's running toward us shaking his fist.

Oh God, what have I done? The tractor driver approaches me, badly winded and red in the face, and lays into me in a thick Irish brogue. In a daze I fish around in the glove compartment until I've found the insurance and the registration. It's a rental. He leaves, still muttering with rage, and I'm abandoned to the woman sitting beside me. She's so upset she can't sit still. She paces up and down beside the car. Rocks in the steep embankment have scraped paint and left grooves on the passenger's side and there's a long, deep gash in the driver's side, caused by the hub of the tractor wheel.

"I can't believe it! What were you thinking, McEvoy?" That's very promising; she knows my name. Apparently, I'm McEvoy. "What the fuck were you thinking?"

She stops for a moment, but then she's on the move again, her arms sweeping wild, exasperated circles in the air.

"Where did you go? What strange planet do you live on?" I dodge the ferocity of her gaze. "I overlooked it the first few times, but you weren't risking me bleedin' neck then." Ah, so we've been traveling a while. "But this is too fucking much. I don't need this!" I'm in total agreement. I don't need this either.

She slumps against the grassy bank and lights a cigarette so I get a chance to study her more closely. She's short, maybe five feet four, and has a mop of black hair that flops into her eyes. Although she's wearing jeans and a loose ragg wool sweater, she seems compact and powerful, exuding a coiled form of energy. There's a tension in her, as if she's using the boyish haircut and clothes to offset the femininity of her face, which has graceful and simple lines, elegant and economical like a Picasso sketch. Her brusque manner is also belied by her eyes, which are an exquisite shade of green.

She finishes her smoke. The calm of the countryside reestablishes itself. There's a chorus of bird song and the faint buzzing of bees in the hedgerow. Apart from the after-shocks of a near-death experience, it's idyllic. She walks up to me.

"Look at you, you big wally. Come 'ere."

She tugs my collar with both hands until my head descends and my mouth meets hers. Her tongue ranges inside my mouth. Then her hands drop and grab my butt cheeks and she pulls my hips into hers. I'm tentatively assuming we're lovers.

But what's the hell's her name?

■

I wait patiently as the landlord finishes pulling the pint. The dark brown liquid is sealed under a pallid blanket of foam that's the texture of meringue. Guinness. Quintessential beverage of the Emerald Isle. The landlord looks over my shoulder.

"Will that be another Pimms, Fiona?"

I'm grateful to the landlord. Her name's Fiona. Another minor embarrassment averted.

"That's great, Liam. Give it to my kamikaze pilot to bring over."

I redden.

"Will the Town Hall do for your show?"

"Not even close, Liam. These are huge pieces."

I have a fat crayon and I'm sketching in the blank areas of my life as fast as possible. It seems Fiona is an artist. I deduce we've been here for a few days. Fiona is good friends with the bar staff while I have a low profile and am more of a stranger. I don't know why I'm here so I guess that I'm tagging along with Fiona.

"Darts, McEvoy?"

In the short time of knowing her, or at least remembering that I must know her, I get the impression that Fiona rarely asks a simple question or makes a simple declarative statement. There's often an implicit challenge.

My first dart finds double top. The second hits the sliver of treble twenty. The third veers slightly to the side and hits nineteen. Another mental scribble with the crayon: I'm a dab hand at darts.

"Bloody show off," she says. "An' I was going to give you head."

We walk arm in arm to back to the B&B. Despite the difference in our heights, we fall into an easy stride. My crayon fills in a new blank area. We've known each other for some time.

The next anxious moment comes in the B&B. I see clothes that I assume are mine piled on one side of the small bedroom. I go to the bathroom to buy time. Scribble. I have a purple toothbrush and use Crest. Scribble. I shave with a hand razor, not an electric. It's not as though I'm inexperienced, but I'm unaccountably nervous as I finish my ablutions and prepare to climb into bed with a stranger.

I needn't have worried. She's curled on her side with the covers pulled up to her chin, fast asleep. I put out the lights and lay awake for a long time before sleep rescues me. It's been a strange day.

■

I wake with a pleasant erection and lie on my back watching the encroaching grey dawn and listening to the finches outside. She's still curled up facing away from me, as if she hasn't moved all night, the sleep of the dead. Then she rolls towards me and nibbles on my ear dreamily. She reaches down.

"Mmmm. Wouldn't want to waste that."

She rolls onto me and sits up, straddling me and shrugging the covers off her shoulders. She reaches down and peels off her white silk camisole and tosses it to the side. The pace is languorous. She wakes up her whole body at once. Her breasts are small and silky smooth and delicate; I reach up to gently caress them. There's a brief pause while tartan boxers and green candy stripe panties are discarded. She rocks on me slowly, mouth parted. The pressure increases until I catch my breath, then with a smile she eases back and slips me inside her.

She controls the horizontal. She controls the vertical. I'm hanging on, enjoying the ride. She rears up until I'm only just contained, then slides down firmly. I'm bedded and embedded. The rhythm keeps me at a slow bubbly simmer. She bends down to give me her mouth and I claim it hungrily. Then she breaks free and begins a long shuddering climax. First she pushes down on my chest, then she grabs my chest hair, and by the end she's pounding me with the heels of her hands, each blow percussively linked to her contractions and sighs. She flops onto me, spent, glistening like a salmon freshly landed. Her skin is hot to the touch.

■

I get up late in the morning. Dim light is filtering through the mist outside and then through lace curtains. Fiona's sleeping but she stirs and asks me to get her a packet of fags. On the way out I pick up the card of the B&B. We're in Clonmany, County Donegal. Clonmany is a cluster of houses and a few farms, barely a hamlet. I follow a road sign saying Lifford two miles.

Ireland is fabulously lush, like Scotland on acid. The landscape is fields, rolling hills, and bogs. Water's everywhere, in ponds, running through the fields in tiny streams, and standing in puddles on the road. Even in the muted light, the green is so livid it hurts my eyes.

It's the preternatural color a blind child might visualize after investing it with the enhanced power of their remaining senses. Except for a tractor bouncing over springy turf in a nearby field and a motorcycle whizzing by, I see no activity on my walk into town.

"Two packs of Capstan, full strength." Interesting. She didn't tell me what to buy and I didn't notice what brand she'd been smoking. My crayon's working unbidden. Things are coming back.

"There y'go. Anything else?" The old man running the news agent has a face overlaid with a gnarled topography of broken veins.

"This Mars bar. Is there a local paper?"

"The Lifford Gazette. Here y'are."

I look for a place I can sit and read. There's a playground nearby but the wooden benches are soaked with rain. I brush the water off a child's swing. Flipping through the paper, a big region of my missing picture is colored in by a boxed item on page three.

"Young English Sculptor and her Traveling Show—Fiona Cooper brings her iconic and controversial work to the Lifford Town Hall from July 10th to the 16th. Cooper, 30, from Chelmsford, near London, has established herself as the enfant terrible of modern sculpture, dating back to her break-out show at the Saatchi and Saatchi Gallery in 1995. Her bold use of monumental metal forms and her controversial themes mark her out from all contemporaries. Cooper is touring Ireland with selected works in anticipation of her much-anticipated installation "The Troubles." Cloaked in secrecy, The Troubles was the winning entry in a competition run last year by the bilateral Committee for Reconciliation Through Art. The public can view the work of this young lioness of the art world from 10am to 5pm daily, parking across from the Town Hall in the Carrick Multistory. For more information, call (045) 38712."

It's a lot to absorb. The lioness of the art world. Mmm. I finger my sore ribs and smile.

■

I'm in the lobby of the Barbican Art Gallery in London with my girlfriend. We've just had a huge row over dinner and the curry is curdling in my stomach. Both of us want to leave but we patch it up with a grudging kiss. We pass through the galleries together but are not connected. I peel off into the main exhibition hall for new artists. There's a buzz at the far end of the hall where people cluster around a huge installation that reaches close to the ceiling, forty feet above my head. It's a series of curving wrought iron pieces shaped like sails that soar and swoop, held together by near-invisible cables. It conjures up an ocean clipper and a metallic explosion. The sculpture is static but it bristles with dynamism. Almost hidden in the throng is a girl wearing black jeans, a white t-shirt, and a black linen jacket. She has the same restless energy as her work. Her eyes roam from the group around her and catch mine. For a moment, everything else in the room flattens to two dimensions. Only the space between us has any shape or volume. Fiona.

∎

"Fuck's sake, McEvoy. Small town Ireland!"

"What's up, Fee." Fee. Yes, that's what I call her.

"I told them we needed their big church, that the town hall wasn't up to snuff. But we're in the town hall anyway. When's the reception? How long have we got to set this lot up?"

"Um. I'm not sure."

"Well, look it up, you big sausage."

Fiona has the flat, slightly nasal accent of the Home Counties. It's basically Cockney with the glottal stops and modulation smoothed out by urban flight. But in her voice, as in her art, she takes something flat and breathes shape and contour into it.

I've no idea what I'm doing but I rummage around my duffel bag until I find a sheaf of paper. The itinerary.

"Lifford set-up: 1pm July 8th." I read off the top sheet. "Reception: 7pm July 9th."

"We'll be alright then. But at the reception you gotta get me outta there when you see the signal."

I've no idea what the signal is but I'll figure it out. "Fee," I turn to her and hesitate for a moment. "Am I your manager?"

"What a daft question." She gives me a worried look. "You know I 'ave a manager. The wanker's probably starting the midday leg of his daily Dublin pub crawl as we speak. I've a manager and an agent and fat lot of good they are. Sometimes I wish I was back on my own. Just me and the metal."

I sit on the bed staring at my knees. She walks over and lifts my head until I'm looking into her eyes as they search mine. She speaks softly, in a lilting London patois.

"It worries me when you're like this, baby. You're my muse and my lover and my friend. You're my person. I've never 'ad my own person before. Never thought I deserved one. I need you."

■

We go into town after lunch in the local pub. Cheese, chutney, and Guinness seem like a plausible diet since you can pop vitamins for all the rest. Fiona goes to the Town Hall to work on her installation while I replace our hire car. The deductible is sky high; I cringe as they run the credit card.

The next evening at the reception I see the tension between her public and private personas. She's confident, outspoken, the center of attention, and always surrounded by admirers. But I've seen the raw energy that bubbles under the surface and know she's giving them a low octane distillate. Everything she says in public is guarded. Behind her easy smile is an animal primed for fight or flight.

"Ms. Cooper, you're often compared to Damien Hirst. Do you like shocking people?"

It's the reporter from the Irish Times. He pulls ranks on the local rabble and buttonholes Fiona just as the wine runs out.

"Damien's trying to do quite different things with his art," she says evenly. "I admire him but I wouldn't bracket us."

"Why does is so much of your work concerned with abortion and pornography?"

I can see she wants to unload on him but she keeps it reined in. "D'you think we live in an equal world, Mr..., Mr. Finnegan?"

"Well, I couldn't say really. Women have lots of opportunities."

"I see. Well, when you've been in the situation where you couldn't control your life and death choices, or when you've been objectified or demeaned, maybe you'll understand."

"Ms. Cooper, tell us about the big work. The government is keeping everyone in the dark about it."

She gives him a syrupy smile. "I can't say. Your government has told me to be discrete, and I'm a model of that."

"What of Ireland? This is your first visit, I understand."

"It's gorgeous. They treat artists so well, I might move here." She hopes she's home and dry but he has one more dig planned.

"Rumor has it that they've paid you fifty thousand pounds for the tour of local galleries. Isn't that a little hypocritical for someone who has decried the commercialization of art."

I wince. I know what's coming. The wine may have run out but she's about to pop her cork.

"Mr. Finnegan, just because you work for the posh paper doesn't give you the right to be a prick. The rumor is wrong. The government is paying my local expenses and nothing more. There's far too much money driving art; it leads to crap and turns artists into whores."

She pokes him in the chest. "I loathe money. But I love being in this lush, beautiful country. Fuck the Green. Love the Green."

He has his headline.

∎

The next day there's an ugly scene at the newsagent as I try to stop her from buying a copy of the paper. She thumps me hard and breaks free and comes out with one. Her bold quote is the headline on the front page of the arts section, with an asterisk tastefully replacing the "u." She rails about the asshole journalist loud enough that people cross the street to avoid us, then settles into a sobbing fury. I give her a cig. She squats on the curb with tearstained cheeks and her feet in the gutter and smokes it quietly. The storm passes.

In the car a few days later, as we head to the next show in the county town of Connemara, she reengages the subject a little more calmly.

"They're bastards, the art critics. If they 'ad balls they'd be off in a war zone getting shot at. They create sod all. Their words are destined to blow around on the street or wrap fish and chips or wipe the arse of a homeless person."

"Forget about them, Fee. They're horseflies."

"Maybe. An' I did step in some shit, didn' I?" She laughs.

I lean over and bite her ear. She's driving. After my last episode it'll be a while before I'm be trusted behind the wheel.

"Why do they always bring up Hirst?"

Damien Hirst is a controversial English artist who's obsessed with death and whose most infamous work involves segmented animals preserved in formaldehyde. He's been arrested many times and once tried to impress journalists by sticking a cigarette into the end of his penis. Fiona seems to know him well.

"I like Damien. We both came out of fucking nowhere. The media are so infantile with art. I do something to make them uncomfortable so I must be the same as this bloke who makes them uncomfortable. It's like saying two people are similar 'cos they like spaghetti."

She looks thoughtful. "Course, a lot of 'is work is crap. But then, I've put out a bit of crap myself when I 'ad bills to pay or the muse was dossing on someone else's sofa."

"What do you two talk about?"

"We don't talk about concepts or themes and stuff like that. Last time I ran into him we compared welding techniques. Like that poet geezer Santayana said, art critics talk about theories of art but artists talk about where to get good turpentine."

■

I write poetry. This is new to me. The morning we're due to leave for Connemara I find myself sitting in chair with a half-written poem. It freaks me out and I'm immediately unable to write any more and put the notepad away. Fiona has also said I'm an inventor. What else do I do that I don't know about? I walk into the bathroom and look in a mirror. It's a strange feeling to see yourself for the first time, which happened to me less than a week ago. Now I'm getting used to that broad, freckled face and mop of fine, red hair. I'm well-muscled with just a hint of thickness about the middle. No obvious lines or sagging bits. I'm guessing thirty, but it's unnerving not to know my own age. Another thought. I'm sure I have a book, a journal, which would fill in most of the missing pieces. It's not in my travel bag. Where is it?

∎

On our way to the coast we buy sandwiches and look for a place to stop for lunch. The road winds through peat bogs then enters rolling hills. We ditch the car and head up a sheep path. The sky is clear and it's doing it's very best to act like summer, but there's capriciousness in the air too, warning us not to take the blue sky for granted.

We do. We tramp over the rolling hills until we find one higher than the rest, a place with a vista of miles of solitude and emptiness. Going back towards the car we cross a virgin meadow. Cows and sheep are kept out by a stone wall and the grass is long, shaggy, and soft.

Fiona kicks off her shoes and runs barefoot through the lush sward. I follow suit. When I look up again she's discarded all her clothes. OK, when in Rome, make like a Roman. We run naked in spirals and figure eights and great looping arcs, like pagans doing etch-a-sketch. Finally we find each other and sink to our knees.

"Do I 'ave sporty tits, McEvoy?"

"You do, Fee, very sporty."

"Do I 'ave a sweet ass, McEvoy?"

"You do, Fee, the sweetest."

"And do I 'ave a fabulous bush?

"Fee, there's no greater wonder."

We roll around in the grass and fuck with joy and abandon. As we lie on our side in the green cushion, with her legs over my shoulders and me moving easily inside her, I feel a shift in the breeze.

We watch entranced as mist slides down the hillside and envelopes us. It's just as private and secluded as a bedroom.

Alive

Fiona's on top of her game. It's a new location every four or five days as her show wends its way down the western coast of Ireland. The physical labor involved in taking down and setting up her work is intense. We have a driver and a helper but by the end of a takedown or setup day I'm usually curled up in the truck, exhausted.

While a show's running we hop around the countryside, choosing small hotels and B&B's at random, to avoid the bloodhound noses of the journalists. Fiona stays up late with her sketchbook. I'm drinking a wee bit too much and she's smoking a wee bit too much. She's getting just a few hours' sleep but seems none the worse for it. I tumble along in her wake; on days when I'm dragging I surf her energy.

■

Driving through County Sligo, we get a sense of the long reach of Irish civilization. There are stone circles and barrows on many of the hilltops. I regain my position of trust as the driver.

"They're my kin," I said. "It's like coming home."

"But are the Scots Irish or the Irish Scots?" she asks playfully.

"We settled the Emerald Isle. It's ours." I sound confident.

"Really?"

"Absolutely. We came to Antrim in wooden boats in 8000 B.C. This was one of the last parts in Europe to be settled. We lived in skin huts that we could pack up and carry on our backs. We stayed on the coast to hunt and fish but it was hard to get a good pint so we left."

"So you say."

"These stone megaliths come from later, the Neolithic period from 4000 B.C. to 2000 B.C. That takes us to the Bronze Age."

"Are you makin' this crap up?" She eyes me suspiciously.

"No way, Fee. Four thousand years ago, Paddy trades in his stones for bronze."

"Bronze, McEvoy. It's my absolutely favorite medium."

"Why's that?"

"Supple but strong. Lustrous but modest. When it's well turned, the sound is pure and sweet. And it was discovered by chance."

"Really?"

"You're such a know-it-all." She pokes me playfully. "Think you're the only person who knows shit?"

"Do tell. I'm all ears."

"It's an alloy of copper and tin. Both are soft and ductile. So who would think that when you combine them you get something harder than either one? I'd like to have seen the look on the face of whoever tried it first."

"OK. I lied. They're not Scots here."

"Then who are they? Who came first?"

"The Scots did come here very early, but that Mesolithic tribe was shifted out by the Celts, who arrived from Europe in 500 B.C., bringing their ironware and whiny music with them."

"You're a mine of information, McEvoy. Here I thought you were just a pretty face and a good fuck."

I smile and continue my mini-lecture. "As the Romans took over most of Britain, the Celts hung on in Scotland and Ireland. When the Romans fell, the Britons conquered the whole island except an enclave in Scotland that was settled by the Celts. Damn, I am Irish."

After I finish regaling her with ancient history, I feel queasy. How can I rattle off this esoteric information while major chunks of my life are still blank? What on Earth is going on in my head? But I'm relieved that at least I can recall the entire brief and tempestuous history of our relationship.

We park by the side of the road and clamber up a hill to see the stone circle at the top. It's mute to meaning but I imagine a compass to the stars built into the large slab of rocks. Coming back down the hill we see hillocks that are too well-formed to be natural. Some have openings that have been boarded up by archaeologists; we stop for a breather on one that's untouched. I lean back onto the grass of the barrow and Fiona falls into my arms. We kiss and paw at each other like puppies. Suddenly the earth behind me gives way and we tumble into a dark cavity.

"Shite." I land awkwardly on the dirt and stone and seem to have dinged my leg and back.

"Are you OK?" I've broken Fiona's fall; she's fine.

"More or less. Christ, that gave me a fright."

Looking around in the gloom I can see a crude stone sarcophagus. Beside it is something striking. Bones are draped like necklaces across large slabs at the back of the tomb; the bones have been tied together with leather. Small bones. Children's bones. I turn around to tell Fiona about this find but she's already scrambled out of the tomb.

She's shaking.

"What is it, Fee?"

She shakes her head. Tears carve paths in the grime on her face.

"Fee. Tell me. What is it?"

Silence. Finally it comes out of her in guttering sobs.

"Oh, McEvoy. I had a baby." She stops and shakes her head. "A boy. I gave 'im up. I never told anyone."

I wrap her in a bear hug and wait until she settles.

"It's terrible. I was sixteen." Another shudder. "I didn' know what to do. My mum said she'd disown me if I kept 'im."

I've never seen her so miserable. "There, Fee. It's OK now."

"It's not OK. It's not. It's not." She shakes her head over and over. "It'll never be alright. But I didn' know what else to do."

■

We head south through Galway and into the savage and beautiful terrain of Connemara. I lose track of all the small towns we stay in—Cleggan, Leenaun, Kilkeiran, Ballyconneely—but the highlight is a crushed coral beach at Corrahoe. I bring a fingertip coated with wet sand close to my eye. The grains are finely crushed sea creatures. They have different shapes and colors; each one is a miniature world. Look don't touch, says the ocean, but we touch anyway, charging into the surf wearing skivvies and goose bumps and getting chilled to the bone in minutes. We huddle together under my jacket and eat hard boiled eggs dusted with sand.

At Clifden, we see the first protesters, a half-hearted gaggle of mostly men holding placards that say "Cooper Go Home" and "God Thinks It's Rusty Junk" and "The Irish Know Best for Ireland." That's before the opening but by the time the show starts a counter-protest is in full gear. These women cheer loudly as Fiona arrives. Their signs say "Fiona Speaks for Us" and "A Woman's Body, a Woman's Choice" and "Pornographers Be Damned."

In a quiet moment one evening after the show has closed I look at her work with fresh eyes. The travelling exhibit has eight pieces and they're all too large for most galleries; at Clifden they're in the lobby of the municipal building.

Her sculpture is abstract. It displays aerial legerdemain that's reminiscent of Calder; the massive curving forms seemed to float in the air, gravity is firmly snubbed. But it's also visceral, reaching right into the solar plexus with its message. Fiona burst onto the scene by speaking out in sculpted metal against anyone who abused women or took away their rights. Early on, when I first met her, the work had been angry and its impact was limited for that reason. Good politics doesn't often make good art. But she has talent and craft to go with her passion. Now she's found out how to meld joy and optimism with unflinching truth. Interpenetrating shards of steel, brass, and bronze are uncomfortable to look at, but in some of her pieces those forms and materials are supple and tender.

"Fee, for someone who hates attention, you're attracting an awful lot of static. The phrase lightning rod comes to mind."

We're driving south into Kerry. The wild peninsular scenery of the north is turning into rural pasture and wooded hills.

"McEvoy, it's so fucked up for women 'ere."

"But aren't they having a vote on divorce in a few months?"

"Yes, and the forces of darkness are lining up against it. It might not fly. Italy has had legal divorce since 1974, Spain since 1981. This is the only Catholic country in Europe that's still stuck in the bloody Stone Age."

"Aye, that sucks."

"It's fuckin' feudal." She pulls hard on a ciggie. In the intensity of her work and the tour, she's smoking and drinking more. The taste of ashtray takes the edge off my kissing pleasure but Fiona's hooked so it's part of the package.

"D'you know 'bout their 1861 Offences Against the Persons Act?"

"No."

"It says, I quote, that any person performing, attempting and or assisting in an abortion is liable to penal servitude for life."

"Surely they don't enforce that?"

"Maybe not, but they could. Imagine the chilling effect. This is the only country in the world that bans information on abortion."

"That's Orwellian."

"Six thousand women a year go to England for abortions."

"Well, they wouldn't be going for the food or the friendliness."

She swings her arm and whacks me in the chest. I wince; my ribs are still tender from rowdy love-making a week ago.

"You're so glib, McEvoy." She smolders. "You can be a right prick."

"Sorry, Fee. Really. You actually scare me when you get going this way. You're totally manic."

We fall silent. I glance over and see her face set, but the flicker of a smile works at the corners of her mouth.

"I know. But I've got so many ideas. It's like my muse is on speed. I 'ave to ride it while I can, baby."

Days flick by. South to Galway, Limerick, and Kilarney, then east to Cork, Waterford, and Wexford. As we head into the rural south, I feel the tide of conservatism steadily rising. Pub banter is restrained. It's Churchy. But the obvious telltale is the protests. We've both stopped reading the papers and we never switch on a TV but Fiona is attracting increasing attention at each stop and most of its negative. The Garda is on hand at all the shows and in Kilarney and Cork everyone has to walk through metal detectors.

In Wexford the mood turns ugly. As we arrive for the reception, Fiona's women are out in force as usual, yelling encouragement and support, but there are an even larger number of men and it looks like they're well oiled by beer. An hour later we leave and walk to the car nearby. A beer can sails past my ear. The Garda hauls away the perp and we bundle into the car. A man flings himself onto the bonnet and leers at us; he too is pulled away. Flustered, I grind the clutch and we lurch into gear. There's a loud whack as a stone hits the windscreen. A large spider's web appears but the safety glass holds. Stones thud into the roof and the door.

I'm worrying about trading in yet another wrecked car when Fiona catches my eye. She's not scared at all. She's energized.

"Fuck, McEvoy." Her eyes are on fire. "Art matters!"

■

The Troubles have barely begun.

The Troubles are the main reason for our trip. All the stops around small town Ireland are side shows before the main event. Everything's leading up to The Troubles.

With a new un-gouged car in hand but another deep gouge in the credit card, we drive north. No stops for tourism this time, no leisurely pub lunches, this is a straight shot up the middle of the emerald. And Carlow and Kildare and Meath are prosaic farming counties so there's little to distract us. We're running late so we eat meat pies and crisps on the road. We slip across the border in the dark and two hours later we're peering at street signs, trying to find an address in the Belfast docklands, an unremittingly grimy and gloomy place. I've driven all the way and I'm played out.

Finally, we see the only warehouse that's lit up so we pull over. Armored personnel carriers bookend the empty street; three soldiers stand at the entrance. As we get out one of them talks into a lapel mike. A well-groomed man emerges to greet us.

"Alistair Castlemaine. Home Office. Miss Cooper, I'm delighted to meet you."

They shake hands.

"And this must be your traveling companion. Mr. McEvoy?"

"Spot on." His grip of my hand is brief. He's tall and gaunt with a razor-sharp nose and a weak chin. An English chin, I think to myself uncharitably.

"I think you'll find everything you need. A crew has been working for a week to set up your shop."

"Thanks." Fee looks anxious. "I can't wait to get stuck in."

"Should I park the car?" I ask. "And where are we staying?"

"Mr. McEvoy, we'll provide the transport for your visit. My men will return your car. A driver will take you to each accommodation."

"And the squaddies?" I jerk a thumb towards the soldiers. "What're they for?"

His smile is ingratiating and his tone is supercilious. "Her Majesty's Government is committed to ensuring that everything runs smoothly."

The interior of the warehouse is brightly lit and piled fifteen feet high with gleaming piles of metal. Most of it seems to be thick copper sheets, but I also see strips and rods and smaller sheets of iron and bronze. A large arc welding rig occupies one corner. In another corner, they've built an open plan office with drafting table, work bench, desk, and filing cabinets. Fiona opens two boxes of papers that were shipped ahead and starts laying out drawings.

"Fee, this is you in your element, isn't it?"

She beams at me. "It's fucking brilliant, McEvoy. They've given me everything I need, but I've got so much to do."

"And this is only half of it? Can you explain that again?"

"The work site is on the border. But as part of the agreement half of the installation has to be created in the North and half in the South. It's part of the reconciliation theme but it's giving me nightmares."

"Like making the body of an airbus in France and the wings in Germany and hoping it flies straight."

"Yeah." She spies something under a plastic cover. "Ooh, they got me oxy. Brilliant!"

"It's just a blowtorch, isn't it?"

She gives me a withering look. "Not even close. Watch this."

With practiced dexterity, she hefts the unit onto her back. It has two small tanks like scuba gear, with tubes from each one joining into a hand-held device with a pistol grip. She opens both valves and hits the ignition button. A bright blue finger of light leaps from the nozzle. It hisses like a snake.

"A blowtorch," she says scornfully, "burns gas and will barely get you 500 degrees. Now a gas welder will burn oxygen from the air but it only gets to 600, OK for soldering and brazing."

"I've always said 600 degrees is quite toasty enough for me."

She ignores me. "This baby mixes gas and oxygen from the tanks. That'll get you 1000 degrees and cut quarter inch steel like butter."

School chemistry dimly swims into view. "Isn't pure oxygen really dangerous?"

"Well you wouldn't leave it around for your nieces and nephews to play with. But in the right hands, it's fabulous."

My Venus is no soft goddess. She's a true lad of lads, Lord of twin carbs and hard metal. She's positively hopping with excitement over her oxyacetylene gear. Women.

■

I need to occupy myself while Fiona throws herself into her work. She's intoxicating to me, like breathing pure oxygen. But she's also combustible and exhausting. She's all the woman I could ever want. When she's on, with pedal to the metal, only food and sex permeate her bubble.

The first few days I walk the streets of Belfast, but it's a dour and drab city with the shell-shocked feel of a place too long in a war zone. All the people I meet are cheerful and friendly but the sum's less than the parts. The military minders tried to chauffeur me but I tell them, very politely, to shove off. Besides, it's not likely to encourage open arms from the locals to be hitching rides with people thought of as armed occupiers.

Then an item in the paper catches my eye: a lecture series at the Armagh Observatory on astrobiology, the study of life in the universe. I've always had a soft spot for astronomy, so I hop a bus for the thirty miles to Armagh and get to the complex of Victorian buildings just as the lecture starts. A suave Frenchman with a thick accent is describing the first discovery of a planet beyond the Solar System a few years earlier. I noticed the story on the front page but hadn't registered the implications. The haul of exoplanets, as they're called, is up to a few dozen and it seems likely that most stars have planets.

I'm intrigued and see on a bulletin board outside the auditorium that there's a research symposium running all afternoon after each public lecture. The symposium is an invitation-only affair but nobody's manning the registration desk so I pick up a packet and a blank name badge and invent an academic affiliation for myself. Most of the talks are dense and technical and it takes my full attention to learn anything but a few speakers have the skill of conveying information at high level but also with clarity. I enjoy the mental workout.

At coffee, a man wearing a blazer and clubby tie approaches.

"I don't recognize you. Were you at the banquet last night?"

"No, sorry old chap." I affect my poshest Edinburgh accent. "The beastly flight was late, and I had a splitting headache, so I stayed in and worked on my monograph."

"I see," he eyes me carefully. "I'm Liam Kennedy, Director of the Observatory here."

"Professor Ian McEvoy, very pleased to meet you." Careful McEvoy, not too plummy.

"And you're from..." he peers at my badge. "...the University of the Outer Hebrides."

"Not to be confused with our sister institution, the University of the Inner Hebrides." I say confidently.

"Mmm. I can't say I'm familiar with it. Do they have an astronomy department?"

"Absolutely. Brilliant skies." I lean in conspiratorially. "Of course it's not much good in the summer."

He faces me squarely. "You're not a professor or an astronomer, are you?"

My best hangdog face. "No, but it was fun while it lasted."

"Look, Mr. McEvoy, if that is your name." I nod. "There's nothing secret or private about our meeting. We charge registration to cover the cost of the lunches, the banquet, and the conference bag. But I'm happy to waive registration for a member of the public who's so keen he's already sat through one of our technical sessions."

"Why that's awfully decent of you." I'm stuck in my upper crust accent and worry that the wind might change.

"Enjoy the meeting, Mr. McEvoy, and if I can help in any way don't hesitate to ask."

The rest of the session is a series of presentations on the method for finding planets so far away. I'm lost most of the time, but get the gist of it, which is that other planets are so dim and so close to their parent stars that there's not a snowball's chance in hell of seeing them directly. Astronomers are sneaky. They look for stars that wobble due to the tug of a Jupiter-sized planet, like someone being pulled around by a manic dog on a leash. The wobble is detected by changes in the spectrum of the star. Something like that.

At the coffee break, I make small talk with a few participants but feel naked, with more pretensions than credentials. I scan the posters about jobs and meetings; there's one in Spanish that I can read easily. Where did I learn how to do that?

■

I'm still fired up with the revelation that our Solar System isn't unique when I get to the warehouse later that evening. The soldiers recognize me and stand aside.

"Fee. I heard some brilliant stuff today. Clever dick astronomers are finding planets everywhere."

She's at her drawing board, poring over sketches. "McEvoy, I need your reaction to this section. Should it be pure copper or have bronze welded to it?"

"They use spectrographs, so it's indirect evidence, but just as real as taking a picture."

"This has to convey liberation to new possibility so I want to move to a new medium."

"Of course, with existing precision they can only find Jupiters, but Earths will surely come."

"Bronze adds huge complications and I've no sodding idea if I can make the welds strong enough."

I'm standing beside her. "This is us not connecting."

"I know. Shit, McEvoy, fuck me. I'm totally horny."

"Actually, I think we should explore our feelings and the reasons for our alienation."

"Fuck me, McEvoy. Fuck me hard."

"But transient physical pleasure will not address our underlying emotional problems."

She stands up and I enfold her in my arms from behind. Her hair smells of smoke. She moves her bum from side to side and I quickly get hard. I kiss her neck and reach under her shirt to hold her breasts. She eases open the buttons of her jeans. I pull them impatiently down to her knees, followed by her panties. Her sweet ass beckons and my fingers caress and knead the smooth, white flesh. I reach between her legs and inside her with my fingers then follow quickly with my cock. She leans on the table and pushes hard against me with each stroke.

"Put your finger in me. Fill me up every way. Go on, baby."

I spread her wider and see the purple rosebud. I ease in my index finger. Impaled by this dilemma, she resolves it by giving in to a fiery paroxysm of pleasure.

A strange counterpoint ensues. I spend my days in a stuffy lecture hall in the Armagh Observatory coming to terms with one of the most momentous discoveries in science in the past century. Fiona grapples with the technical and artistic challenges of a sculpture that's supposed to recapitulate and resolve thirty years of religious strife and sectarian conflict. Are we the twain that can never meet?

∎

"Life will be found everywhere. Ganz bestimmt!" Franz Eberhard gives everyone around the table a fierce look and lowers his pint of lager emphatically, splashing froth on the table.

That stills the conversation momentarily. Eberhard is a world expert in the niche field of extremophile microbiology. He studies microbes that thrive under conditions that would be intolerable to humans. He sports an Indiana Jones leather hat, well-worn and tilted at a rakish angle. He's seventy but brims with youthful vitality. When he removes his hat, grey hair sprouts like a stiff brush from his head. It also springs from his eyebrows and from the end of his chin. He's over six feet tall and has huge hands.

It's day three of the astrobiology conference. Some attendees stay at the observatory and eat limp sandwiches and fruit salad. I call them the astro-zombies, though not to their faces. Others walk down the hill to eat meat pies and quaff beer; that's the group where I feel kinship. They don't mind that I'm an interloper. It's a younger crowd, mostly postdocs and graduate students. The conversation is ribald and free-wheeling.

"Franz, have you cleaned your kitchen lately?"

"Unsightly stain in your bathtub getting you down?"

"My steak and kidney pie. It's alive! Aaaaargh."

"Is it true extremophiles lurk in those hard to clean places?"

Eberhard wants to take a break so I walk with him to the park rather than heading up the hill to the Observatory for the next talk. I'm glad to be able to talk to him on my own; the young astronomers have too much technical knowledge for me to be able to keep up with the conversations. Eberhard is patient with my lack of background and he's happy to have someone open-minded to talk to. Or as I would put it, someone whose slate is unsullied.

"They're so rigid. Life can only be in the habitable zone, they say. What is the habitable zone? The place where life can live. Ha!"

I nod. I'm sure I'd never want to be his graduate student or his adversary in a debate.

"These people think life needs Darwin's warm pond. They look at the Earth and say you can't have biology unless it's not too hot and not too cold, not too salty and not too acid, the pressure not too high and not too low." He waves his hands and uses a German-accented singsong to convey his contempt for such lack of imagination.

"What's wrong with saying that?" I ask gingerly, because it makes sense to me too.

"Der erste, we shouldn't be surprised that life does well here, on the temperate Earth. If it didn't we wouldn't be here! That tells us nothing about the chance of life in more extreme habitats. Der zweite, we have found life in highly unusual places, from the deep sea floor to a desert where it rains once in a century. Life is happy in the most unpleasant places on Earth. Der dritte, life started here on the Earth when it was molten and volcanic. An inferno! If life can start here, it can start anywhere!"

"So Earth's not really the Goldilocks planet?"

"Ach, ja. The temperate surface is just right for us," he says. "But it is just one environment that life has adapted to. At the ocean floor there are entire ecosystems that thrive in darkness. The superheated water near a volcanic vent is 700 degrees and a hundred atmospheres pressure. Does that remind you of anywhere?"

All I can think of is the tip of Fee's blue flame. I fail this small test. "Er, no, sorry."

"Venus! A liquid equivalent to our evil sister planet, a place nobody imagines would support life. Why should we be so sure?"

"I see your point. So microbes might live on a range of planets."

"Genau, genau. And we should not be so sure only microbes.

More advanced forms of life on other worlds might have evolved strategies to deal with physical conditions we think intolerable."

We walk back to the Observatory. Even with a slight stoop, he's a large man and looms over me by several inches. He stops at a boulder in the park gardens.

"What do you see, Mr. McEvoy?"

"Not much. Just a rock."

"Look closely."

"Um. Well, guess there's a bit of moss, and some lichen, and over here some tiny white flowers!"

"Das ist es ja eben! If you looked with a microscope you would discover hundreds of different microbes. And if you broke the rock, within it you would find dozens more, all living with no sunlight and almost no air and water! Tell me, Mr. McEvoy, how do you think life started?"

"Well, not with some bearded bloke working flat out for six days, if that's what you mean."

"Then how?"

"I haven't thought much about it. I guess simple molecules in the water stuck to each other and got bigger, and eventually they got big enough to turn into cells and have conversations like this."

"It sounds impossible, doesn't it? Fast unmöglich. But it happened in only 100 million years, a blinking eye in the 4.5 billion year history of this planet. And all when the Earth was being bombarded with large meteors and the oceans had just condensed from steam."

"So what kind of life do you study, Professor Eberhard?"

"Microbes that can live above the boiling point of water, or below freezing, microbes that can live in battery acid or drain cleaner, and microbes that live happily at Chernobyl. Leben ist verwunderlich."

I look at him carefully to see if he shows any obvious mutations or signs of radiation damage. Those eyebrows are pretty scary. "How do they do that?"

"They have a short genetic code and keep multiple copies of their DNA in tidy piles so they can repair it quickly."

"And these creatures all have our DNA?"

"Not exactly the same, but all life on Earth shares the same genetic code. Life on Earth is one thing—ist eins—just one example of biology. We'll have no idea about the general case until we find new examples of life among the stars."

"Amazing. How did you get into all this?"

"I liked chemistry as a child. I made messes." He winks at me. "Explosions sometimes."

"But how did you know you wanted to study weird life?"

"I visited a volcano as a child with my family. Everyone else got sick but I wouldn't leave. Ich liebe den Geruch von Schwefel! I love the smell of sulfur!"

■

Back in the warehouse, huge sections of metal are taking shape across the warehouse, held upright by a complex system of pins and pulleys. Fiona works flat out during the day when people are there to help, takes a short nap in the late afternoon, and then powers through the evening making drawings and testing welds. We have some middle ground; our bodies meet and shared intense pleasure there, but Fiona mostly dwells in a place beyond my reach. Our best connections come in the evening, when I get back from Armagh and Fiona realizes she's not eaten all day. A plain, unmarked sedan takes us wherever we want in the city, waits outside or discretely round the corner, and then takes us back to the warehouse.

■

By the end of the week, Eberhard has taken me under his wing. He talks about me proudly at coffee as if I'm a young faculty protégé, not a professional wanderer who doesn't have any science O levels.

"You with your habitable zones." He pokes his fork in the direction of the planetary science contingent of the pub crowd. He has a slightly disgusting habit of talking while he eats; when you work on extreme life forms I guess you aren't too squeamish about food splatter. "Just how many planets might have life?"

One of the postdocs pipes up. "Using a strict definition? Earthlike planets near Sunlike stars with liquid water on their surfaces? Maybe 100 million in the Milky Way."

"Gut! And with a generous definition, to allow large moons of the giant planets, like Europa or Titan?"

"Hmm. An order of magnitude more. Maybe a few billion."

"Sehr interessant. Now, what do you think will happen on all these planets, with energy and the chemical ingredients for life available? Do you think they will all end up with life like Earth's?"

Uncertainty sets in. People look at each other. One of the students says hesitantly, "Well, maybe not…"

Someone else chimes in. "A few might have complex life."

A third. "I'm not really sure…"

"A billion Petri dishes under warming Suns." Eberhard pauses for effect. "I think the possibilities are legion. Leben ist sehr seltsam. Not just stranger than we imagine, life is stranger than we can imagine!"

We leave the pub and the others walked ahead while Eberhard and I take our regular detour through the park. He has old world decorum, tipping his leather hat to women we pass and occasionally offering a breezy "Guten tag!"

"Life is surprising, don't you agree Mr. McEvoy?"

"I'd say so, yes."

"Even what we think we know about our own mechanism is not the whole story." He rummages in his pocket and pulls out a business card that he gives me.

"This woman has found clues to a wonderful mystery. If you are in the south and want to engage your deep brain again, visit her."

I glance at the card. Professor Devi Chandrasekhar. Department of Genetics. Trinity College. Dublin.

"Astronomers have started a bold adventure, Mr. McEvoy. I hope I live to see the answers."

"Aye, my brain is totally bursting from this week."

"Within a decade it will be commonplace to find large planets near other stars," he said. "Clones of Earth will be found soon after. It will be difficult for astronomers to inspect them for signs of life from afar, but I think they will do it."

"What will they find?"

"Ach! That is the question." His eyes are bright. "The microbes I study are just the first steps on a long, unpredictable journey. Here and in millions of other places in the galaxy, advanced life might be indistinguishable from magic!"

∎

I'm avoiding Fiona and the pressure cooker of her work. Usually we go for a meal then she returns with the minder while I find a pub and make fast friends over beer and darts. Castlemaine checks in from time to time, and once makes a dry allusion about how hard she's driving her daily assistants. I offer to pitch in but she shrugs it off, saying the vital bits of the project are all in her head.

When Fiona's deep in the act of creation her tether on the world slips away. She forgets to bathe or eat. Her smell is sexual and feral. Her gaze is uncomfortable. Her abundant energy fills the cavernous space with electricity, but it's raw and unfocused.

One night she's slicing bronze into strips with a circular saw so she can braze them onto larger pieces of iron. It's tricky work; bronze is brittle and can shatter if stressed too much. I hand her bronze sheets and put the strips into a neat pile. We both wear goggles. The grinding whine suddenly turns into a shriek of metal.

"Shit! Fuck, that hurts." She calls out plaintively, "McEvoy!"

She's pushed the cut too hard and a section has splintered. She turns with her arm held out to me. A needle of bronze is projecting at a shallow angle from her forearm. Blood runs down her arm from the entry point.

"Hold still, Fee." She bites her lip. "Christ, you just missed a vein! It's in an inch or more. I'll try and be gentle."

I ease the metal shard from her arm. I apply disinfectant. As I'm bandaging her I say, "You really need to use softer drugs."

Late the next night I find her with a dead cigarette in her mouth hammering rivets into a copper sheet with a large mallet. Clanging reverberates through the cavernous space. I touch her shoulder; she turns with a start.

"How's it going to end, Fee?"

She looks at me blankly. I pull her gently to me and fold her into my arms. She's tightly coiled, stressed like one of her metal sheets. Neither of us speaks. I hold her for a long time and very slowly she begins to unclench. Her steel morphs to bronze and bronze turns to copper and copper eases to soft, malleable gold. She melts into me. Stroking her hair, I whisper to her.

"How does it end?"

Whiteness. I'm suddenly struck by this thought—it ends with the blank pages of my wee book.

The Descent

It's the pivot point of The Troubles. Half of it has been built in the Belfast warehouse and we have another all-day journey back south to a warehouse in Crumlin, near Dublin, to complete the other half. We leave behind towering piles of metal, but Fiona insists on taking the oxy rig since finding out she can't get one like it in the Republic.

Fiona's almost back to her old self in the car, pawing and hitting me, full of acerbic social commentary. That blend of pleasure and provocation that I love. But it doesn't fool me. It's bravado. She's going through one of her changes.

■

The vibe in our southern digs is much gentler. The warehouse full of hardware is similar but there are no soldiers standing guard and Castlemaine's counterpart is a jocular man from the Republic's Ministry of Culture called Roddy Sullivan. Our hotel is a short walk away. Roddy offers us a car and driver for getting into the city, but seems content when we say we'd rather take the tram.

"First breakfast in Dublin, Fee, what do you fancy?"

"I fancy you but I'll leave that appetite 'til later."

I scan the menu. "I'm looking for grilled mutton kidneys with the fine tang of faintly scented urine, but I'm having no luck."

"Why not do bangers and mash instead."

"Right, and a stout pint of Guinness."

She raises an eyebrow. "Breakfast of champions?"

"My body is a temple. No lesser beverage will do."

She wants to get stuck in right away but I persuade her to see the city until lunch. We get off the tram at Phoenix Park and buy a bag of stale bread to feed to the swans. We flit from bookstore to bookstore. We scramble down a stairwell on a busy shopping street for a quick snog. We buy religious kitsch for souvenirs: a snow globe with John Paul II giving a blessing, nun soap on a rope, and a rag doll of Saint Brendan in a sailor's shirt. We choose some nice cheese for snacking on later. Corpse of milk. We walk along the Liffey. It's almost like the early days of the trip.

"I've got to get back, baby."

"I know. I think I'll roam a bit more."

"See you for dinner?"

"Aye." I kiss her. As we part I see a hint of tentativeness in her eyes. Very un-Fee.

■

Fishing in my jacket pocket, I find the card. Devi Chandrasehkar. Trinity College is in the city center and just a short walk away. The building is old and ivy-clad but the lab inside is new and gleaming. A student fetches her. She makes slow progress moving between the lab benches, walking on half-crutches. Polio. As she gets close I loom over her by a foot, she's very petite, her skin dazzlingly dark against a crisp white lab coat.

"You're a colleague of Eberhard?"

"Not a colleague, really. Not even a friend. He sort of took me under his wing these past weeks, he's been teaching me about the microbial world."

"Eberhard is an excellent scientist. A visionary. That's not an easy role. Scientists can be quite defensive when their conventional wisdom is challenged."

Her English is crisp, perfect, and unaccented.

"How can I help you?"

"I know you're busy, but Eberhard said you had a project that was threatening to rewrite the book on the genetic code."

She smiles. More white, crisp perfection. I know Indians who never brush their teeth yet have immaculate teeth. Genetics.

"I do. It's my dirty secret. I will only publish when my position in the university is secure. My husband earns a modest salary and I have three children. Today, I have to run a difficult set of sequences that require my attention. Tomorrow I can explain it to you. This afternoon one of my students will give you enough background so that what I say will make more sense."

Siobhan, a first year graduate student, sits with me in the snack shop downstairs and over a coffee gives me a primer on genetics and molecular biology. A single genetic code in all life on Earth, from fungi to elephants. A four-letter alphabet of base pairs—A, C, T, G—laid out along the twinned strands of DNA. Three billion of those letters making up the human genome, their combined syntax forming an encyclopedia about each of us: the book of life. Then she tells me the idea that's so central to the subject that it's called, with mock irony, "The Central Dogma." Genetic information hard-wired into DNA is transcribed into little packages made of messenger RNA, and each package contains instructions for the synthesis of one or more particular proteins. The proteins control all the functions of every cell. The Central Dogma is simple: DNA makes RNA, RNA makes proteins, and proteins do all the heavy lifting of biology. But she leaves me with the impression that it might not really be so simple.

■

That evening, for the first time in weeks, Fiona actually needs my help. She's checked out the welding rig, set up her portable oxy and is unpacking boxes of drawings and design specs.

"Fuck. McEvoy, I'm not finding all my sketches."

"Not to worry, Fee, they're here somewhere. There wasn't a scrap of paper in that place when we left."

"I know, but some of the sketches I've found seem wrong." This is also very unusual, Fee doubting herself.

By midnight, we've found most of what she needs. In past weeks she would have cranked up the gear and tested spot welds on the new materials, but tonight she walks back to the hotel with me and flops into bed and into an immediate deep sleep.

I'm restless and lie awake for a long time. Finally, I go to the desk, switch on a low light, and try to write. The words won't come. I feel a tremor of Joyce: no pen, no ink, no table, no room, no time, no quiet, no inclination.

The next evening, it seems to be going more smoothly. Fee is in a flow, doing spot welds and singing softly to herself. I'm reading a slim volume of Seamus Heaney. The poetry is earthy, soothing. I glance at her and instantly fling the book aside and lunge across the room. With a second to spare I slap the box of matches out of her hand. It skitters across the floor.

"Jesus Christ, love, what were you thinking?"

She looks at me, dazed. "I was…it's…fuck…I dunno what to say. I've never done that before."

Lighting a cigarette near a 1000 degree flame and two tanks of highly explosive gas is not recommended.

She looks shaken. "I 'ope we survive this, baby."

My heart is still pounding. "I hope so too."

■

Chandra, as she prefers to be called, gives me a tour of her lab the next morning. I'm taken aback by the rows of machines and robots in a subject that I've always associated with lab coats and pipettes.

"What are they all doing?"

"The work of ten thousand biologists," she says proudly.

"How do you mean?"

"They are reading the genomes of everything from a bacterium…" she points to a small machine with flashing lights on his left, "…to an elephant." She points to a similar machine to his right.

"You feed an elephant into that little gizmo?"

"A mocker is never taken seriously when he is most serious."

"A fan of Joyce." I nod in recognition.

"You're a kindred spirit, I see. Naturally, one reads." She gives me a reflective look. "Genomics does not stimulate all parts of the brain."

"Why did you come here, Dr. Chanda?"

"Ireland's the lion of Europe. Rapid growth, an educated workforce, and little government regulation. The software industry is doing so well they're luring back second generation émigrés from San Francisco and Boston. Biotech is the next boom. I'm the first woman in my family to go to university. I started with engineering. But being the only girl in my class at the Madras Institute of Technology was a bit…" she pauses to select the right word. "…disconcerting. I had some skill in the lab so was able to advance in academia. The government of Maharashtra was building an Institute for me, but my days and nights would have been consumed with umpteen kinds of paperwork. When they offered me a lab here I accepted."

I try and imagine the obstacles she has elided in this condensed version of her career path.

"Sorry, I interrupted your explanation."

"The double helix is separated like pulling apart a zipper and then chopped up. It goes through a polymerase chain reaction and…"

"Hold your horses, Dr. Chandra, I'm a neophyte in genetics."

"Apologies. Base sequences are assembled to make complements to the sections of single strand DNA, like hands and gloves, and then the DNA is split apart and the process repeated.

This device amplifies the DNA by factors of millions, which gives plenty of material for the sequencers."

"Those R2D2 units over there?"

"Yes. Each sequencer can parse 100,000 base pairs per hour."

"Not too shabby."

"Genetics has entered the industrial age. We've found genes that regulate and control Alzheimers and autism and Graves disease and a host of other ailments. If the 20th century was the age of physics, the 21st century will be the age of biology."

"You're giving me this glowing sales pitch for genetics. But you're going to drop the other shoe any minute."

"Correct. We're reading books we don't understand in languages we cannot comprehend."

"How d'ye mean?"

"The first clue is the fact that organism complexity has very little relationship to genome size, or the amount of genetic material. For example, the puffer fish genome has is a tenth the size of ours but it has the same number of genes. Even more perplexing is the genome of a unicellular organism called Ameba dubia, which has two hundred times the DNA of a human."

"That's freaky."

"Only 10% of the human genome is associated with any biological function. The rest is called "junk DNA" but that's just an admission of ignorance, like astronomers calling invisible stuff in the universe dark matter or neuroscientists saying we use a tenth of our brains."

"I see your point. In my wildest dreams I use ten percent." I'm intrigued. "But there must be speculation?"

"Absolutely. One idea is that junk DNA represents evolutionary relics, sequences that once served a useful purpose but now are scrambled and obsolete. Since our genome is continuously evolving and the tree of life links us directly to the first organisms on Earth, four billion years ago, this is not unreasonable. Another idea is that most of the DNA is involved in regulating and triggering genes. Since genes don't map simply—one gene for each disease or one gene for each attribute of the organism—some of the code might have this function."

"But I can tell you have your own ideas."

"I collaborate with a cryptographer and he tells me emphatically that the base pair sequence between identifiable genes isn't random. And it doesn't correlate well with surrounding genes. There are true patterns there and there must be meaning, it's just…"

"…that we don't know what it is!"

"I am glad the excitement is contagious, Mr. McEvoy."

"Why's so hard to figure it out? Look at all the horsepower you're throwing at the problem."

"True, many clever researchers have thought about it. Part of the problem is reductionist thinking. Looking from the bottom-up, at base pairs to amino acids to proteins to genes, misses the higher levels of organization. The Central Dogma might be wrong."

"Who's closest to cracking the problem?"

"I thought you'd never ask, Mr. McEvoy." She bestows on me her widest, whitest smile. "Two years ago, researchers at Johns Hopkins discovered a second code superimposed on the traditional genetic code. It controls the placement of little protein spools around which DNA is looped. The spools protect and control access to the DNA; it's like a gatekeeper code."

"And you?"

"We've found evidence of at least five additional codes imprinted in different ways in genetic material. This might just mean that layers of complexity arose independently, each one serving a purpose for living organisms, except…"

"Except…" I'm leaning forward. She has my total attention.

"…except that deep combinatorial analysis shows all six codes are related, but in a way we don't yet understand. There is some master architecture that controls everything."

■

On the way back, I duck into a newsagents to buy a Mars bar.

I'm about to leave and have already unwrapped it and taken a bite when my mind goes blank. Literally. There's nothing there, no memory of where I am and why I came to be standing in a newsagents. I walk slowly down the street and try not to draw attention to myself. Panic won't help. I sense this has happened before and so I must trust that I'll find a way out.

I start with the mundane. I'm chewing something sweet and sticky and chocolaty. A Mars bar. Yes, I like them. From this simple epicenter I work outward. A bustling town. People with accents. Dublin, yes, I'm sure of that. In my pocket, a card with an Indian name on it. It means nothing. My wallet has a photo of a ginger-haired man and a pretty black-haired girl laughing in a pub. Yes. McEvoy. Fiona. My life.

Images flood my head, blending together like a montage sequence in an old movie. Fiona with her brow furrowed and a cigarette hanging from her bottom lip. An old Indian with crooked teeth. Sitting in a cold stone chapel while a massive priest chants a liturgy. My life. A crystal bowl shattering at my feet. Looking across a table at an old man with gnarled hands and hooded eyes. A burly black man wearing a colorful waistcoat. A canyon bathed in starlight. My life.

The images are accompanied by bursts of smell, taste and sound. As this multi-sensory input buffets me, I stop walking and I'm dimly aware of raised eyebrows and leery looks as the locals flow past me, like river water diverting past a boulder. The blank cipher fills in but my relief is mixed with unease because the visions are so sharp and fresh. How can I be sure I'm filing away memories? What if McEvoy's story already exists and I'm accessing fragments of it—past, present, and future?

Like an abandoned house where the owner goes around and flings open shutter and doors, light steadily returns. And with it my sense of self. I have a terrible foreboding. Fiona needs me. I love her. For her sake I must avoid the abyss.

■

When I get back, famished, I root around in the fridge that's in a back room of the warehouse, but all I can find is curdled yogurt and stale sausage rolls. Their DNA's of questionable provenance so I pass. Fiona is at her drawing table, immobile, poring over a blueprint. I fall into one of the two chairs they've brought to make it more homey and pick up the local paper I was reading on the bus.

"Fee, if you get ahead of the game, let's take an evening off. The best fiddlers in Donegal are coming to the Sheep's Head on Swift Row. That'll be magic."

No reaction.

"And if that doesn't rock your boat, they're speed-reading Ulysses in Phoenix Park."

She hasn't moved and is still in her bubble.

"Fee?" I walk over, and am immediately alarmed. She's just staring at a half-finished drawing, and has been since I got back.

"Fee. What is it?" But I know. I've been here before.

"I can't do it, McEvoy." Her voice is as slender as a thread. "I just can't do it."

"Of course you can. You're halfway there. It's more of the same."

Joyce speaks. My words in her mind: cold polished stones sinking in a quagmire.

"No." Her tone is quiet and final. "No."

■

She steadily hollows out, until there's less and less Fiona there. Talking to her is like talking to someone at the bottom of a deep well. But we've come too far and she's worked too hard to give up. As she recedes deeper into shadow I scribble hard to preserve some texture and to give the shadows strength and depth.

To have someone you deeply care about disappear while you're watching is an intolerable loss. The broken piece is invisible but it profoundly compromises her whole. Fiona's told me of the gamelan, where metal instruments are forged from a single vat of bronze in the ideal proportion of 10 to 3 parts copper to tin. A single crack in a gong or a saron creates intolerable disharmony; the only recourse is to melt everything down and re-forge all the instruments. Fiona can only be reborn after she has melted down.

Our little world is hot and smothering: a Venus only lovers could love. There's no rejoicing at days that bleed into each other: Moanday, Tearday, Wailsday, Thumpday, Frightday, Shatterday.

No more the intellectual dilettante, I spend my days assimilating her sketches and plans, trying to comprehend the fantastic, metallic jigsaw she's constructing. Roddy the Culture Minister does his part with some extra pairs of hands, metalworkers from the Sandymount Shipyards. Fiona directs the activity in a whisper and the dockworkers and I try to make metal obey the remains of her will. Luckily, they're skilled and committed to the cause so we make a good team.

For a few days it seems to be going well. Large sections are being assembled, welds seem to stick, and the physical objects match the engineering drawings. I allow myself to anticipate success. The hopes are dashed when we realize we've duplicated a section that had been made in Belfast and we're running out of the tempered steel that only comes from one small plant in Wales.

"Enough, McEvoy. Enough." Late in the second week, the deadline is approaching. She throws in the towel. "It's not worth it."

"Have you eaten today?" I have to ask, or she'll forget.

"Yes, I had something or other."

"Have you taken your meds?"

"Yes. No. I don't know." A half-hearted shrug.

She's curled up in a chair like a dried leaf. I touch the pale skin of her cheek. It's damp from tears.

"Don't worry, McEvoy. Delirium passes."

Joyce again. He echoes her phrase, applying it to himself. "What am I to do?"

She looks up.

"You're crying too."

It's true. And I never cry. "I can't bear seeing you like this."

"Baby, don't you remember? You just buried your mother."

It is as painful to be wakened from a vision as to be born.

∎

I just buried my mother. She was 58 and had been in poor health for some time. Living with her sister, my aunt, in Corstorphine on the edge of Edinburgh. The death certificate mentioned respiratory failure and emphysema, and while her lungs were weak, it failed to mention the internal organs that had been weakened over the years by John McEvoy, my father. The death certificate failed to mention the slaps and blows to the head. It omitted all the cigarette burns. It somehow deemed insignificant the savage punches to the stomach and ribs and the numerous tumbles down the stairs.

My family obeyed decorum. Annie was out of detox for the funeral; she could barely breathe or stand still. Nobody went up to my father and called him out or spat in his face. To my eternal shame, neither did I. There was a reception at my aunt's house after the cremation. But I couldn't face the bland lies and the homilies. I had a tidy parcel with half the ashes and went straight to Waverley Station. Five hours later I was on the ferry from Mallaig to Skye. I stayed in a quiet B&B. By late the next afternoon I was climbing the Black Cuillin. Under a churning grey sky I scattered her ashes from the high point on the ridge, one of the few places I ever remember her laughing.

∎

Night in the warehouse. The hotel is abandoned. We sleep on the floor and eat from tins and cartons like hobos. I think: we end it here or it never ends. Joyce's ghost visits me again. He could hear nothing: the night was perfectly silent. He listened again: perfectly silent. He felt that he was alone.

Roddy comes by the next morning. There's enormous pressure to make the official opening date. He's painfully polite.

"I've come from the Prime Minister's Office. The Taoiseach asks if there's anything he can do personally?"

I gesture towards Fiona. She's asleep on a cot with her slim limbs splayed and her shirt riding up to show pale midriff and a jade navel ring. Her face twitches as she dreams. She's a lost teenager.

"Not unless he has insights into the mysteries of brain chemistry and the creative process. Tell your Prime Minister that art and artists can't be rushed."

He gives me a pained smile. "McEvoy, you're doing your best, I do know that. But the stakes have become higher in the past few weeks. Both governments have invested their credibility in the outcome."

"That's supposed to make me feel better?" My voice hardens. "If you imagine we can spill more of our guts into this work, please tell me how. We didn't cause your cursed troubles."

"It's not just that." He looks uncomfortable. "Hard core factions on both sides gain if the Good Friday Agreement fails. This installation has become a symbol of the agreement. There've been some threats, and some letters."

"Is that what you've got there?"

He holds a clutch of letters and I can see Fiona's name on the top one. "Yes. You probably shouldn't read them. It won't help."

"What the fuck have you got us into?" My voice rises almost to a shout. I know he's doing his best but we're deep into the shite now. Fiona stirs. "It's OK, Fee, back to sleep my love."

"Please accept our protection from now on."

"Is that supposed to give us the warm fuzzies?"

Another pained smile, too identical to the first to be genuine, and Roddy Sullivan takes his leave.

Giant's Work

Our next drive through the countryside isn't carefree at all; we're in a discretely armed convoy. In a grinding blur, with me acting as the eyes and hands of the sculptor, the work in the warehouse gets done. Fiona sleeps much of the time. She gets up at all hours and wanders around like a fevered child. She's lucid long enough to issue critical instructions, and also at the end when she gathers her drawings and gets me to put her treasured oxy gear in the rental in case she needs to do spot welds on site.

The border in this country is arbitrary. There's no mountain range or major body of water to separate Northern Ireland from the Republic of Ireland. Brooks and wild animals and birds all cross innocently and freely. Green is just a wavelength. Rich sod spreads seamlessly across the divide; no blade of grass is different from its neighbors.

This boundary is conjured by people not nature and the weight of their unforgiving history hangs heavy along country roads lined with squat brick houses and muddy fields. Religion and tribalism are as concrete as the Berlin Wall. Dozens of men have died from blunt force trauma in these woods and farm sheds, and hundreds of women and children have been bullied and bloodied.

Our convoy stops along a narrow winding lane. We wait. Fiona's asleep in my lap. I hear scurrying in the hedgerows and birds warbling in the trees. British Army armored personnel vehicles approach from the opposite direction and stop. The lead vehicles are fifty yards apart. Castlemaine and Sullivan emerge from their cars and solemnly shake hands. It's the handoff. We're back in the tender care of Her Majesty's Government—our government—but I'm hardly reassured. We use an open gate and paddock to turn around and I slip our car into the pack of vehicles heading north. The convoy is emphatically punctuated with armored Sarazens acting as brackets. Soldiers in the turrets scan the meadows with their eyes and their machine guns. The government has commandeered a B&B for us in the small town of Roslea. Somewhere in the nearby countryside, under smothering security, Fiona's destiny is waiting.

■

"Tell them to fuck off, McEvoy. I've got too much to do."

"Fee, they're saying it's important. They swear it's the only one you'll have to do. Some crap about obligation and taxpayer's money."

The handlers are insisting that Fiona do a BBC interview.

"Bugger. Well I suppose I 'ave to." She gives me a wicked look. "They do know I 'ave a foul mouth, don't they?"

"I'm sure their fingers won't stray far from the bleep button."

"Fuck. What am I gonna wear? My welder's overalls?"

"We'll find something. C'mon."

Near the bottom of the suitcase are black velvet pants, creased, but nobody will be able to tell, and a burgundy cashmere sweater. Fiona dabs at herself with makeup but she still looks pale and drawn. She cheers up a bit when I give her a massive hug and a big sloppy kiss. I tell her she looks like dynamite.

Our escort turns on the flashing lights and gets us to the nearby town of Enniskillen in twenty minutes. The BBC has set up a mobile transmitter and studio in a van the size of a large coach.

"Welcome back to BBC News in Depth. This is Kay Rankin and I'm with Fiona Cooper, the young artist behind a monumental work called The Troubles, which is taking shape under a shroud of secrecy in the Northern Ireland border town of Roslea. British and Irish governments have invested the work with great symbolic importance as they try to implement the Good Friday Agreement and end decades of sectarian strife. Good morning, Ms. Cooper, how does it feel to be at the center of a maelstrom?"

"Actually, I'm not bothered. I've got me head in the metal."

"Meaning you're so busy the politics don't bother you?"

"Yeah, more or less. It's a sculpture; it's art. A pile of metal isn't going to stop people fighting any more than liking classical music turned the Nazis into nice people."

I wince. Fee's not exactly PC. It looks like a live feed but maybe their wizards can use the five second delay to edit it out.

"I see." The interviewer changes tack. "You've never attempted anything so ambitious. How are approaching the work?"

"One steel plate at a time, one rivet at a time, one weld at a time. I admit it freaks me out sometimes thinking about it."

"What was your reaction when the U.N. Reconciliation

Commission picked your idea from over two hundred entries?"

"I was over the moon. I knew it would change my life but I didn't guess how much."

"You're often compared to Maya Lin, who designed the Vietnam Veterans Memorial, another young woman with a strong vision."

"I'm flattered by the comparison. Maya is a brilliant artist, but she prefers stone. My real hero is the American sculptor Richard Serra. He can make steel do anything he wants. I have to beg."

It's going much better. I relax. Fiona looks sharp and sexy. The BBC makeup woman tried to tame it but her hair is still wild.

"Extremist elements from the IRA on one side and the UDF on the other have said they'll try to disrupt the opening ceremony. Are you concerned?"

"Like I said, I'm in me bubble. I 'ope the wankers just go out and get drunk instead."

The finish is pure Fiona. Brilliant!

■

I'm helping full-time on the site, where the two poles of the work are being reunited and integrated into the landscape. Fiona is still very weak and has no stamina. She uses her occasional bursts of energy to make major decisions and always works far into the evening.

The installation site spans ten acres of fields and meadows and is surrounded by a high perimeter fence with soldiers on patrol outside. After sunset, arc lamps on high poles flicker on, casting us in a harsh white light. I hear the occasional whir of helicopters overhead. This high level of security successfully fends off journalists, who have not managed to take a single photo of the installation.

As we're escorted back to the B&B, I whisper to Fiona. "Let's sneak off and get a pint later."

"I thought you were gonna lick my ear."

"I'm really wanting to lick your clit, but you've been standoffish."

"Have I?" She seems shocked.

"Maybe not. Distracted, let's say."

"McEvoy." She takes hold of my hands. She's very serious. "When I'm like this, pleasure is alien to me. I'm adrift in a vast, churning sea with a small piece of driftwood to hang onto."

"You don't have to explain. I'm happy to be your flotsam."

The soldiers are on guard front and back so it's relatively easy to find a side bathroom with a window big enough to crawl through. At least it's easy for Fiona, who's compact and lithe. My bulk turns it into an origami exercise.

The fifth pub we pass seems warm and lively. We figure that even if they come looking for us, it'll take them a while to go into all the pubs, and by the time they get to this one we'll have had time for a quiet drink.

We play darts and I reestablish mastery over Fiona, but she evens the score with dominos. We're halfway through our pints when an old man in a cloth cap passes by. He seems to head for the door but then veers toward us. He gets within a foot of Fiona and spits directly in her face. I'm so stunned I don't move for a few seconds and by the time I get up he's gone. The barman gives Fiona a clean towel to wipe her face and several locals offer their apologies and say that the old man isn't a regular or anyone they know.

We're shaken by the incident but try to shrug it off. After we've finished our pints we leave the pub and have just turned the corner when a voice reaches us from the shadows.

"What're ye doin' here? Mind yer own fecking business."

"Leave us alone!" I yell, scanning the darkness. "We're not doing you any harm."

"Ye've sold out the Republicans. Ye'll fecking pay."

"Look pal, go home. Sleep it off." I'm tensed for action but can't see anything; my eyes are still dazed from the light in the pub.

Something harder than a fist slams into the side of my head and my body seizes up with blinding pain. I slump to my knees.

"Run, Fiona!" is all I can manage to say.

Shapes emerge from the shadows. Four men in dark clothes with pale and pinched faces. The first one steps forward and swings his boot into my stomach. A split second later I feel a boot connect with my lower back and another towering pillar of pain overwhelms me. I've been in this situation before, or close to it, so I know what to do. Submit and survive. I topple over and curl into a ball. Even protecting my head and guts, there are many places to inflict suffering. I will the blackness to come.

■

"You're a very lucky man, Mr. McEvoy." I slowly open my eyes. It's Castlemaine. "My men were on the scene quickly."

"And Fiona, is she…"

"Ms. Cooper is unharmed. She would have been next. That's why you're lucky we were alert. Your infantile antics have jeopardized this project, Mr. McEvoy, and that's unacceptable."

My pain is dulled by serious drugs. I pause to gather my strength, and pump as much volume into my voice as I can manage.

"Look, you supercilious prick. We're working to help a situation your type has fucked up for thirty years. You want an artist to come and help you. You wouldn't know what was good for Ireland if it was branded on your balls."

Jaw clenched, Castlemaine raises a faint smile. "I've been told I have to tolerate you Mr. McEvoy. But I know your type. You're rude and ignorant. My patience has worn thin."

"No, it's your hair that's thin. It's your dick that's thin. It's your humanity that's thin. Get the fuck out of my sight."

■

The work continues. The pressure is relentless and Fiona works on fumes. I'm the only person looking out for her. Her sense of riding the juggernaut of history is the only thing keeping her upright. The act of creation is too far in the past to savor; now the grind of execution is wearing everyone down.

She tells me that the night of the attack there were soldiers at a nearby street corner. They ran to her as she fled the scene but she had to beg them to go to the pub and intervene. Castlemaine might have had his men protecting her but he was happy for me to take a beating. I'm hoping the bastard comes back to check on us so I can give it back with interest, but he doesn't show his face.

Two days before the unveiling, Fiona and I come up with a detailed set of final instructions and then have to wait for them to get carried out. With nothing to do I catalog my aches and bruises. We're both going stir-crazy.

"Let's play hooky, Fee."

"After what happened last time?" She looks incredulous.

"We won't go to pubs or hang out with locals. It'll be fine."

He face brightens. "Why not? I'm going loopy here."

Slipping out of the B&B and finding the car is no problem. They must assume we wouldn't be daft enough to go out unescorted again. Neither of us is sleeping well so at 4am we escape under the cover of darkness. We head north from Roslea. I want to get as far from the border as possible. A few hours later we're standing on a bluff looking out toward Scotland. Venus hovers near the horizon like a milky eye, marker of the rising Sun. The water is dark and forbidding.

"The snotgreen sea. The scrotumtightening sea."

"Look," says Fiona, reading a sign. "In 1588, the Girona sank on the reef. It was the largest ship in the Spanish Armada."

"I wonder how many fools drowned themselves for her gold."

Fiona squeezes me round the waist. "Don't worry, baby, it'll be over soon." She looks at my swollen, bloody face. "Did you 'ave a bloody clue what you were getting yourself into when I asked you to come 'ere?"

I laugh.

∎

The rugged headlands of County Antrim lie ahead. We pull into a coastal area called the Giant's Causeway. Basaltic rocks project into crashing surf. The rocks have naturally formed an amazing array of interlocking hexagonal columns. They're like giant geometric stepping stones heading into the sea. There are forty thousand of them.

It's a bizarre sight. One placard gives the folk explanation. Finn MacCool was a rowdy giant and leader of the Fianna, guardians of the King of Ireland. Finn got into a pissing contest with Benandonner, a Scottish giant. To sort him out, Finn ripped stones from the cliffs and built a causeway to Scotland. But he was tired and had to rest so the Scottish giant ventured over the causeway to do Finn harm. All Finn could do was hide in a crib in his house and pretend to be a baby. So when Benandonner arrived, he tried to touch the baby, so Finn bit his finger off. If this is the size of the baby and what he can do, thought Benandonner, I want nothing to do with the father. Finn prevailed. Reassuringly for the legend the "other end" of the causeway can be seen at Fingal's Cave in Scotland.

A second sign says 17th century scientists and theologians debated whether the formations were due to the hand of god or natural. In the scientific explanation, rapidly cooling pools of lava contract horizontally rather than vertically. With such stresses the most efficient cracking of the rock forms hexagons and sometimes octagons and they then erode to different heights.

I incline toward the explanation in geology, but it seems too neat, too glib. Could nature really make polygons as vastly different in size as a multi-atom crystal and a column of rock like a Parthenon pillar? Suddenly, I have a sharp memory of strange stones from the Arizona desert that I was given by an Indian when I was young. I think about my conversations with Chandra the about a hidden genetic code. In a debate over natural and unnatural forms, we don't have the answers. If I were a playful god, I'd leave them strange stones to puzzle over. But if I were a sublime god, I'd write poetry into their DNA.

"Let's climb up." Fiona tugs on my hand. She's wearing a crimson blouse, a short tartan skirt, and calf-length boots.

I scramble to keep up. We reach the crest of a hill. We're all alone. The hexagonal pillars are all around us, some the height of a chair or a stool, and some towering overhead. She pulls me to her.

"Not enough time for us, McEvoy" She puts her head in the crook of my neck. "It's sad, but I forgot what you smell like. I wore tartan so you'd have an ancestral memory."

"I like it just fine, Fee."

She kisses me softly and traces her fingers over the scar tissue and discolored flesh on my face. I reach under her skirt; she's wearing the skimpiest panties. So skimpy, in fact, that the waistband snaps in my hand. She unzips me and holds my cock in her hand. I lift her and find a perfect spot nearby, one of the giant's stones at waist height. I place her gently on a giant's chair. Rough stone bites into her pale flesh.

"There, Fee, I've put you on a pedestal."

"Don't do that, baby, be close to me. Consume me."

I drop to my knees and bury my face in her mound of Venus. My blind tongue touches cold granite grit and cool soft moss and then her musky juice.

She pulls me to my feet and guides me in. I press deep into her wet grip and she wraps her legs around my waist. Her head is thrown back and the sinews of her neck are taut under the skin. My heart is pumping hard.

"I want you, Fee."

"You have me. You have me."

"Not this. Not just this. I want you."

"Oh. Oh." She's entering her place. Her legs tighten their grip on my waist. Her fingers dig into my shoulders. "I'm yours, baby."

"Then come with me, Fee. Come away with me."

"And then I asked him with my eyes to ask again yes and then he asked me would I yes and his heart was going like mad and yes I said yes I will yes."

■

Halfway back to Roslea, we stop for snacks in the drab town of Ballymoney. I park near a grassy space in the town center and head into an Indian grocery for crisps and Mars bars. Fiona has curled up under a blanket on the back seat so I decide to let her rest. Walking away from the car, I see two men in a nearby car talking.

As I leave the grocery, I know something's terribly wrong. Out of the corner of my eye I see two men running away across the park. In a flash I'm sprinting toward the car, bellowing for Fiona. I'm halfway across the road, in full stride, fifty yards from the car, when it ignites in a deafening roar and a vortex of flame. I'm flung to the side and off my feet. A moment later, I hear a series of crashes as chunks of glass and metal fall to the asphalt.

My world is about to implode when I see Fiona. She runs out of the Ladies Room on the park green and stares in amazement at the fiery devastation.

•

We're rescued by an Army helicopter. Twenty four hours later the same helicopter whisks us from the edge of Roslea to The Troubles. Speeches from the British and Irish Prime Ministers are timed to go out live on the ten o'clock news. The opening ceremony will follow shortly after. The helicopter drops from a dark sky. Below, contained within a floodlit ellipse of light, The Troubles look ugly, like a gash in the ground. I'm unsettled.

We land and while Fiona is whisked off to be prepped for the ceremony, I walk the length of the installation. This is nothing like the Vietnam Memorial. There are no names, there's no soothing water, no smooth expanse of black marble to touch and be comforted by. This is violent and elemental. Starting at ankle level, almost invisible in the grass, a strip of copper appears. It rises up and undulates, bending slightly and sagging this way and that, but growing in strength. Then as it climbs above head level, iron and bronze join the theme. There are jagged scars and clefts in the metal but it retains its unity and oneness. I walk on and just when it seems the metal wall must blot out the stars, it ascends steeply, bifurcates, and turns on itself. The broad sword becomes a soaring flower.

In my hand is something I've kept in my pocket for the past few weeks: the bronze needle from Fiona's accident. It's a piece of all this. It's a piece of her.

She breaks away from a cluster of organizers and politicians and walks up to me. Her monolith reflects us dimly and gives us its flat embrace. Joyce said men are governed by lines of intellect—women, by curves of emotion. He was wrong.

"I can't do this, Fee."

"I know."

"This is you. It's not me."

"It's not you. It's me."

"I miss you already."

And I turn and leave her pool of light.

6 GOLDEN STATE

Normal

I've lost my life. It just disappeared. Without a trace, not even a ripple. I joked about it with Pam this morning. Next month I'll be thirty nine. The big four-oh is after that and then, surely, oblivion.

"Let's do something special," she says.

"Celebrate the incipient crisis, the wheels coming off?"

"Silly man. A trip. Maybe Santa Barbara."

"Aye, we could. I'm due a few days."

"Late closing tonight. Can you cook?"

"Can I? I can if it comes in a can."

"Ian." Her hands are on her hips. "Will you cook?"

"Sure, sure. And it'll be rippling with riboflavin."

"Got to go." She picks up her briefcase and cell phone.

"Me too." I grab my satchel. It's bulging with paper.

A brief kiss, and then we drive together through the quiet morning streets of Monrovia, with the San Gabriel Mountains appearing vaguely through the smog, parting company on the 210 into Pasadena.

■

"Opposites attract, Mr. McEvoy?"

"No Dylan, we're looking for Isaac Newton here, not Dr. Phil."

Loud snickers.

"The third law. Any takers?"

A hand in the back. Abby. Bright girl.

"The law of action and reaction."

"Good, good. But what do the words mean?"

Her smile dims. "Something about equal and opposite?"

"Getting there." I walk up the aisle and stop by a boy with tousled black hair who sleep-walks through every class.

"Nestor, what would happen if you pushed Isaac Newton?"

A trick question. "He'd get mad?"

Another hand. "Yes, Jada."

"He'd push back!"

"Exactly. Of course he's been dead for 350 years and his moldy body is buried under a stone slab in Westminster Abbey. So if you tried to push him now they'd lock you up." A few giggles. "But Jada's right, he'd push back. Even if he didn't actually push back he'd resist your force."

Another hand.

"Darryl."

"Mr. McEvoy," his brow is furrowed. "It doesn't make sense. How can it be equal? If I push Rafael," he gestures to a very small Hispanic boy two rows away, "I'm a whole lot bigger than him. My push must be bigger than his push."

"You'd think so, Darryl. But in physics there are no bullies. The resistance he presents you as an object with mass means that his force equals your force. Oh sure, you could cause him harm. But it works both ways. Anyone here doing jujitsu or karate?"

A few hands go up.

"Then you know about action and reaction. Anyone doing martial arts understands Newton's Third Law better than I do."

"Let me put it another way," I continue. "Why don't you fall to the floor?"

Puzzled looks.

"Cos we're not retards!"

"Yes, Tyler. And in polite company we say mentally handicapped. The other reason is that our chairs push against our bums with exactly the same force that our bums push against the chair."

Titters at the word bum.

"The forces are in balance. Everyone can sit and hear my pearls of wisdom. But what happens if an unfortunately overweight person visits the classroom and sits next to you?"

"Gordo crashes to the floor." Tyler's on a roll.

"Precisely. The wood in the chair isn't strong enough to match the force presented by his humungous bottom."

I have them do an exercise in the workbook. I relish the texture of the classroom: activity and moments of insight mixed with boredom and chaos. Sixth grade is best: a limbic time between the simplicity of childhood and the maw of hormones and peer pressure to come. They are fresh and partly-formed, a putty of possibility.

I spot restlessness. Ten minutes to go, it's time to get them up and moving.

"What stops you from just floating off into space? Anyone."

"My mom would get mad." The serious Nestor again. Snickering around the room.

"True, and it's not recommended as a way of getting out of chores. Anyone else?"

"Gravity!"

"Yes. Gravity is one of those equal and opposite forces. We'll talk about it more in the next unit. But you actually pull on the Earth with the same force that the gigantic Earth pulls on you."

Darryl pipes up. "You're messing with us, Mr. Mac."

"No, Darryl, it's true. And it works with push as well as pull. If you jump, you push the Earth. It doesn't move very much since its mass is so big compared to your mass, but it does move. Let's try it."

Everyone just looks at each other.

"Come on, get up. Get up!"

They stand, tentatively, very unsure of what will come next.

"Now, on the count of three, jump. Jump as high as you can. Jump as if your young life depends on it. If we all jump together our forces will add and we'll move the Earth more. Next time we'll figure out how much we shifted the planet."

They're sheepish and excited in equal measure.

"One. Two. Three. Jump! My, what a ragged rabble you are. Let's try and do it all together. One. Two. Three. Jump! Almost. Nestor, you seem to be on a different planet, remind me not to dance with you. OK once more. One. Two. Three. Jump!"

I join in and we're still bouncing up and down when the bell rings. The point of the exercise is long forgotten, we're just happy, jumping fools.

■

Woodrow Wilson Middle School, Pasadena, in beautiful southern California. After seven years, I'm the most senior science teacher. I can't claim any particular expertise; the attrition rate is so high it's more a case of last man standing. They offered me a fat raise to go into admin, but I like the kids and the classroom far too much. Let other people push the paper and deal with the governing board. I'm careful to screw up just enough to stop the onerous jobs from being sent my way.

For a while, it looked like I would crash and burn. I had too much potty mouth and I was too free-wheeling and subversive for the liking of the Principal and the PTA Board. McEvoy in charge of children? Why he's little more than an overgrown child himself. I concede that, but I trimmed the sails of my vulgarity and avoided any epic meltdowns. Seven years in the harness smashes all Guinness records for McEvoy job longevity.

The students are half white, quarter black, and quarter Hispanic. Not each one but in the aggregate. It's a Wonder Bread sandwich of chocolate spread and peanut butter. They're savvy, innocent, naïve, jaded, bored, and blissed out on technology. A few are totally fucked up and disruptive but mostly they're just kids. I'm in the trenches of seeing just how hard grown-ups can make it to be a kid.

Pam works five miles away, in South Pas. She's the manager and recently part-owner of Nuts and Twigs, a small health food shop in a strip mall. Our schedules rarely let us lunch together. We met when I was living in an apartment in Pasadena and she had just moved here from the mid-West. The old Rialto near her work was showing Capra. Sullivan's Travels. I accidentally spilled coffee on her and we chatted. We bonded over black and white films and espresso. We dated. That turned smoothly into sharing an apartment and a year later we were married. It seemed like a natural thing to do; I can't remember who suggested it first. Houses are expensive in Pasadena, so we found a tidy tract home on a half-acre lot in Monrovia. I'm living a mid-scale version of the California dream—what's not to like?

∎

"Hitchcock's coming to the Rialto?"

"Mmm." She's doing accounts at the kitchen counter. I've set my pile of grading aside on the couch and am flipping through the local free paper. The radio is set on the smooth jazz station. I find it bland to the level of annoyance but by concentrating I can filter it out.

"Many in today?"

"Pretty typical," she says, and looks up from her work. "I'm going to have to let Julie go. She messes up too many orders and she's been mislabeling things. I don't know where her head is."

"Pam," I say gently. "You were nineteen once, too."

"Yes, but I always took care of my responsibilities."

I'm sure you did. I look at this woman. My wife. As she leans over the paperwork her bangs falling forward like a dark curtain. Pam is the most harmonious arrangement of the parts to the whole of any person I've ever met. Her face is wide, open, and framed by dark brown hair in a pageboy cut. She has large brown eyes, broad cheekbones, and smooth milky skin. The body: trim although tending to middle-aged fullness. She favors mid-length skirts and blouses, solid colors not patterns, and low pumps. Minimal jewelry and make-up. Her look speaks of reassurance rather than challenge.

And like the Edinburgh rock of my childhood—candy where the pattern runs all the way through—her personality is equally pleasing. Her vibe is calm and competent. She inspires instant confidence. I take for granted the fact that I can bring her insecurities and doubts, minor woes and frustrations, and she'll soak them up like the sea absorbs the rain. In our relationship she's placid and I'm mercurial, but tranquility rules because my tempests are in a dimly remembered past.

"Remember, Joy's coming this weekend."

"OK, right." I'd forgotten. Joy is her older sister, a nurse. "I've got poker tomorrow, and a school outing to La Brea tar pits on Saturday. I may not be back until mid-evening."

"Ian." Mild admonishment. "You know Joy likes your company. And I want you around to fend her off from talking about children."

The kid thing. For the first few years of our marriage I was evasive and reluctant. More recently, as end of the "window" looms for Pam, we've been giving it a go, but there are problems, her tubes may be blocked. I'm secretly relieved. But she's feeling the heat: of five girls in her large family, Pam's the only one who hasn't yet delivered any grandchildren.

"How about a hike on Sunday? Get above the smog layer."

"Joy's not in great shape. Maybe a short one."

"Right. Annapurna, the gentle route." I go back to my grading.

■

Sometime later, I sense Pam is staring at me. I pretend not to notice, then look up.

"Did I forget to take the recycling out?"

"No." She's still staring. It's unlike her. She usually speaks her mind. Directness rather than reflection is her style.

"An unsightly zit perhaps? My come-uppance for too much sugar."

She doesn't say anything. Now I'm unnerved.

"Ian, are you happy?"

"What a strange question."

It's not strange at all; it's one of the most important questions in the world. It's just unlike Pam to ask it.

"I'm not unhappy." I say. Is that true? I'm not sure.

"I see changes in you. Before you make a joke out of it, I don't mean mid-life crisis, sports cars, going to strip clubs. I sense some restlessness in you but it never gets to the surface."

"Honestly, Pam, I don't know what you're talking about."

"I know what you do, Ian. And I know what you like. But I

don't know what you truly want." She purses her lips. "It's hard to say this to someone you love and are married to. But the pieces don't add up to a whole."

∎

"Hit me." I say.

"Changing one. It's a total con. He's got bupkis."

"Look at his eyes, Eli. I dunno."

"I don't mind his luck. But he's such a smug fuck."

"And dashingly handsome, Walter, you forgot that," I add.

"Play the cards, McEvoy. And cut the crap."

"House rules," Eli's right, I am smug. "The host can goad his opponents."

Walter, Eli, Carlos, McEvoy.

Bank loan officer, doctor, ad man, teacher.

Negro, Jew, Latino, extreme Causasian.

Four middle tier, middle class professionals who gather on Friday evenings to play nickel-dime-quarter Texas Hold 'Em and live slightly larger and louder than they do the rest of the week. Wives complain—that's expected—but they know how harmless it is. There's nothing more sinister going on here than lite beer, nachos, Ben and Jerry's, and the odd cigar. Once Eli paid extra for a cable porn channel but it embarrassed us so much we settled back into football or baseball as the ambient video.

I fetch four more bottles from the fridge, open them up, and pass them around. I raise mine at a pause in the betting.

"Here's to quiet desperation."

"Joyless sex."

"Male pattern baldness."

"Balloon mortgage payments."

As often happens, I end up ahead. Nobody wins or loses more than twenty or thirty dollars at these games, but my success grates a little with the others. I don't calculate the odds like Walter, and I'm not a student of poker like Carlos. I simply win. And I know it's because I'm a stunningly good liar.

Lying comes effortlessly to me and I assume it always has. I see this as a burden and an obligation rather than an opportunity. I have to practice what I preach in the classroom, and Pam's guileless; I'm always straight with her. Like a 7th dan black belt, I can cause great harm. I must use my power wisely or not at all.

■

School's hit by flu so everything's in chaos. I'm sturdy and haven't succumbed but teachers are dropping like flies and we can't scrounge up enough subs to cover. I'm pulling twice my normal heavy load. So when our staff meeting is cancelled I'm happy to play hooky and meet Pam for a late lunch.

"Be with you in a minute, Ian."

She's in a powwow with her accountant in the back office. Nuts and Twigs has a large vitamin section and Pam says it accounts for most of the profits. I wander the aisles, musing over the enormous number of additives and remedies. If we need this stuff how did we survive when we were literally eating nuts and twigs on the savannah?

"This is a nice surprise."

"Aye, it's hellacious in the salt mine right now. Thought I'd come for a bit of conversation and sanity."

We're in a sushi bar nearby. After years out west, this Scotsman has finally traded his fried cod and chips for uni and wasabi.

"Was that you cooking the books?"

"We're doing fine. But I need to add some new lines. There's a lot of competition right now."

I switch tack. "Pam, how about a trip?"

"We're going to San Francisco. For your birthday. Did you forget? You're so absent-minded." In her navy blue jacket and skirt and white blouse, she looks supremely competent and professional. I admire her for that; I wing it and don't usually look the part.

"Not that. I was thinking of a meatier trip."

"Maybe. But it's a busy time of year. I have inventory to do and tax season coming up." She smooths her skirt. "And you know I can't take as much vacation as you."

It's a point of slight friction between us. Pam's her own boss so she has to work like stink. Small business is precarious but most years she makes more than I do. I get long summer vacations which I usually fill teaching at summer science camps for inner city kids, but those take me away from home and the pay's shite.

"Chicago? New York?" She suggests.

"No, I meant farther afield. More like Brazil or Nepal."

She looks askance at me.

"That would be expensive and not very practical. We have beaches and mountains here in California."

"I just thought it might be good to step out of our routine. Push the envelope a wee bit."

She regards me calmly. "Is everything alright, Ian?"

Yes and no. But I don't say this. I say yes, and leave it at that.

■

Sex with Pam is very tidy and squared away. I like turning her on and she makes love with careful vigor but the boundaries are clearly drawn. Sex happens in the bedroom and it happens at night. There's no opportunistic, half-clothed coupling in unfamiliar or semi-public locations. Muff diving and giving head are only for special occasions. Sex during her period is a big no. Anal sex is an emphatic no. Body oils and lace negligees define the boundary of acceptable erotica but they're to be sparingly used if at all.

■

Snap out of it, McEvoy.

I loathe self-pity, so when I find myself moping around the staff room during a lunch break I give myself a stern talking-to. There isn't one part of my life that's sub-par. I have work that matters, a loving wife, decent friends, and a life that flows with no major obstacles. I'm not smart enough to win a Nobel Prize, fast enough to play for Celtic, tall enough to play for the Celtics, or pretty enough to be on the TV, but so what, I knew all that years ago. As for craving adventure, the truth is I've been content being a homebody for nearly a decade.

I'm not depressed, I don't have existential angst, and my body is holding up nicely. Maybe you need a religious conversion, McEvoy. It's like converting your gas guzzler to biofuel; the conscience is eased and the planet is a wee bit happier. I'm happy to leave a door ajar for the possibility but I'm not going to bank on the outcome. My gut tells me this is the only hand of cards and I don't get to change them or sit out a round. Play your hand, McEvoy. Just play your hand.

That should've done it. The interior monolog and pep talk should have cast out all doubt and questioning and let me get to period six: geology of the Earth with my 7th grade class. But as the bell rings and the other teachers stream past me, I have an overwhelming sense of unreality. Not just the feeling of being apart from the flow of people and time around me. And not just the illusion of matter as substance, when it's in fact a shimmer of electrical forces. It's not even knowing the transience of those atoms in a fabric of time that dwarfs my small piece of cloth. It's a strong suspicion that the complex construct of my life is a shadowy chimera with no tether in reality.

Genius

"This side of the railings, Shona and Jada. If you toss that wrapper Tyler, I swear I'll make you clean up the litter in the whole parking lot. Darryl, no ice cream on the bus. Finish it right now."

We're on Mount Wilson. The hundred-inch telescope that Hubble used to discover the expansion of the universe is no longer any good for research but it's been opened for tour groups. We also get to climb up the solar heliostat tower. The Sun's projected image is the size of a manhole cover. We count fifteen sunspots; I tell them Galileo would have been proud.

The worst part of these trips is crowd control. In school, only the miscreants misbehave. It takes someone fresh out of Teacher Ed or totally devoid of self-confidence to lose control of a class. It's like the school building itself moderates behavior. Fair enough—it's a kind of prison. But out in the real world these bonds are loosened, and small primates must be true to their nature, I muse philosophically.

I watch the kids being totally engaged in the act of being an age they'll never experience again and I'm aware that I'm treading water, marking time. I love teaching and I love the kids but each year they advance or graduate while I stay put. Kids grow up to become adults but a dog is always a dog. Am I just a dog? I love teaching and it's a vocation, but perhaps I avoid difficult personal choices by doing this for a living?

"Mr. McEvoy, can we go look at that?"

"Wow, are they really jumping?"

"Hey, everyone, check this out!"

"Back to the bus!" I bellow.

Authority bent but not totally broken I lope after them to a railing at the edge of the parking lot. Beyond, there's a small area of sloping rocky ground then an almost sheer cliff face. Greater Los Angeles is spread out below like a vast puddle of houses and roads that have mysteriously crystallized into a rectilinear grid. The horizon isn't a sharp edge but rather it's a blurry band connecting endless sky to endless city.

A group of young men and a few women beyond the fence are assembling hang gliders. I've always thought of hang gliders as sails on metal frames, but that's as fanciful as imagining that clippers still ply the sea. These conveyances have diverse shapes and seem to be made of mylar and other high-tech materials. They're light enough that the skinny young men in front of us lift them effortlessly.

"Cool!"

"Awesome."

"I want to try that!"

Flattered by avid attention from twenty kids, the guy nearest the fence is chatting with some them. He wears a Caltech t-shirt.

"Hey, Mr. McEvoy, have you ever done that?" Darryl asks.

"No, I'm a bit of a landlubber."

"I bet he's scared." It's Rashid. That's fairly bold for him.

"Somebody's got to get you back to school," I point out.

"Ms. Peterson's on the bus too." Darryl again. The teacher's aide doesn't like to exert herself so she's reading a book on the bus.

"School's over anyway when we get back." Nestor chips in.

"Alright you lot, sightseeing's over, back to the bus." Authority is reestablished. "Anyway, there's no room for me on one of those."

Caltech shirt speaks up. "My rig can take two, no problem."

At this point the dynamic subtly shifts. Having been seconds from getting everyone back on the bus, I'm now faced with explaining why I'm not going to take a joy ride on a hang glider.

"This is silly. Get on the bus! We're done here."

Caltech shirt again. "It's totally safe. I've not lost anyone yet." He isn't making it any easier. He's enjoying the little charade.

"Go on, Mr. McEvoy."

"Please, just this once."

"I dare you." A quiet voice. Nestor! Small and unassuming in class, he's a delta dog choosing this moment to assert himself. Golding was right. Kill the pig and spill his blood is just a thin veneer away.

"Don't be ridiculous, Nestor. I'm not in 7th grade."

"I double dog dare you."

Nestor again. Now the group falls quiet. It would have been very easy to shut him down, bark an order to leave, and they would have filed meekly onto the yellow bus. But in the pantheon of challenges, verbal and physical, a Rubicon has been crossed. A double dog dare. You don't fuck with a double dog dare. Everything's on the line.

∎

"OK."

A loud cheer from the throng. I climb over the fence. Caltech shirt introduces himself as Günther, a grad student in Physics. He helps me into the harness and climbs in alongside me. He gives me a helmet, which I don't find reassuring given how high up we'll be. His parasail looks as inconsequential as a child's balloon. It's time for instructions.

"In the air this bar controls the motion. Left to go left, right to go right, push to go down, pull to go up."

"OK, got it." Very efficient teachers, these Germans.

"I'll be doing most of the flying."

"The take-off?" I ask, though I'm trying not to think about it.

"Just run as fast as you can."

"That's it?"

"Don't slow down and don't stop running. That's very important." He pauses to make the point. "If you do—big problems for us."

While putting on the harness I check out the take-off zone. It's thirty yards of gently sloping rock slab followed by a thousand foot drop. Other pilots pause to watch the newbie and my kids are pressed against the fence, mesmerized by the fact that their teacher is actually going to abandon them by jumping off a cliff.

Suddenly we're running. This is lunacy, I think. For one madcap moment our legs work against nothing and the sail drops sickeningly. Then it bites the air and we're thrust powerfully upwards until the mountaintop is below us and my kids and the bus are arranged like figures in a Toyland tableau.

"God, this is incredible. It's so smooth and quiet."

"Yes, I'm hooked. Doing this will probably add a year to my Ph.D. but I don't care."

We introduce ourselves aloft. Günther is from Baden-Baden on the edge of Germany's Black Forest. He's working in gravitational physics with a big name prof at Caltech.

I turn to him. "Interesting. You do battle with gravity in your spare time as well as in your day job."

"Yes, I want to know gravity in my gut as well as in my head."

"I'm in the physics trenches too," I say. "Teaching it to those kids we just left behind."

He's delighted. "When I was that age, it was one science teacher at my small school that got me into physics. I should introduce you to my advisor; you'd enjoy each other I think."

I neglect to mention to Günther that I don't have a science degree of any kind. It seems like such an inconsequential detail.

For a while I soak up the experience. I tuck away the thought that by abandoning my charges I've done something rash and foolish; I'm likely to be suspended, or maybe worse. The updraft from prevailing winds rushing up the face of Mount Wilson gave us a free thousand foot boost but now we're gradually descending. We slide along the ridge to La Cañada where the vast Jet Propulsion Lab complex nestles in the valley. Just past that I see the Rose Bowl and the old Colorado Street Bridge. We're low enough to make out people on the street. Günther points the sail with precision over a grid of streets towards a fancy neighborhood of large pink houses with Spanish tile roofs and swimming pools nestled among palm trees. The tidy Caltech campus slides into view below us.

"Günther, is what we're doing legal?"

"Approximately."

It's a physicist's answer and good enough for me. I'm pretty sure hang gliders have to land in the foothills just below Mount Wilson and we're now breaking a number of FAA rules. What an incredible way to get to work.

We circle like a metallic hawk over the campus, and then spiral in to an olive-tree-lined patch of grass between what look like dorms. We land with no more impact than from jumping off a low table. There are a dozen or so students nearby. Several give us brief but uninterested glances and the rest don't even look up.

"That was fabulous." I'm energized. "Thanks for the experience."

"Help me pack this up," says Günther. "Then I'll introduce you to the Bard of Gravity."

■

"Zell Abernathy. Call me Zell."

"Ian McEvoy. Call me McEvoy."

He's a tall and burly black man with a shaggy grey-tinged afro and a bushy mustache. He's quite sharply dressed for a scientist, clad in a midnight blue waistcoat covered with swirling bubble chamber tracks. His large hands are adorned with chunky rings.

"Zell's an unusual name, Zell."

"What, you don't think I look Jewish?" He laughs. "I'm a liberal misfit. Zell's my grandfather's surname. My father liked the sound of it. I got my mother's last name. She was an activist working with the Black Panthers. He was a San Francisco lawyer doing pro bono work on their cases."

"You're a child of the '60s then?"

"I was conceived in a swirl of sex and drugs and race riots. It's a pretty typical American story."

"Brothers and sisters?"

"No, just me. My parents have both passed on."

It takes an expert liar to spot another one but I'm certain that one or both of Zell's statements are not true. I only met him a minute ago so it would be easy to let it go. In for a penny, in for a pound.

"It's your business, Zell, but you're not being straight up."

The temperature drops and he stiffens. He glares at me and the silence in the room elongates. I'm ready to be dismissed but his face and body soften.

"What's your story, McEvoy?"

"Not much to tell. Born in Edinburgh. Hardscrabble childhood. Got out by going to sea. Bummed around the world for a while. Many odd jobs. Fell into teaching and it fit. Came to the land of opportunity."

It feels strange to realize, as I summarize my life in a few dozen words, that I'm not really condensing anything.

"Reinvented yourself, eh, McEvoy? Several times."

"You could say that." I change the subject. "But I'm thrilled to meet a famous scientist."

"Günther said you were teaching physics."

"At middle school, Zell. That's diddling in the hillocks compared to your Himalaya. I fell into that too. I started out teaching history and social science, but the science and math teachers were all bailing out and it was dire having it taught by the basketball coach, so I thought I'd pitch in. A bit of night school, a bit of reading, most of it I picked up as I went along."

"Some of the sharpest minds I've ever met were autodidacts."

"Zell, I feel like an unclean heathen sullying the temple."

"Try not to take a dump on the marble steps, OK?"

∎

We like each other immediately. I'm intimidated to be standing in the office of a Nobel-caliber physicist; it makes me think of the vast amount of physics I don't know and will probably never know. Zell is friendly and without pretense though I detect a substantial ego that might emerge when he's with his peers. With me, his banter comes very easily. I'm guessing that he's rarely called out the way I did just after we met.

I look at his whiteboard. Rather than the usual welter of math scrawl its large expanse holds a single equation: $G\mu\nu = 8\pi T\mu\nu$.

"I'm afraid to ask."

"Never be afraid of the truth, McEvoy." Zell gazes lovingly at the whiteboard. "There's more power there than in a decade of TV."

"What is it?"

"Einstein's field equation."

"Gravity, right? General relativity. 1916."

"Yes. Beauty is truth, truth beauty that is all ye know on Earth, and all ye need to know."

"Keats, right? Ode to a Grecian Urn. 1820-ish."

He raises his eyebrows and gives me an appraising look. "Yes. This is the symbolic form, so condensed it's useless for actual calculations. It unpacks into ten interrelated equations. But even that's extreme shorthand; laying out all the tensor components would take pages."

"Is that what's on your ring?" I've noticed some symbols on a gold pinky ring on his right hand.

"Yes. It's a brotherhood with very few members."

"And even now I can tell you're watering it down. Go on, hit me on the chin, I'm man enough to take it."

"OK, you asked. General relativity involves the solution of a set of ten coupled hyperbolic-elliptic nonlinear partial differential equations." He winks. "Of course, I usually save that for when I'm out a date and trying to get laid."

"I'm a ploughman with the math, Zell. What does it mean?"

"GR in a nutshell? Mass curves space and space is curved by the matter in it. John Wheeler put it this way: matter tells space how to curve and curved space tells matter how to move. The left side of the equation, G, contains all the information about how space is curved. The right side, T, contains all the information about the location and motion of matter, and energy, which Einstein showed is equivalent to matter."

"You make it sound simple."

"It is simple, if by simple you mean elegant. Of course working out the math can be fiendish. I remember waking up with the cold sweats in grad school because I couldn't solve a GR problem. In physics there are technicians, grinders who just crunch through the calculations. But there are far fewer, maybe a few dozen worldwide, who understand it at a deeply intuitive level."

"How does it speak to you?"

"I experience relativity just below my solar plexus, about here." He points to the center of his rather expansive gut.

∎

"How was it today, Ian?"

"Golden."

"No more problems with the ADD kid?"

"He's not acting out but I think he's filching school supplies. I've got him down to see the counselor tomorrow."

Pam and I navigate in the confined space of our kitchen, moving easily and seamlessly around each other. She's late for a networking meeting for small business owners and I'm heading back for parent's night at the school. We're both eating on the run.

"Don't you want to throw some sprouts on that?" She looks in mock horror at my sandwich.

"And spoil the symphonic texture of all this meat?"

"Ian, really, take some carrots or an apple with you."

"I was thinking more of a can of Jolt and a Mars bar."

"If you follow my advice, your colon will thank you."

"If my colon starts talking, lock me in a rubber room."

It's one of our little rituals, to play these exaggerated roles. In truth, I can happily go a week without meat, and I watch out for the cholesterol and the salt. And Pam may be the owner of a heath food shop but she's no dietetic saint; I've caught her rummaging through my emergency stash of candy bars.

Our relationship is built on doing. We're good at dovetailing two busy lives but less good at communicating through the place Zell had spoken of, the gut. I don't fault Pam. She's loyal, honest, and cheerful. She has less artifice or guile than anyone I know. So what about you, McEvoy? Where do you stand when it comes to artifice?

■

I look at the scrap of paper in my hand. It's the right address but Zell must have made a mistake. A dingy neon sign reads "The VaVoom GoGo Club." It's a seedy part of Burbank near the airport. Zell said to meet him there for a lunchtime primer on relativity and gravity. Inside, it's dark and a loud Donna Summer groove hits me; my ears and eyes slowly adjust. I spot Zell's raised hand and beaming brown face in a booth in the corner. Five Japanese salarymen are deep in conversation at one table. The bartender is reading a tabloid paper. Apart from that, the place is empty. Two strippers gyrate lethargically near the end of the runway with flashing Christmas lights. On a salubriousness scale from one to ten, The VaVoom GoGo Club is barely a two.

Zell orders bourbon, straight up. Makers Mark. I stick with a lite beer, feeling a bit self-conscious about my thickening middle, a battle Zell has already lost.

"How's the blackboard jungle?"

"Same as ever," I say. "I liked the way Sidney Poitier graduated from being the student in '55 to being the teacher in '67."

"To Sir, With Love. McEvoy, you're full of surprises. A film buff."

"Aye, but I'm here for weightier matters. Thanks for giving me the time. I'm sure you've got lots on the go."

"A pleasure. Your casual cynicism never fooled me. You're hungry for knowledge." He sweeps his arm across the tacky tableau around us. "And I have trouble getting colleagues to come with me. Let's eat! We'll start with Newton."

So it is that Zell begins to school me weekly on gravity. I relish his quicksilver intellect and feel like Mercury orbiting close to his intense light and energy. His choice of venues is unconventional, to say the least. The VaVoom GoGo Club is so loud that we have to sit close and almost shout to be heard, but Zell is clearly partial to the sensual beat of Rick James, Barry White, and the diva of divas, Donna Summer. He starts each session with a neat pile of cocktail napkins in front of him, which he scribbles on with a black felt marker.

"Before Newton, Earth and sky were irreconcilably different. It was very bold to imagine the motions of everyday objects and dots of light in the sky might be due to the same force."

"How did he make the connection?"

"He knew that gravity was a force that declined with the square of the distance."

"Right, I've got that down pat." On this, I'm confident. "You move two objects twice as far apart and gravity is four times smaller, three times further apart, it's nine times smaller, and so on."

"So he realized that the falling apple and the orbiting Moon follow the same force."

"You're not gonna tell me he really got bonked by an apple?"

"No. But I made a pilgrimage to his childhood home in England a few years ago, and there's an old apple orchard out back."

He beams with pleasure at this thought. Zell's concentration is formidable. He's not only able to filter out the music but he doesn't appear even slightly interested in the curves and undulations of the strippers. I'm having slightly more trouble maintaining focus.

"OK, so what's the connection?" I yell.

"Newton could easily calculate how fall an apple or any object will fall under the action of gravity in one second. The Moon is sixty times further from the center of the Earth than we are or he was, so by the inverse square flaw, the force on the Moon is 3600 times smaller. He then calculated how far the Moon would be deflected toward the Earth in one second. It was the same distance!"

"So the falling apple and the orbiting Moon obey the same force?" I'm shouting above the booming bass line.

"Exactly. Heaven and Earth unified."

"That's brilliant!"

"It's dangerous to be too brilliant," Zell winks at me. "Newton died a virgin."

He's very methodical in his tutoring. He numbers each napkin so I have a pile of "notes" to refer to. After an hour of lecturing and three shots of bourbon he beckons the strippers over. I fear he's going to mix theoretical physics with lap dancing, but they've partially covered up with silk dragon robes and are on their break. They each lean over and peck Zell on the cheek.

"Bree, Jazmine, meet McEvoy. My most promising student."

They nod in greeting. Jazmine has slid into the booth next to me and her parted gown reveals fantastic and unnatural cleavage. Bree sits next to Zell and is similarly and fabulously endowed. The three of them chat for a while. Zell seems to know and empathize with all of their tribulations: dead-beat boyfriends, unscrupulous employers, problems with child care. He isn't just a good lecturer, he's a good listener.

"Bye, Bree. Bye, Jasmine."

"See you next week, Zell."

The girls each kiss me lightly on the cheek; I'm quite chuffed. Zell gives them lifts home because they live in dangerous neighborhoods. I've done research on Zell. He's a physics wunderkind. Degree from Berkeley at age 17. Ph.D. three years later. Caltech snapped him up and made him a full professor at thirty, the youngest ever. He's won the Fields Medal and he's a Fellow of the National Academy and has a dozen honorary degrees. I'm surprised that Zell is willing to share his time with me; his brain and career are powered by rocket fuel while my two-stroke motor chugs along on two star. But I'm proud to call this iconoclastic genius my new friend.

Lookback Time

I'm sprawled on the floor working my way through a fat stack of chemistry workbooks when Pam gets home. One of her two assistants has quit so she has to cover evenings in the shop three days a week. By the time she gets home she's beat. She pours a glass of wine and flops onto the sofa.

"This isn't what I imagined when I bought in. I thought it would get easier because I could delegate."

"You're too good-natured. Rose is taking advantage of you." Rose, the other part-owner, is hard-nosed and ambitious and very happy to let Pam do more than her fair share.

She sighs. "I know. But we seemed to have more time for each other before I took this on, and before you got promoted and they upped your workload."

I look up and she's standing over me. She reaches for my hand and tugs.

"Come on, Ian. Put that aside. Let's make love."

This is unusually direct for Pam. This isn't our "night" so it usually ends with Turner Classic on TV or a rented video and either or both of us falling asleep while reading in bed.

In the bedroom, we follow habit. I close the blinds while she turns down the bed. She lights the candles while I put on the soft jazz that she prefers. We brush our teeth side by side. We undress and put our clothes in neat piles on bedside chairs.

I sit on the edge of the bed. She approaches and places her hands on my shoulders. Her tits are full and milky and delicately veined and she likes it when I play with them so I massage them and take her nipples into my mouth until they're fat and hard. She works me with her hand. We follow our loose script but she's much more aroused than usual. Her tongue probes more, her grip is stronger, her skin hotter. With one of her legs raised over my shoulder I slide into her easily. I hook her other leg over my shoulder and press down on her folded body and deep into her until she reaches her orgasm; I follow her moments later.

■

"Whoa. That rocked." I'm dripping and sated.

She's flushed and spread-eagled. She rolls over onto her side and looks at me.

"Ian, we don't have many moments like that."

"Well, we don't have sex that often." I'm defensive.

"You know that's not what I meant."

"Och, we share moments. Making an Italian meal together. Putting our feet up and watching a Bogart movie. Chatting on the phone while you're stuck on the 210 and I'm crawling along the 134."

"Yes, but we don't have a connection like that very often, where the other person matters more than anything else in the world."

I'm quiet. It's true.

"Maybe this happens to all married couples," she says. "But I don't care about them. I care about us. I want us to work."

And suddenly we're slap bang in the middle of one of those times after sex when the gal wants to talk about the relationship and the guy wants to go to sleep or flick on the TV.

"There's no one else, Pam. I'm true to you."

"Yes, though I'm not happy with the places that physics

professor takes you. Why can't he teach you at Caltech or in his house?"

"Zell's a true original. I don't touch the strippers, though I might ogle them a wee bit." I blush at this admission.

"I know. I don't think you're unfaithful. It's something else."

I dread what's coming.

"I don't know who you are, Ian McEvoy."

Total silence. One of the candles gutters out. Inconsequential jazz flutters in the background.

"You know everything I do. I don't keep secrets."

"Now. And maybe since we've been together. But I know very little about your life before me. Just little vignettes, tidy little stories. We've never been to visit your family and they've never come to see us. You seem to have almost no friends that predate us. It's unsettling."

"C'mon Pam. We can't afford to go to Scotland and you know what little family I have is fucked up. I got my life on track when I moved out here and met you. I don't look back."

But she's right. The past nine years are like a path through a forest with plenty of landmarks. Looking back further, the path disappears in a trackless wilderness. Everything earlier has the flavor of things I've been told rather than things I've experienced.

"Ian, I like it that you enjoy the moment and are optimistic about the future. But the past matters. It's who you are too."

She touches my tattoos, and the scars on my forearms. "When I hear your stories, it sounds like you're telling them about a different person, like you don't even believe them yourself."

There's nothing to say, so I say nothing.

"There's something else."

I wait. When she speaks her voice is very soft.

"Everyone has tics and favorite expressions, and I love your sense of humor. But you say things to me with no apparent awareness that you've said them before."

She pauses. "It's as if you're hollowed out."

Neither of us speaks. The room holds its breath. I avoid her eyes and stare helplessly at my bare feet.

"Pam, this is me. This is all there is." But dread seeps through me. I'm afraid that everything I say and do is an echo. Is my life is a series of meaningless, repeating epicycles?

Tears run down her cheeks and follow the folds at the corners of her mouth. "I can't live with a shadow person or with someone I don't know. I've said this before, but nothing changes. Please figure it out, Ian. And if you can't, get help."

▪

Zell arranges for my class to visit his lab at Caltech. Theorists don't normally get to work with hardware but he's so preeminent he's been named the lead investigator of a visionary new experiment to detect gravitational waves. A prototype for the detector is housed deep under the physics building. Tons of ultra-fast electronics and lasers rest on a steel slab that floats on mercury to insulate the gear from possibility of slight tremors; we're just thirty miles from the San Andreas Fault.

"Darryl, you come out of there!"

"Nestor, put the klystron down."

"Abby, I said no gum on this trip. I don't want to have to guess where it'll end up."

I appreciate Zell's invitation but the tour's giving me an ulcer. There are hundreds of ways my kids can get in trouble in a physics lab, most of which involve damage to very expensive equipment. We have four grad students to act as minders, but they're unaccustomed to eleven year olds so they're useless.

"Who wants to see how gravity really works?" Zell's dapper and in great form. His waistcoat today has a set of four colorful paintings of Albert Einstein, a riff on Warhol's montage of Marilyn Monroe.

Hands shoot up and the kids crowd forward. They recognize Zell as a showman.

"What's in this tube?" He holds up a clear tube that's a few inches across and as tall as he is, sealed at both ends.

"A golf ball?"

"Very good! And what's in this tube?" He holds up a second one that's similar.

"A moth?"

"A bit of Kleenex?"

"A feather?"

"Excellent! A feather." He lowers his voice so they'll pay closer attention. "Here's all you need to know about these tubes: the air has been sucked out. The only force in there is gravity."

They're all watching raptly. I wish I could grab their attention this completely in class.

"When I turn these tubes upside down and the golf ball and the feather start falling together which one do you think will reach the bottom first?"

"That's easy!"

"The golf ball, of course!"

"Do you think we're morons?"

"OK. You seem quite sure. But let's be fair and vote. How many of you think the golf ball will reach the bottom first?"

Every hand goes up.

"How many think the feather will reach the bottom first?"

Nobody moves.

"Let's see." Like an expert cheerleader he twirls the tubes through one hundred and eighty degrees. The two objects sink like stones and land at exactly the same time. Gasps.

∎

I continue my weekly tutelage with Zell. He's mortified to find out how little I know of Los Angeles so he decides to vary the locales.

"You're a flatlander, McEvoy. You need to get out more; this is a great city."

"That's harsh, Zell. Monrovia is quite cosmopolitan."

"Don't pull my chain."

"Upton Sinclair lived there. We were declared an All American

City by the National Civic League in 1995."

"I'm not impressed."

"Try this. Patrick McDonald opened an unassuming hamburger joint at the Old Monrovia airport in 1927. Decades later, Ray Kroc pressured his sons into selling out. The rest is history. By my estimate, Monrovia has increased the mass of the citizens of the U.S. by a million tons and killed two hundred thousand of them, more than all wars since WWII."

"Now I'm impressed. You're a mine of truly useless facts."

"Thanks, Zell. Coming from a Fellow of the National Academy of Sciences, that means a lot to me."

Our second stop is an ice cream parlor on Melrose in Hollywood. The clientele is yuppies and punks, but these punks are colorful and sanitized compared to the punks of my youth, who were scabby and punctured and looked like they'd give you head lice just by looking at you. The next week we meet at a taco bar on Figueroa. It's the heart of gang-banger country and once again I'm amazed by how well Zell can shut out the potential hazards in his surroundings and concentrate on the physics at hand.

After that is a strip club in the Valley, Canoga Park, where Zell's familiar with all the strippers and they greet him like a favorite uncle. I'm suspicious that these relationships aren't platonic; Zell admits to being divorced three times and he's a large man with lusty appetites for most things. Following that are a conveyor belt sushi bar in Little Tokyo and an Anglophile pub in Santa Monica stuffed with Toby jugs and hunting kitsch. The variety seems endless, but I deduce that he's partial to acres of voluptuous flesh—strip clubs form a leitmotif of my education.

Poker night has fallen by the wayside. I'm consumed by Zell and his larger than life intellect and world. I feel a pang of regret for the loss of that easy camaraderie.

■

"My turn to pick."

Zell climbs into my beat-up Mazda. Instead of going to a locale of his choosing for our physics lesson, I pick him up at Caltech and say I'll decide this week.

"Which side of the tracks are you taking me to, McEvoy? Should I have brought my piece?"

He's joking but I can tell that Zell is uneasy as we drive down the Pasadena Freeway. He's used to being in control and in charge. After twenty minutes on the Harbor Freeway, we take surface streets to a non-descript jazz club in Inglewood. Dee Dee's.

The dozen or so tables are sparsely occupied. Zell can't get his favorite whiskeys so he settles for Red on the rocks. When the band comes out and he sees the bass player he freezes. I guessed right. Without saying a word Zell gets up and walks out of the back of the club. I follow. He's pacing in a flickering pool of neon light.

"What the hell are you're doing!" He's livid. I worry that I've really screwed up. "How dare you interfere in my personal life! Who do you think you are?"

"I'm just putting it out there. My sis is a hard core druggie so I do know how that feels."

"McEvoy, you crossed the line." He's still pacing and fuming.

I try to catch his eye. "But Zell, it doesn't help you to pretend he doesn't exist."

We drive back in silence, with the physicist brooding beside me. When I looked up his storied accomplishments, I found a youthful picture that made me wonder; someone standing next to him looked so similar they had to be kin. It took some work but I tracked down a minor jazzman called Nathan Abernathy who was about Zell's age and from Berkeley. I watched him play in a couple of seedy bars down in Compton. At one, a casual conversation with the manager confirmed his talent and tendency to disappear for weeks. At another, as I stood next to him at the urinal I saw red eyes, track lines on his forearms, and gauntness. A smackhead. Zell minus a hundred pounds.

■

I resign myself to having blown it with Zell. Weeks pass and I'm consumed by the hurly burly of teaching. Then I get a call. With no mention of what happened, he asks if my physics class would like a treat for spring break. He connects me with an astronomer he knows at the SETI Institute up in Mountain View, near San Francisco. I piece together a five day trip that starts at the Stanford Linear Accelerator, passes through San Francisco to visit the Exploratorium, then heads north to Hat Creek where an array of radio telescopes are beginning a new search for intelligent aliens.

I'm exhausted by the time we're on the third lag of the trip. Pam and I never had kids but I have eternal status as the meta-parent for three dozen eleven-year-olds. Ms. Peterson, the teacher's aide, nudges me awake. We're at the Hat Creek Radio Observatory in the foothills of the Sierra Nevada. Luckily, the observatory's used to school tours, so the locals escort my class off to see the radio dishes. I drag myself into the cafeteria and buy a large coffee.

∎

"Mr. McEvoy? Mr. McEvoy?"

I jolt upright. "We can pay if there's damage. We have insurance." The words tumble out automatically. I'd rested my head on the table and fell asleep, coffee untouched.

"It's OK, there's no problem. Your class is in good hands. I got a call from Zell Abernethy that you'd be coming up. I'm Carol Mornay, project scientist for the Allen Array."

"Hi, very pleased to meet you. I probably look terrible. These little bleeders can take it out of you."

"You have a hard job, Mr. McEvoy, teaching is a real vocation. My father was a teacher."

Carol Mornay is about fifty, with short salt and pepper hair and sparkling eyes. She's dressed in dark and conservative clothes but something about her says that's just for public consumption.

To help me revive, we move outside into the bracing spring air. We're at four thousand feet altitude and the snow on the high Sierras almost extends to the plateau where we stand. Dozens of white radio dishes are scattered around us, each one twenty-five feet across and looking like a glorified satellite dish.

"I know what you're thinking," she says. "They're not impressive. We went for a larger number of small high quality dishes rather than one very large one. We have 40 now, and there will be 350 when we are fully operational. By combining the radio signals, we can act as if we had a much larger telescope than we do."

"Why radio telescopes rather than optical?"

"Good question. Maybe we should back up. What we're doing here is SETI, the search for extraterrestrial intelligence."

"I bet you get tired of the little green men jokes."

"I do. But I want people to understand." She radiates a steely and resolute commitment to her subject.

"My kids have grown up on sci-fi and X-Files reruns. Many of them think we've got aliens stored on ice."

"I know." She sounds weary of dumbed-down alien monoculture. "But the science of the search is as exciting as the fictional stories. It starts with the fact that there are probably a hundred million planets capable of supporting life in the Milky Way galaxy."

I know this. But how? I can't recall reading any book or article on the subject.

"So," she continues. "There are many biological experiments out there. It only takes a small fraction of them to have evolved species with our level of intelligence and technology for there to be potential pen pals."

"OK, I'll buy that." I decide to play devil's advocate. "But maybe intelligence and technology aren't inevitable. Look at Earth. It took four billion years for evolution to produce us and there have been hundreds of millions of species, but we're the only ones with cell phones and SUV's."

She smiles. "You're a perceptive debater. However, consider this. There have been stars making carbon and the other heavy elements needed for life since a few hundred million years after the big bang. That's thirteen billion years for planets to have biological evolution. Earth might be unique but it's very unlikely. In fact, there may be Earth clones where life is eight billion years ahead of us."

I nod. "Aye, I get it. If we traveled into space and found a planet with pond scum, we wouldn't be impressed because it was four billion years behind us. But there may be Earths out there with four billion years on us. They'd be to us as we are to pond scum!"

"Exactly. It's called the timing argument. We've had technology and the ability to travel in space for such a small fraction of our time of evolution, anyone we encounter will logically be far more advanced than we are."

"Won't they just laugh at our pathetic radio telescopes?"

"Possibly. But we use radio waves to communicate since they're the most efficient. Radio waves take the least energy to create and they easily penetrate gas and dust. We're also using pulsed lasers since that technology can outshine the entire light of a star for tiny fractions of a second."

I struggled to absorb her arguments. I waved at the radio dishes around us. "What can this lot do?"

She glowed with pride. "In just one year this array will be able to gather a thousand times more data than has been acquired in nearly 50 years of similar searches. It can detect radio waves beamed from the equivalent of Arecibo—Earth's largest radio dish—out to 1000 light years, a distance that includes a million stars."

"That's a lot of alien real estate. What have you heard so far?"

Her face falls slightly. "Nothing. But the game is just beginning. I've bet my whole career on this."

I think of people who never have a hit record or get passed over for CEO or never get their shot to go into space, after a career spent trying. It doesn't seem so quixotic to listen for signals from intelligent aliens when the consequences of success are so enormous. There's a question I've been itching to ask.

"Dr. Mornay. Your personal story sounds very familiar. Were you involved in that Carl Sagan film about alien hunting?"

"Contact. Yes." She smiles modestly. "Ellie Arroway, the

heroine played by Jodie Foster, was a composite of me and another woman scientist. The name's a hybrid of Eleanor Roosevelt and an Anglicized version of the hero in Voltaire's Candide."

■

I debrief Zell on my meeting with Carol Mornay. He claps his hands in delight as I tell him about her speculations about aliens.

"I love it! They say I'm mad to be looking for ripples in space-time. I'm glad there are scientists even more out there than me."

"Is that what you really think, Zell?"

"No. But I think it's a long shot." He looks around. "What's a guy got to do to get a drink around here?"

We're in a strip club in Duarte, but one with an unusual thematic twist. It's a faux cantina decked out to look like a family restaurant. The waitresses are topless and have big hair, plastic chili peppers in place of g strings, and garter belts in the colors of the Mexican flag.

"Herradura anejo, double shot, no salt, lime on the side. And some generic hop-inflected water for my low rent friend here."

Zell always orders top tier: $15 drinks in even the sleaziest places. He doesn't know any of the conchitas who serve us so I assume we're scouting a new location. I regard this larger-than-life man.

"Zell, you don't sound Jewish."

"Wait until you hear me speaking in tongues."

"Zell, you don't look black."

"I believe I have transcended race and color."

"Zell, you don't smell like a physicist."

"Watch it, kilt boy, I'll take you down."

We settle into the weekly lesson, doing battle against the canned Mariachi music. I collect the pile of cocktail napkins and put them in my pocket. I had a scare the week before when Pam discarded my whole lecture series, assuming the napkins to be trash. Now I keep them in a shoebox on a high shelf in the bedroom closet.

■

The second round of drinks arrives and Zell raises his glass.

"McEvoy, thanks. Really. Some have said that I'm a bully and an egomaniac. It takes a real friend to push back against that."

I drink but am not sure what we're toasting.

"I reached out to my brother Nathan." He looks glum. "Physics is hard but this is much harder. Last week we visited my father."

I say nothing. When we first met he'd said his parents were dead. A waitress walks by and winks at us. Zell swirls the tequila around in his glass and stares into it.

"I don't know about this alien business, Zell. Part of me thinks it's bogus, because they have to make unreasonable and anthropocentric assumptions about technology and communication."

"All true. I have the same issue in my gravity wave project—not knowing what a signal will look like. In their case they don't have to decode the signal and understand the message. That happens all the time in science fiction but language is so culture-specific that true communication is extremely unlikely. We can't talk to apes yet we share 99% of our DNA with them. What chance do we have of being understood by an alien of unknown function or form?"

"Then what's the point of the experiment?"

"You have to rule out all natural causes. If you find a pulsed signal with a pattern that's not random but not caused by any known natural phenomenon you've hit the jackpot. But that's hard because ruling out natural causes assumes you can recognize all natural phenomena."

Zell slams his shot back, brushes the residue from his mustache, and raises a chunky ringed finger to order another one.

"What about the timing argument?"

"It's a good one. Logically, we're unlikely to be the first civilization to go technological in the galaxy. If we're not, the alpha dogs will be pretty impressive."

"You mean phasers and transporters and such?"

"Maybe. But that's kid stuff. A physicist I know at Princeton did a calculation of the capabilities of a civilization that could harness all the energy from a star. Earth intercepts only a billionth of the Sun's light and we don't use that very efficiently, so this is a civilization using a trillion times more energy that we do. They'd do it by building a hollow sphere around the star to capture all the energy. It sounds ridiculous but it's just a few centuries extrapolation of our current technology."

"What could they do?"

"They could make a Truman Show simulation of our world."

"Fake dome and all that?"

"Better. They could render the surface of the Earth in great detail and a small fraction of the crust since we've barely scratched it. They'd construct the Moon and all the planets we've visited but just as hollow spheres since we've only seen the surfaces. They'd paint the fake sky with the stars and galaxies at the same level of detail we see with our telescopes and we'd be none the wiser."

"Wait a minute. That's ridiculous. Why would they do that?"

"Who knows. All sorts of reasons. The point is they could. Without breaking a sweat."

"It seems like a stretch, Zell."

"Not at all. Aliens with this capability almost certainly exist. How do we know it hasn't already happened?"

As usual, Zell likes to challenge, but now he's messing with me. I reel with the possibilities. We drink in silence for a while.

"Zell, we've talked about gravity up, down, and sideways. But you haven't told me much about your gravity wave experiment. I'm really curious."

He looks at me as if he's very carefully weighing me up.

"How much truth can you take, McEvoy?"

Ripples in Space

I've killed a man.

■

I wake up with a start, my body rigid. Luckily, Pam's in a deep sleep and doesn't stir. No dream comes with the awareness, no story, no broader context. Just raw, absolute certainty that I've murdered someone. I lie awake staring at the plaster swirls on the ceiling, dimly visible in the streetlight that filters through the curtains. A dog barks. An occasional car passes. Hours later, I'm still lying awake as dawn finally comes.

●

Zell's in his office with a couple of visiting colleagues so I wait in the corridor. Mixed in with posters announcing conferences and a bulletin board with job openings there are a series of framed bets. Twenty years ago Zell and Stephen Hawking began challenging each other with wagers on gravity. Each wager is written out and signed, set below a photo of them. Zell's so massive compared to Hawking it looks like he could pick him up like a rag doll.

When Hawking was having doubts about the inevitability of the singularity he bet that black holes would not exist. Zell happily took that bet and won a case of Kentucky bourbon when Cygnus X-1 was shown indisputably to be a star that had collapsed beyond the event horizon. Next was a bet on Hawking's "no hair" hypothesis for black holes; Zell conceded that and ponied up a three-year subscription to the satiric British magazine Private Eye. Then there's one so esoteric I can't make head or tail of it, something on the conformal nature of a Brans-Dicke metric. Anyway, Hawking won lifetime membership of the Cambridge Rowing Club for that one. I'm musing on Hawking's choice of prize—with his wasted body he was light enough to be cox, perhaps they prop him up in the stern and he calls out strokes in an amplified mechanical voice—when Zell appears at my shoulder.

"Ah, another of my vices. Gambling."

"You're down two to one, Zell. Hawking has your number."

"This will tie things up," He walked over to another bet. It was the only one that hadn't been stamped paid in full.

I read it. Something about information loss in black holes. "Explain it to me, will you?"

"Stephen showed in 1982 that things falling into black holes didn't violate the law of conservation of energy. Virtual pairs of particles and antiparticles are in constant flux at the event horizon, and when one disappears inside its partner escapes. If the antiparticle escapes it will quickly meet a particle and annihilate into radiation, so the net effect is that the black hole emits radiation. Are you following me?"

"Barely. But I'm chuffed that you think I can keep up."

"So black holes emit a feeble amount of radiation and they've a temperature as well as a mass. It's called Hawking radiation."

"What's that got to do with information?"

"Radiation is unstructured. It has low information content or high entropy. I pointed out that when an object falls into a black hole its structured information is lost to the universe because it's replaced by radiation. Toss an encyclopedia in and the information's gone forever. But if you fall in with the encyclopedia you know it still exists. Stephen didn't like this paradox so he bet that somehow the information is not destroyed." Zell gives me a conspiratorial grin, relishing the fact that he may have put one over on Hawking.

"What does he have in mind?"

"He thinks partial information about everything that went into a black hole is coded on the event horizon. Like a hologram. He even speculates this is true of the universe itself."

"You sound skeptical."

"I'm a hard-nosed theorist, not given to flights of fancy." A wide smile. "I think Stephen's going down this time."

"And the bet?"

"A fine encyclopedia, of course. The 1883 first edition of Burton's translation of the Kama Sutra." He sees my eyebrows rise. "I know what you're thinking, McEvoy. But the Kama Sutra's not just about sex; that's only one chapter. It's a manual on how to live a sensually full life."

"Umm. How on Earth are you going to settle that one?"

"Not on Earth, in space. The only real way to resolve it is to do an experiment. We'll build a pair of machines or robots that can generate coherent quantum information across the distance between them. It's called entanglement and it's been done in the lab over a distance of a few meters, so this is harder but not impossible. We'll toss one of the robots into the black hole and see what happens to the quantum state of its partner. Bingo."

.

"Zell, I've mentioned this before, but you're not very black."

We're sitting in the tea garden of the Huntingdon Gardens, a very genteel choice for the raunchy physics prof.

"You'd prefer that I spout ebonics?"

"No, it's just that you don't seem to have a color at all. Back where I'm from we get so many stereotypes of African-Americans."

"It's true, I wear my race and culture lightly on my sleeve. In the world I inhabit the currency is ideas and intellect and it really doesn't matter a damn what color you are. Most of the time…"

"But you must be an icon. What fraction of physicists is black?"

"Less than a percent." He chuckles. "There's a lot of white bread in my game. My mother instilled in me a sense of the struggles she went through, but she buffered me from that growing up. She never let me have any doubt that I could be whatever I wanted to be."

"That's special."

"Yes, it is."

We admire the soothing formal gardens for a while. Zell tells me Hubble's papers are on display at the Huntingdon so we spend some time looking at the notebooks of the man who expanded the universe.

"Zell, I need your help." We're walking in the gardens again.

"You look very serious. Are you in trouble with the law?"

"No, no, nothing like that." As far as I know.

"It's hard to explain." I struggle to choose words. "I feel like I'm coming unglued. I have memory fragments that make no sense. When I think back to childhood and early life I have recollections but they're flat, two dimensional. They're isolated and there's no connective tissue to make it feel like a real life. When I try and draw from the well of my life I come up dry. Zell, it's scaring me."

"I think I have an explanation for that."

"Go on."

"In relativity, space and time are connected. We think of space as something we occupy and time as something that flows. They seem to have nothing to do with each other. But there are some situations with space-like and time-like aspects. Add in the concept of curvature and you can have regions when space is pinched off and discontinuous, we call that a wormhole, and situations where time is pinched off too. It could lead to disconnected memories, amnesia, even precognition."

"Zell, are you bullshitting me?"

"Yes, I'm bullshitting you."

"What do you really think?"

He pauses and stares at me.

"I think you're crazy, McEvoy."

"Oh, God."

Zell is somber; all hint of levity has gone. "There's something that I haven't told you about myself: I have total recall. It's a blessing and a curse. It's been useful in my career and for my learning, but because everything's retained, I have to continuously and consciously purge my memory to avoid being saturated."

"That's amazing. I'd love to have a photographic memory."

"No, you'd probably hate it."

He reaches into his jacket pocket and pulls out a well-thumbed black notebook. I've seen him use it to jot down ideas.

"Soon after we first met," he continues. "I noticed something very peculiar. You'd repeat yourself from one meeting to the next or from one month to the next."

Pam said this to me too. "So? Everyone has catchphrases."

"Yes, but these were entire chunks of speech, whole paragraphs, word for word the same. My total recall allowed me to recognize them and match them when they came around again. Look."

I flip through his notebook. Every few pages, marked with an

"M," he has written a verbatim quote, sometimes a hundred words long. They all look like things I would have said. There are dozens of them. Some are repeated three or more times.

I blanch and fight back a wave of nausea.

"The odds of that happening by chance are infinitesimal."

"Christ, I'm a fucking automaton!"

"No, McEvoy, I've watched you exercise free will. But something very strange is going on in your brain."

■

We approach the problem scientifically. Psychotherapy will be the last resort. A week later we're in Chinatown eating dim sum. Zell is invested in the power of the brain so he naturally starts the therapy with willpower.

"Let's get started." He pops a shrimp dumpling into his mouth. "I'll take care of the food, you need to concentrate."

"I'm brain putty for you, Zell. Tell me what to do."

"Think of the most distant memory you have. Bring it clearly into your mind, then push on its boundary, test its limits, try to expand its details or go back even further."

I still my mind and slowly shut out the oriental chatter around me. I reach for an old memory. A good memory.

"I'm in the living room of a small house, my grandfather's house. He's sitting in a chair reading from Just So Stories by Kipling. I'm at his feet in front of the fire and I'm fascinated by his boots. They're hobnail boots he's had for ages, since the army. He's a retired miner. He coughs a lot. I'm happy. I'm ten years old."

"Good, good." Zell says. "Now think of something earlier. The first time you read with him. Remember when you could sit on his lap."

I try. "No good, Zell. The memory's discrete and limited; it doesn't connect to anything else."

"Never mind, try a different starting point."

I refocus. "OK. I'm in a park with my mum and my sister Annie. Annie's in a pram so I must be about eight. It's a blustery day. I'm happy playing on the swings and the roundabout. Annie's asleep. My mum's sitting on a park bench crying, bawling her eyes out. I ask her why she's crying but she just shakes her head over and over."

"Now think of a time when Annie wasn't there, before she'd been born, or think of why your mom was crying."

"No good, Zell. These memories are like tumblers of liquid, they contain just so much and no more."

Willpower fails. Each memory fragment seems unconnected to the larger whole. There's no connective tissue of a life lived, no narrative. Just isolated beads on a string. I realize this is why I'm such an expert liar. It's not so much lying as invention; with no continuous story to draw on I constantly have to make things up to connect all the dots. Most of the time I'm not even aware I'm doing it.

Also, there's a hard limit to my early memories. As Zell phrases it, using terminology from cosmology, my lookback time hits a wall when I was seven. I don't have to be Einstein to figure out that I suffered some trauma at that age, but why are the subsequent memories such a patchwork quilt? And why do they feel like events that I've been told about or things that might as well have happened to someone else?

■

Plan B. Zell and I go to the Mile High Country Inn in Idyllwild, a mountain resort in the San Jacinto Mountains an hour out of LA. He's got some special deal with the owners, who seem to be aging hippy types. We're enjoying cocktails in the hot tub when he lays out his plans for the morning.

"I'm going to order us up a mushroom omelet, McEvoy. OK?"

"Sure, why wouldn't it be?" I pause, and then I put two and two together. "Oh, you mean that kind of mushroom. I dunno, Zell…"

"Trust me, McEvoy, the only problem with 'shrooms is a variable dosage of psilocybin. But Josh and Peggy have been serving up fine psychedelic experiences for twenty years. You couldn't be in better hands. Of course, I won't be able to act as the objective observer, since I'll be joining you in a mountain high."

It's a side of Zell I haven't seen before. But recalling his radical Berkeley roots, it makes sense.

"How is this going to help me?"

"First of all, to allay your fears, 'shrooms are non-addictive and less toxic than aspirin." Zell gets his prof on. "Increased ability to concentrate on memories is a primary effect, which is why we're here. Side effects include enhanced sensory perception, hilarity, synesthesia, and at high doses, ego death. You might experience mild nausea and weakness in the limbs. The symptom duration is five to seven hours, depending on metabolism." He winks at me.

The next morning we tuck into granola, omelets with the special ingredient, and freshly squeezed orange juice. I've braced myself for profound Castenada-level experiences but all that happens is heavy churn in my color palette and the disconcerting tendency for all hard surfaces to become supple. And mirth. Zell and I succumb to inanity and lavatorial humor until late in the afternoon. Other than that, it seems to be a bust.

∎

When I let slip to Pam that I've been getting help from Zell, we get into a big row.

"Let me get this straight. You've got serious problems with memory loss and you've been getting counseling from a physics professor?"

"He's knowledgeable about many things."

"Ian, if you need help, get help! Don't do something this important with a science quack."

I realize it was wise to keep mum about the mushrooms. Accepting Pam's advice, I find a psychotherapist and submit to six sessions. But impermeable boundaries will not yield. Added sessions of hypnosis fail to yield a breakthrough.

∎

I know the scars on my arms are self-inflicted.

∎

"Is the gravity doctor in?" I knock on Zell's open office door.

"Yes, but he has weighty matters on his mind and may not be able to talk to you for a while. What seems to be the problem?"

"I have an overwhelming feeling of heaviness. Even walking feels like a burden."

"I see." He strokes his mustache. "How's your love life?"

"It's the same problem. What goes up must come down."

"Seriously, McEvoy, how are you doing?"

"I'm stuck. I get these memory morsels from the other side. But mostly it's a set of disconnected puzzle pieces"

"I'll level with you. My colleagues don't know any of this—they'd be aghast—but I experimented with psychedelics out of pure intellectual curiosity. As shiny as my career is, I've only had a handful of moments of searing insight into the workings of the universe. I wanted to know if hallucinogens could provide an additional portal."

"And?"

"Sadly, they've not. I've had some entertaining times and some truly memorable sex while under the influence, but no epiphanies."

"Aye, I'd give my left testicle for an epiphany right now."

"McEvoy, I hate to say this, but maybe you should let it be."

"What do you mean?"

"A few weeks ago told me that you found a pile of poems in your bedside drawer? They were in your handwriting yet you said you had no recollection of having written them. You brought me a few and—I hope you don't mind—but I shared them with some colleagues in the humanities. Do you want to know what they said?"

"I'm afraid to ask."

"They were uniformly impressed. They said it was work of unusual sensitivity and technical skill. Almost certainly a professional poet."

"Bloody hell."

"Mystics, artists and even scientists have craved a pure form of creativity that doesn't emerge from the application of intellect. Your strange mental disassociation carries with it some special powers but they're dangerous powers; to explore them you must venture to the boundary between genius and madness. And you know the problem with that?"

"No."

"Most madmen who claim to be geniuses are simply madmen."

∎

"Here's where we listen for the harmonies of gravity."

After several postponements, Zell finds time to give me a tour of his gravity wave experiment. The test rig is in the basement of his building at Caltech, but several video screens show vistas of the newly-commissioned facility on the Hanford Nuclear Reservation in Washington State.

"For the entire history of astronomy, we've learned about the cosmos through light from stars and galaxies. In the past fifty years we've opened up the spectrum from radio waves to gamma rays but they're all versions of the same thing: electromagnetic waves."

"So this is a new way of seeing the universe?"

"Absolutely! General relativity says that when matter changes its shape or configuration it sends gravitational ripples or waves out into space at the speed of light. Hulse and Taylor got the Physics Nobel Prize in 1993 for showing that gravity waves exist but they did it by inference not direct detection."

"Why is it so different from light?"

"Because with light or other electromagnetic waves, we see matter indirectly, by the way it emits or interacts with light. Gravity waves let us see the universe with gravity eyes."

"So what exactly are these ripples?"

"They're fleet-footed messengers so they streak to Earth without interruption across space and time."

"And how do you detect them?"

"See the long tube here, with a metal rod at one end and a laser at the other?" He points to a cylinder running the length of the lab. "The tube has all the air sucked out. When a gravity wave passes through the equipment, it changes the shape of space very slightly and so the length of the metal rod changes very slightly. We detect the change by bouncing a laser off the rod. The change is extremely subtle, less than the diameter of a proton."

"And that gear?" I point to the video monitors, one of which shows two long tubes stretching off at right angles into the far distance.

"The Hanford facility has tubes five kilometers long; it's sensitive enough to detect astronomical signals. We're part of an international collaboration. The whole experiment cost $400 million."

"Hang on. You're saying you persuaded governments to give you close to half a billion dollars to detect invisible wiggles in space that are smaller than an atom that nobody has every detected before?"

His grin is as broad as his girth. "McEvoy, I told you I'm good."

■

"So what have you seen with your fabulous gizmo?"

"We've started to detect the signals we had hoped and expected to detect: two neutron stars spiraling into one another, or two black holes merging, or a neutron star merging with a black hole. So we know the equipment works and the team is busy interpreting that data."

"There's more, isn't there? Zell, if you came to my poker night we'd clean you out. You're like the cat that got the cream."

"Do you know about the inflationary theory of the universe?"

"I've heard the universe began in a mega-dense and mega-hot state 13 billion years ago, and we know this because of microwaves left over from the big bang."

How do I know this? I never read it anywhere. It's another little example of knowledge I have with no obvious source.

"That's the basic, vanilla big bang. It's had one major modification over the years, the addition of the idea of a rapid phase of expansion in the first tiny fractions of a second that expanded the universe from the size of the nucleus of an atom to the size of a basketball."

"And that's inflation?"

"Yes."

"What's it good for?"

"Inflation explains features of the universe that would otherwise be mysterious, such as its overall smoothness and the lack of ruptures in space-time called strings and monopoles."

"You're flying over my head so I'll take your word for that. What's supposed to have caused it?"

"Inflation is physics of the very early universe, where energy from quantum fluctuations causes a minute bubble of space-time to inflate dramatically and become our observable universe."

"Wow. You theorists have vivid imaginations. Were any 'shrooms involved in the invention of this theory?"

Zell ignores my crack and continues. "We have evidence from the microwave radiation that inflation actually happened, but it's indirect, like the evidence for gravity waves before this experiment. However, inflation has a fascinating implication."

"Do tell. Heal my ignorance, Doctor Gravity."

"If our universe inflated from an iota of space-time, then other parts of the quantum space-time foam may have turned into distinct universes. They'd have different properties from our universe. They might be long-lived or they might die young. They might host life or they might be stillborn. This idea is called the multiverse."

Not for the first time while talking to Zell, my head swims. A whole universe from a quantum bubble? Many parallel universes?

"Gravity waves are the frontier of cosmology." Zell waves his arms like a preacher. "This experiment is probing the origin of the universe in a new way!" Beads of sweat form on his brow. He mops them with his sleeve. "McEvoy, I'm overheated. I've got to calm down. Let's go get a drink."

∎

In a crowded biker bar on Colorado Boulevard, Zell delivers the denouement of his story. As always, he's comfortable anywhere, but I've spotted the blades the biker chicks are packing and I keep a low profile. We toast each other with Jack on ice.

"You've discovered something, you clever bastard."

"McEvoy, it's huge." He knocks his drink down and waves for a refill. "The rest of the team has been working on the black hole and neutron star data, which is exciting in its own right. Everyone shied away from looking for cosmological signatures because they didn't know what to look for. The data's very noisy so you have to filter it with sophisticated algorithms."

"No data's too noisy for the Bard of Gravity."

"I used a set of new routines I've written that tease information out of the most stubborn data. They worked. Remember what the expectation is: the big bang is a time when the entire universe was just a dot of energy. There was no structure, no information. All the amazing things that happened since—the formation of galaxies and stars and carbon and planets and life—are a result of natural forces acting over thirteen billion years, nothing more."

He pauses for dramatic effect and takes a slow sip of bourbon.

"C'mon, man! You've got me on tenterhooks."

"I've found highly complex information imprinted in the gravity waves from the very early universe."

"You're bullshitting me, right?"

"No, my friend, this is real."

"Christ, Zell, what does it mean?"

"I don't know how to interpret it. But there's data embedded in the big bang."

"Are you saying the universe has a bar code?"

"Something like that."

My head is spinning. "So it's unexpected because the big bang was supposed to be simple, right?"

"Exactly. The big bang was an iota of space-time where the forces were merged into one and there was no differentiation between matter and energy or particles and radiation. Exotic, but very simple. There's no way in the theory that any complex or coherent information could have been present at the beginning."

"When you go public with this, the god-squadders will be all over it, saying it points to a deity or an intelligent designer."

"God, intelligent aliens, there's no reason to jump to a particular conclusion. But it does mean that the universe is a whole lot more interesting than we thought."

We amble to the pool table and play the bikers for drinks, losing three times, which is probably wise. Then Zell and I play a final game against each other. There's no wager, but after he loses Zell pulls off his general relativity pinky ring ceremoniously and gives it to me with a bow and a flourish.

"McEvoy, I don't know what the future holds for you, but you've earned your gravity wings. Wear it in good health."

∎

I replay the murder.

∎

Jackie and Robbie and I come barreling out of the pub like rats out of a burning ship. We lean against the alley wall breathing hard. Ewan, skiving bastard, has gone to scam beer money. We have to be back on board at dawn but we're juiced and ready for more action. A couple of toms are eying us across the way but they look right skanky. Then the Ruskies come up to us, full of jaw and piss. It's shoving first, but one of them clocks Jackie in the face and it's on. No shivs, just fists. We're one man light—fucking Ewan—and sucking hard. Jackie's down, face trashed, and I'm in a clinch with an ugly bastard who smells like vodka and tooth decay. I miss the butt and I'm blind with pain, nose spurting blood. I grab his head and slam it on the brick wall. He spits at me and I'm whacking his head against the wall again and again. Then he shits himself and I let go. He drops like a sack of coal.

∎

And I know it's not the last.

∎

Dawn light seeps into the bedroom. I look over at Pam and know she deserves better. There's no happy ending for us and no graceful exit for me. I gather a few items from the bedside table and dress quietly. In the closet, I grab a change of clothes and a duffel bag I keep on the top shelf, next to the shoebox with Zell's lecture notes. It's one of the few things I own from a time before California. By the look of it, I've had it since I was in the merchant marine.

Interesting. It feels like there's something stitched into the lining. A book of some kind. Looking through a tear in the cloth, I see that duct tape has been applied to the cover. I pack the duffel and take a last look at my wife. Her breathing is even, her face is calm, and her eyes flutter as she navigates a dream.

In the living room I write a long note. I tell her as much as I can and I leave nothing out. I say I might be back and mean it. But if all I have is wrecked and hollow pieces she's better off without me. I have to get whole to be with her or not come back. I've no plan. I'll pull the next step out of thin air. Literally.

I switch on the TV and keep the sound soft. I surf across the game show where the host gives a clue and contestants respond in the form of a question. Jeopardy. One of the categories is Europe. That'll do. I bide my time and wait for the thousand dollar question. The clue: it's the location of the largest university in Scandinavia. I've got no idea, but the mousy woman with big glasses knows. She pipes up: where is Göteburg, Sweden? I switch the TV off, put on my jacket, and leave.

7 THE FROZEN NORTH

Crystal

There's no up, no down, no sideways. I stare ahead and try to find a purchase on the horizon but all I see is softly glowing whiteness. My hands are on the steering column of a small plane and its high-pitched drone reverberates in my head. Apparently I know how to fly. He gives me the occasional word of instruction and reassurance. We head north into the twilight.

■

She's curled up in a chair reading. Looking relaxed in a chunky knit sweater and jeans, blonde hair piled up casually on her head. I watch her read. A clock tick and the occasional creak of the wooden walls as they breathe are the only sounds. She looks up. Her glasses have slid down on her nose; it's such a pretty nose. She needs nothing at this moment. She's perfect and perfectly self-contained.

■

The rhythmic clack of ski and binding blends with my breathing. My muscles ache from the unfamiliar motion. There's no sign that anyone has come this way; my skis crunch into untouched snow. Birch forest slides by on either side and sunlight filters gently through its tangle of snow-clad branches. The trail is endless. I move purposefully towards the vanishing point.

■

I spend hours on the phone with her. The cost is ridiculous but I don't care. We talk about trivia. We talk about trauma. We lapse into the code we used as kids. We talk to fill in the many years we've left blank. I tell her what I can, what I remember. She tells me everything. Her life is a sprawling ruin.

■

Göteburg is a bustling city on the coast. It's working class with a busy port and a major university. I check into a city center hotel with tiny rooms and play tourist for a few days while getting over jet lag. Riding trams, I visit the Cathedral, the Volvo Museum, and the replica of an 18th century Dutch tea clipper. The food's pedestrian and heavy; dark bread, muesli, and cured fish predominate.

It's March and the equinox approaches but Sweden is still in the grip of winter. The streets are clear but snow blankets the parks and the red rooftops. A raw wind blusters off the Baltic and dark flattened clouds scud across the sky. The nighttime high is minus three and the daytime high is plus three Celsius. This Nordic country straddles the freezing point of water with equanimity.

Caprice brought me here but there's nothing to keep me. This is not my destination so I move on. I take the train north and east to Stockholm. There's more to divert me in the capital: museums and parks and cafes. Hotels in the city center are too expensive so I ask around and take the metro out to Kista, a northern suburb. A hotel near the station is reasonable. The room is clean and paneled in pale pine; it includes a tiny kitchen but I'm sharing a communal bathroom down the hall. Inside it's small and cramped like a doll's house and I get claustrophobic when the blinds are drawn but I'm only traveling with a sailor's duffel so it will do fine.

Lack of immediate purpose keeps my head clear. If I stay here for long I'll have to work, but for now I'm content to wander. The suburb has a big immigrant community, mostly Turks and Slavs. Their shops and restaurants line the streets. I'm also an outsider. I take the metro to Gamla Stan, the old town, and walk its medieval streets. I'm drawn to the window of an antique shop that has nautical items. The ship's bells, capstans, and gleaming brass gauges remind me of my days at sea. I go in.

The shop is stuffed to capacity. I duck and navigate carefully to avoid bumping into the clutter hanging from the low ceiling. Backing up to admire a mahogany captain's sea chest I bump into someone.

"Aaaah!" The sound of glass shattering.

"Oh God." I turn around to see what I've done.

A woman crouches on the floor. Fragments of a cut crystal bowl are scattered at her feet.

"I'm so sorry." I stoop down to help her gather the pieces. I look into the pale blue eyes of a classic Swede. She's stunning. I'd guess around thirty, ten years younger than me. Her cheekbones are high and flushed from upset over the breakage, the only disruption in a face that's pale, cool and perfectly proportioned. Straw blonde hair is tied back but wisps fall across her slender neck. I've been in Sweden long enough to see that genetics has been kind to these people but staring at perfection up close is unnerving.

"Let me help. Maybe it can be fixed"

She bites her lower lip and is close to tears. "No, it's not possible."

"Maybe there's something else like it." I look around the shop but see nothing similar. "Of course I'll pay for the broken one."

"There is no replacement." She's distraught.

"What do you mean? Perhaps you can try other shops."

"The bowl is from a town further north. My grandmother's home town. It was a birthday present. She will be ninety."

McEvoy, you fucked up big time. Move like a lumbering oaf and make the pretty woman cry.

I stare at the bowl. It isn't actually shattered but is broken into a dozen or more pieces. I try again.

"It might be salvageable. At least let me pay for it."

"Perhaps. I don't know. I'm upset." She looks pensively at the floor.

"If I'm going to apologize properly, let me know your name."

She hesitates. "Sonja. Sonja Amdahl."

"Ian McEvoy, and I truly regret what I've done. I'm sorry, Sonja. And if I can make it up to you I will."

"It was an accident. Don't feel bad. I have to go." She ties the belt on her dark wool winter coat, turns on her heel, and briskly exits.

I pay the man behind the counter for the bowl and I'm halfway out the door when I stop. The shopkeeper is moving to clean up the mess with a brush and pan when I catch up with him. I ask if I can take the pieces. He shrugs.

This is why I'm here. Things that are broken have to be put back together.

■

That evening, I call Pam and explain why I left. She's not happy but says I should take the time to get help somehow. I even sense relief in her voice. She admits she was thinking we needed a trial separation. Then I nest a little, arranging small items I picked up in Gamla Stan around my hotel room in Kista. There's something else I have to do. I unpack the remaining items from my duffel then use a pocket blade to cut through the lining. I extract a tattered notebook and put it on the table.

My wee book.

For ten years it was hidden in plain sight. Before that it was my constant companion. My hands tremble as I open it and flip through the stained and dog-eared pages. My life. I approach it is I would a twin if we'd been separated since birth, with excitement and some trepidation. I turn to the first page.

And I read.

Sunlight is angling through the window by the time I'm done. I've spent the night vicariously as a rambunctious bairn and troubled teen in Scotland, and as a young man traveling in Arizona and living in New York and wandering in China and South America. I've fallen in and out of love and I've had my heart broken in Ireland. It's authentic; it feels like my voice. Yet there's there so much described in these pages that I can't recall. And so much missing that I'm incapable of filling in. The childhood memories are merely fragments and the adventures are full of incident but they leave most of my life unaccounted for.

My eyes ache so I flop onto the narrow bed to rest them. When I open them again the Sun has slanted across the sky but its light is still pallid. There's more to do.

I grab a pen. I try to write about California. The whole story: my life, my wife, my job, the kids I taught, and the places I visited. But it's like squeezing a rock. After struggling with my obdurate recall, I settle for writing about the time when the fog clears and events come into view. I write about Zell and my inability to be whole with Pam. I write with shame about my dissolution and departure. As I notice the Sun rising again I'm writing about a striking face and a shattered bowl. Full circle and a new beginning.

What comes next?

■

I've not eaten for two days and I'm ravenous. There's a place two doors down from my hotel called Pasha's Turkish Café. It has a small grocery section, a delicatessen with a few small tables in front of the cold case, and an area with piles of junk that seems to be the place where everything from watches to shoes can be fixed.

An old man approaches. His brown face is wrinkled like a walnut and his apron is spotlessly white. I glance at the menu. It's printed in Turkish and Swedish, but fractured English has been added by hand below each item.

"I'll have a coffee. And something to eat. What's borek?"

"Pastry with meat or cheese. You will like."

"Like a pasty back home. I'll have a borek, please. Meat."

There's a pleasing bustle around me. Turkish people shop and chat. The men wear plain work jackets and some sport fezzes; most women are in plain veils.

The next day I come in for coffee and breakfast and the wizened owner strikes up a conversation.

"Again! You loyal customer."

"Aye, could be. I'm staying just down the road for a while."

"You not from here. Red hair, too many speckles."

"Freckles." I laugh. "No, I'm from Scotland by way of other places."

"You like my coffee?"

"It's, ah, an acquired taste. I'm still getting used to it."

"Strong!" He grins to reveal a half set of nicotine-stained teeth.

"Yes, the first one passed through me like the Flying Scotsman."

"My beans ground the old way. Add sugar and water. Boil in copper pot. Leave to settle. Absolute best!"

"No argument here."

"Have another. Over the house!"

"I think you mean on the house. My guts may regret this, but sure, thanks." I hold out my hand. "Pleased to meet you. I'm McEvoy."

"McCoy."

"No, McEvoy."

"Mavoy."

"Close enough. Tell you what. Let's use rhyming slang. McEvoy, the Real McCoy, shortens to Real. Call me Real."

"Real?"

"Real."

"Good to know you, Real. I am Hikmet Oktar, owner."

"Hikmet. That's a mouthful too. Listen, in honor of the tasty but dangerous refreshment you sell, I'll call you Hazmat."

"Hazmat?"

"Hazmat."

He grins broadly. We're fast friends. He runs the store with his two brothers. They live with their wives, seven children and two uncles in a three bedroom apartment. I make a mental note not to feel bad about the size of my hotel room again. I tell him my misadventure from the day before.

"My brother can fix."

"Are you sure?" I glance at piles of broken appliances and worn out shoes on the far side of the café. "This is pretty delicate."

He folds his arms. "You not trust your new friend?"

"Oh, c'mon, Hazmat, don't get your knickers in a twist. I'm sorry. I'll bring it in later today."

I bring the broken bowl to him in a shoe box, but I don't hold out much hope. It's high quality hand-cut crystal. I had rummaged on the floor to get the small bits when it broke but was bound to have missed some.

Next morning I'm sipping coffee at Pasha's again, thinking I might get addicted to this rocket fuel, when Hazmat walks up with the bowl proudly held in front of him.

"Bloody hell, Hazmat. That was quick."

"Should not be doubting Thompson."

"Thomas."

"Thomas."

I rotate it in my hands and hold it up to the light. Incredible. The large cracks are almost invisible. There are just places where an edge or corner had shattered, leaving tiny surface divots. And many of them have been expertly filled in by glue. From a few feet away, it looks brand new.

"Hazmat, you're a genius."

"My brother did this."

"The eponymous Pasha?"

"Not understanding Real's English. Pasha is our father. My brother find special glue to match lead in glass. Good, yes?"

"Bloody amazing, yes. Anyway, thank him from me and let me pay you for this."

We arrange a barter. In exchange for this wizardry with glass I'll give his two youngest kids five hours of English lessons each.

"Is that fair, Hazmat? Your brother did a lot of work."

"Sure. After this we're even Sven."

"Steven."

"Steven."

As I'm leaving he calls out. "Real!" His eyes twinkle. "Come back if you need help to find the girl."

■

In truth, I've been distracted by her for days. I scan the Stockholm phonebook and note many pages of Amdahls, maybe three thousand. Now I look at the bowl. It has a beautiful forest scene and some words in Swedish below, but I recognize Uppsala as a place name. I walk to the post office and look in their regional phone books. My heart sinks. Uppsala is twenty times smaller than

Stockholm but there are nearly three hundred Amdahls.

I realize the implausibility of my quest. So I assume and hope that it's her paternal grandmother and that Sonja hasn't changed her name through marriage. The only other thing I know is that her grandmother is turning ninety. From my hotel I call the office in Uppsala where they stored birth records but the only woman there speaks no English.

"Greetings, Hazmat, my toothless Turkish delight."

"Now you want help to find the girl?"

"Am I so transparent? I've come for your fabulous beverage."

I explain what I need him to do. He leaves his brother in charge and makes the call. It takes a very long time. He returns with thirty different Amdahls on a scrap of paper. Matching with the Stockholm phone book brings that down to nineteen.

"What else you know, Real?"

"Nothing, Hazmat. Wait, she was wearing a fancy wool coat, very expensive. Her gran would definitely live in a posh part of town."

That gets us down to six.

"We make cow's eye!"

"Bull's eye."

"Bull's eye."

I'm in business. Before I leave Hazmat makes me describe the object of my infatuation.

"She's statuesque. The palest milky blue eyes. Silky blonde hair. Cheekbones to make the gods envious…"

I've lost his attention.

"This is Swedish woman. They look very sick. Why you not want a woman with color? Shiny black hair. Big brown eyes. Extra fat to get through hard winter. That's beauty! If Real wants, I introduce you to friends of my wife."

■

As I set off across Stockholm it occurs to me that searching for a woman I met once and who was rightly mad at me is at best quixotic and at worst obsessive. Worse, it's avoidance. I've traveled across the world to recover my life by resolving a mass of gaps and contradictions called McEvoy.

But I set those thoughts aside. The six addresses are all in affluent suburbs on the edge of the old town center. The first two apartments are dark and nobody answers the buzzer. The third address is a town house; a taciturn man answers to the door and closes it quickly and emphatically when he decides I'm not worthy of further attention. At the fourth, an old woman's voice comes faintly over the intercom. She speaks no English so I say what I hope is her granddaughter's name and hope for the best. The door clicks open.

She's a tiny woman, barely past my waist, yet she stands in the doorway in a wide stance as if she's confident that she can repel the Celtic attacker. I hold out the crystal bowl and watch her break into a delighted smile as she takes it. That seems to be that. With no way to make further conversation I half bow and turn to leave. But then she raises a bony finger and scurries back inside. She presses an envelope into my hand. Outside, I see it's an invitation in ornate Swedish script, sporting an address, a date and a time. Bingo!

■

To my great pleasure, I'm adopted by Hazmat and his extended family. I've already seen many of them in the café but I have trouble keeping names straight. Hazmat invites me to a gathering. Nothing special, just a way to bring together relatives living in the far-flung suburbs of Stockholm.

"Real! Real, come and meet my family." Hazmat gives me the tour. After the shyness and awkward smiles, we quickly get on with it using their limited English and my expressive gestures.

"Eat! Kofte, kebab, dolma, borek, manti, what you want!"

It's all delicately spiced and delicious and I realize what my palate has been missing with the stolid local cuisine. Later the old men bring out the instruments: the banjo-like baglama, the bass-like kemenche and the recorder-like zurna. Two teenage boys in the group roll their eyes and beckon me to join them in a bedroom. We smoke cigarettes and listen to something called Anatolian Rock that's no doubt edgy for a kid raised in a strict Turkish household, but to me it sounds worse than watered-down Abba. Their names are Aydin and Aslan.

"Bit of a trek from the Mediterranean to the Arctic Circle, isn't it?"

"We were born here." He shrugs. It's Aydin, I think. Hard to keep sorted when the names are so similar and they share the same dark eyes, black hair in a pudding bowl cut, and slender physique. But I'm sure Turks think all Scotsmen look the same too.

"What's it like?"

"It's OK." Another shrug. Aslan, this time.

I'm going to have to try a bit harder.

"D'you like football?"

"Yeah. I'm a lot better than him." Aslan jerks his thumb at Aydin. "Do you play?"

"Aye, I've knocked it around a bit in my time."

"You can watch us if you like. We've a club." Aslan allows himself a small smile. "You could play in goal."

In football, it's the fool's errand. "You might regret it. How is your school?"

"Bad. The Russians beat us up. The Poles take our stuff. And the Finns are always cheating to get ahead."

"Sounds dodgy. What about the Swedes?"

Aslan looks at me blankly.

"The locals. How is it with them?"

"They don't go to our school. They think they're better than us. There's just a few skinheads."

My illusions are dented. I thought Sweden was a grand, egalitarian social experiment. I'm sure it's more fair-minded than most countries, and maybe it's harder to be gracious when you're poor. But the idea of blonde neo-Nazis is unsettling.

■

A week later I see how the other half lives when I arrive outside an elegant apartment building on the Strandvägen. It has a view across the water to the Opera House and the Royal Palace. I'm buzzed in and climb a sweeping stone staircase to the second floor. Nervousness and awkwardness vie for supremacy as I walk into the crowded room and immediately wish I'd stayed in my hotel. Everyone's stylishly-dressed, poised and sophisticated in an effortless European way. Polite laughter and bright conversation bounce off white marble walls. I feign a deep interest in one of the tables of canapés when she speaks.

"You have come. I'm glad. Welcome, Mr. McEvoy."

She's dazzling. I take in the long black sleeveless black dress, the creamy white skin of her arms, and the black pearl earrings and gold choker that complete the picture.

"My pleasure. I'm glad I could make up for my clumsiness."

"Farmor was so pleased to get the bowl." She makes a sweeping, graceful gesture to a table where it is doing yeoman service among many others to hold hors d'oeuvres. My pride ebbs.

"I want to wish her a happy birthday before I leave."

A man appears at her shoulder. "I'd like you to meet someone," she says. "This is my fiancé, Mats. Mats, this is Mr. McEvoy. He's visiting Stockholm. We bumped into each other in the old town."

Mats is tall and steely-eyed; he's from the same superior genetic stock. His grip is firm, authoritative, and slightly challenging.

"Mats is a junior partner in an architect firm," she continues. "He works very hard; if he becomes senior partner I'll never see him."

She looks up at him fondly. Her diction is so smooth and crisp and mellifluous that I go into a momentary trance.

"Mr. McEvoy? Mr. McEvoy? You seem far away. We must visit with family. Stay as long as you wish."

She places her cool hand in mine and leaves it there for a moment. I pass on another bone crush from Mats. Barely a minute after they've disappeared back into the crowd I slip away.

I walk off my disappointment and my humiliation in a park on the island just across from the Strandvägen. The snow has melted during the day into an archipelago of white scabs on the flattened grass. A keen wind slices through my thin jacket.

Stupid, stupid McEvoy. You're a grown man acting like a besotted teenager. What on Earth are you thinking? What ego-ridden, deluded fantasy makes you think she'd even give you the time of day? You're just a hideous pink gargoyle who stumbled into Valhalla and has been sent packing. Her life is perfect. Her course is set. You're as welcome as a fart in a spacesuit. Grow up, McEvoy, and get a life.

Self-pity is ugly, but it has a place in the psyche. Unfortunately it's a social beast that never drinks alone.

Reality Bites

I'm in my bed, but when the racket starts downstairs I know I'm needed elsewhere. I slip into her room in the dark and step into the even greater darkness of the closet. She's in her bed, curled up under the blankets like a wee sack of potatoes, snuffling from cold. I'm using every iota of my will to keep him away. Clumping up the stairs. It's too late. The door bursts open and ricochets off the stop. Heavy breathing. A moment of pure silence. Hope rises. Then falls. What're 'ye pissing about now? Don't we feed you? Don't I drag my arse around all week so you can eat, so I can go without my fags and beer? Eh? Eh! Heavy breathing. A small whimpering sound. Then a slap, loud as a gunshot. Another. I bite my arm but it's not enough. I take out a used blade I found in the rubbish in the bathroom. Outside, the percussive sounds continue. I score myself with the blade, one arm then the next. Again. Again. But I cannot deflect her pain. I cannot take it away.

■

"Fuck. I must've got into a kerfuffle. I feel like shite."
"You look like you have had better days."
"Where the fuck am I? Who the fuck are you?"
I wince as I sit up. I'm wearing a blue t-shirt, gray sweatpants

and canvas slippers. I'm in a small bedroom with white painted walls and a small window looking onto an empty courtyard flanked by a high wall. Across from my bed, a man sits on an identical bed, wearing identical clothes. He's bald and has the biggest forehead I've ever seen.

"In order: Langholmen Prison and Oddbjorn Engvold."

"My head's like a fucking war zone, pal. Play it out slow."

"Very well. You're in prison. Langholmen is on a wooded island in the middle of Stockholm. It has partly been converted into a hotel but we're in the section that retains security features. I'm a professor of philosophy at the University of Stockholm."

"Did they say what I'm in for?" The previous eighteen hours have disappeared from my memory.

"Uve, the guard, said you had obviously been drinking heavily. You were picked up in the old town. You were lying in the snow bellowing." He smiles faintly. "The charges include disorderly conduct and extreme Scottishness."

"And you? What's a professor doing in the slammer?"

"I was arrested for civil disobedience. I chained myself to the gate of the Parliament to protest the right of Sikhs to wear turbans while riding a motorcycle."

"Christ. What a pair we are." I absorb my surroundings. "It's nicer than the hotel I'm staying in. You Swedes are bloody civilized. I doubt I'd get a mint on my pillow at the Bar-L."

A genial guard escorts us to breakfast, an excellent spread of meat and cheese and muesli, with piping hot coffee. The few other inmates are quiet and very polite. Afterwards, Oddbjorn suggests a sauna.

"Sauna? Bloody hell, how do you Swedes ever keep on the straight and narrow?"

"We're generally very well-behaved."

"I'm McEvoy. Can I call you Oddbjorn? That guard seems to know you pretty well. Are you an old lag?"

"I find myself here every few months. One mustn't live inside one's head, McEvoy. My work is very esoteric. I'm compelled to act out my principles in the real world."

"So what is that gets you so bent out of shape? Hasn't this place been run by socialists for fifty years? I couldn't imagine a more liberal country."

"A civil society is a continual compromise. We allow constraints on our freedom in return for security and social order. Sweden does well, but we fall prey to smugness and complacency and we can always try to do better."

"Surely women do just fine here. Aren't half of your members of Parliament and ministers women?"

"Yes. Those battles are mostly won. The leaders of women's right movements have moved on to other matters, such as the right to bare their breasts in public."

"You're shitting me."

"Not at all. The Bara Bröst network goes topless as an act of civil disobedience. They want to desexualize the female body and see this as an equality issue." He's perfectly deadpan.

"I'm behind them on the practice but I'm afraid they've lost me on the principle."

"My concerns are animal rights and equality for minorities. Sweden has 350 members of parliament but only are members of any of the immigrant communities. Proportionally, we should have thirty. There are many political, cultural, and social barriers to people not of classic Nordic stock."

The sauna does wonders to clear my head, and I enjoy the high intellectual octane of this man of philosophy. His Saturnine demeanor is reassuring. As my breakfast settles and the warm vapors ease my aches, I think: this is the perfect place to be bent.

∎

Leave or stay? After a few weeks in Sweden I'm in limbo. I've a strong sense of otherness, which gives me an empathetic bond with my adopted Turkish family. Swedes are aloof and I return the favor. But unfinished business weighs on me. I don't know why but I sense impending closure here.

My life is a series of disconnected episodes. I felt it when reading my wee book and I feel it now when I draw on memories. Can I make a piece of whole cloth from these strands? On an impulse, I call Pam. Her voice is heavy but calm as she talks about how difficult it was to live with my mental dissolution. Our disembodied voices flit instantly across five thousand miles, trailed by awkward silences. I am seeing someone, she says softly. Right, I reply, it's probably for the best.

Later, I feel a wave of guilt over my infatuation with Sonja. But I suspect if I can work past that superficial reaction Sonja might hold the key to the resolution I seek.

■

I work a deal on a lower weekly rate for my hotel room but I'm running out of money. Hazmat says Ericsson is up the road; they're the biggest employer in Stockholm. I arrived with almost nothing and I've bought items of clothing that make me look more like a local. At the interview I pull out the stops to present myself as a solid, boringly reliable worker, and not someone prone to alcoholic binges, memory loss, obsession, hallucinations, and getting tossed in jail.

It works. The next day I stand in a brightly lit, cavernous building next to a conveyor belt as a steady stream of mobile handsets slides by. My job is to pick one up, do a quick physical inspection for flaws in production, switch the unit on, then pass a wand over it to detect radio interference or unwanted emissions. They use a sampling approach. I pick out one in a hundred and am glad not to be responsible for them all: making me gatekeeper for 200 million units a year would mean a lot of angry customers.

The job's fairly mind numbing but once I get the hang of it I find I've time to think. Wasn't this how Einstein did his best work? On a break in the bathroom I see my reflection. Who's this strange man with a white lab coat and a white hair net covering ginger hair? The stylized Ericsson "E" reminds me of three sausages; I imagine myself as a high-tech butcher, purveyor of mobile meat for the masses. I've got a job that Swedes turn their noses up at, and I suspect I got the nod over darker applicants because at least the Celts are worthy of carrying bath water for the Norse.

∎

I start playing football again after many years fallow. I cheer on Aslan and Aydin's under-16 team and then wander over to the adult pitches. The muscle memory kicks in and I can hold my own with the young Turks in the playing fields of Kista. Some days, there's a pick-up game at the plant during the lunch break; the teams are rainbow-hued. My "family" looks after me well, and Hazmat is an avuncular guide to the occasionally hidden rules of Swedish life. An hour every evening I give pro bono English lessons to a growing gaggle of family members, kids ranging from eight to eighteen, all recent immigrants. But I'm not sure my English is legit enough to serve as a model for anyone trying to grasp a new language.

Stockholm is a cultured city, and I rekindle my engagement with music, mixing jazz and classical concerts, turning up just before the show time to get the cheap, unused tickets. It's at a concert at the Grünewaldsalen that I see her again. The program is a set of Mozart quartets for flute, violin, viola and cello. She plays flute. Her tone is pure and sweet, gliding pitch-perfect over the strings. The crowd is modest, the applause polite. I wait at the stage door afterwards in a pool of lamplight, braced against the evening chill. She appears with the other musicians and after giving them a wave, walks over.

"So, Mr. McEvoy, this time you're brave enough to talk to me." A coy smile plays at the corners of her mouth.

"This time? I don't get you. And please let's not stand on formality. To my friends I'm simply McEvoy."

"You were at my concert a few weeks ago. I saw you very clearly, though you showed no sign that you knew me."

"I'm sorry, but that wasn't me. This is the first time I've seen you since your grandmother's bash."

"How very strange. I was so sure it was you."

It's an awkward moment. I wonder whether my memory lapses

really include something that I'd be so unlikely to forget. Meanwhile, she no doubt harbors the suspicion that I'm a crazed stalker.

"Listen," I cut through the silence. "Do you want to get a drink?"

"I should be going…"

"But you haven't let me compliment you on your playing."

"You're kind. I don't practice nearly enough." She tilts her head equivocally. "I suppose I have time for a quick drink."

We adjourn to a nearby hotel bar. And there, in surprising and unanticipated ways, we click. The itinerant, world-traveled, rough-hewn, sod dweller turns out to share a wavelength with the stylish, effortlessly-accomplished, native of the archipelago. We talk about music and poetry and science. I make her laugh and it's a fabulous sound, like water cascading through a pyramid of wine glasses. As I talk about places I've seen and the twists and turns in my life, I see her grow wistful.

"Whenever a door opens, you seem to jump through it, without asking where it leads, or whether it's the best choice."

"Sure," I said. "That's what doors are for. And if they don't swing open, that's what your shoulder is for."

"I have not done that." She looks solemn and distractedly winds a strand of hair around her index finger. "I've decided with great care what the best choice is and I've followed that path. Always."

"Sonja, you've traveled through Europe, and beyond. Christ, you speak five languages, which is four more than me, five if you include my imperfect grip on English. You're ludicrously cosmopolitan."

She laughs again, and covers her mouth with her hand, a gesture both disarming and appealing.

"You don't understand. I holiday with other Swedes. We travel the world and make mental notes but what we see just confirms that the best of everything is right here. None of my friends or family has ever lived more than a year out of the country."

"You obviously have a full and rich life."

"Yes. I do. My music means a lot to me. Mats is a good man,

we'll make a fine life together. Children. A holiday cottage down in Öland." I'm parsing her voice for doubt but find none.

She glances at her watch. "And now… I do have to go."

The interlude is over. I watch as she winds a long black silk scarf around her neck.

On a whim, I blurt out. "My best friend Hazmat, well, that's not his real name, he's got a birthday coming and they're having a wee party. Do you want to come? And Mats, of course. I want to return the favor of being asked to your gran's birthday. Hazmat's the closest I have to family. He's a good man, if you overlook the half set of choppers and the slightly suspect personal hygiene."

McEvoy, you manage to turn self-effacement into an epic art form. I regroup. "Sorry, that didn't come out very well…"

"Perhaps. I'm not sure what we're doing next week."

I write the information on a scrap of paper and watch her slender silhouette glide away into the night.

■

To my great surprise, she shows up. Alone.

Hazmat's in rare form. He charms her right away. Twenty people are crammed in the living room and kitchen of their small apartment and there's no structure to the conversations; they ebb and flow and loop in different people and seem to embrace the four corners of the room. It's warm and chaotic.

Sonja eats daintily but tries everything, urged on by the mothers and aunts who obviously think she's not only woefully pale but also dangerously thin. By the time the sweets are brought out, the helva and the baklava, everyone's groaning.

"Real, she's sweeter than my best coffee." Hazmat joins us and is grinning broadly. "I see why you broke her bowl."

"Hazmat!" I redden and then turn to Sonja. "He's a very silly man, you must excuse him."

"Please marry him, and give him many pale children with spots." Hazmat is irrepressible; I'm glowing like a stove hotplate.

"Hazmat, I swear I'll disown you."

"You have good eye. She is pretty like a frame."

"Picture."

"Picture."

"You are most kind, Mr. Oktar." Sonja smiles warmly.

"Aydin! Aslan!" Hazmat calls into the back room where the youth brigade is holed up watching TV. "Come show shirts!"

They come out, trying to look as bored as possible. Each wears a red football shirt with Ericsson emblazoned across the front.

"Real got his company to sponsor team." A gap-toothed smile. "He will soon get promotion. Become a mongol."

"Mogul."

"Mogul."

I doubt Sonja has ever been in an immigrant family's home so I watch with interest from the side. Her social skills are finely honed. She's warm and animated and a good enough sport to try the zurna when the instruments are brought out; she plays it beautifully. But her reflective surface is designed to dazzle and deflect. I sense an interior that's intact and undisturbed.

"Thank you, McEvoy. You were rude about your friend, but he's a wonderful man, and his whole family too. I had fun."

We stand on the street outside the darkened café. Sonja pulls on her gloves.

"Come up for a minute," I suggest. "I'm only two doors down. Hazmat gave me a special copper pot and taught me well; I make a mean Turkish coffee."

She sits on the only chair in my room while I boil water in the tiny kitchen area. She takes off her gloves but not her coat; the apartment is cold. She's showing me she doesn't intend to stay long.

As I finish preparing the coffee she's looking at one of the few bits of nostalgic decoration in the apartment: a watercolor of a Highlands fishing village I found in a flea market. I place the coffee on the table and walk up behind her. She turns. Her lips are slightly parted. I lean in slowly. Our lips touch. There's exquisite softness and no resistance. My entire essence, the hard reality of McEvoy, is muted as I dissolve from solid through liquid and on into pure vapor.

She stiffens and pulls away, eyes bright with panic.

"I must go!"

And she flees.

•

McEvoy is strong. He's in the best shape of his life. For the first time in a decade he's completely off the sauce and he's even taken a sabbatical from his beloved Mars bars. He runs in the Hansta nature reserve just north of Kista. When he cruises along the wooded trails, pulling pine-fragrant air deep into his lungs, all his senses are turbo-charged. He has little body fat and grudgingly admits that the naked Scotsman in the mirror is not bad looking.

•

McEvoy is lucid. He's always had the ability to be present in his dreams, partaking in the illusion and relishing its clarity, while being aware of its unreality. He knows that the lucid dreamer can become seduced by their nether world so he builds in nonsensical items and other clues as reminders that he's in a subconscious bubble. In his waking world, he registers everything with crystal clear clarity.

•

McEvoy is scared. In quantum theory, indeterminism is built into nature. No two quantities can be known with perfect precision. If the velocity of a particle is well-determined its velocity is unknown. If the time of a particle interaction is short enough the energy involved can be arbitrarily large. His newly sharp physical presence coexists with a fear that his psyche is becoming unmoored and unknowable. Hazmat calls him Real, but is he?

•

One evening there's a message pinned to my door that was called in to my hotel. Weary and bleary from hours of testing phones, I just want to crash on my bed. It's an invitation to join Professor Oddbjorn Engvold at his club for dinner and sauna. How can I resist my favorite criminal philosopher? Oddbjorn is a lifetime member of the Stockholm Yacht Club, with imposing views of the Kungliga

Slottet, a 18th century royal castle with 608 rooms. He's reading a newspaper in the lounge next to the dining room when I arrive.

"How much do they pay you professors? I thought philosophers weren't in it for the money."

"Purely inherited, to my moral shame."

"And what did the Engvolds make? Gaskets for Volvo? Grommets for Ikea?"

"My grandfather invented the perfect container for the shipping industry. His specification is called the Engvold protocol."

"Any more weekends in Langholmen since we last met."

"No, I've been deeply immersed in the problem of evil."

"Tell me more, that I might recognize it in my own heart."

I listen to Oddbjon's lightly accented, perfectly modulated voice elaborate on the problem of evil from an academic perspective. The insights are very clever but don't seem like they'd be any use if you had to deal with genocide or had pissed off a bloke with a knife.

He asks what I've been up to. He perks up when I tell him about Sonja's conviction that she'd seen me weeks before I met her at the concert.

"Do you know what a doppelgänger is?"

"Some kind of shadow of a person?"

"Not shadow. An exact double. The appearance of a doppelgänger can portend death. A number of literary figures claimed to see them. Guy de Maupassant's double entered his room near the end of his life and began dictating a short story. John Donne saw his wife's double in Paris holding a newborn baby at the same time that his wife gave birth to a stillborn child in London. Shelley saw a doppelgänger. And there's Goethe, perhaps the most interesting story. Goethe was riding on the road to Drusenheim when his double approached, wearing a gray suit trimmed in gold. Eight years later Goethe was traveling the same road in the opposite direction, when he realized he was wearing the same gray suit trimmed in gold that he had seen on his double eight years earlier. Raising the question, had he seen his future self?"

"I dunno, Oddjborn. Sounds a bit fishy."

"Agreed. I don't accept the doppelgänger as a literal double but they're intriguing in what they say about perception and reality."

"Are you saying that Sonja saw my double?"

"No. I'd guess she had been thinking about you and projected that thought into her situation. A pure case of wishful thinking. But it's an interesting account. In Norse legend, a vardøger is a ghostly double who precedes a living person and performs their actions in advance."

I'm not real to her and she's not real to me, I thought.

■

After dinner, we move to the spa area of the club and both have massages before facing the rigors of the steam room and the sauna. There's a full bar just outside the sauna.

"The experience is completed by schnaps," says Oddbjorn. "If you think you can stay on the rails, I recommend it."

"I'm clean enough now that I can have just one with you." I say this with confidence, and it's true.

We sit in the smothering heat, pores slowly opening, with aquavit in our hands. It tastes of caraway, coriander and fennel. I look closely at Oddjborn. With his translucent skin and domed head he's just like a child's stereotype of an alien, an impression accentuated by his overly precise diction. The best terrestrial proxy is a Beluga whale.

"Oddjborn, I'm worried. Most of the time my life has the crispness and unmistakable heft of reality. But there are times when it all just comes apart."

"Perhaps it's the moments of confusion and unreality that are lucid and the bulk of your experience that's mere comforting illusion."

"You're not making me feel better. What do you mean?"

"Are you ready to consider a somewhat extravagant idea?"

"My mind's as open as my pores."

"You've studied astronomy, McEvoy. You know it's almost

certain that there are intelligent beings out there. The odds are that some of them are far more technologically advanced than we are. If we follow this logic we're led to consider the likelihood that we are not actually biological entities, but instead we are part of a computer simulation created by a more advanced race."

"Oddjborn, you've either been hitting the aquavit, or reading too much B-grade scifi. That's the storyline from the Matrix."

He nods genially. "Yes, there's a slight resemblance but the movie supposed that some advanced race would keep human brains in tanks to produce power, which is ridiculous. No, the simulation hypothesis, as it's called, is quite serious, logically rigorous, and surprisingly hard to completely refute."

"Go on, my attention is undivided."

"The argument starts with a few assumptions. One is the fact that the processes of the brain are the result of a complex electro-chemical network. Our brains are manifested in biological neurons, but suppose they could be manifested non-biologically, such as the silicon circuitry of a computer."

"I guess I'll buy that. Biology's just one way to make a brain."

"Next, we ask what would be the requirement to simulate all our thought processes in silicon or a purely computational environment. It's not hard. Extrapolate Moore's law by fifty years and you predict a computer that can store all the thought processes of everybody who ever lived. Extrapolate a bit more—still only slightly more advanced than us given the vast amount of cosmic time available for technology to evolve—and you conclude that such advanced civilizations could trivially simulate minds like ours and could cheaply simulate almost infinite numbers of them. We'll be able to do it in a century. So why should we be the first?"

"I can't find a fault in that, as creepy as it sounds."

"Now, the argument itself. Logic says at least one of the following three hypotheses must be true. One, essentially all species at our level of technological development go extinct and so never reach the level of making simulated civilizations. Two, no advanced civilizations that can run such simulations choose to do so. Three, we're actually living in a simulation."

I scan his face for signs that he's pulling my leg, but he's totally inscrutable. "Christ, Oddjborn, my brain just hit the rails! That's an awful lot to take in. And how do we decide which of those three is actually the truth?"

"We can't. But one or more of them must be true, and ruling out the third possibility is extremely hard."

"Break it down for me."

"You might think it unlikely that all advanced civilizations become extinct just after our level of development so if the first proposition is false there are many civilizations capable of making simulations of minds like ours."

I nod. "Right, civilizations might be unstable beyond some level of technology. But it's unlikely that none of them would get there. I don't like option one."

"You might think it unlikely that no advanced civilization would run simulations of creatures like us; after all, we do it all the time with our rudimentary computers."

I nod again. "Aye, video games are awesome and they're getting more realistic all the time. I'm sure if you had killer computers you'd use them to create your own wee world. I don't like option two either."

Oddbjorn adjusts his face into a slight smile.

"Then you're left with the third choice. For if the first and second propositions are both false there are vastly more simulated than real intelligences. The mediocrity principle means you're likely to have a simulated mind rather than one running on biological neurons."

I peer at Oddjborn through the steam to see if he's still smiling or if he's wearing an ironic expression. He is perfectly deadpan.

"So if I don't like one and two, I have to accept three, is that what you're saying?"

"Yes."

"But what about those times when life feels totally real? Sharp and crystal clear. I don't feel simulated then."

"Of course not. You wouldn't; it's part of the simulation. Others will feel real too but their conviction is no more well based than yours. If the simulators choose not to reveal their existence there's no way we would know."

I'm getting exasperated. "C'mon man, you don't seriously believe this?"

He stares at me calmly, without blinking. "It's not a question of belief, McEvoy. If I believe in Santa Claus or gremlins or God, it's my choice, my belief. This is a matter of supposition and logic. Accepting the suppositions, there are few logical choices."

I try to imagine how it would change the way I act or view my life if I knew I was living a simulated reality. Interestingly, it doesn't seem to remove the need for a moral framework or for sensible actions. The world would still have an internal logic, governed by the interactions of the simulated entities within it. Then I realize that there's no way to be sure the civilization that simulated us wasn't simulated in turn by a yet more advanced civilization. The regress might continue infinitely.

That thought causes my rational mind to shut down.

■

When my attention returns to the real world I'm alone in the spa. Minutes must have passed. Oddjborn returns, dressed in a blue velvet dinner jacket, white shirt, white pants, and white patent leather shoes. His pale skin glows pink from the sauna, making him look even more like a new-born than usual. It also makes a contrast with the ebony skin of the striking woman he's with.

"McEvoy, I'd like you to meet Dr. Oba Okoye. She's visiting from Nigeria, doing research at my Institute."

There's a moment of mild embarrassment; I'm naked in the spa. Then I recall the healthy Scandinavian equanimity about the body. I reach up to shake her hand.

"Hello. Please excuse my extremely casual attire."

"It's quite all right."

Her graceful fingers are cool to the touch. Oba is very tall and very slender, an impression accentuated by her long neck and her towering and braided black hair. She wears an emerald green skirt and jacket. I'm thinking: supermodel. Why do philosophers have all the luck? She has a lapel pin with the symbols "h+" formed with tiny diamonds.

"You might like to visit the Institute." He handed me a card.

"Sure. Is it part of the university?"

"No. This is my independent work. It's a little too avant-garde for the Academy."

"What do you mean?"

"I'm an experimental philosopher. Come and visit. I think you will find it meaningful."

Full Circle

My sister Annie had a twin. I had another sister. He killed her.

∎

The equinox is close. Equal day and equal night. The cusp when north dwellers celebrate spring and the return of life-giving warmth and their mirror images in the south begin to hoard food against the encroachment of winter. Equinox. Half darkness and half light. The shadow and the fear and dark dreams it brings recede but they will return. They always return.

∎

I spend hours on the phone with her. The cost is ridiculous but I don't care. We talk about trivia. We talk about trauma. We lapse into the code we used as kids. We talk to fill in the many years we've left blank. I tell her what I can, what I remember. She tells me everything. Her life is a sprawling ruin.

Reconnecting with Annie is the best thing I've done in ages. She's in a shelter, on methadone. There have been letters and a few phone calls but the last time I saw her was Mum's funeral.

"You got away, Ian. You had to."

"Aye, but I left you and Mum in the shite."

"Don't say that. Don't think that way. It's not true. We found our own way out."

I wince to think of her life as a smackhead. When I saw her last she was a frail waif, less than a hundred pounds, her skin sallow and dry, only twenty four but looking like an old Chinese woman.

"I'm done with skag," she says. "I've got a job. I like where I am. People here understand me. I've even got a cat."

"Boyfriend?"

"What, and risk my recovery for so little?"

I laugh. She's my kin and her voice is soothing and familiar like the sound of waves on a distant shore.

"What about you, Ian? You always jumped into things, tried your hand and ignored the doubters. Your blood runs hot. I worry that you hanker for women that can make mincemeat out of you. Who's been special in your life?"

"I'm married, Annie. But now I'm separated."

"God, Ian, I never knew. What happened?"

"I was in the States. Pam's a good woman and I do love her but I was coming apart at the seams. It wasn't fair to her."

"Is it over?"

"Aye. I've called her since I got here. We talked it through. I told her as much as I know, which is bad enough. She forgives me. She's already moving on."

"You shouldn't be alone, big brother. You've got too much to give. Your squander your talent. It makes me mad."

"I've had an amazing life. There were connections. I wish you'd met Fee. She was burnished bronze: the softness of woman and the suppleness of art alloyed into something fierce and strong. That was the heat I couldn't handle."

"And now? Something's going on, I can tell."

"Ah, well, some days it's the yearning that gets you out of bed. I don't believe in soul mates, Annie. We want the melting, that loss of self. But this time it's not real. It's a test."

"What do you mean?"

"I'm done chasing shadows. It ends here."

·

I'm writing poetry when there's a soft knock on my door. I have few visitors. Sonja. I hadn't expected this but I'm not surprised. She comes in and looks around; it takes her only a few seconds to size up the cramped quarters and a few grace notes I've added. She takes off her coat, scarf, and gloves. She undresses slowly. Reaching up, she unclasps her hair and it tumbles down her back. Facing me now, she draws her shoulders up and hugs herself. Her clavicle casts a pool of shadow. She tilts her head slightly to the side; it's a question with no answer. Neither of us speaks.

The pale blue of her irises recede; she has the eyes of a cat. Her breasts rise and fall with her breathing. They're shaped like perfect translucent tears. Her gaze is steady but there's awkwardness in the way her arms hang by her side and the way her legs turn inward to shelter the pale hair of her pubis. I fold her in my arms and hold her tightly for a long while.

We make love, wordlessly. Then we lie face to face on our sides on the narrow bed. We stare at each other. She drifts off and I softly kiss her flushed cheeks and the tip of her nose. I can't take my eyes from her face. She stirs and quietly slips silky clothes back onto her graceful curves, and brushes her lips against my cheek. I blink and she's gone.

·

This never happened.

·

I know I've conjured up a fantasy but that knowledge doesn't let me off the hook. The spell is deep; I'm utterly contingent. For several days I don't go out. Every evening I listen for footfalls in the corridor outside. Sonja will hurt me as she will hurt all who fall under her spell, even the inestimable Mats, because she's translucent. Her light shines but doesn't permit a view inside. Her substance is air. Air is essential but it's unfathomable. After a brief tangent, our arcs will diverge. She's made of the finest cut glass while I'm heading towards an amorphous fugue state.

■

The theatergoer knows how it ends but there can be enjoyment in the final act of a tragedy. With the power of the lucid dreamer I script an ending so I can escape my twilight. I crave at least one moment of hedonistic perfection. The curtain rises on the last act when she invites me to her family cottage south of the city.

What Sonja calls a cottage is a sizable house with six bedrooms and gabled windows that looks out onto a sheltered bay of the Baltic. We have it to ourselves. We turn on the heat and listen to the wooden house creak and groan into life.

On a long walk in the woods she's effervescent and playful, pelting me with snowballs, and easily evading my grasp by dancing between the trees. She edges out onto the ice at the lakeside and beckons me with a teasing finger, sure that my greater weight and my unfamiliarity with her winter world will make me tentative. Kissing with chapped lips and runny noses we draw warmth from each other's mouths.

At night we melt together under a thick duvet. The skin of her hips and thighs is hot to the touch as she folds into me like a cupped hand. I bury my face in her golden hair. She sleeps with a sighing breath as I lie awake listening to night sounds.

Late the next morning, we make a feast and eat until we're sated. She practices the flute in her underwear, hip and elbow at a jaunty angle. I tinker with some poems I'm working on. We make love on a rug in front of a fire of pine logs that snap and pop. She's quicksilver in the flickering light. I caress her from neck to ankle then move down and reach inside her with my tongue. My fingers massage her nipples and she undulates under my touch. I slowly lick salty sweat from her navel and the hollow of her neck. We lock in motion until the melting point of crystal is reached.

She's curled up in a chair reading. Looking relaxed in a chunky knit sweater and jeans, blonde hair piled up casually on her head. I watch her read. A clock tick and the occasional creak of the wooden walls as they breathe are the only sounds. She looks up. Her glasses have slid down on her nose; it's such a pretty nose. She needs nothing at this moment. She's perfect and perfectly self-contained.

▪

What's next is real.

▪

I see her for the last time. The music is Schubert. The concert opens with Death and the Maiden, written after the composer learns he has syphilis and his health is ruined. As the last plangent strains fade, I glance at Sonja. I'm on an aisle near the back of the orchestra section, while she's four rows ahead and to the side and appears not to have seen me. She wears black and accentuates the look with gold jewelry and black lipstick. The Swan song follows, composed when Schubert was thirty and stricken with typhoid fever. It's suffused with supernatural morbidity. The song cycle ends with Der Doppelgänger, which starkly depicts the climax of madness at the realization of rejection and imminent death.

At intermission neither of us leaves our seats. She talks to no one; she's apparently come alone. Out of compassion for the audience, the closing piece offers uplift from the man Liszt called "the most poetic musician who ever lived." Shubert's String Quintet was written two months before he died and was laid to rest next to his idol Beethoven. With an added cello, the lower register is gripping. The message is of the possibility of repose with the infinite. I'm immobilized in my seat by the music as the applause fades and people start to file out. Sonja rises to leave and, barely pausing as she passes my row, hands me a small white silk handkerchief. I open it. A black kiss.

▪

The next day I dig up the business card Oddbjorn gave me. After calling to make sure he's there rather than at the university, I go. By strange coincidence, the Institute for Transhumanist Studies is a few miles north of Kista in a wooded science park; I've seen it often from afar while running in the nature reserve. The building's shaped like an H and on top of the roof there's a brushed aluminum sculpture shaped like a three-dimensional plus sign. I recall Oba's diamond pin, with its similar design. I've done some research; transhumanism is a small but growing worldwide movement with a goal of radical life extension and transcending the human condition. It sounds fairly fringe.

"Excellent. Excellent." Oddbjorn is pleased to see me. "Let's do a quick tour."

He wears a cream suit and mauve shirt. His head gleams. Pointing to the two wings of the Institute, he says, "Independence from body. Independence from mind. Let's do away with the body first."

We walk down a corridor past a series of labs, with glass windows looking in on gleaming equipment tended by technicians in white lab coats. I was expecting something more exotic.

"You're disappointed. But a geneticist would give up an important body part to work in a lab like this."

"No, Oddbjorn, I'm bloody impressed. You run this lot, and I think most philosophers wouldn't be trusted with tying their own shoes." In fact, I'm thinking that his university vita and his interest in animal and minority rights would give no hint of this huge facility.

"Harsh, but I accept the compliment. We do follow conventional approaches to senescence. One is trying to trick the telomeres."

"Come again?"

"It's repetitive DNA that caps a chromosome. As cells divide the telomere is consumed and the genetic material degrades. Nature's built-in aging mechanism."

We reach another set of labs. "Whoa. Only a mother could love that. But if it's lunch we're taking about, then I prefer it grilled with butter, rosemary, and a twist of lemon."

A large tank holds several large orange fish. They have rough skin, large downturned mouths, and are stunningly ugly.

"Rockfish. They live over two hundred years. The oldest specimens are not physiologically inferior to young fish. They don't age."

Oddbjorn is oblivious to the fact that he's as strange-looking as the rockfish. He points to a smaller tank in an adjacent lab. Peering at it, I see it contains hundreds of tiny jellyfish.

"Turritopsis nutricula has solved the problem. It can endlessly and indefinitely revert to the immature polyp state. It's truly immortal. We try to learn new tricks from these species."

"I always thought the boon of immortality would be wine, women, and song. It's a tad dull if you have to be a jellyfish forever."

"We are quite eclectic. We will follow any promising avenue. Gene therapy, dietary supplements, and yes, even cryonics. Life extension will be achieved but it will be a difficult road."

∎

Oba joins us for the second part of the tour. It's hard to take my eyes off her. Prominent cheekbones, a tapered face, large eyes, and skin with the luster of black marble. Oddbjorn sees me staring.

"How old do you think Oba is, McEvoy?"

"Ah, I don't want to be rude."

"Go ahead, she doesn't mind." Oba nods her assent.

I look more carefully at her face. Her skin is smooth, supple, and almost flawless.

"I dunno. Twenty eight. Maybe thirty, tops."

"I am sixty three." It's the first time I've heard her speak.

I'm gobsmacked. Something else bothers me about Oba but it's a while before I can pinpoint it. She never blinks.

Oddbjorn smiles. "We've had some success. And here," he points down the corridor, "we engage in fundamental neuroscience."

The second wing of the Institute is similar to the first, rooms filled with computers and lab hardware. But I stop in front of the window to one room that has six people in chairs with computer screens flashing images in front of them. They're wearing metallic hair nets. I look at Oddbjorn quizzically.

"Neuro-mappers. We perfected the technology. You probably know about EEGs, which measure brain waves using 20 electrodes. We have several thousand sensors and we use timing measurements between them to holographically reconstruct full brain activity. We can localize down to the level of a neuron cluster."

"Neat. But isn't it hard to figure out what it all means?"

"That's what all the computers are for, and a team of some of the best programmers in Sweden. We've made real progress in correlating thoughts with waveforms."

I pause at the next room where two technicians monitor a bank of fifty or more video screens. The scene in each one is slightly different but each screen shows a bedridden patient viewed from above or from the side. They're all wearing the neuro-mappers. Oddbjorn anticipates my next question.

"Patients in hospitals all around the country. They're in a persistent vegetative state."

"But are they cabbages or swedes?"

Oddbjorn looks at me blankly.

"Growing up, we called them Rangers supporters."

The slightest flicker of a smile.

"Professor, you're a tough crowd. So you're measuring their brain waves too?"

"Yes. In fact, we can push data as well as pull. Create thoughts as well as harvest them."

"Do these people know they're part of your experiment?"

"They are fully conscious, but unable to communicate."

So unable to give consent. An unnerving thought occurs to me. What if his partner hospitals think they're using neuro-mappers as a clinical tool, while Oddbjorn hacks the signals for his own purposes? And do they have any idea that he's pushing signals and maybe even fully-fledged thoughts into the brains of all these people?

I'm not wearing a hair net but Oddjborn reads my mind anyway.

"Indeed, there are ethical issues. Philosophers have debated them for millennia, with no progress, which is why I conduct experiments. We are addressing profound questions about the nature of mind, self, personhood, and free will."

The import of Oddjborn's experiment is sinking in. "You can target specific thoughts."

He nods. "Yes."

"How good is the technology?"

A prim smile. "Quite good. The specificity is improving steadily."

"Paint me a picture. Is it like reading and writing to a hard drive?"

"Not yet. We can insert the kernel of a thought, perhaps a person or a place or an event. We leverage what's already there; the nearby neural network adds details and a context."

"Give me an example."

"I could create in you the thought of a particular person, such as the young blond woman you're infatuated with, or your sister, or her twin. They would be quite realistic."

"But what for, Oddbjorn? What's the point?"

He looks at me as if I've asked a truly stupid question.

"Independence from mind. The goal is replication and storage of the mind in silicon, where any person can be uploaded or downloaded at will. I believe it's within reach."

I blink. Oddjborn doesn't. He's surely a madman.

■

We finish the tour back in the lobby, a gleaming cube of glass and brushed aluminum. Oddbjorn and Oba are seeing me out.

"Wild stuff, Oddjborn. Thanks for showing me around."

"I hope it expanded your mind."

"It made me think of our last conversation, about the simulation hypothesis. Aren't you heading down that road?"

"You flatter me. These are still very simple experiments."

"What if we're all just parts of another civilization's dream...?"

Oddjborn is impassive.

"…or worse still, just epigrams, or non-sequiturs?"

I attempt levity but something is troubling me. Nobody outside my immediate family knows my sister had a twin.

∎

Normal life resumes. I go to work, hang out with Hazmat and his family, and try to forget the strange things I've seen. Every evening I make an entry in my wee book. There are only a few pages left; soon I'll be taping in extra pages or embarking on Volume Two. I'm muddy and bruised from a football game at work when the phone rings just as I open the door to my apartment.

"Ian. I need you to be here with me." Annie.

"What is it? What's going on?" I'm alarmed. Her voice is eerily flat but tinged with urgency. I know she can't afford the call.

"I'm inside. He left the back door unlocked. I've done a reckie, Ian. I know the nights he goes out and gets blitzed. I cut some clothes line from out back. I've got to put the phone down a minute."

"What is it? Annie! Where are you?"

But I know. With crushing certainty. The FB. Dear old dad. John McEvoy. But why?

"Annie, for God's sake get out. What if he comes around? Get out of there right now!"

I strain to listen. The line is too noisy and I can't make out words. Everything's indistinct. I hear yelling. Then a man's voice.

"Annie? Annie! Speak to me, for Christ's sake."

"You there? I'm back." She's out of breath. "He's tied up now. He's not going anywhere. I got the jump on him and hit him with a brick. I got a toe rag from the kitchen and stuffed it in his ugly gob. Ian, you should see his eyes bugging out."

I keep my voice calm. "Annie, this is madness. Get out of there. If he gets loose…"

"Don't fret, big brother. He's tied up like an old sow. I'm enjoying looking at him like this, all helpless."

"Annie," I plead. "Leave it be."

"No, Ian. It's time. This cost me a month of wages. Way purer than I could ever afford. Nothing but the best for our dear old dad."

"Don't do this. Please, Annie. Don't!"

A long silence. I'm helpless.

"There. He's quiet now. Good. And Ian? I used a clean needle. It was better than he deserved."

Ice World

There's no up, no down, no sideways. I stare ahead and try to find a purchase on the horizon but all I see is softly glowing whiteness. My hands are on the steering column of a small plane and its high-pitched drone reverberates in my head. Apparently I know how to fly. He gives me the occasional word of instruction and reassurance. We head north into the twilight.

Oddbjorn is in co-pilot's seat, head tilted back. I look closer and see no sign of breathing. I nudge him with my elbow. No reaction; he seems dead. Ten minutes later he stirs.

"You're doing extremely well, McEvoy. Stop when you get to the end of the world."

We fly for another two hours. Oddbjorn takes over as we approach Kiruna, 200 kilometers north of the Arctic Circle. He's invited me to his cabin up north, where he goes to think, work on papers, and meditate. He has a jeep with snow tires parked near the airport. We bypass the town and drive north on smooth, snow-packed roads. Oak-less boreal forests slide past on either side. This is the taiga: one of world's great biomes, spanning the northern expanses of Canada, Scandinavia, and Russia. The soil is very young and poor in nutrients; only lichens and mosses cover the vast tracts between regions of forest.

Oddjborn's cabin is utterly isolated. The quiet that first night is so absolute that I bundle up and go onto the deck. Northern lights flicker like ribbons near the horizon. I recognize Saturn low in the sky like a pale, unblinking eye, the symbol of a domineering parent, and twin to Cronus, spending the last years of his life in the unremitting gloom of Tartarus. The cold is shocking. I'm quickly forced inside. Everything I own is in my duffel, but not any clothes thick enough for this place. I lie awake most of the rest of the night. Next morning we're drinking coffee in his living room.

"It's bloody remote here, Oddbjorn. What happens if you get taken ill or have an accident?"

"If there's someone at the other end of the short wave radio I get help. If not I'm out of luck."

"Trust you to be philosophical about it."

■

Another sleepless night for McEvoy. We eat breakfast. The Sun oozes above the horizon. Its flat arc is that of a lazily skipping stone. At noon it will only be a quarter of the way to the zenith.

"Being here is loosening my grip on reality, Oddbjorn."

"Perhaps your grip was never so strong in the first place."

"What do you mean?"

"How confident are you of your back story, your base reality?"

"I don't get you."

"It would take a tedious set of calls, but you could confirm salient details about your family. I assume you're never tried."

I stare at him uneasily. "No. There are some things that I feel in my gut—I don't second guess them."

"And you've never questioned the chance encounters that have defined your path through life, such as bumping into Sonja a few weeks ago?"

"No." I take a deep breath and exhale slowly. The double-glazed windows and thick walls of the cabin admit no sound from the frozen wilderness outside. All I hear is the rhythmic tock of an old-fashioned clock on the kitchen counter. "Why do you ask me that?"

He ignores the question.

"My work acquaints me with the frailty of the construct we call reality." He looks austere and a little intimidating.

"You mean solipsism? The idea of questioning everything?"

"No. That's just a simple mental malfunction. I mean the insights from physics that underlying the material world is an essence whose nature is fundamentally intangible."

"You got me there. Explain."

Oddbjorn tents his fingers and speaks over the top of them. "The current best bet for a theory of everything, a theory that unifies the four forces of nature, is a geometric formalism called E8."

"E8?"

"Yes. It's a purely mathematical concept first recognized in 1887 by Sophus Lie, who was born a few hundred miles away in Norway. It has 248 dimensions and the equations took 120 years to solve."

"That doesn't sound particularly simple."

"Not simple, but exceptionally elegant. There are only a handful of other geometric frameworks that are as fundamental."

"OK, geometry. So what has that got to do with physics and tables and chairs and the real world?"

"Physicists have learned that E8 can be used to describe all laws of physics. It makes predictions for a few dozen new subatomic particles that physicists can search for. It takes the seemingly arbitrary masses of particles and strengths of forces and explains them in one sweeping framework. But it's physics without physics—pure geometry."

"So what's the so-called real world then?"

"Just a projection into three dimensions of space and one of time of this more extensive and beautiful mathematical reality."

"But why would the universe be arranged that way?"

"My, my, McEvoy." He looks at me impishly. "You're quite full of questions today. I suspect you may be a philosopher."

I spend most of the next few days exploring Oddbjorn's extensive library. The living room and all the bedrooms have three walls lined with books and one wall with a floor-to-ceiling window. A lot of the books are dense, technical philosophy but I also find a few on Norse mythology written in English. I go for brief walks in the blinding white snow but the cold is so intense I can't stay out for long. The cabin sits in the middle of a trackless birch forest. Four narrow trails align with the cardinal points of the compass. I've only slept a few hours of the past sixty but I'm energized and euphoric.

■

Who is McEvoy? He's a chameleon, a trickster. Even his voice, that distinctive Scottish burr, is used for deception. Sometimes it's smooth and insinuating, a tool of seduction, like a cat's purr. It can be crude, like a cheap rug curled up at the end, or mean, like the curled lip of a sneer, or menacing, a low growl. He's forty years old, halfway through his nominal span, but he faces a Rubicon. He's loaded with talent and equally burdened with flaws. He has infinite promise and a big heart but he often chooses to flirt with doom. All that holds him together is the electrical force of his atoms, and that life force is frayed.

■

That evening Oddbjorn suggests we bundle up and go for a walk. I'm not sure why we're engaged in such foolishness. After ten minutes of walking, a sulfurous smell hits me and we enter a clearing. A deep volcanic seam reaches the surface; there in the starlight is a wide pool of water fed by a bubbling hot spring.

"Be very careful, McEvoy. One wrong step and you'll be scalded. Follow me closely."

We navigate the knife edge between extreme cold and heat. As I stand naked waiting for him to disrobe I feel ridiculously vulnerable. Then we slither across the shallows and I join him at the sweet spot, the place that's hot but tolerable, where flat rocks under the surface allow us to sit with our chins just touching the water.

I exult. "A place fit for the gods!"

"Indeed. My own private Valhalla."

"Tell me about the real Valhalla, Oddbjorn."

"Valhalla is the great hall of slain warriors. It's in Asguard in the realm of Odinn. There are 540 doors, each of which leads to a room that can hold 800 warriors. The roof is made of their shields. They all spend their days fighting and their nights feasting until Ragnarok, the day of the final apocalyptic battle."

"And they just keep coming back?"

"Yes, warriors die, are made whole, and return to battle."

I laugh. "Bloody good. Oddbjorn, when you took my head off with that double-headed axe I never saw it coming. But wait 'til tomorrow. I've a cunning revenge planned. Meanwhile, let's toast! Barmaid, a hundred drinking horns of Kvas."

"I believe you would fit right in."

"What about the Valkyries?"

"In the oldest Norse tradition, the Valkyrie is a corpse goddess, represented by the carrion-eating raven. The word means chooser of the slain. The Valkyrie is related to your Celtic warrior-goddess, the Morrigan, who may also assume the form of a raven."

"That's a bit grim. I thought they were supposed to be hot."

"Around the 8th or 9th centuries, the Valkyries assumed a benign aspect. Amulets show them as beautiful, blonde, blue-eyed and fair skinned, welcoming fallen heroes to the afterlife with a horn of mead."

"That's more like it."

"The chief of the Valkryies is Freyja, goddess of love and fertility. Freyja travels on a golden-haired boar or in a chariot drawn by cats. The Valkyries carry out the will of Odinn in determining the victors of battle. They bring fallen heroes to Valhalla and send the unworthy to the goddess Hel in the underworld."

"It's a bloody good yarn."

"It crosses over to the real world with the legend of the Raven banner. Canute had a banner when he triumphed at Ashington in 1016. It was woven of the finest white silk and carried no image or legend. But in a time of war a raven was always seen as if woven into the silk. The raven's demeanor dictated the outcome of the battle."

"Oddbjorn, you've just made my blood run cold." I tell him about Sonja and her parting gift.

"Very interesting. This woman either has a keen eye for history or a very strong sense of the macabre."

We fall silent. At the far edge of the pool small chunks of ice drop into the water, float away, and melt. In this wild place my memories are also emerging and floating free, like floes calved from a sheet of ice. Just over Oddbjorn's shoulder there's a miraculous place where the ice meets both water and steam. The triple point. It's rigid, fluid, and evanescent, yet it's one thing. I've been here before—the lunatic, the lover, and the poet are of imagination all compact.

The sky is almost bright enough to cast shadows. Thousands of stars litter the sky, blazing with Byzantine waste. They're remote and aloof, yet their dust is insinuated into our being. I look at Oddbjorn. He's preternaturally pale. The whiteness of the whale. His unblinking eyes regard me calmly. I've never seen him register emotion, never seen the slightest ripple in his equanimity.

"Oddjborn, are you made of the same carbon as the rest of us?"

"What a strange question." He continues to stare at me.

"But I notice you don't answer it."

■

Another sleepless night; another breakfast in the netherworld with the enigmatic Oddbjorn Engvold.

"Today is the equinox," he says. "Seasons change here subtly. In the local Sami tradition there are eight seasons rather than four and twenty words for snow and ice."

"It's bleak but gorgeous, sure enough."

"I hope you're keeping up with your journal." He sips black coffee.

"Aye, lots to write about up here." But I never mentioned my wee book to him.

I take a deep breath. "Oddbjorn, what's really going on?"

He looks at me for a long time before speaking. "You are our most successful experiment. Quite exceptional."

My throat instantly tightens. I taste bile at the back of my throat.

He continues. "We've never achieved anything so densely

textured. The twin motif, the detailed sense of place, the allusions to Joyce and Shakespeare. The game show twist that brought you here was a nice touch, don't you think?"

I stare at him. I feel a dull, hollow ache throughout my body. My mind seems like it's filled with static. "What happens next?"

"Whatever you want."

What he has said changes everything and it changes nothing. "I want to venture out today and see the wilderness."

"Very well. I have extra equipment. Can you ski Nordic style?"

"Sure." Actually I've never tried but how hard can it be?

"I suggest you go north. I've created something you might enjoy three kilometers away. I hire Lapp herders to maintain it while I am away. You can't miss it."

"Is your property extensive?"

"Yes."

"How far does it go?"

"Farther than you can travel." He said enigmatically. "The paths are deceptive. They appear straight but they slightly curve; it can be disorienting. If you go too far you might meet yourself coming the other way." At this, he laughs. It's the first time I've ever heard him laugh. He glances up to the clear sky.

"Be careful. A change is coming."

I wear all the clothes I brought and an outer layer borrowed from Oddbjorn. Before putting on my gloves I fish around in the bottom of my duffel for my wee book. I touch the familiar and reassuring layers of tape on the cover. I open it. Blank. Another page. Blank. As if from above, I watch myself flicking in panic through the pages, all of which are unsullied by marks from pen or pencil. Total whiteness.

∎

The rhythmic clack of ski and binding blends with my breathing. My muscles ache from the unfamiliar motion. There's no sign that anyone has come this way; my skis crunch into untouched snow. Birch forest slides by on either side and sunlight filters gently through its tangle of snow-clad branches. The trail is endless. I move purposefully towards the vanishing point.

After half an hour of effort that's made me sweat, trees fall away on the right and there's a large clearing. In the middle: an ice palace, its smooth surfaces gleaming in the slanting sunlight. I dimly recall that Empress Anna, niece of Peter the Great, ordered an ice palace to be built in Saint Petersburg to celebrate a major victory over Turkey. Oddjborn's palace may not rival Anna's but it's magical nonetheless. The shallow Sun glances off its outer surface, casting prismatic shafts of color onto the snow nearby.

Inside, the ceilings are domed so the ice blocks can support the weight. The floors are made of individual ice tiles. There's furniture made of ice, there are lamps made of ice, and in the large bedroom the bed, with mattress and pillows made of ice. I lie on the bed, which is covered by an animal fur. It's very restful and I do so need to sleep. The light filtering through the windows dims so I look outside. A band of low cloud has slid across the Sun and turned the sky grey.

I must move on. I reach inside my parka for the leather drawstring bag I've brought. I lay seven objects on the bed.

∎

A perfectly circular stone
A sonata written in blood
A tiger's eye
A fossilized pine cone
A bronze needle
A golden gravity ring
A black kiss on white silk

∎

At the bedroom door I look back. A raven perches at the end of the bed. I blink. It's gone. I smile to myself? Myself. Who is that exactly? Am I reduced to a metaphor or a literary illusion? An irreducible kernel of McEvoy resists the notion. But while I can easily posit McEvoy I can no longer demonstrate him.

■

I walk on foot down one of the trails. Every hundred yards there's a bench made of ice, as if for a precession. The cloud has lowered to the treetops and turned into a fog bank. The dull light offers no hint of the Sun's direction. I'm not alarmed. I walk confidently down the trail. My senses are raw and heightened. I catch the rank whiff of an animal carcass. I can hear the tiniest twigs cracking in the forest. I feel alone but am not alone.

I sit on one of the benches to rest. The fog descends gently to the ground. Far away I hear an echo of the snow falling faintly through the universe, and faintly falling, like the descent of their last end, upon all the living and the dead.

A mist of gossamer ice particles swirls around my head. As I blink, I feel thin rime on my eyelids. Suddenly, I'm very tired. I think I will lie down for a while. I smile to myself because this too has happened before. I know how it ends.

***

ABOUT THE AUTHOR

Chris Impey is a University Distinguished Professor and Deputy Head of the Department of Astronomy at the University of Arizona. He has over 280 research and education publications and he has won eleven teaching awards. He is a past Vice President of the American Astronomical Society and has been an NSF Distinguished Teaching Scholar and the Carnegie Council's Arizona Professor of the Year. He has written many popular articles on cosmology and astrobiology, two introductory textbooks, and four popular science books: *The Living Cosmos* (2007, Random House), *How It Ends* (2010, Norton), *How It Began* (2012, Norton), and *Dreams of Other Worlds* (2013, Princeton), with two more in press. *Shadow World* is his first novel.

www.ingramcontent.com/pod-product-compliance
Lightning Source LLC
Chambersburg PA
CBHW070214260626
47160CB00002B/554